I0674206

Strays Welcome

An Uplifting Family Comedy

E.L. Phoenix

with

Chance Stevens

Strays Welcome

Publisher's Note

This is a work of fiction. Names, characters, businesses, places, events and incidents either are the product of the author's imagination or are used fictitiously, and any resemblance to actual persons, living or dead, or to actual events is purely coincidental.

Second Edition

Copyright © E.L. Phoenix, Chance Stevens, 2015, 2016
All rights reserved.

Front Royal, Virginia

Cover Design by Brent Meske

ISBN: 978-0-9897483-9-1
Printed in the United States of America

Scorecard

One Cub Scout troop leader rolls in dog poop.

Fifteen Cub Scouts learn valuable lesson: Stop, Look . . . drop and roll.

Three Frosties: Two vanilla; one chocolate.

Zero calls home from school.

"Lizzie, did you learn something from math homework tonight? About how you can't compare unlike things? Like apples and oranges?"

"I love oranges," cries Lizzie.

"I have an ice cream headache," groans her father. "And no ice cream."

Three homework assignments; one still not completed. Two hundred eleven subscribers to email newsletter.

Impending release date despair.

Three hysterical phone calls, several cross replies, and many, many I love yous.

Chapter 1

I met Bad Doggy one dark and stormy winter's eve, a few nights after Christmas. Cold rain fell from a purplish-grey Northern Virginia sky, and nary a star shone from above. My hard-working husband William and our three kids were milling around the driveway, messing with my eldest daughter's new telescope and re-stringing broken lights, and I was picking up shreds of soggy material from the white paper bags that had held our votives. To make these votives, you folded a white paper bag over, set it on the street beside the curb, poured a handful of sand into a white bag, rooted a tiny candle in the sand, and then lit the wick. Then you poured more sand in an identical white bag, shoved in another candle, and you kept repeating the process until your entire curb burst forth into a splendid light show.

Everyone in the community was expected to light these votives, so late at night, after dinner, you could walk around and gaze at your candle-lined street. The candles are supposed to light the way so that Santa Claus can avoid a crash-landing into each kid's yard. It's one of those community things that everyone does together, and it's supposed to make you feel good about living in the suburbs—until you get soaking wet.

My name's Sally Lane Brookman, but my kids know me just as "Mom," and I'm generally okay with that. When you're a mom, you're somebody to someone, and that's all most of us really want to be. I'm not perfect. For example, I hate votives, especially when a cold rain has turned the bags into freezing, messy sand piles, and *of course I was the one picking it all up*. I was also picking up my neighbor Sandy's piles, because she's getting older and I don't want her arthritic hands to seize up on her. My hands will be all twisted and knotted up too when I'm 60, but until then, I can handle helping my neighbors as long as I can complain a bit.

Brett was trying to throw a Frisbee into the bushes "because it seemed like a good idea at the time," which is pretty much a phrase he uses several times a day. In fact, William must have taught him that phrase, because he also uses it a lot, and right now, he was trying to explain why he bought a slingshot for Junior. It has something to do with squirrel population control in the suburbs, which certainly does not appear like something that could ever seem like a good idea at the time.

Todd, the shade tree mechanic from across the street, gunned the engine of his 80's vintage Camaro and he exchanged manly waves with my supposedly saner half.

"Hey! Will!"

Junior, who's named after his father William, looked up from his slingshot.

"You should add paintballs to it! One time, we took out some possums—"

"Todd!" Sherry, his girlfriend from Tennessee slapped him on the arm from her vantage point in their oil-spattered driveway. "That's cruel."

"Aw no baby, the possum didn't mind a bit. Just kept on about its business. And scared the bejeesus out of my ex-wife. She was raking the yard when suddenly this neon-orange possum came scuttling past her. Thought she'd been accidentally prescribed the red pills instead of the white ones."

I'd been staring so intently at Todd as he 'splained all this I'd lost track of Brett, who'd gotten several steps up the 15-foot ladder William had left leaning against the garage to use for restringing the lights that Brett had knocked down with a racquetball.

"William!" I stood up and grabbed a trash can lid.

"Uh, yeah, William," drawled Todd, "Reckon you better grab the little man before he says, 'Hey Mom, watch this.'"

I love Todd, but I was kind of relieved when he rumbled off in his muscle car, probably to buy another Smith and Wesson or some deer urine. It seems like whenever Brett and Junior and even William spend even a few minutes around him, one of them promptly suffers one of those "temporary lapses in judgment" as William likes to call it. William pointed to a spot next to the moon, which was *waxing fingernail*, or whatever the more scientific terminology is, and I shivered as a gust of wind hit me. I had wanted to go for a short run before it got pitch black outside, but the wind was making me think otherwise.

I stood up, grabbing the grey, thick plastic trashcan lid I'd been using to stash the piles of sopping paper in, and lurched a little as I hefted it toward the driveway. Once I got the heavy lid stacked and slammed shut on the stinky trashcan, I leaned back and stretched, and for a moment, I felt peaceful.

That's when Aaron from next door came out of his garage carrying this ball of black fur, and if only I could have told Sally what I know now. If only I could have whispered, "Run Sally, run! This is the last moment of peace you're gonna have. Just run!"

Chapter 2

I should have run away then and there, but I didn't. Bad Doggy dashed over and tramped right through my pile of cold sludge. His pointed, muddy toes spread my sludge from curb to mailbox and then across some broken pieces of driveway, and some of the sludge must have made it underneath the leg of my pants, because I was feeling something cold and wet near my ankle. But before I could check, Bad Doggy jumped up in the air and rolled like a soldier evading zipping bullets. His little feet were still moving while he was airborne, and when he landed, he fell in a tangled heap on William's feet. Before he got himself sorted, Bad Doggy lifted a leg and peed on William's boot.

I wasn't sure what William was going to do. In life, there's the things you plan for, or if you're a wreck like me, do anything to avoid planning for, and then there's the ones you could only imagine if you weren't right in the head. And the real test for what sort of man you are is how you react to the former. What did William do?

He leaned down and scratched Bad Doggy's ears. "Gosh, he's got a lot in common with Junior and Brett," he drawled, one side of his mouth lifted in a smirk. "Both christened the doctor before they even made it to their mother's boob. This one," and he gave

Aaron's daughter Petunia a nod, "This one's gonna fit right in round here."

Petunia, with the pinched up face of a wanna-be Southern belle, put one hand on her hip and made a pirouette in front of Brett to show off her new outfit. Brett ignored her. Then Petunia issued a massive sigh-shrug and murmured, "Figures. Oh my God." And with a flounce, she gave Lizzie, who was dressed in her usual eccentric mix of post-apocalyptic girl warrior meets punk rocker, an eye flutter and a hair flip.

Lizzie jumped up from the chalk drawing of a Zombie-Alien-Barbie Doll she was making in the wet asphalt just in time to avoid another squirt from Bad Doggy. "Hey, Petunia," she said with an easy grin.

"Oh, my God! Bad Doggy!" Petunia was squealing and I wanted to take a shovel to her head, but I knew that was a bad thought. Petunia turned toward Lizzie and performed another flounce-hair flip-pirouette. "My BFFs are calling me 'Tune, but maybe you can call me—"

Brett tripped on a piece of chalk and it sent him flying sideways. He landed on one foot in front of Lizzie and Petunia and howled, "Tunie-Petunie!"

Petunia opened and closed her mouth, once, then twice, and then flounced away huffing, "Like, Oh my God, really? Really Brett? Oh my God." Over her shoulder she added, "If you were one of my BFFs, you could call me Tune."

Lizzie smirked at Brett and made eye contact with me. After I nodded, she replied, "I think I'll just stick with Tunie-Petunie."

Meanwhile, Aaron kept checking his pocket for his cell phone. After he finished scrolling through it, he gave an absent-minded nod toward Bad Doggy. "Ain't he just the cutest little thing ever?"

"Adorable." I agreed, and glared at William when he issued another ear scratch.

I was determined to dislike Petunia's dog. I resolved then and there to write it into my next novel. Yeah, I know, I'm mean. But I promised Lizzie, who somehow got wind of what I was planning, that I wouldn't kill off the dog. I never liked movies where dogs got killed. The big secret here is I'm a softie. Just don't tell Petunia.

Scorecard

2 bowls Cap'n Crunch
1 bowl Kashi Crunch
75 balls thrown,
32 caught
One prayer offered,
Several more answered.
4 hamburgers cooked, only two enjoyed
We can't eat burgers without ketchup!
One password lost
Three new passwords generated
Three laps, 15 arguments, 20 unlawful touches, one Ninja takedown
One website fixed, six passwords changed
13 hugs, 18 I love yous.

Chapter 3

That's what I do in real life. I write books about, as my kids would tell you, "stuff." In reality, I write about us. And about our past lives, and about characters I create from nothing other than the people I see and hear about, and sometimes I just create a character who makes me smile. I like to smile a lot. I'm one of those people who laughs at my own jokes and smiles at the things my characters say.

My life, in other words, is about a little more than merely the pitter-patter of little feet, and the scrubbing of windows smeared with grimy fingerprints. I'm also a minister of sorts, but even that's a little confusing, because I don't quite have a church. It's more like I help people, but I do it quietly. I got a big settlement from when a bus hit me, and I use that money to pay people's electricity, to buy food for hungry single mothers, and whatever else comes my way, I pay it if I can. And I talk to people.

I listen to their problems and sometimes, I just listen. It's what we all do, really. At this church I went to the other day, the lady who was talking said that in the early Christian church, everyone acted like a priest, and there were no actual priests. Just everyone helping out the best they could with what they have, and because I have a little more, I help a little more. And I write. I write stories that make me smile.

So it was wintertime in Northern Virginia. It was that time when the snow is turning grey and the skies match the grey snow. And I was between book projects, staring at those skies, gazing somewhat disconsolately at a yellow notepad. Trying to think about a good story I could tell.

In wintertime here in Northern Virginia, the suburbs run on lower-grade fuel. We live a good bit south of the Mason-Dixon line and folks around here complain about the temperature once it dips below 40 degrees. I didn't see too much of Bad Doggy in January, February and March. Every once in awhile, we'd run into Aaron scrolling through the phone numbers on his cell phone, or Petunia, who now went by *Tunes*, pacing along beside Bad Doggy. Petunia was always as deeply into conversation as Aaron was into the important thing he was reading on his cell phone, but they'd always stop so that Junior and Brett and Lizzie could pet Bad Doggy. Sometimes, we'd see Bad Doggy zigzagging behind Petunia's big sister, who'd long since adopted the nickname *Rhodie*. I suspected her actual name was Rhododendron, but no matter how bad I tried, I could never make the issue come up in conversation.

One late March morning, someone knocked on my front door, and I knew it wasn't the UPS guy, because he always taps the doorbell, and I can hear his diesel engine firing up before I even reach the landing at the bottom of the steps. I opened the door and Aaron, who was wearing a business suit, stood there with a smile as goofy looking as his red bowtie.

I was on a ministry call, and he made the motions as if to say he'd come by later. I scanned the doc he was holding in his hand, and recognized the letterhead. It was from our Homeowners' Association, which I adore. It's sad to say for a freethinker like me, but I kind of dislike neon-colored houses.

"Whatcha building?"

"A fence, and if it's not a good time—"

I reached my hand out. "Nope, it's a great time. You just need me to sign, right?" Without waiting for him to answer me, I clicked my ballpoint pen, fine, blue ink, and scrawled my name all over at least two of the wrong boxes before I found the right place. It was like signing a contract, or a treaty, without any need to promise anything.

Aaron made some nice social noises, and I slammed the door shut, thinking I'd have peace now that he was gone. And I did. At least, that afternoon I had peace.

A couple weeks dripped past. The leaves got greener. The lawbirds and the robins and the sparrows showed up, and so did the poor bird, who we nicknamed Narcissus, who visits our back deck each year. I know he's here because of the tapping sound I keep hearing on the glass beneath the window in my study. He always falls in love with his own reflection in the family room window, and knocks himself silly trying to give himself a kiss. Each year, I tape a photograph of a hawk to the window to save Narcissus from himself.

One day, Narcissus flew away, leaving a trail of droppings and a nest on top the grill cover, and I thought I'd finally have some peace and quiet. I even popped a can of root beer to celebrate.

And then, right after the children got on their school bus, and as I was sipping my morning coffee, I heard a brand new sound: Ka-CHINK. I set my steaming mug beside my laptop, praying as I always did that it wouldn't spill all over my keyboard in some horrific karma-induced tragedy, and approached the line of windows on the back of our five four and a door to investigate.

I heard it again: Ka-CHINK! It sounded like an industrial-sized stapler, and the emphasis was on the second syllable. I sort of liked the sound. It sounded like I was standing on a factory floor somewhere in the Midwest, or so I imagined. I closed my eyes and pretended I was having an adventure. *I was on the line, and we were building cars and this massive monster of a machine was swinging around, grabbing wheels with the hulking arms and—*

Ka-CHINK!

I loved the sound. Just adored it. For about the first fifteen times I heard it.

The sixteenth time, I started to pace and get a little frantic. *What the heck was it?* Then I caught a glimpse of a stack of wooden boards through the slats in our two-inch plantation blinds and realized that Bad Doggy was finally getting his fence. I loved the look of the fence. I still do, actually. It's made out of a lightly-stained wood, three long boards held together by vertical planks set about seven feet apart, with chicken wire bound between the boards. It looks rustic and rugged. I could handle—Ka-CHINK for another day or Ka-CHINK so. Maybe.

Chapter 4

Within a few days, I realized I'd signed a treaty about as equitable as any of the ones the Indians signed with the white man. In effect, by signing Aaron's HOA form, I bargained away a lifetime of peace and quiet in return for a little neighborly goodwill and about five minutes of peace. Being the ridiculous woman I am, I hadn't even earned much goodwill when Aaron coerced me into signing his doggone HOA form.

The first morning, I thought Bad Doggy was having a bad day. Like the whole thing was a strange anomaly. I mean, shoot, every dog loses his or her mind on occasion right? Even Sandy's dog Louise loses her mind on occasion, but only when Louise gets consigned to the patio. She has a workman problem, or to be precise, a bad habit of biting anyone who comes near Sandy wearing a badge or a clipboard.

So when Bad Doggy barked for two straight hours, I tried to ignore him. Then I started pacing and mumbling under my breath. Finally, I threw my mouse down and called William to whine about "bad working conditions." Then I drove to Starbucks and told everyone in earshot I was a writer, which is one of my more dreadful habits, because then everyone asks, "Whatcha writing?" Usually, I murmur, "Stuff," and imagine the dollars that aren't adding up in the cash register. Like you know the sound of money going, "Ka-Ching?" I hear it not ringing, if that's possible. It's why I need a manager.

Oh, and I made the mistake of complaining to one of the mafia moms about my very loud neighbor's dog. This mom, call her Leanne Little, is good friends with Aaron's wife, Esmerelda. Somehow I forgot about this in the middle of my monologue, which Leanne accidentally taped on her cell phone. I know it sounds like a stretch, but it's true. And then, even worse, she played it to a bunch of her friends at book club, and they were drinking wine and . . . well. Facebook. YouTube. There you go.

And so this virtuoso performance of mine, by far not my worst in a historical sense, but certainly my most widely watched, explains in part my unfortunate place in the local social hierarchy. I belong somewhere at the bottom, right there with the pot dealers.

At least they will hang out with me.

•••

Junior and Brett had taken over the entire family room coffee table with a model ark they were assembling. We'd ordered the ark for Christmas, and it had taken them a few months to get started on the project. Almost each week now, I had been driving them out to the arts and crafts store, the hardware store, and even the music store (best reeds around, and reeds are good for masts) to acquire more supplies. The funnest trip we had made though was to a specialty toy store. We had seen a flyer for after-Christmas sales of farms, and sure enough, we had snagged an entire farm, complete with sixteen different types of farm animals, for only $19.99. And we had discovered a display that had free-standing zoo animals, so for another $32.97, we had bought two each of zebras, lions, tigers, monkeys, hippos, bears, and rhinos.

Now, the coffee table had become a veritable animal farm. One of the kids had spilled a half bottle of cement glue on the antique surface, and to hide the evidence from William (and perhaps in a fit of naughtiness), Lizzie and I had affixed the animals atop the still sticky glue. Right beside the glop of glue stood a box of recycled Popsicle sticks, which we were using for the planks on the decks. And now the ark had reached its fourth and final deck, and

Junior was using an Exacto knife to carve a door into the bottom deck, which was by far the largest of the decks.

On the other side of the table, Brett was kneeling, a paintbrush in his hand. He had several popsicle sticks glued together, and was applying coats of varnish to seal in the light brown paint we had used for the side boards that led up to the space for the massive door, which was where the animals would enter the ark once the flood waves hit the sides of the tub. William, thank goodness, was not home to see just how much paint we were getting on the table, which was looking like something out of a Halloween nightmare—garish, but oddly appealing to the eye.

Now, Lizzie was asking me questions about the ark, and I was frowning over a mast I was gluing to the rigging that was yet to be affixed to the top deck.

"Mom, did it rain for just forty days and forty nights? Or was that just the story they told in Genesis?"

"Well, I think it rained a lot longer actually, like most of the time for a couple of years, but once the story got filtered down to Gaddarison—"

"—That's who wrote Genesis?"

"Yeah, he was Moses' main scribe."

"What's a scribe? A writer?"

"Yeah," I said. "So I think what happened based on the meteorological record—"

"—What's meteoro . . ." Junior scrunched up his face trying to pronounce the word.

"Weather-related," Lizzie said.

Junior made a face at her.

"It stands for weather, yes," I said. I paused and gave them both a long look, and they both got the message and stopped making faces at one another. "So the meteorological record shows that the poles probably shifted around 9500 BC. Basically, imagine that the South Pole was to the right of Antarctica, and the North Pole was over top Canada. So if the poles shifted like this," I showed my hands shifting to the left on the bottom and to the right on the top. "If the poles shifted, the ice would be melting in those spots, and that means water would be moving all around and flooding all the surrounding sea sides, which is usually where cities are situated, so all the major populations are getting flooded, and people are having to move to the mountains, or they're fleeing their homes in boats and ships—"

"—Wow, sounds like a massive cataclysm," Brett gasped.

"Much worse than the sinking of the Titanic or the Lusitania," Junior agreed.

"Yes," I said. "It was a world-wide event, and it affected every city on earth, even the ones on higher land because they had to deal with waves or survivors or immigrants."

"Oh," Lizzie said. "Lots of refugees to help, I bet they had to feed them and give them shelter." Lizzie glowed a little at the thought of it.

I smiled. "And the neat thing is this flood is spoken of in indigenous tribes all over the world, in their oral traditions, so it must have affected the whole world."

Lizzie grasped a mast and then fumbled around with it until it tumbled sideways into the opening of the blue paint bottle. Brett was using blue for the flags, which he was fashioning in the style of Israel's Star of David. Lizzie made a rueful face and shook her head. "I think this one is hopelessly blue where it's sposed to be white," she giggled.

"You could make it into an interior furnishing," Brett said.

"Oh no," I groaned.

"Oh no, what?" Junior said.

"I forgot we were going to decorate the interior, so I need to raid a doll's house for sofas and chairs, but I threw out Lizzie's dollhouse in a cleaning fit."

"Oh Mom, your cleaning fits are so inconsistent," Lizzie said.

"Yeah," I said, "But you were on an *I hate Barbies* kick, and your entire closet was taken up by the doll house, I never thought to turn the furniture into ark salvage."

"Mom?" Junior started to say.

I held up a hand. "Just a sec. I know," I said. "We can try to get a used dollhouse from the Goodwill store in town, and we can also give them some old clothing."

"Great, so long as we don't get any Barbies," Lizzie said.

"Don't be too particular," I chuckled. Then I turned to Junior and said, "What were you going to ask?"

"I understand if the poles shifting caused flooding, but what about all that rain? What's that got to do with? Why would it have rained for so long? Did the pole shift also affect the jet stream or something? Or cause more weather fronts to develop?"

I thought about it for a moment, and the answer came to me with a dead certainty of it being true. I shook my head, because it almost felt like someone was speaking to me, but it was a thought rather than the sound of someone's voice. "I think that in order to facilitate the pole shift, you have to oil the ground so to speak."

"Oil?" Lizzie made a disgusted face.

"Oh, no honey, that's not what I mean, I mean, like, you know when the door squeaks and you put some WD-40 in it? To oil the hinges so to speak?"

Lizzie nodded.

"Mom, you need to oil my closet door," Junior said. "But is that what you're saying the rain did? If it rained for months or years or the like, the rain oiled the ground and the liquid maybe filtered down to the tectonic plates . . ." Junior's forehead wrinkled in concentration as he tried to visualize what the ground would have looked like after a year or so of continuous or near-continuous rain.

I listened and thought about it and what he was suggested sounded accurate. "Yeah, that sounds right," I said.

Brett set his brush down and jumped to his feet. "I'm gonna go test the bathtub, make sure the waves get high enough."

"Oh gosh, Brett, remember to turn off the spigot this time."

"At least before Dad gets home," Junior said.

"Yeah, he'll make you bathe in the laundry tub if you flood the bathroom again," Lizzie said.

"Oh, he said that?" I shook my head and put the cap on the blue paint.

"Yes," Lizzie said.

I thought about cooking dinner, but wasn't really feeling like it. And I thought about the calls I needed to make for the ministry, but those calls really could wait. Last, I thought how badly I needed to take a walk and get a moment alone. But that could also wait.

"Maybe I should supervise," I finally said.

Brett burst into a big smile. "You will?"

Chapter 5

I was between book projects. From a practical standpoint, this meant it was time to clean the house. I used to keep a clean house, before I worked. And there are still times I keep a clean house. Usually I will finish a book and it's kind of like I'm once again aware of the environment around me. It's about then I'll go and tell the kids to clean their rooms and I'll run around for a couple days dusting and vacuuming and painting rooms and rearranging furniture and for at least those few days, I'll act kind of righteous about the whole clean house thing. Or at least the idea of the whole clean house thing.

It didn't take me long to realize I'd met my match. In fact, after I finished the last book, which I almost but did not name *Bad Doggy* (see, he inspires me), I went into Lizzie's room and started in on how nice it would be if she got her things set in order. Lizzie was busy penning one of her stories. She was writing about rescuing kittens and giving them new homes in loving families. So it took me several tries to get her attention, but I was rolling. I was really leaning into this lecture, actually. I was saying, "Now, whaddya say Lizzie, don't you think you could get your homework done more easily if you could find your pencils, your pens, and weren't always misplacing your blue binder?"

Lizzie had given me a thoughtful look and then glanced longingly back at the Harry Potter book she was reading between the paragraphs she was composing. "No, I don't think so, not really Mom," she said.

"Really? Huh." I leaned against her doorframe and let my eyes linger over a pile of laundry that was impinging on her desk area. "I don't know how you can possibly manage to answer the harder of the math questions when your desk is in such a state of . . ." I gestured at her desk, "Look at the six shirts, five socks, ten rubber bands . . . and a partridge in a pear tree sort of . . ." I waved my hand at the mess in front of me, and finished with, "It's a disastrous sort of disorder."

"Well," she said, "Here's the thing. Have you looked at your office lately? How many pens, markers, empty coffee mugs, bottles of fancy oil from Doe, telephones, wires, cords . . . and yes, what did you say, partridge in a pear tree disastrous disorder surrounding all your papers and writings oh and don't forget newspaper clippings." Lizzie was smiling.

So was I.

I had no response for this. So I turned and while I was on my heels, I heard Lizzie mutter, "Chalk that one up for Lizzie."

•••

I don't want to give the wrong impression about Lizzie. I adore her. She's a wise soul and she is a joy to parent—in most cases. Or so I was reminding myself one Sunday afternoon, as I was going over some proofs of one of the books I'd written. I was sitting out on the deck, kind of supervising the children. They were supposed to be picking up sticks in the backyard but every few minutes, Lizzie was coming up and showing me just how badly she didn't want to pick up sticks. Of course, she wasn't saying that. Not in every so many words.

"Hey Mom, how big should the sticks be?"

"I don't know, sticks."

"Well, but how big? Dad says we don't usually have to pick up twigs."

"Okay."

"Because the twigs don't hurt the lawnmower. But bigger than twigs hurts the new lawnmower." We'd gotten an environmentally friendly lawnmower that was as ineffective as it was friendly. But it was green and we liked it.

"Okay."

A few minutes later, she was back. "Hey Mom?"

"Yes."

"What if the twigs are near a bee's nest?"

"I don't know, are there any bee's nests out there?" I looked over the post at one of the azaleas in the backyard. Next to it was a recycled milk jug that contained some sort of bee killing potion in it, or so William had explained to me one night when I wasn't really paying attention.

"Brett saw a bee, so there might be a nest near the bench."

"One bee doesn't make a nest," I said.

"Two bees?"

"I don't know, no. Not two bees."

"Well, what if I see three bees?"

I sighed and returned Lizzie's stare. Finally, I said, "Please go pick up sticks and let me know if you see more than three bees within the same zip code."

"Zip code? How wide an area is that?"

"Please. Lizzie. Sticks."

"Okay," she said.

Five minutes later she was back. "Hey Mom."

"Yes."

"How many sticks? Dad usually gives us a set amount or divides the yard into thirds and then gives us ice cream when we finish or says whoever picks up the most sticks gets ice cream and the other two kids don't get ice cream. He says he's teaching us about incentives. I think it's mean. Don't you?"

"Um," I said, "I don't know."

"Junior usually wins and then he gets ice cream and Brett and I don't." Lizzie frowned. "So how many sticks?"

"As many as you can pick up, okay Lizzie?"

"In how much time?"

"In how much time what?" I sighed and turned the page of my book.

"Mom, you're not giving me enough guidelines. How can I get this job done and supervise the boys getting their part of it done if you don't give me clear guidelines?" Lizzie did one of her hair flips-nose pinch-smiles and then said, "So perhaps you'd like me to help you with the editing instead?"

That's when I remembered one of the stories Archangel Raziel used to tell me in heaven. It was the Reluctant Cow Sacrifice Story, and she told it to me lots when I was a baby soul. I always loved this story, and now it was my turn to regale a miscreant child with it.

"Hey Lizzie, wanna hear one of Archangel Raziel's stories? From the time she was Moses?"

"Oh yes, Mom, I love Raz's stories," Lizzie said.

"Okay. Come sit next to me," I said.

I grinned to myself. I was feeling like the wolf when he first caught a glimpse of Goldilocks . . . well, that was kind of a weird thought. "Okay," I said. "So you remember Moses and the group of people he was leading through the desert, out of Egypt, and how he got the Ten Commandments and all that?"

"Yeah, he dropped them the first time because they were worshiping a golden calf—hey Mom, was it really gold? As in they made a calf out of gold?"

I nodded. "Probably, yeah, they had a lot of gold, Moses was rich, so were a lot of the priests who followed him out of Egypt."

"Oooh so that's some of the buried gold you and Brett are always talking about?" Lizzie's eyes gleamed.

I rapped the table and leaned in closer to her. Brett and I were always studying maps of the Middle East and Egypt, plus islands in the Mediterranean. We were both kind of obsessed with what had been buried in the sands centuries ago, but I'm getting ahead of myself and, I realized, Lizzie was about to get me off-course. "Yes, yes," I said, with just a tad of impatience. "So anyway, that's the background, right? These people were kind of a pain in Moses' butt, okay? You with me?"

"Yeah, they never listened, kind of like how you say Raz says you never listen," Lizzie said.

We grinned at one another.

"Yep, that's true. So one day, Moses goes back up to the mountain and talks to God. Then he comes back down and says, 'Right, so now we need to sacrifice a heifer to God.' And he—"

"—What's a heifer?"

"It's a cow. So anyway, Moses says they gotta sacrifice a cow. Now, the leader of the group says to him, 'A cow? You sure? Can you double-check with God about that? You sure he doesn't want, oh I dunno, maybe a goat?' And Moses rolls his eyes, can you imagine Raz rolling her eyes?" I traded eye rolls with Lizzie and we both giggled.

Then I continued, "Moses is like, 'Oh okay, I'll double-check, fine,' and he goes and talks to God and then he comes back and this time he tells Aaron, who does most of his talking for him, to do the talking. So Moses is standing next to Aaron and the village head, his name was Simple—"

"—Was it really?"

"Nah," I said, "Just making sure you're listening. But Simple's a good name for him. When Aaron tells Simple to go ahead and sacrifice a cow, Simple's like, 'Okay a cow. Wow. Okay, well, how big of a cow?' And Moses shakes his head and whispers to Aaron, 'Middle-sized cow, a cow,' and Simple says okay. And a few days later, Moses sends for Simple and Aaron's not around so Moses says to Simple, 'Hey, how about that cow? Aren't you worried God's gonna be upset with you?' And Simple says, 'Oh, um, yeah, about that cow, how old should the cow be? Should it be a baby calf? Shouldn't it be, I dunno, maybe a really old cow?'"

"Like one that's about to die?"

I nodded at Lizzie. "And Moses was like, 'No, not a baby calf, course not, but not one that's decrepit and senile either.' So Simple goes off, right, and Moses is waiting and waiting, and then he sends off for Simple again. And when Simple comes to talk to Moses, he's still not got the cow. Moses is like, 'Simple, where's the cow?' And Simple says, and he's talking really slowly now, he says, 'Well, should it be a female or male cow?' Moses is thinking he's wanting to strangle Simple and strangle Aaron too because of course Aaron should be handling all this, but Moses is real patient. He says, 'A female cow is fine. Now go! Go and sacrifice that cow for the Lord.'"

"Oh man, so did they sacrifice the cow?" Lizzie was breathless now and I was getting all theatrical, more and more so as I told the story. I was having fun with it.

"Well no, not yet. Moses waited a couple more days and he sends for Simple again. He's says, "Simple, how about that cow?' And Simple kind of hesitates and then stretches his hands out in supplication and he's like, 'Well, what if the cow is about to have babies?' Moses is like, 'Come again? That's stupid, if the cow has calves suckling from it, no, don't sacrifice that one.' So Simple turns to go and then he's like, 'Wait, how about if the calves were weaned within the last year?' And Moses is like, 'Just go, get God his cow, man.'"

I paused again, and Lizzie was looking downright murderous now. She didn't interrupt though, so I continued, "Okay, so where were we? Ah yes. Simple still hasn't come back with the cow yet, so Moses sends Aaron to get him and he has Aaron ask Simple, in the clearest language possible, 'Where's the beef?' And Simple's like, 'Oh. Right. You're still waiting on a cow, right?' Aaron says, 'Right,' and then Simple says, 'But you never told us what color cow.'"

"Oh my God, just go and kill a cow!" Lizzie was screaming next to me and I waited for her face to turn back to its usual light shade.

Then I turned to her and said, "That's exactly how I'm feeling about those sticks you're supposed to be picking up, you know?"

Lizzie's mouth opened and closed. Then she said, "But how about the cow? What happened?"

I stood up from the chair and put my hand out. She took it and stood beside me. Then I kissed her forehead and said, "Once you go and pick up the sticks, you come on back here and find me and I'll tell you how the story ends."

Lizzie gave me a bit of a look. Then she mumbled, "Fine. You win this round. I'll be back."

Chapter 6

Speaking of Lizzie, she and I were taking a walk, or a walk and talk. This is when we do most our talking, or in most cases, she talks and I listen. Sometimes I know what to say, but Petunia and one of her friends had made fun of Lizzie's mismatched toe and nail polish, and one of the girls had drawn all over Lizzie's lunch box. I had no idea what to say. I don't like saying over and over again, "Gosh, Lizzie, I love you, and kids can be jerks, so just play with someone else" each time she gets slighted by Petunia or Rhododendron (I decided that's gotta be her actual name, and I tested it out the other day by calling her it and she gave me the greatest eye roll and flounce head-roll, so I knew I was right). I was struggling to make Lizzie feel better though about what Petunia and her gang did to Lizzie's lunch bag. Everything I tried that usually worked—a few kind words, and a lot of elbows to the ribs, and some funny stories about my favorite archangels, weren't helping.

So I called my best friend Stevie, and put her on speaker. For reasons I'll explain later, I call her Mama.

"Hey Mama, I'm here with Lizzie, we're walkin' and talkin', how are you?"

I could feel Stevie's warm smile in her voice. "Hi there, hi Lizzie," she said.

"Hi Stevie!" Lizzie and Brett generally omit a "Miss" from Stevie's name when they talk to her, unless William is around. Junior usually calls her "ma'am," but he's been calling her "Stevie" too, and it's not a lack of respect. It's because she's so comfy and familiar.

"So you're outside? I bet it's nice and warm there." Stevie lived out in Montana, which always seemed ironic to me, because I liked the cold and Stevie hated the cold and much preferred the hot weather of Virginia. Said it warmed her bones and that the cold was a general affront to her soul, which always made me laugh.

"Ugh, at least ninety in the shade." I swatted at a gnat and Lizzie quipped, "Mom's slaying innocent bugs again."

"There are no innocent bugs," I said.

"But Sally, they're outside, you're bugging them in their natural habitat." I could envision Stevie rolling her eyes at me with a dramatic raise of her eyebrows, and it made me smile even wider.

"Ha, was that word play, or a rhetorical device?" Lizzie's forehead knit into horizontal thought lines.

"Probably word play," Stevie replied.

"Like what Petunia and her friends are doing to my lunch bag?"

"Um, what?" Stevie's voice rose. "Someone's messing with your stuff at school? Isn't Petunia the girl who lives next door to you, who's been calling you 'Dizzy Lizzie' and whatnot?"

Lizzie nodded.

I tapped her arm and gestured toward the phone.

"Yes, that's the girl, and now she's gone too far. A couple days ago, she and her friends took markers in art class and scribbled 'Dizzy Lizzie' and some other stuff on my lunchbox and—"

"—Wait," I said, "Why was your lunchbox with you at art class?"

"They stole my lunch box the day before, and I got it back that morning, and I didn't want them to take it again, and we have art right before lunch, so I just took it with me," Lizzie explained.

"And why," Stevie said, "Aren't you saying anything to these girls, Lizzie? Why are you letting them steal your stuff?"

"I'm afraid they'll report me to the teacher, Petunia's a patrol leader, all the teachers think she's the bomb, they won't listen to me, I'll get in trouble if I tell on her . . ." Lizzie's voice trailed off as she listed her string of excuses. It was as if she were losing wind like a balloon that's been popped with a pencil in the side.

"That's nonsense," Stevie retorted.

"What, that her teachers won't believe her?"

"No, I get that but it's ridiculous to be afraid of the repercussions." Stevie took her time pronouncing that last word, so much so that I found myself thinking of a mallet hitting a drum with percussive effect.

Aloud, I mumbled, "Maybe Petunia needs a percussion shot to the head."

Lizzie giggled. "We're not allowed to hit people."

"Yeah," I said, "True—"

"—But you're allowed to stand up for yourself, and you're not doing that Lizzie, you can't be afraid of these girls or else they will keep torturing you, stealing your stuff, writing on your things, lying about you, once they start down this route and they see that you're scared, they'll just keep getting more emboldened, they will think you're weak and they will stomp all over you, and you can't allow that, you need to stop being scared of them." Stevie was still speaking slowly, pausing to hit certain words with emphasis, and the entire time Lizzie's eyes were riveted on the phone.

"Don't just stand there and stare at the phone or at the girls for that matter," Stevie continued. "If they take out their pens, snatch them away. Stand up straight, look them in the eye, tell them to keep their hands off your stuff, it's not their stuff, their hands belong to their stuff, not yours. You will not lack a backbone, do you hear me Lizzie?"

Lizzie nodded.

I shook my head and whispered, "Answer aloud, 'kay?"

"Yes ma'am, okay, I just can't hit them, right?"

"Use your backbone," Stevie said in her peculiarly forceful but feminine voice. "Don't let anyone treat you as less, don't be less, because you're more. Don't let anyone bully you, not under any circumstances, not ever, not for any reason, and do not be afraid to stand up for yourself."

"Yes ma'am," Lizzie said, this time without being prompted.

Stevie's voice softened ever so slightly. "I love you, now Sally, take me off speaker."

"Love you too, thank you Stevie," Lizzie said.

I hit the little red button on the phone and pressed it to my ear. "What, you gonna yell at me now?"

"How did you guess?" Stevie chuckled.

"Because I'm sposed to be teaching my own kid stuff I haven't learned so good?"

"Well," Stevie said, "You are a leader, it's why you've been called, you are to call souls Home, but you also need to call your own kids, right?"

"Yes ma'am," I said, almost automatically.

"Why are you hesitating with that?"

"I dunno, just a sec," I said. "Lizzie, can you run ahead, I gotta talk to Stevie and it's private."

Lizzie wrinkled her nose and shuffled her feet.

"Go on, just gimme five minutes," I urged.

I watched Lizzie's tennis shoes tap the asphalt on the walking path for a few seconds, and then I said to Stevie, "I don't know why I'm a caller really."

"Because God wants you to wear your piece of the robe, it's your mission to call souls Home. That should be enough for you. It's not about the why of it, it's about doing what you're here on earth to do, and doing it to the best of your ability. And yes, I wanted to remind you that calling souls Home starts with the souls that you bore. You need to teach them better, Sally, you need to teach them how to be the best souls they can be, and that includes standing up for themselves and not being afraid of the consequences, it means you do your job."

"But what if no one listens?"

"Oh my god, Sally, you sound just like Lizzie, you ever think about maybe why she's scared to stand up to the mean girls at school may have something to do with you being scared to call?"

I groaned.

"What was that?" Stevie's voice got higher and took on a comical pitch, and I laughed and smiled at the phone. "So you're saying I got a piece of the robe, I guess that means robe of righteousness, like in Isaiah or Revelations?"

"Something like that, I gotta go pick up Desi." As usual, Stevie's response to one of my biblical or godly questions was cryptic.

I sighed and said, "Oh all right, I'll go figure it out myself, it will probably take me hours of research."

"Good," she said.

"Good?" I repeated.

"You should be reading the Word more anyway, gotta know it well to teach it, right?"

"Yeah, yeah."

"I love you," Stevie said.

"Love you too," I said.

•••

After I got the kids to bed, and after William also went to bed, I sat in my study and felt confused. Stevie had been telling me that I was supposed to call souls Home, and I only sorta understood what that meant. She had told me to read the scriptures more intently, so for about the tenth time, I'd gone through the Bible. In the Old Testament, I'd read the chapters and verses about prophets especially. I studied how they lived and how they taught. I'd followed the travails of Jeremiah and Ezekiel the most closely, and watched as Jeremiah kept getting sent to prison and Ezekiel kept seeing visions of heaven.

In the New Testament, I'd also studied John the Baptist and Jesus really closely, and I saw how hard it was for them to talk to people, or to call souls Home. And I was trying to figure out if I was a prophet or what I was supposed to do. And I wasn't understanding when I was gonna get a robe. Maybe it was an imaginary robe; maybe it just meant that I had words of truth and the robe symbolized speaking God's truth.

I was thinking all these things, and I was thinking, "I wish someone would tell me what to do," when a flash of light and a whir of motion caught my attention.

I dropped my Bible, I was so surprised. And frightened. Because when I turned my head and focused on the space to my left, I saw a beautiful, tall man standing next to me. And he had wings. Wings with an array of glorious light blue and pale yellow feathers. His wings swept up to the ceiling and his long, curly black hair touched his shoulder. Flowing white robes stretched from his broad shoulders to his feet, which were covered in brown sandals. I stared at him for several moments with my mouth open.

"Hi, Sally," he said. "Don't be scared, my name is Gabriel."

My hands were shaking.

"Really, it's okay, you're not in trouble."

I tried to speak but the words didn't come out, not until he smiled and repeated his introduction.

"You said Gabriel, as in the great archangel Gabriel?" Tears ran down my cheeks and I wanted to fall to my knees and kiss his feet.

"You don't need to do that, Sally, it's me yes, I'm here to help you." Gabriel's eyes were twinkling, but he also looked serious.

"You can read my mind?"

"Yes."

"It's really you?" I shivered and then the tears stopped falling, because I could feel an overwhelming sense of comfort and safety.

"It's me, yes. Most people are scared when they see me or another archangel, yes. And God sent me to talk to you, to explain that you've got the robes now and you're to call souls Home by speaking and writing His truth."

"Wow," I said. "That sounds like what Stevie told me. She uses the same words."

"That's because she's one of his servants too." Gabriel shifted his weight to one foot and then projected an image of Stevie, but she had a massive set of wings on top her shoulders.

I gasped. "She's a servant, or you mean she's an archangel?"

"All archangels are servants of the Lord, Sally."

I nodded. I was thinking I felt stupid.

"Don't feel bad, you don't remember anything yet, but you will, she's an archangel, she's a servant, and now that you wear the robe, you'll be serving too, what you don't remember is that you serve at Home. This isn't new." Gabriel sent me another image, and in this one, I was taller, still with long blonde hair, but younger, and I was wearing robes. And wings?

"No, I'm not—"

"—Yes, you are, and you're here to help other humans, so stop doubting what I'm telling you. Stevie's in charge down here, listen to her. She knows her mission; she also knows what you're supposed to do." His eyes widened as he flashed me a reassuring smile.

"This is almost too much . . ." I closed my eyes and blinked really fast. But when I opened my eyes, Gabriel was still there.

"You'll get used to it," Gabriel said.

"Why does Stevie say I have a piece of the robe? That's confusing to me."

Gabriel chuckled and said, "One time you lost it, so she doesn't like to give you the whole robe, but I'm sure God will let you have an entire robe."

"You're sure?"

"I am, come on Sally, I got something to show you." Gabriel put his hand out, and I said, "Where are we going?"

"Well," he said, "You're not actually leaving your body but I want to show you something so it will feel like you're in heaven, it's more like a vision, you know what that's like?"

"Um, like Ezekiel saw, right?"

"Yes, like that. It's real, but you're going to stay here in your study on earth, but it will feel like you're traveling, I want to show you some things."

I reached out and realized as I tried to touch Gabriel's hand that he was in soul form—he looked real, but he didn't feel like anything physically. But before I could ask him how that worked, I felt like I was moving at some crazy speed, and then I wasn't in my study anymore. I was moving across the earth, and at a high rate of speed.

We zoomed through the atmosphere for a few more moments, and then we alit just above a hospital. An angel was part-flying, part-carrying a somewhat smaller soul, a human. I somehow knew she was an old lady.

"Watch this," Gabriel said. "Her guardian is gonna take her home to her family."

The scene shifted, and now we were headed to heaven. The guardian and the old lady floated through a tunnel, and at the end of it, they emerged into a light-filled atrium. At the entrance to the atrium waited three other souls, and as soon as the old lady reached them, she shouted, "Miriam!" And then she jumped into the arms (but it was more like jumping into a swirl of bright color, with a face that looked like a happy young woman) of the awaiting family member.

"Oh Rose, I'm so happy to see you!" Miriam exclaimed.

"Who is that?" I asked.

"It was her sister on earth, and it's her mother back Home," Gabriel explained.

I watched as Rose and Miriam hugged and chatted for a few moments, and then they floated through the atrium, which opened onto a rock-lined road.

"Where are they going?"

"To their home here in heaven, they live a few clicks down from the town." Gabriel nodded toward a gorgeous city that stood astride a green-blue river, and then pointed up the hill. "Wanna see where we live?"

"Wait," I stuttered. "But are you telling me that we start living in heaven, then come down to earth, then we go back Home and we live with our families? And 'Home' is what you call Heaven?"

Gabriel started to move up the hill, and then he stopped and gave me a slow smile. "Yes, of course, we live, we go back, we live again, we come Home, and it's not just what I call Heaven, it's what you call Heaven."

"Me?" I took a tentative step and realized I was now in a different form. Like Gabriel I had wings and as soon as I thought about it, I lifted off the ground and so did Gabriel.

"I can fly?" I giggled, and then flapped my wings and glanced at them. Colors rose and sparkled in the golden light, and with a few more flaps, we rose high above the pink, orange, brown and tan rooftops. In all directions, I could see houses and buildings of various shapes and designs. Aside each house appeared a mixture of flowers, trees, grass, and an occasional fence, and there were souls moving to and fro, as if they had business to attend to somewhere in town. I felt content, and everything seemed familiar.

"Seems like it."

"Are you sure I'm—"

"—You're part angel, yes, you belong to God."

"You mean I serve? And what do you mean, I'm part-angel?" I glanced at my wings and couldn't contain a smile.

Gabriel's dark locks glistened beneath a setting sun, and a look of bemusement crossed his visage. "Well, how about if we ask God himself?"

"God?" I was choking on my words.

Gabriel landed on a walkway that wound to the top of a hill. I alit beside him. To my right was a white colonial mansion with columns and white shutters. "That's your house, isn't it?"

Gabriel nodded and pointed to a tall building that stood at least ten stories high. "That's called the Frat, it's where you grew up, it's where most the Master Archangels, those are the top ones, there's about twenty-seven of us, that's where they live, and that place next to it, that's the University, it's where angels and humans can attend classes and receive training, and that house there, it's where Jesus and Mary live." We were passing by a pretty structure that was almost salmon colored, with slightly darker shingles, a cupola and balcony sticking out from the second floor, fronted by a garden full of hummingbirds and butterflies.

"Um, I thought Jesus sat at the right hand of God?"

"Well, his house is to the right of God's house, but what did you think, that God and Jesus sit around all day, judging people?" Gabriel rolled his eyes and added, "And that of course is God's house. You should know it well."

"You mean they're busy, taking care of us? Of things back Home, of people living on earth?" I peered at a white house, built in a mix of Greek Revival and Renaissance styles, with maybe a hint of Tudor styling. The home was white, and Caribbean ocean blue shutters adorned it.

"Yes, but don't just take what I tell you on faith. You can ask Him yourself."

Before I could open my mouth, the door opened, and a handsome middle-aged man with flowing blonde hair stepped out onto the terrace. He waved at me, and He looked happy. "Sally," He said, "You were asking about the robe I believe. Do you see what you're wearing?"

I peeked at my torso, and gleaming robes covered my multi-colored swirls. "You mean, I'm wearing the robes, the ones that mean I'm serving, you mean . . ." I froze and then stared into God's blue-grey eyes. ". . . And you're . . ."

"Yes." He shut the door and then spread out His arms and gestured towards me. "I'm God, and I'm speaking to you, it's okay, Sally, look at me, I love you."

I realized my eyes were centered on the ground, which was covered in cobblestones and dotted with white and pink flowers. "It's . . . you're . . . beautiful." I shifted my gaze and then I was looking into His eyes again. "You love me?"

"Of course I do," He said.

"What do you want me to do?"

He motioned towards me again, and I moved into His arms, and He hugged me tight and whispered, "Just write and speak what I give you, I'll be talking to you more, I love you."

I sighed and felt His warmth, His love, His beauty, and I said, "I love you too, thank you God, I'll do anything you ask me to do."

"I know," He said.

"And you work all day? You're busy, so is Jesus?"

"Yes," He said.

And then everything shifted; it was like the world receded and changed; and I was back in my study.

I felt the hint of a kiss on my cheek.

And then Gabriel was gone, and I was sitting in my chair, smiling, and missing Home.

•••

I dreamed that night of Home. God was there, and His blue-grey eyes were smiling at me.

I smiled back at Him and said, "Are you here? Or am I there?"

"I'm with you. And you were asking, I think about the robe again?"

"The robe?" I looked down, a little embarrassed.

"Yes," He said. "Whether you only got a square of it or the whole robe, it's your pride, you're missing the real story because you're caring about inconsequential things." He spoke so gently, His words didn't hurt.

"Yeah, I guess it doesn't matter," I mumbled.

"It's not that it doesn't matter, because you wanted to understand, and that's okay, He said."

"It's okay?" I felt a little better, and once again, I was seeing the kindness in His eyes.

"The issue isn't that your pride makes you bad, it's that it takes over sometimes, and you forget, and now you need to remember."

"Remember what?" Before He spoke, I saw an image of a young man, and he seemed a little frantic, like he was searching for something. He spoke to one lady, and then he waved, and smiled, and looked worried again. Once he was out of her sight, he ran to another house, and he asked the man there a question. The man he visited shrugged, and then the man, and I knew at that moment the man was me, but from another time, and I was searching . . .

"Wow," I said. "Is that me, from another lifetime, and I lost the robe, the robe I was supposed to wear, and I was looking for it?"

"Yes," God said.

"But why do I need to remember? Why is that more important than having too much pride?"

"Well, if you remember your past lives, you will remember not only the lessons you still need to learn, but the lessons you have already learned, yes?"

"What do I need to remember exactly?"

"Other times you've worn the robe, Sally."

I stood and stared at Him. I had so much to ask Him . . ."

"Don't worry." God smiled again. "I'll be back, listen for me when you're out walking, I'll walk and talk with you."

"You'll talk more with me?"

"Yes. I love you Sally. Just listen. And remember."

I started to say *I love you too*, but then He was gone. And I awoke to the singsong of larks and blue jays outside my window, and to the wisps of clouds obscuring a rising sun.

Chapter 7

Later the Same Day

It was still morning. Bad Doggy was barking. Brett the geologist was channeling Forrest Gump.

"And this is green opal which is Dad's birthday stone well kind of; at least it's a type of opal and that's the October birthday stone. And this is peridot which is your birthstone, for August, but you don't like that one so we're gonna pretend you're born in March because that's aquamarine and you like blue. And this is carbon and this is slate, check it out, this is carbon with gold streaks and if I got my pick I could chisel it down and then we'd have gold which is Au on the periodic table and it has a hardness of three which is a lot lower than diamond which has a hardness of ten. That's the hardest hardness.

"Oh and this is pink graphite don't you like the pink streaks? And this is glass diamond I wish we had diamond my birthstone I told you diamond's the hardest there is, harder than granite even, they use diamonds to cut stuff did you know that? When Dad took me to see the Hope Diamond it was amazing but it's actually really small you know and it can be worn as a necklace did you know that Mom?"

I groaned.

"And this is magnetic hematite which is a type of hematite but it's *magnetic*; don't ever *ever* no matter what put it near the computer because it will destroy it and look Mom it's got paperclips and scissors stuck to it. The magnet on the fridge is not as strong and maybe that's because it's painted hematite not hermaphrodite which Dad says he'll teach me about when I get older. And this is turquoise and you like blue so maybe we can change your birth month again . . ."

This went on for at least two hours. I kept whimpering and begging Brett to leave me alone, let me read the Bible and drink my morning coffee. Lizzie and Junior cleared out of the kitchen after the fifteenth citation of the word peridot, but only after Lizzie unsuccessfully tried to correct Brett on the MOH Hardness of diamonds.

"Oh please, Lizzie," Brett snapped, sounding like an adult. "Everyone knows diamond is hardness level ten, please."

Lizzie had rolled her eyes and left the kitchen.

"I figured out why Jesus died on Easter," Brett said.

"Oh yeah? Why?" My mind sped ahead to the cross and the resurrection and I was trying to figure out how to explain it.

"Because Easter's in April. And April's rock, you know, birth stone is a diamond. And diamonds are the hardest of the rocks. Hardness is ten. So they're the best rocks and April's the best month and so Jesus—"

"—Is the best, right?"

"Right," Brett said. "But I don't think diamonds are as good as quartz actually you know why?"

"Um, no, why?"

"Come on Mom, for the same reason you're always saying jewelry is boring."

"Come on, I'm too tired to think, just tell me."

"Okay, because quartz—"

"—Hardness level seven, like granite," I quipped.

"Yeah, but that's only how hard it is to scratch. Granite has a bunch of different minerals or types of things in it, and once you meld them together, what happens is," and Brett had taken his fingers and interlaced them together, "You get a snowflake sort of pattern, like this."

"But snowflakes are soft," I said.

And then Brett had almost glared at me, but in a friendly way, and explained, "No, listen Mom. The hardness of granite results from its interlocking mineral structure. This happens when crystals grow out of a molten state. As different minerals reach their point of crystallization, they form in whatever space is available and after they're all done forming, they've tightly interlocked, and that looks like the snowflakes you draw in class, not so much like the ones that fall except for when they get really big, and that's when the arms, the six arms of the snow flake lattice form according to the varying temperatures met by the molecules as the snow crystal tumbles through the air." Brett had gone on about hexagons and facets and crystalline lattices and I'd tried not to count how many times Bad Doggy was barking through all of this.

And I'm serious about this: Bad Doggy was punctuating every sentence with a bark or a yelp. After Brett finished his dissertation on crystalline lattices, I realized Brett had never explained why quartz was better than diamonds, so I asked him about it.

"Oh, of course. Quartz lets us talk to God. Diamond is just shiny and pretty. Really kind of silly dontcha think, wanting diamonds when quartz can get you Home?"

"Mmm," I said. "But diamonds are great for cutting the quartz, so they are useful, right?"

"True," he said. "Better to use your mind to do the cutting."

"Think you can use your mind to make that dog stop barking?"

Brett shook his head seriously at me.

"How about if we go to the pool?"

"To escape the barking?" Lizzie came back in the room and heard the last bit of our conversation.

"Yes, Lizzie," I said. "We're gonna go to the pool to escape a barking dog."

"Sounds good," she said. "But maybe you can ask them to take the dog in?"

Chapter 8

Maybe I should have done that. Maybe I should have asked Aaron and Esmerelda to make their dog stop barking. But I didn't. In fact, I thought I was coping beautifully. Rather than yell at my neighbor, I'd go for a walk. Go to the pool. And I was sane. I was under control. Not mad. No. Not at all. I have seen the mad side and chose to be on Luke Skywalker's team instead.

But Bad Doggy had been barking for five straight days. I'd gone from pacing in the family room, and round and round the circular layout of our main floor, which had three separate entry ways and made for an amazing roller derby practice setup, to pacing up and down the stairs and then around the derby loop. Then I'd started calling William and whining.

"Sally," he'd say, his voice all reasonable and patient, "Why don't you just tell Aaron Bad Doggy's annoying you?"

"No. I don't accept this. No. I wanna slap Aaron. Do you hear him William?" My voice was rising higher, almost to glass-breaking vibration level. "Do you hear that little jerk barking?" I pulled the phone away from my head and held it closer to the back windows. "Ya' hear him William? He's been barking all dadgummed day."

"Aww gosh, Sally," came William's voice, all mellow and smooth. "That's pretty awful, isn't it?"

"Yeah," I sniffled. "I'm gonna crack William. Gloria called and she needs my rewrites, like yesterday." Gloria was my long-suffering agent. I loved her except when she made me sob with her mounds of rejection letters. The publishing industry is a cruel beast of a business.

"Aw, Sally, can't you ask Esmerelda to keep Bad Doggy inside for a couple hours? Just tell her you're working and you got a deadline."

"She hates me. I swear she does. She thinks I'm a weirdo Will. I saw her yesterday and I swear she called me a bad word in Spanish."

"But you don't know Spanish."

"Exactly." I gestured wildly with my hands as I circumnavigated the main floor again. "Exactly. She knows I don't speak Spanish, so she's communicating to Aaron, like a secret code."

William was typing something on his computer. I could hear his keyboard clacking away. "You're working, aren't you?" My voice sounded one parts accusatory and two parts jealous.

"Yep, sorry. Got a deadline. Why don't you practice on me?"

"Like, saying what I would say to Esmerelda?"

I could hear click clacking, followed by an "Uh-huh."

I was totally quiet for a moment, just thinking about it. And then, voice quavering, "Please make it stop, please, I can't . . . think . . . write . . . brain hurts please make it stop, please, please, Essy." I paused.

"Wow. That's . . . " William was giggling.

"Yeah. Brilliant stuff." I glared at the phone and waited for William to sound contrite. "No. They hate me. Everyone hates me."

"Bad Doggy doesn't hate you."

After I hung up with William, I ran through a checklist of ideas. Buy a pack of cigs and grab some cheap American beer, and drink some beers out on the deck until the kids came home from school? Tempting. Pick up the phone and call Aaron? Knock on the door and ask Esmeralda to . . . groan. *I'll go out for a walk instead.*

I trudged past the rose bushes that rise like overweight, past their prime rock stars toward the sun that streams between the houses on the side of my yard and paused. A weird bouquet of aromas greeted me. At first, a hint of fuchsia, or maybe melon, or maybe Merlot . . . *stop it Sally* wafted in front of something decidedly less pleasant. Downright pungent in fact. It was the same smell I'd noticed when we stayed in a cabin somewhere near the Appalachian Trail, within the Shenandoah mountains.

It was—*uh oh*. A Skunk. I dropped my red bush trimmers, which have since disappeared, and I'm somewhat suspicious about that crazy Yolinda down the street, and skedaddled down to the creek behind our house. Just in case the skunk aimed one of his fear-stink sprays at me. As William the Eagle Scout had told me at least a dozen times, there wasn't a harder smell to eradicate than skunk smell.

Once I got down to the creek's edge, I took a deep breath and peered behind the huge elk tree, the one that's clinging to the edge of the embankment and is growing sideways. There's something exciting about the elk growing at a 45-degree angle. We keep planning to chop it down when William's on a business trip. You know, for fun. I think that's why William hardly ever goes on business trips. The last time he left for a night, I chopped down half of the dogwood tree. Apparently, I did a lousy job at it, because the other half looked like a misbegotten popsicle stick. *William wasn't amused, so maybe it would be a bad idea to take a hack at the elk tree*, I reasoned. *Oh, right, Sally, the skunk.*

No skunk. I gulped. It sure smelled like skunk. So I tiptoed under the "troll bridge" that crosses the creek. My kids like to hide under that bridge and scare the heck out of joggers who run across it. It's really fantastic, in an awful, *you know you shouldn't laugh* sort of way, when a grown man takes a three foot vertical leap in the air when your tiny four-foot troll screams, "LEAVE OR I'LL EAT YOU." I always pretend I don't know what's going on when I'm out in the back digging up worms and weeds when that happens.

No skunk.

I shrugged, and decided to think things through while I walked. I got about ten steps, and Bad Doggy tore across the yard and started yapping at jet airplane decibel at me. He skidded right up against the fence and stuck his little black nose under the fence at me, grinning. I glared at him, but he just kept barking happily. He pawed at the ground and yipped. It was like he was asking me, asking everything around him, to play. I walked away, shaking my head, and tried to tune him out.

Then the phone rang. It was William. He'd forgotten to pick up the keys for his Cub Scout meeting. He's the den leader, which irritates me, especially since he's always calling me in the middle of the day asking me to pick up stuff like soda bottles for their scientific experiments, so I grumbled something.

"What's wrong Sally?" His voice sounded all sweet.

"Besides your calling me to bug me about stupid Cub Scouts stuff?" I smiled as I said that, so it didn't sound as mean as it might look on paper.

"Yeah, besides me bugging you about stupid Cub Scouts stuff."

"I think we got a skunk in our yard." I wrinkled my nose. "Maybe it's built a home under the troll bridge."

"Oh? Maybe you can build a crumbs trail to Bad Doggy," William chuckled. "Like Hansel and Skunkel."

"Oh, wow," I smirked. "I like the way you think."

"Yeah, that would be—"

I heard his other line ringing.

"—Oops, gotta go. Don't do anything crazy," William added hurriedly.

"Me? Never." I was already smirking before he hung up the phone.

Chapter 9

We still had some leftover jellybeans from Easter, so it didn't take long to skulk inside and grab a handful of them. With a hoe thrown over my shoulder to give me cover, I walked between Bad Doggy's house and mine, and every few feet or so, I dropped a jellybean or two. Red, green, yellow, purple, and an occasional black jelly bean toppled from my right hand to the ground, and I made sure I stomped on them a little, so that they weren't easy to spot in case a cop was flying overhead. A little preparation is the best guard against *jail time*.

Once I got to the corner of our property, I turned left and walked right up to Bad Doggy, who was still standing there, nose stuck under the fence, yapping away at the passing butterflies. I dropped several jellybeans about six inches from his snout, and then I slouched away in the other direction, trying to appear all innocent and nondescript.

Bad Doggy barked a whole lot the rest of the day, but we had a busy night, and I sort of forgot about the whole thing. I didn't even tell William what I'd done until he'd gotten home from Cub Scouts and I'd gotten back from taking Lizzie to soccer practice, and we'd fed everyone large Slurpees for dinner. That was of course my idea. So we were lying in bed, talking about our days, and he asked me if I really ate an entire bag of jellybeans out of spite.

"Whaddya mean?" I pinched my nose in disgust. "I hate jelly beans."

"But I saw an empty bag of them in the garbage."

"Oh, what, now you're going through the garbage," I huffed. "Really?"

He looked up from his iPad. "You didn't feed them to Bad Doggy?"

I shook my head. "Not exactly."

"You did what I told you to do, didn't you?"

I nodded.

"But Sally! I was just joking."

"Crap," I gulped. "Think I should go out and pick up the jellybeans?"

He grinned at me and grabbed hold on my arms. "Nah. Come gimme some sugar."

I thought that was the end of the jellybean incident until Lizzie came running in from the bus stop the next afternoon. She was breathless, and it took her a few moments to catch her breath. From the very few words she was able to spit out, it was pretty clear that the jellybean incident was now the skunk-Bad Doggy-Petunia-orchestra incident.

"Whoa! Slow down, Busy Lizzie!" Brett and Junior tumbled in the garage door and toppled into me and Lizzie, where we were still huddled together in the laundry room. Some families gather in kitchens, but for some reason, mine seems to prefer the laundry-mudroom. We always seem to be coming or going.

"Mom, I had a horrible day," moaned Brett. "Mrs. Peters took my card down."

I hugged Brett, and tried to hear what Junior was saying about black holes, and through it all, words and asthmatic coughs were spilling out of Lizzie.

"Petunia got skunked!" she finally managed.

"Okay, okay, just a sec Lizzie." I grabbed their lunchboxes out of their backpacks, signed Junior's learning journal, and promised I'd read his thing about black holes and the Big Bang in "just a minute," as Brett hopped around and tried to tell me about his bad day. In the background, of course, Bad Doggy was barking.

After I poured Lizzie a glass of water and promised to buy Brett a toy *if he'd just be quiet for five minutes*, I leaned against our granite counter top and issued an imperious nod to my hysterical daughter. "Okay, start. Take it from the top."

"The top?" interjected Brett. "What does that mean?"

I grimaced and tried not to snap at my son. "From the start."

"Idiot," flounced Lizzie.

"Don't call him that!"

"But Mom—"

"—No. We don't talk like that."

Lizzie started to roll her eyes but thought better of it, and by then, Brett had bounced out of the kitchen in search of his fuzzy pillow. Then she half shrugged and squinched up her face in a way that made her freckles stand out. "Well, okay, like, this morning, you know, like Petunia came running out of her house to the bus stop just as the bus was coming. And I didn't notice it at first, but she smelled, like," Lizzie made a spinach face. "Yucky."

I swallowed uncomfortably. "Um, like cat pee?" Esmerelda had about a half dozen cats, so I was hoping it was a cat pee problem.

Lizzie shook her head. Crap. And she's already said something about skunks.

"Not like a skunk?"

Lizzie nodded. "Yep. Apparently, Petunia had been out in the back before school with Bad Doggy. She was dressed up in a brand-new outfit for today's Orchestra performance." Petunia was a sharp dresser, no doubt about it. She put the g in girly-girl, and she'd gotten all dolled up for her solo singing performance in the children's spring performance.

"So then what?"

"Well," Lizzie brushed her thick auburn hair out of her eyes. "He jumped up to grab a treat from her, and she grabbed him to kiss him. He'd gotten sprayed, or something like that, and from what Petunia was saying as she cried to me in the bathroom—"

"—She was talking to you at school?" I gave Lizzie a scoffing look.

Lizzie narrowed her eyes and thought about it. "Well, yes, now that you mention it. No one else would talk to her. She smelled kind of bad, Mom."

"That was really kind of you, to listen to her."

Lizzie nodded and then continued, "And it got worse. Paul drew a picture of Petunia on the chalkboard. Used black and white chalk, and put a tail on her butt."

I groaned. "Then what?"

"Then we were supposed to go to lunch, but no one would sit next to Petunia."

"Except you?"

Lizzie nodded.

"Well, I'm proud of you, sweetie."

She smiled at me. "Hey Mom?"

"Yeah?"

"I invited Petunia to come hiking with us on Saturday. She asked if we could bring Bad Doggy. Can she Mom? Please?"

"We'll see." I half-groaned, just to buy a little time.

First Day of School Scorecard

Two phone calls from school.
One visit to the nurse.
One case of vomiting in school toilet.
One trip to school to pick up sick child.
One safety patrol belt brought home.
Two school lunches bought.
One lunch brought.
Two homework assignments.
One chattering kid.
One laughing kid.
And a silent kid.

And that's a wrap.

Chapter 10

Somewhere around now is when I found out my best friend in life is an archangel and a little later I found out I was something similar but different. See, when God made me in heaven, he used a different mold. He grabbed a bit of human prophet, added a big chunk of an archangel's wing, and to top it all off, he added some of his own soul DNA and some of Jesus's soul. He also added something he mysteriously refers to as "liquid crystal, it's what makes all the pieces work together, you'll see, Iz," he later explained. He calls me Iz, which is short for Israel. That's my name in heaven.

Whenever God sends me to earth on a mission, he sends Archangel Raziel to look after me. In this lifetime, Raziel was living in the body of my best friend Stevie, who's a girl not so named, kind of like Johnny Cash's "Sue". When God made me, I was something entirely new, so he needed someone to raise me, look after me, teach me how to be what he calls a "hybrid" and that someone turned out to be Archangel Raziel.

The way she explained it to me was there was no one else in First Heaven who had the wherewithal to handle me and she also had a good home, which she named "The Frat," so one day God handed her this Rubric's Cube and said, "Here, I need you to figure out how this creature works . . ." and when Raziel coughed and asked what the creature was exactly, God smiled and said, "We'll figure that out as we go." And Raz took one look at this strange creature . . . which as a baby looked quite strange indeed . . . and then another look. She really had no idea what to do with me, because I wasn't the usual angel, nor was I human, and I wasn't like Baby Jesus either. But she raised me as her own in The Frat and she often says, in her gruff way, that she's proud of me.

If you're wondering why I didn't find out I was something not exactly human until I was all grown up, then there's something else you need to know about Archangel Raziel. She's the Keeper of Secrets and the Protector of the Sacred Mysteries. As in that's her Job Title. Keeper of Secrets, Protector of Mysteries. She's also God's top adviser . . . so it's sort of a big honor to have her as my jumper.

Raz was the first jumper. She was studying alongside God, a couple chairs down from him, and she was watching all sorts of bad stuff go down on earth, so she asked God if she could go fix things. Because of what happened with the Fallen Angels under Lucifer, angels weren't allowed to fly down and live on earth like they used to, back in the days of Atlantis and prehistoric earth. Stevie had to get a special waiver to jump from heaven to earth. And when she jumped, she lost her wings . . . and took on a human body. Like me, like you, she is born as a human baby, and like me and you, she's born forgetting who she is and all of her past lives.

Unlike most of us, she does remember who she is, but only once she becomes an adult and is ready to deal with finding out she's an archangel. In case you're wondering, there aren't many jumpers. About twenty-eight total. Jumpers are a different breed of angel. They keep their angelic soul but take on human bodies.

To get any answers to all my questions out of Stevie, the conversation is always amusing. It's amusing because she's really funny, and it's also amusing because she loves to keep secrets. She also speaks in riddles and she's also supposed to tell me stuff, and we both know this. We both also know she tells me as little as she can get away with and I'm thinking some of this has to do with what I am. See, as a prophet, I'm supposed to talk—a lot. I'm not a good keeper of secrets. It goes against my grain just as much as telling secrets goes against Stevie's. So here's what a conversation between us goes like.

"Okay, Sally, so you get a square of his robe and with it, you're supposed to share his word with the people."

"What do you mean, 'a square of his robe?'"

"It's an expression. His robe."

"I don't understand what you mean by robe," I said. "I'm like picturing a big white robe, so how can there be squares of it?"

"Well, go look up robe in the Bible, then ask me," she said.

So I go and look up "robe" and find out it refers to a robe of righteousness, which is what the prophet Elijah wore. And then I get distracted by the story of Elijah. See, he had this robe from God that he wore and this robe seemed to allow him to perform miracles. But it wasn't the robe that was magical—the robe just signified that the wearer of it was God's messenger and as God's messenger could perform miracles. In other words, if you're filled with God's righteousness, you can perform miracles. The robe is great but it's a symbol. If a thief stole the robe, he'd still be a thief. But when a rightfully-appointed prophet wears God's robe, the prophet can do all sorts of neat things.

Speaking of Elijah, I got all distracted when I read about him. When he had reached the end of his time here on earth, he sought out Elisha and insisted that Elisha take the robe. Elisha made Elijah mad when he said he had to say goodbye to his parents; in fact, Elijah sort of yelled at Elisha and the whole story always made me giggle. Maybe it's because I knew who Elijah and Elisha actually were. See, I know almost all the major players in the Bible. In Elijah's case, he has always been one of the great prophets. He's been Moses. He's been John the Baptist. He's beautiful and wonderful . . . he also can get annoyed kind of easily.

Like one time in First Heaven, I kept asking Elijah questions about how God sent manna down from heaven. I must have asked a million questions about what kind of bread it was, and how much did God send, and how did they divide the bread . . . and finally Elijah just sort of glared at me, if you can imagine a swirl of colors glaring at you, crossed his arms, and exclaimed, "Iz! Sit still please, I'm trying to get some work done."

I'd scurried away, giggling of course . . . and returned about ten minutes later to ask him another series of questions.

On this afternoon, when I was trying to figure out what it meant to be given a square of God's robe, I ran into a brick wall asking Stevie for answers. All she would say is, "Yes, a square of his robe, you're a prophet."

"But how big a square? Are you talking about a quilt like with tiny squares, like just three inches long?"

"A square, come on Sally, I gotta get back to work," she said.

So I went and talked to God about it. *God*, I transmitted, *what does it mean I get a square of your robe? How come I don't get the whole robe?*

God had laughed and not answered right away. Instead, he sent me images of white robes.

But how big is a square? Is it tiny? Sort of big? How many times do you divide it? I sent him my own pictures of quilts with tiny squares.

Oh, bigger than that.

Okay, right, but why only a square? Is it because I'm not ready for the whole robe?

God transmitted an image of a white robe and then an image of the robe wrapping around me. *There, Sally, how's that?*

Mmmm, I like that.

Good, God sent. *Stevie didn't mean anything by "square", just a term she came up with when she was writing gospels.* That's another thing you need to know about Stevie. She's written a lot of the gospels. God has too.

So later that night, I called up Stevie and told her that I now was in possession of the entire white robe.

"Good grief, how did you get it?"

I smiled at the phone. "Just asked. Hey Stevie, were you Elijah?"

Stevie chuckled and didn't answer.

So I said, "Elijah was really annoyed with Elisha, reminds me of that time I was annoying you in heaven—"

"—Oh my gosh, Sally, which time would that be? Like every day?"

I snickered. "Come on, wasn't that bad."

Stevie was still laughing on the other end.

"So were you Elijah?"

"Elijah was wonderful," she said.

"Aw come on, stop that," I whined.

"Wonderful soul, that Elijah," she added.

I glared at the phone. "So," I said, "About this robe. What does it mean exactly, to be a prophet?"

"Mightn't you have asked that before you went bugging God for the entire robe?"

I grinned. She had a point of course. "Come on, Mama."

"Don't you go mama-ing me," she said. "It's always "mom-this mom-that" when you want something."

"Yeah, I want the Manual."

"Manual?"

"Yeah," I said. "You're telling me you didn't write the Manual? There's gotta be a 'Thou Shalt Say, Thou Shalt Not Say' kinda book for prophets, come on, there's gotta be a coherent set of rules, there's just gotta be, like for example, how do you use wrath and what not? Like don't you angels have rules on wrath?"

"Hmmm, sorta," she said. "Well, yeah I'm more of a 'please not today soul, ugh ok shoot today—'swipe flat handed to the right banishment and flick my wrist—smite thee.' I got banishment taken away once then I said fine I will just kill them all."

Now I was laughing, picturing a massive and glorious swirl of lights, which is what souls look like, smiting demons. "God told me I wasn't allowed to use wrath unless it was in self-defense or in protection of loved ones, so I thought it was kind of frowned upon."

"Yeah," she chuckled, "It was a lot more acceptable back in the day."

"Like when Lucifer left and you were at war with millions of fallen angels?"

"Yes."

"So did they give it back, wrath I mean?"

"Yes, He told me not to wave them off so much, more 'flick the wrist I smite thee.' That's where that came from."

"Okay, but what about the rest of the manual? Are you saying there's a manual for angels but not one for prophets?"

"Yeah, well, my daughter," she chuckled, "No prophet before has ever whined about it."

"I am not whining!"

Stevie didn't say anything. She was waiting, and sure enough—

"—Seriously wish I had some sort of manual, like come on, what if someone asks me about other religions or other prophets, how do I know what to say and when, this is gonna be too hard, mamma," I said, and by the end of it I was grinning because I knew I was whining and sure enough, she was laughing. I could always make Stevie laugh even if she wouldn't answer any of my questions.

Stevie remained stone silent. Like silent as a stone, so long as it's not one of the talking ones (but I digress).

"So were you Elijah," I continued. "Come on tell me."

Instead of answering, she said, "If there was a manual, you wouldn't read it."

"How do you know that?"

"Because you never read the Book of Guidance for Angels."

"Yeah," I said. "Because it's stupid."

"Sally," she gasped, but she wasn't really shocked or anything like that. I was always kind of naughty like that. "How could you know it was stupid if you didn't read it?"

"I don't know," I shrugged. "Guess I kinda skimmed it."

"And asked me about a million questions."

"Yeah," I said. "'Hey Mama, why's this gotta be like this?' And a few minutes later, 'Hey Mama, why's this gotta be in here? Nobody dresses like that anymore, not since y'all stopped living as Watchers on Earth.' And then, before you could answer that question, I'd be, 'Hey Mama, why's there gotta be this about this, and that about that?' And then you'd be shaking your head at me, your swirls starting to glow in irritation and whatnot.'"

"And amusement, too, my girl," she said.

"Yeah, cuz I'm always amusing, aren't I?"

"Yep."

"So were you Elijah?"

"He was really quite lovely and in that scene you were quoting me, with Elisha, I'll have you know that Elisha was being a punk, probably got a cuff on the side of the head too," Stevie said. "Oops, that's my brother calling, gotta go, love you buckets."

"Elijah?"

"Bye, love."

"Awww, Mama . . . love you too," I said.

In case you're keeping track, no she didn't answer my question about Elijah. And I'm still waiting for a Thou Shalt Not Book for Prophets. Last time I talked to God, he said that if I want one so bad, maybe I should write it. And then we both started laughing. Because God knows I don't do well with rules and regs.

Chapter 11

Junior's diary.

Dec. 10, 2013.

Hi, I'm Junior Brookman. Mom is really annoyed about the dog next door, because it barks ALOT. Brett's annoyed by him too. Mom and Brett are wired differently than I am. That's how Mom explained it to me once. It means that loud noises upset them more and they can't help it. Just like Bad Doggy can't help barking all morning and all night, Mom and Brett can't help that it gives them a headache.

Bad Doggy's name isn't really that. Brett nicknamed him Bad Doggy and now that's what we all call him 'cept when Tunie's parents are around. At first Mom said we shouldn't call him that but then she said it once accidentally and she laughed and said the name was rather apropos. I asked her what that meant and she told me to look it up. Here's what the online dictionary said:

ap·ro·pos
[ap-ruh-poh] Show IPA
adverb
1.
fitting; at the right time; to the purpose; opportunely.
  2.
Obsolete, by the way.
adjective
3.
opportune; pertinent: apropos remarks.
Idioms
4.
apropos of, with reference to; in respect or regard to: apropos of the preceding statement.
  Origin:
1660-70; < French à propos literally, to purpose < Latin ad prōpositum. See ad-, proposition

I guess that means the word fits but what I don't get is why the word says it's appropriate and before Mom said we could call him "Bad Doggy" she kept saying it was inappropriate. Guess Mom changed her mind. Or maybe it's just not appropriate to be apropos when Mr. Aaron and Ms. Esmeralda are listening.

That, she says, would be most likely not apropos. Mom changes her mind a lot like that. Anyway, here's a little about me. I am nine years old, I am totally obsessed with Just Dance, and I have a ton o' friends.

Chapter 12

We were all piled up in the laundry room again, except for Brett, who was missing a sock, a hat, and at least one other item he never did find. "Brett!" I bellowed. "Come on! We're gonna be late!"

Lizzie made a face at Junior, who was telling her about his favorite elements on the periodic table. Junior's like that. He reads high school chemistry textbooks for fun, and the really scary thing is he wants to be a genetic engineer. Brett also says he wants to be a genetic engineer, but what he really wants to be is a mad scientist so that he can turn himself into a hamster. He's probably the only human being on this planet aiming to be a hamster.

"Mom! Lizzie pinched me!"

I glanced over at Junior, who now bore a welt on his forearm. "Aw, Lizzie, that was mean."

She tossed her hair, which was already frizzy from the humidity, and retorted, "He's breathing too loud and he's annoying me."

"Oh? So you pinched him? Say you're sorry—"

She folded her arms and shook her head.

"Or no Slurpee after soccer practice."

"Fine! Sorry." Lizzie opened the garage door just as Brett was tearing around the corner, and he tripped on Junior's feet and slammed into Lizzie.

"Ow!" Lizzie reached her hand out to swat at Brett, and I raised an eyebrow.

"Slurpee."

She let her hand fall to her side, but I could tell she was waiting for me to turn my back before she pinched, poked, or swatted one of her brothers.

"Mom! Can't find my new shoes!" Brett was breathless.

Junior peeked at the thick book he was holding and I suppressed a smile when William came bounding around the corner holding a soccer ball, a few water bottles, and two or three mismatched cleats.

"You really bringing a book to practice?" William shook his head in disgust at Junior, who was the spitting image of his father, especially with the thought crease in the middle of his forehead.

Junior ignored William. I ignored Lizzie, and we all ignored Brett, who was rambling about hamsters and asking where his shoes were. His new shoes. His perfect purple and blue and black shoes.

""Never mind." William checked his watch. "Everyone get in the truck. We're late."

"As usual." I thought it was hilarious that we were late of course. Especially since William was performing what he calls a "belts check."

"Lizzie. Belt."

"Normative."

"Junior. Belt."

"Stand by. Normative."

"Brett. Belt."

There was no response.

"Brett? Belt?"

"Hey, Brett," screamed Lizzie. "Seat belt check!"

I could feel Brett's feet kicking the back of my seat, and I groaned. "Normative," he finally called back.

As I was pulling out of the driveway, I caught a flash of purple and blue in the corner of my eye, and realized Brett had left one of his new shoes lying on the apron of the driveway. This wasn't unusual for Brett. Sometimes he takes his shoes and wildly throws them across the yard or out the back of our SUV or drops them out of his backpack. He's got a thing about losing or misplacing his shoes.

"Brett, is that your new shoe lying in the driveway?" I hesitated, with the Mazda in reverse, tilted at a 45-degree in the road beside our house.

"Mmmm," he mumbled, barely paying attention.

"Just go!" Lizzie's voice was loud, even from the third row.

William tightened his jaw. It really bothered him when "the kids left their stuff lying all over the place." But it also drove him crazy being late. "Yeah, go," he agreed. So we went.

And we had an awesome time. The boys and I tossed a football around while Lizzie practiced soccer. We drank multi-colored Slurpees for dinner. And about two hours later, we pulled back into the driveway. As William hit the garage door opener from about three houses away from home, I made a mental note to grab Brett's shoe before we drove over it.

But his shoe wasn't in the driveway. And I wasn't the only one who noticed its absence.

"Where's my new shoe?" Brett's voice rose higher, and I heard the seat belt lock unclick, and the metal clanged against the side of the door. "I saw it there, right before we left."

I could tell Brett was about to leap from the back of our SUV while it was still moving, so I tapped the brake and turned around. He froze in place as soon as I fixed him with a deathly glare.

"Sit. Down."

As soon as I heard his seat belt click back into place, I pulled into the garage, and then we did our best A-Team imitation. Lizzie threw her shin guards and her cleats in a heap, and forgot her soccer ball and her water bottle. Junior clung to his book, mumbling about acid dense sublingual somethings. And William, with a look of quiet consternation, took Brett by the hand, and led him on a search for his missing shoe.

We live near a forest, and it's not unusual to hear a chipmunk or rat or other rodent screeching horribly while being hunted or consumed by a cat. At first that's what I thought I was hearing, until I caught a backbeat of caterwauling child. *My child.* I sighed, and headed back outside. I hadn't made it past the laundry room, and had been busy glaring at eleven pairs of shoes blocking the entrance.

The garage door slammed shut behind me and Brett collided with me before I got both feet off the single concrete step leading out to the garage. Still shrieking, he tugged at my wrist and I followed him to the edge of our property. William was kneeling down, inspecting a dark pile of something I couldn't make out.

Clutching a beer and missing a shirt, Todd ambled over. "Well, dang, something heaved up something pretty gross, eh, William." Todd grabbed a stick and pushed the pile around.

William stood up and put an arm on Brett's shoulder. "I suspect it just might be Brett's shoe. But it's, um, hard to say, seeing that it's been partially digested."

Todd gulped some of his cheap American beer. "Then upchucked! This reminds me of the time we was bear huntin' and—"

Brett interrupted Todd's story with another wail.

Todd opened his mouth again, but before he could tell his bear hunting story, Bad Doggy staggered outside in our direction. Usually, Bad Doggy is wagging his tail so hard when he sees anyone, his whole body shuffles, but this time, he seemed like a overloaded cab dragging a huge trailer.

"Oh my," giggled William. "Looks like we've found the culprit."

Just then, Bad Doggy starting turning round and round in circles, faster and faster, with an almost insane look on his face. Counter-clockwise, he went, until he stopped, and then and there, right in the middle of Esmerelda's marigolds, he dropped the load he'd been carrying.

It took awhile. And I was staring, I must admit. Maybe because it wasn't the right color, or maybe it didn't look normal, the way it was coming out. It looked like a very narrow, long, thin snake . . . but not a snake. Something blue.

Oh no. A shoelace. The shoelace that belonged on Brett's new shoes. Brett's shoelace.

And Brett realized what it was a split second after I did. The strange thing was, he stopped crying and wailing. He just turned on his heels, and stalked away without another word.

I should have known he was up to no good.

Scorecard

2 soccer uniforms, red and blue
one child obsessed with digging for crystals
one child obsessed with boobs and bras
one child obsessed with unmarried teacher
A barking Schnauzer
24 Ritz crackers, eight double-stuf Oreos consumed
at snack time.
No calls home
"What are sports bras?"
three perfect behavior charts
one mean girl at lunchtime stared down
12 birthstones memorized
four long sleeve shirts
and acorns raining on deck.

Chapter 13

The next morning was a Friday. I didn't get up until way past seven-thirty, not that there's anything wrong with that. I think I'm supposed to feel guilty for sleeping in later than any of the other moms who post their wakeup times on social media, but I'm an incorrigible night owl. So forget the mock guilt.

Lizzie is also a night owl. Thursday night, she stayed up reading a Stephen King novel past midnight. And yeah, I told her to go to bed about a dozen times before she finally did. I've read some articles that say you can cure a person from being a night owl, but whoever wrote them hasn't met me or my Lizzie. I don't yell and scream at her like my mom did to me each morning. It doesn't fix anything. I don't want to fix her or anyone really.

I just want to get the kids to the bus on time. So when she dragged herself out of bed, blearily feeling around for her glasses, at around 7:55 a.m., I handed her glasses to her and then whispered, "Bus in 15! Hurry!"

Junior was sitting at the kitchen table, hair combed, wearing a Redskins t-shirt and orange shorts. His royal blue backpack hung on the back of his chair. A glass of milk and a bowl of cereal sat in front of him, and he glanced up from his farmer's almanac with a genial nod. With a bleary smile, I ran my hand through my hair and looked around for my French Press.

"Where's Brett?"

Junior took a bite of his green and orange Apple Jacks and shrugged.

"Have you seen Brett at all, Junior?"

My son, all four feet five inches of him, seemed more man than boy as he considered my question. He slurped the last bit of milk from his bowl and the lines in his forehead creased together as he spoke. "I have. He was talking about turning into a hamster, getting back at Bad Doggy and," Junior waved his hand at the pantry, "He made a mess out of the crackers."

My head swiveled over to our pantry. It's more like a closet that overflows with boxes and cartons of mostly empty food containers. It makes passing between the kitchen and the laundry room an adventure, and it drives me crazy that we can't shut the pantry door without it getting stuck. A pile of crumbs spewed from the pantry all the way to the kitchen table.

I sighed, and was about to reach for our industrial strength shop vac when Lizzie's voice, screechy and excited, echoed from the top of the stairs all the way down to me.

"Mom! You better look outside! Brett's painting the fence!"

I spun so fast at the thought of my youngest child holding a can of spray paint, as if in homage to a street artist, I slipped and fell on a stray, half-eaten box of animal crackers. The lions, tigers and bears went flying all around me, and a few even landed on me, because I hit the floor so fast.

"Oh, oh, ouch," I howled, clutching at my wrist, which I'd sprained one time while I was holding Lizzie and Junior when they were still babes. For some reason, I had picked that moment to kick the truck door shut, and I had hit the hard cement while still cradling my two children. They'd been uninjured that time. Anyway, as I lay there beside the pantry, with cracker crumbs and animal crackers strewn from one side of the kitchen to the next, I thought of that time, and a silly grin broke out on my face. Just the thought of my Lizzie and my Junior as babies . . . made me all warm inside.

The crunching of more animal cracker crumbs snapped me out of it.

Junior and Lizzie both dashed over beside me, and Lizzie got down on her knees to make sure I was okay. Just like Brett, I fell a lot, so this was pretty much standard operating procedure.

"Mom?" Her sweet blue-grey eyes stared into mine, and she stroked the hair out of my eyes. "You okay?"

That same dumb smile tugged at my cheeks. "Yeah, just give me a minute and then I'll go see what Brett's doing."

"Swear I saw him painting."

Junior plopped down next to Lizzie. "Can I paint some too?"

"You serious?" I tried hard not to grin.

"Yeah, really," snorted Lizzie, "Junior, like really?"

"Come on you two." I groaned as I stood up, rubbing my back. There was going to be a bruise for sure.

As I limped to the laundry room, the door from the garage swung open and clocked me in the shoulder. I whimpered, then half-yelled, "Ouch! Oh, oh!"

"Oh, sorry, Mom," Brett's voice sounded tiny, even adorable, and I felt bad for cursing. At least, I felt bad until he emerged from the other side of the heavy, white door.

He was covered in paint. Covered. And the bus was going to be here in . . .

"BUS!" screamed the safety patrol.

I shook my head at Brett.

He smiled at me. All three dimples showed. I fought against smiling back at him with every muscle I had. I smiled anyway.

With a pained smile on my face, I motioned to Junior and Lizzie. "Come here. Huddle up. Okay, you two run and catch the bus."

They hugged me and ran, Junior in his awkward duck shuffle, Lizzie with her beautiful, natural marathoner's strides, just in time to get in line for the bus. I waited for the flashing lights to turn off, and listened to the diesel engines blast power to the wheels, and waved to my older children as the bus turned left in front of our house and chugged up the hill. Then I looked at my paint-encased, crusted, covered son, and grimaced.

"Wanna show me what you did with all that paint?"

"He had it coming to him."

I gulped. There wasn't an ounce of remorse in Brett's expression.

How do you punish a kid who isn't sorry? And what exactly was I punishing him for? Worst, I had a feeling it was going to make me laugh, whatever it was. Where was William when I needed him? Like the time Junior ate the Christmas tree and got a needle stuck in his throat? Were it not for William's quick fingers, we'd have ended up at the ER. I'd better not call him though. Not today. Not in the middle of the class he's giving.

I put my arm around my son's diminutive shoulder and kissed his rainbow-colored hair. The real question was whether I'd send him to school looking like a 50-pound lollipop.

"What did he have coming to him exactly?" My voice sounded good and steady still. No cuss words. No giggles.

"He ate my new shoe. And he woke me up, barking. He had it coming to him. " Brett repeated his mantra. "He is a Bad Doggy."

"So that's what I did," Brett continued, and I realized I was staring at my own rose bushes while my son made a dramatic gesture toward the fence. He skipped a few steps ahead of me, and my hand rose to touch the yellow rose bush, as if in touching the petals I could cancel out the aching, crushing sadness of its thorns. *No, you're not here now, pop. It's just me, and my kid, and everything is all right now.*

"Oh, wow," I gasped. In several different colors, a different one for each letter, the words Bad Doggy had been scrawled across the fence. It was graffiti, and yet it was also artistic, stunning, and resplendent. *It was a very, very bad act, done very, very well.*

Chapter 14

I really didn't know what to say to my son, so I just stood there, letting the morning breeze ruffle my messy blond hair. *Come on Sally, you gotta deal with the paint.* I sighed again, and rolled my neck around in a circle. The truth was, I just didn't care about Brett's graffiti right now. I was exhausted from being strangled, if only in my mind, and I was too grateful to be standing in my own backyard, safe, not only loved, but full of love . . . to care.

I tried to paste an earnest look on my face, one that expressed concern and mild dismay and a hint of disappointment. I needed, no he needed, some parental guidance, and I was the only parent around. It felt like my face was set in plaster as I spoke to him. *I was that tired.*

"Where did you get the paint?"

"Pinewood Derby." William was the Den Leader for Brett's Cub Scout troop, and in February, they'd raced little wooden cars down a ramp for their annual Pinewood Derby competition.

I nodded, and tried to stop touching my neck. Junior and Brett both raced cars, so we had a lot of different paint colors.

"And this seemed like the right thing to do at the time, but now you're super-duper sorry?"

Brett scratched at some of the paint on his fingers, and shook his head. "I didn't spray the paint on their house. I knew that would be wrong. Because of the story you told me, about sketching Angel's name on her house with your key. And all the trouble you got in for doing that."

I chuckled. I had gotten creamed for that, and I hadn't meant any harm by it. It had seemed like a good idea at the time, I guess, which is as much reason as many of us have for doing much of anything.

"But you're sorry, for spray-painting the fence? I'm thinking it will be better for you, when your dad gets home from work, if you tell him you're sorry."

Brett shook his head again. "Not sorry, no." He was, at least, a model of consistency.

"Son, come on, work with me." I held my hands out in supplication. "Give me something to work with."

Just then Bad Doggy came loping across the backyard. He looked like a canine version of my paint-covered child.

"Well," Brett conceded, "Maybe I shouldn't have painted Bad Doggy too."

"Oh, Brett." I was trying not to gasp, but I sounded like I was either asthmatic or at the best rock concert ever. "You painted Bad Doggy, too."

Bad Doggy barked at us several times, and then just when I was about to say something at least vaguely parental, he executed one of his counter-clockwise pirouettes and right then and there, pooped out more bright blue shoelace.

I started to laugh. I couldn't help it. Brett's ears were getting redder and redder, and I was doing all I could to stop laughing—

And then Brett screamed, "I hate you Bad Doggy." And he jumped on the fence like he was about to go thrash his four-legged arch enemy.

"Hey! Stop. Now. It's time to turn the other cheek and let it go."

Brett let go of the fence, and over his shoulder, mumbled, "He doesn't have cheeks like we do."

I wasn't sure what Brett was talking about, so I caught up to him and waited for him to ask his next question.

"What does that mean? Turn the other cheek?"

I felt Brett's hand on my wrist and returned his stare. I must have left for awhile. Lizzie's old enough to call me on it, when I get lost in my thoughts, or in my characters, but Brett gets just as lost as I do in his big ideas. He doesn't ever say anything when I pause mid-sentence, or forget to answer a question.

"Turn the other cheek?" He repeated.

I took a deep breath. "It means you don't fight back. You let your enemy slap your other cheek, instead of slapping theirs. It's what Jesus said to do."

"But, I don't see how that works. I mean, Bad Doggy had it—"

"—I know, coming to him. But it's complicated, Brett. Can we please talk about it tonight? We gotta get you off to school, and I need to talk to dad about the fence. Then we can talk about it tonight."

Crap, I probably need to talk to Aaron and Esmerelda too. But not right now. I could just let William handle that too.

Brett sort of inclined his head, and then he started to suck his thumb, and I realized he was probably a lot more upset than I really could understand.

I hugged him close to me, and then we trudged back up the hill together. "So, hey, do you wanna get showered up?"

He hesitated. I was determined not to make a big deal about how he looked. On principle, I won't tell my children what to wear. I had no control over what I got to wear as a kid, and I hated that.

"Well," he allowed, "I guess I should scrub some of this paint off."

"Okay."

"Um, will you help me?"

"Yeah. But your hair might still be pink and green."

"Cool!" He seemed more relaxed now, and he was done sucking his thumb. So I didn't say anything more about the paint that morning. I did take a few minutes and read to him the Parable of the Unmerciful Servant. I sat him on my lap and read aloud:

> *Then Peter came to Jesus and asked, "Lord, how many times shall I forgive my brother or sister who sins against me? Up to seven times?"*
>
> *Jesus answered, "I tell you, not seven times, but seventy-seven times.*
>
> *"Therefore, the kingdom of heaven is like a king who wanted to settle accounts with his servants. As he began the settlement, a man who owed him ten thousand bags of gold*

was brought to him. Since he was not able to pay, the master ordered that he and his wife and his children and all that he had be sold to repay the debt.

"At this the servant fell on his knees before him. 'Be patient with me,' he begged, 'and I will pay back everything.' The servant's master took pity on him, canceled the debt and let him go.

"But when that servant went out, he found one of his fellow servants who owed him a hundred silver coins. He grabbed him and began to choke him. 'Pay back what you owe me!' he demanded.

"His fellow servant fell to his knees and begged him, 'Be patient with me, and I will pay it back.'

"But he refused. Instead, he went off and had the man thrown into prison until he could pay the debt. When the other servants saw what had happened, they were outraged and went and told their master everything that had happened.

"Then the master called the servant in. 'You wicked servant,' he said, 'I canceled all that debt of yours because you begged me to. Shouldn't you have had mercy on your fellow servant just as I had on you?' In anger his master handed him over to the jailers to be tortured, until he should pay back all he owed.

"This is how my heavenly Father will treat each of you unless you forgive your brother or sister from your heart."

When I finished reading this to Brett, I said, "So what does this mean?"

Brett gave me a winsome smile and said, "Forgive people when they've been bad. Just like you forgive me, Mom."

"Of course I forgive you sweetie. What about Bad Doggy?"

"Oh," he said. Then he raised his voice as if talking to the dog and said, "Sorry Bad Doggy." Brett paused and added, still in a high-pitched voice, "But you're still a bad doggy." Then Brett flashed another one of his dimpled smiles.

I giggled and hugged him close. "Well, you're trying to forgive, so that's good, sweetie. Okay, ready to go to school?"

"Do I have to? Can't we go to the doctor's and then get donuts?" Brett and I had been on a lot of doctor's visits over the last year and we always turned them into an adventure.

"Yeah, gotta go to school, yep," I said, and hugged him again.

I dropped him off a few minutes after first bell and then I drove back home and found a quiet spot on the floor in my study, to sit and talk to God for awhile.

Chapter 15

Later that night, after William got home and talked to Brett and after William and Brett talked to Aaron, we were sort of watching a show together as a family. It was called Ancient Aliens and basically, I was letting the kids stay up late and watch it so that they could broaden their grasp of history. Before we all sat down with popcorn to watch the show, I said, "Okay, so who wants to hear why we're watching this show?"

"Why?" Lizzie reached out for her bowl of popcorn and before I could answer she said, "Because you're obsessively watching this series to help you with your book research, I guess for the series you're writing about the History of the Earth or was the Earths, Mom?"

I laughed and said, "Good, so you're paying attention. Yes, I'm working with Jesus and with God on a history of the worlds, with earth of course taking center focus. The thing about mainstream history is that it missed almost all the signs of advanced prehistoric civilizations and most historians, archeologists, and religious scholars hewed to the belief that humans had developed slowly, gradually, and in a straight line."

"Um, Mom," Junior said, "Could you explain that again?"

"Yeah, using words we all understand?" Lizzie tossed a piece of popcorn up in the air and managed to catch it before it landed on the ground.

"Okay, okay," I said. "Most scientists believe in something called incrementalism, which means, well, imagine you're a tiny ant and you're marching across the desert—how long do you think it would take you to get across the sand?"

"Years? Centuries? I mean," Junior said, "If an ant lived that long and they don't . . . it would take years."

"That's true Junior," William said.

"Yep," I said, "So imagine the earth changes very very slowly okay? And it's true. The continents move away from one another a few inches or whatever every year, and all sorts of changes happen, like the mountains rising, the ocean levels going up or down, the ozone disappearing—"

"—Actually," Junior said, "That's happening very fast and so is the rising ocean levels."

"Exactly!" I said. "Right now, we're affecting the earth, we're making it change really fast, and in the past, humans have done the same thing. Also, so has God. He's created—either acting on His own or through nature—massive and sudden changes here on earth. Can you think of any good examples of that?"

"Oooh," Brett exclaimed, "Meteors crashing into the earth!" Brett made explosion sounds with his hands.

"The Great Flood? Was that real?" Lizzie asked.

"Yes, it was real, it happened when the last ice age ended and the glaciers melted, but it happened earlier than the Bible suggests. Around 9,500 BC. That's also when the poles shifted."

"What's a pole shift?"

"Well, you know where the North and the South Poles are right?"

"Antarctica and the North Pole, right?"

"Yes, Junior. Well, before, the poles used to be in different locations. But the entire earth crust shifted and the poles moved like hundreds or thousands of miles. Take North America—it used to be covered by ice, huge sheets of it covered half the continent, like all the way down to New York, and that was only about fifteen thousand years ago. And Antarctica, Siberia, places like that, they were habitable and totally different from what they are now. In fact, we've discovered maps of Antarctica the way it looked before it was covered by a mile or two of ice. This theory of how the earth changes, by the way, is called catastrophism, which just means major changes, major bad changes happen suddenly and these affect the way the earth looks."

"But can this theory work with the mainstream theories, what do you think Sally?" William gave me a smile. He knew I was enjoying teaching the kids about our history.

"Well, according to incrementalism, which was supported by most scientists and geologists, humanity, like earth, changed slowly. In addition, humans started off primitive and really only started to develop more advanced technologies about 5,000 years ago. Naturally, those who interpreted the Bible as containing the full and complete and absolutely correct interpretation of God's word believed that the Flood had occurred around 4,500 years ago—and that was incorrect. The actual Flood occurred in approximately 9,500 BC. But let's see what the show says," I added.

The show started off really cool, but unfortunately I picked the show that was about angels, and I know far too much about angels to be able to sit there when someone says they're not real. And that's pretty much what the main people on Ancient Aliens were saying. The main commentator was the famous author Erich von Däniken. He had written a controversial series in the 1970s in which he showed how the gods and angels spoken of in the Bible and in Sumerian and Babylonian texts had in fact been extraterrestrial beings who had interfered with activities here on earth.

Now Erich and this other guy, this guy with big hair, were going too far and I kept interrupting it and complaining that what they were saying was BS. Erich was saying, "It's obvious that angels aren't real," and the guy with big hair was insisting that the Hebrew word for angel was "messenger" and that the whole concept that angels could fall from heaven and could rebel against God was 'preposterous'.

"After all," he scoffed, "Why would God allow that? What kind of God would that be?"

And Erich had basically said, "The concept of angels flying around with wings is absurd. We need to bring modern interpretations to these religious texts and realize that the people were misunderstanding what they were seeing. Angels with wings? I believe they were seeing powerful beings who could fly."

"Right," said the guy with big hair, "And the concept of giants? I think," and he grinned and rolled his eyes, "That if there were giants we'd have found giant bones, right?"

"Wait, Mom," Lizzie interrupted, "Didn't the angels sleep with humans and create the giants—what were they called in the Bible again? Nephil . . ."

"Yes, some of the angels or Watchers as they were called in the Book of Enoch slept with humans and they created offspring called the Nephilim, or giants."

"What were the giants like?" Junior asked. "And is it true there's no bones found by archeologists digging in the places the giants lived?"

"No, it's not true at all," I said, "Bones have been found. Of course some have decayed, but lots have been found. Lots and lots of bones. And as far as what did they look like, some were just huge humans, but a lot of the giants were scary looking, like the Cyclops and other things you've read about in Greek myths, I think some of those were based on real things, on these Nephilim, who were never meant to exist, I mean, angel genes and human genes just don't work together so well, you know."

"And they weren't really seeing giants," the guy with big hair continued. "It was super powerful beings from other worlds who could do things the people, the primitives here on earth couldn't do. Anyway, the concept of angels sleeping with humans and creating giants—again, it's ridiculous. If there really was a god, why would he allow that?"

"William, turn it off, I can't take it anymore," I said. "I don't know why it's so hard for these guys to understand just how much God loves us." My eyes filled with tears, hot tears filled with indignation and love. "Why is it so hard for them to understand that God created angels and he created humans and he gave us, he gave both types of beings free will?"

"For what it's worth, the guy with the big hair is not someone I take seriously," William said.

"I know but it kills me, it hurts when people don't wanna know God," I said.

Then I was pacing around the kitchen making coffee. Lizzie came up beside me and laughed. "Oh Mom, you're the only woman I know who drinks coffee at this time of night."

"What time is it anyway?"

Lizzie tried to look still and silent like a statue. I checked the clock on the microwave and it blinked 9:34 at me. "Oh, no, oh wow, y'all, it's late. Up to bed right now, go brush your teeth, go on, Brett, listen, time for bed, Junior, good, thank you, I love you too, seriously Brett, upstairs now," I leaned over and returned Lizzie's hug, "I love you," I said. Then I called after Brett, "Brett, brush your teeth and get in bed, I mean it."

It was quiet in the kitchen now. I was staring at my coffee, which was one of those International Coffees, Suisse Mocha, more like hot chocolate than coffee, and I was trying to get a handle on why I was so upset.

"What's wrong, Cutie?"

"It's just killing me William, how people misunderstand the nature of free will. We all want it, we want all this freedom."

"Without the consequences," he agreed.

"Yes," I exclaimed. "We want all this freedom but we want God to come and fix everything when we go and screw it all up. We want freedom, we want to do whatever we want, and we want him to come and make it right when we commit all these sins . . ." My voice broke. William had paused the video and the screen was frozen on this old stone statue of one of the fallen angels and I was pretty sure she knew which one it was. "Oh my god," I whispered, "That looks like Lucifer." The angel on the statue was beautiful but also broken looking, with red ochre paint smeared on his lovely face and a look of absolute sorrow and pain and something else I couldn't identify.

"That's Lucifer after he fell," she said.

William was quiet.

"You know what the Watchers were doing?"

"Well, according to this show they were teaching the humans how to build things and they were sleeping with them," William said.

I sighed. "I wish that's what they were teaching the humans, but if you study the Book of Enoch, yes, they taught us some things, shoot, that was their job, to watch over and protect us! But when they fell, they taught us how to make swords, how to use makeup, how to build jewelry and other clothing that would beautify the body . . . they basically taught us how to kill one another and how to love the body rather than the soul . . . and they were creating these horrific giants who were destroying us, destroying the earth. In other words, they were corrupting and hurting the humans they were sent to protect. But you know what just kills me, Will?" I tore my eyes away from the statue of the fallen angel and fixed my eyes on him.

He turned the TV off and looked at me.

"These commentators act like God doesn't love us," I said. They act like God doesn't care what happens to us. They act like God didn't do everything he could to fix what went wrong and it just kills me, it hurts me so bad, because God loves us all so much. He does, and people are reading these books and watching these shows and they're learning just part of the truth, not the whole truth, and it hurts. I want them to know the most important truth."

William got a glint in his eye and stood up. "Like how God and Jesus built the pyramids and Jesus is coming back soon?" William crossed to where I was standing and placed his hand on the wall above me and grinned. "Or about how much this man loves to kiss this woman?"

Chapter 16

I forgot to tell you something else about the family. Well, I didn't really forget but I figured by now you'd be attached to us and wouldn't mind knowing that our youngest son is also an angel. Actually, I just didn't know how to work it into the story and I wanted to make it all fancy and then Gabriel came down and taught me something about writing. Gabriel is like the patron angel of artists, especially writers, so when he comes to talk with me about the craft of writing, I listen.

Okay, he yelled at me actually. He was like, "Sally, you gotta stop being so proud and refusing to explain stuff simply to people, just tell the story, get out of your own way, the story is what's good, right? Not your writing. Not you on your own doing your own thing trying to be special, trying to be the best writer or this or that generation. That's pride. And it's making your writing worse, not better. You're listening to other people tell you how to write and you need to listen to me and to God. Not to men."

And it smarted a little and I was like, "Why you gotta be yelling at me Gabriel?"

"Come on, Sally, really?" He said.

"Yeah. Everyone yells at me. Raz yells at me. Jeremiel yells at me. God yells at me. Even Jesus yells at me."

"You really asking why we yell at you, come on Sally," Gabriel said.

"Yes, it's like I'm deaf or something," I said. "Oh my God," I started to laugh really hard, "That's so funny. I'm like the deaf prophet."

Gabriel wasn't laughing. "No, you're the prophet who for your first several lifetimes didn't always listen."

I felt really bad when he said that, and Gabriel knew it. That's the thing about archangels. They can be tough but they're also kind. "Aw come on, kiddo. You've done great lately. And you are listening. You're doing great. Just tell what you're given, tell it in a way that makes it easy for people to understand you, and you'll be fine."

"Thanks Gabriel," I said.

And that's when I stopped trying to write the next Great American Novel.

It's kind of funny actually, how I stopped being such a fool as a writer and as a woman and found out my son was a jumper, here to help me dig up lost treasures he buried many lifetimes ago. These treasures he buried happened to have been some of the lost gospels that he and I and many other religious figures wrote during the time Jesus walked the Earth. In other words, I found out what it really means to be a prophet had nothing to do with being thought of as anything other than another soul with a story to tell. A story that was not my own and a story that I couldn't tell without a lot of other souls helping guide the way.

That's the deal with my son. He was made from Raziel's wing about 11,500 years ago and his main job in First Heaven, aside from fighting demons, is to work as a builder. His job, for everyone in heaven had some specialization or way of contributing, was to work as a manifester and builder of worlds. He builds structures in the heavens and he's been helping God build the new planet, Israel, that I'm named after . . . the planet we're gonna hopefully colonize in a few hundred years, after the Final War with the Enemy, or with Lucifer and the other Fallen Angels.

Sometime in this lifetime Brett's being promoted or in God terms activated to the rank of archangel. For now, he's just a kid with a very active mind and a lot of memories of adventures he's had during prior lifetimes. In fact, Brett preferred to be called an adventurer, for building worlds and living and roaming about the heavens is just one big adventure that never grows stale.

To have him here with me is an honor and a joy. He's fun and full of energy in a way that's constantly been misinterpreted. In fact, his preschool teachers said that he was gonna end up in jail when he got older if he didn't calm down. Turns out he was seeing demons, which is something he and I can both see, and they were tormenting him all the time. So he was fighting back and in kicking and yelling at entities most humans cannot see, he came across as kind of fierce, maybe a little as they now call it "oppositional" but he's anything but difficult. Unless you're a demon trying to attack him or his mother. In that case, Tiziel, who goes by Brett on Earth, is a worthy opponent.

Scorecard

One safety patrol belt worn.
Two last minute clothing changes.
One-half tank of gas used.
One entirely fascinating author visited.
One pinching.
One note home.
Two homework assignments.
"It was an accidental pinching. I swear."
"You swear?"
"I swear? Well, please don't tell Dad."
Breakfast served: Hershey's Kisses and Captain Crunch.
One pair corduroy pants hidden.
One set red cheeks.
And that's a wrap.

Chapter 17

"Dad, Brett is trying to guess the c-word."

"If Brett 'guesses' the c-word, you lose TV for a week."

Dishes clatter around the dinner table.

"Hey Brett? Guess what rhymes with 'rick?'"

"Stop it!" I said, laughing.

Lizzie smirked over her shoulder at me, and then said to William, "Why do people like to cuss so much?"

"I don't know—ask your mom. On second thought—"

"Because it's easy to say the words?"

I try to stop laughing, but I know Lizzie's watching me. "Well, in my case, maybe because a lot of words rhyme with it."

William rolls eyes, puffs out cheeks. "Ohhh, like 'truck?'" "Wow. Sally. Clever."

"Kids think I'm funnier than you, William."

"Oh bull."

"40,000 fans agree."

"Yeah, because you steal all my material."

Scorecard

9/11 One nation remembers. Not much else to say.
24 cupcakes baked by a happy man
not wearing a white apron.
Nine presents bought
including A Barbie astronaut
Wearing pink boots, not high heels, thank goodness.
"Do not forget your function, which is to forgive and be happy."
Two cupcakes consumed in the dark.
"Please mom, can I have a play date after school tomorrow?"
Last jung-su class for one child.
Pancakes, bacon, hot dogs, and a granola bar
Eaten for dinner.
One tantrum, lots of tears, and a gentle, close hug.
No showers for children. No cupcakes either.
But set your alarms, get up early, and maybe eat cupcakes
for breakfast on your sister's birthday.

Chapter 18

"Hey Mom ya wanna hear something funny?" Lizzie was sounding breathless, so it was no surprise when she grabbed her inhaler tube and took a deep breath of the medicine.

"Sure," I said. I was suspicious because Lizzie's voice had something extra in it. It had to be about her nemesis. It just had to be.

As I was thinking, Lizzie had already started talking. "So I was, like ya know walking at the playground and Petunia and her gang came over and Petunia said, 'Hey Lizzie are you trying to, like be Anna Desman or something like a frickin' circus clown, 'cause ya are lookin' like one.'"

"Hmnn, that wasn't nice, was it?"

"Exactly!" Lizzie gave an emphatic nod. "So I tried to say something and then she was goin' off on me some more and her whole pack was there of course, know what I mean Mom?" Lizzie sighed with maximum *sturm und drang*.

I grinned and mumbled, *love me some Sorrows of Young Werther under my breath*. Then I grimaced and thought of how much worse it was gonna get when Lizzie was actually a teenager. Aloud, I said, "Okay, then what?"

"So next she screamed, 'Shut your made-uped mouth, 'else you'll regret it,'" Lizzie said. "And Petunia said a lot more abrasive things; then I ran off."

I tried to suppress a smile at the use of the word 'abrasive' but it didn't get past Lizzie.

"What? Why are you smiling?"

"Oh, because you're so good with words. Okay, then what?"

Lizzie's grey-blue eyes lit up a bit at my compliment. She wants to be a writer when she grows up and I'm her favorite writer mostly because I'm the only one she knows. "Well," she said, "At Spanish class, we all had, like this project to do—"

"—Ah I remember," I interrupted.

"Mom!" Lizzie sighed and frowned at me and once again I tried not to grin back at her. "Anyway," Lizzie continued, "We had certain Spanish speaking countries and on 12-inch poster-board we had to write all about their characteristics in Spanish. So I, like . . ." Lizzie giggled, then went on. "I kinda you know snuck over to her perfectly perfect poster and I kinda got a marker and made her report all about Colorado and not in Spanish . . . and I also wrote all over it, in her handwriting, 'Spanish Sucks!' She kinda ya know, didn't notice what I did to it, and she kinda like read it to the class and she got suspended."

Lizzie stopped talking and we looked at each other and I tried very hard not to smile at her. I mean, this was terrible. And I did say aloud, "Wow, this is very terrible," and her sweet little face was trying to figure out which way I was gonna go with this. I mean, I had a number of good sentences ordered up, ranging from, "Sorry Petunia was mean but you and I both know you shouldn't have said that about Spanish sucking, not in her handwriting" to "Shoot, we've been over the whole 'turn the other cheek' principle lots lately, haven't we love" to a simple shake of the head and a wriggle of the eyebrows. I was ready, oh so ready . . . for a teaching moment.

Then Bad Doggy started barking. I bit my tongue and then Lizzie giggled and then Brett came running around the corner and screamed, "Darn dog, can't get any praying done." There was something so strange about the thought of screaming at a dog for keeping you from praying and it struck me and Lizzie at exactly the same instant.

That's when Lizzie rolled her eyes and said, "And the warm, cuddly cycle of hate started all over again."

Needless to say, she and I both almost fell over laughing.

A couple of hours later, I asked Lizzie if she'd go on a walk with me. I had been contemplating what to say about her spat with Petunia and decided to try and get her thinking about the concept of forgiveness. But I wanted to do it indirectly, without making her feel bad.

Lizzie of course wanted to join me, and Junior wanted to come to and as much as I wanted to get through to Lizzie, I didn't want Junior feeling left out, so I said "Sure, come on." Once we were outside, I asked Lizzie to recite the Lord's Prayer. Lizzie sort of froze. She said, "Oh Mom, I never can remember prayers, is that like the worst thing?"

"Nah, even worse would be—"

"—Oh I know what would be worse!" Lizzie said. "Having to recite it aloud for the entire class."

"With Petunia and her friends listening," Junior added.

Lizzie stumbled over one of the roots in our backyard. Every time we go down the hill, seems like one of us trips over the roots . . . I gave her a hand and then said, "That's what I wanted to talk to you about actually."

But first Lizzie said, "Mom, is it easy for you to talk to crowds?"

"Mmm," I said. "Depends. I am usually dreading it ahead of time but seems like God gives me the words once I start speaking and I almost always have fun while I do it."

Lizzie was giving me that *wow I want to be like you when I grow up* look so I figured it was a good teaching moment.

"Right, so anyway, the Lord's Prayer is simple. It goes: 'Our Father, who art in heaven, hallowed be thy name. Give us this day, our daily bread, and forgive us our trespasses as we forgive those who trespass against us. And lead us not into temptation, but deliver us from evil. For thine is the kingdom, and the power, and the glory. Amen.' Okay," I said, "You got all that? What's God telling us to do?"

"Um, be good and eat our bread?" Junior said.

"Well, he's telling us to be thankful for the bread we're given," I said. "What else? Lizzie?"

"Forgive others? Like he forgives us?"

"Exactly, good, Lizzie. That's what I wanted you to focus on. I want you to think about forgiving others because you know what God does?" I paused and waited for Lizzie and Junior to catch up with me. I'd been walking a little faster as I talked.

"Um," Junior said, "He forgives us?"

"Good," I said. "And how many times does he do that? Once? Twice?" I grinned a little and waited for Lizzie or Junior to remember one of their favorite lines Jesus spoke. For some reason they all loved this one.

"777 times 7 times, right, Mom?" Lizzie looked at me from behind her glasses. "Isn't that from the Parable of the Unforgiving Servant?"

"Unmerciful Servant, yes," I said.

"Oh, I remember that one," Junior said. "The servant was mean, wasn't he?"

"Yeah," I said. "And is that how God wants us to be?"

"Nope," Lizzie said. "He wants us to forgive just like he does. I get that Mom. But what about Petunia? She never says she's sorry, you know? So are we supposed to forgive her anyway?"

"Well," I said, "You're supposed to try, right? We can forgive before someone says they're sorry . . . right? Because that forgiveness helps us, makes us feel better, doesn't it?"

Lizzie was quiet. She was thinking it over.

"I mean, does it feel good to be all mad at Petunia?"

"No, not really, but I don't want to have to be nice to her over and over again and have her keep saying mean things to me," Lizzie said.

"Well, sweetie, you don't have to be BFFs with her, do you? I'm not saying you should walk into school tomorrow and throw your hands around her. What I am saying, I think, is you can do your best to forgive her in your mind and at a minimum stop plotting revenge and stop giving her so much rental space over your feelings, okay? I mean think of it like your heart is a storefront, right? Are you putting your favorite products on the store shelf, the stuff you really want people to see and purchase, or are you placing your angry, hurt, vengeful thoughts right out there, front and center, for all the world to see?"

"Guess my angry ones," she said.

"So what if you put your loving thoughts on your shelves, or let those be what's stored in your heart? Don't you think that would be better for you and for everyone else you see tomorrow?"

"Yes ma'am," she said.

"So we write love on our hearts?" Junior was giving me a funny smile.

"Yeah," Lizzie said, "Guess it makes for a better storefront don't you think?"

Junior leaned over and picked a yellow flower and handed it to me. He didn't say another word. We just smiled at one another and then Lizzie was talking about her favorite stores and Junior was talking about video games and I was walking and talking with God.

Chapter 19

Apparently there are thirty-seven messages on our home answering machine. Of these messages, twenty-two are from my mother in law; five are from Will; five are from people or businesses I am avoiding. Oh, and Will is cursing under his breath about either the other five messages OR the twenty-two said messages from his mother. And me? I'm smirking helplessly because I've been bad and ignored HIS MOM for too long again.

Will hates country music (yeah yeah but wait) . . . he heard Garth Brooks' "Friends in Low Places" the other day (my fault). This morning, as he was making coffee, he groaned at me.

"I got Garth Brooks playing in my head, over and over. Worst part about it? It's the extra twangy version."

I took all this in and was about to leave the room. "Wait, but Garth isn't that twangy."

"Exactly. I really have a problem."

I just had to shake my head and walk away, but inside, I was screaming, "In lo-ooow places . . ."

Will came into our bedroom holding a big handful of laundry. I was sitting in the rocking chair looking out the window. I held up a hand so that he wouldn't interrupt the flow of words in my head. "Might look like I'm doin' nothin," I murmured, with my fingers vaguely circling the air, "but I'm writing . . ."

The great thing about William is? He shrugged and didn't say another word. I'm thinking I just bought another two hours of pointless window staring. Man, the writer's life.

As they say on Twitter, LOL, with self-important hash tags, #amwriting.

I just shared a midnight snack with Brett, who is as nocturnal as I am. We ate Goldfish and Ho-Ho's. As he munched on orange crackers shaped like fish (in case you're reading this in one hundred years, we did not eat live goldfish!), he was scribbling something on a sheet of plain white computer paper.

"Whatcha making?"

Brett pointed with his pencil at a series of symbols. "New language."

"Wow, does it have its own alphabet?"

Brett squinted at the paper and then drew several quick squiggles. "Yes, it has twenty-three letters and three wildcards, they can be whatever you want them to be, so if you're not sure how to spell something, you can just use a wildcard. It's like a get home free card," he explained.

I laughed and grabbed a handful of goldfish. "That's genius. So you can adapt your language to whoever's reading? Say, maybe if it's a kid, you would only use one wildcard, but if it was an adult, you could use all three?"

Brett considered this for a moment, and I checked the microwave clock. It was 11:37, and I wondered how long it would take for us to both fall asleep, and how many hours of sleep that would leave before the alarm went off. Then Brett said, "No, I just am tired of having to spell words the same way every time, when the meaning isn't the same. Like if someone says, 'No,' it sounds different if they're smiling. Sounds a lot worse if they're mad at me. So the language should sound different."

I tried it. I said "No" aloud with a smile and then with a frown. "Huh," I said, "It does sound different."

"So it should be spelled different."

"Maybe you're right, maybe you're hearing "No" too often," I mused aloud.

Brett was busy drawing and he didn't answer. After a few more moments with him lost in his drawings and me lost in my thoughts,

Brett said, "You need a flower, I love you, here." And he grabbed another sheet of paper and drew a red tulip on it.

"Tulips are my favorite, thank you," I said.

"Thank you also sounds different when you're smiling," Brett said.

"Am I smiling?"

"Yes," he said.

•••

Once Brett went to bed, my cell phone rang, and I grabbed it on the first ring.

"Hi, is it Oprah?" I giggled.

"Oh my gosh, Sally, you know it's me," Stevie said.

I grinned. "So why hasn't Oprah called?" I was talking about the famous talk show host, Oprah Winfrey, who has single-handedly made writers famous. I had been thinking about her because Stevie had told me that Desi had a dream in which I was on Oprah's show and Desi was in the audience as one of my guests. The concept delighted me far more than it should have, but that's okay I think. It's not a terrible thing to want your writing to make it to the people. It's only bad if it changes who you are.

"Oh gah, you can't just wait for her to call, you need to send letters, make calls, you know that, right?"

I groaned. "I feel like Peter the Rabbit when the sparrow tells him to exert himself."

Stevie laughed.

"'Now you're quoting from Beatrix Potter'" I said in Stevie's nasal accent.

"My voice is that screechy?"

I grinned. "Almost. But you're saying I gotta actually call and write to people? Now I'm groaning."

"Yes, that's exactly what I'm saying."

"Yeah, yeah." I paused and glanced with longing at the coffee pot. "Do you think it would be wrong to make a pot of coffee? I'm freaking out about Thursday." It was two days before Thanksgiving, and as usual I'd been arguing with William all week about my mother in law.

"Is it ever wrong to make coffee?"

"I don't know, I'm asking you," I chuckled.

"No, of course not. Why are you freaking out?"

"Oh," I waved my hand. "She hurt her arm, but she won't let us host, she has to host, so we said we'd cook three or four of the dishes, and then she was like, 'Woe! What about the green bean casserole? Woe! What about the Jell-O casserole!' And I said to William, okay, we're already having green beans, I hate the casserole, it's yucky, and the Jell-O is yucky, and we're already bringing rolls, and we're also peeling all the potatoes and bringing those, but I put my foot down on the casseroles."

"I think it's just because you don't like anything green," Stevie cracked.

I laughed and scooped coffee beans into the grinder. "Hold on, it's gonna be loud for a second, but I guess I'm always loud."

Stevie laughed. "Yes."

"I like some green things," I protested.

"Like what?"

"Does mint chocolate chip ice cream count?" I smirked and poured the beans into the French Press canister.

"No!" Stevie was laughing really hard, and so was I. "But really, why does she need all those casseroles? How many dishes is she serving? I imagine there's the turkey, potatoes—"

"—And sweet potatoes, and stuffing, and corn, and cranberry sauce, that reminds me, I loved this children's book about the Cranberry family . . ."

"So that's at least ten dishes? And yes, I remember that book, I loved it too."

I smiled and was quiet for a moment. "And she keeps moaning about how hard it is, and I kept telling Will we should have Thanksgiving here, but she said no way, but then she calls him and goes on and on about all these dishes she wants to make, but can't—"

"—Sounds like she wants to have them, not have to make them," Stevie said.

"Yeah," I said. "And I can't, no, I won't make them, but I also can't tell her that, not directly, so I know we'll go there Thursday with our six or seven dishes, but no green bean, no jelly bean—"

"—You just said jelly bean, I think you're still feeling guilty for your jelly bean plot," Stevie said.

I froze and felt the hair rising on my arms. It wasn't that cold in the kitchen, but I was that shaken up by what Stevie said. "I didn't tell you about that," I finally said, "Nor did I write about it on Facebook. How did you . . ."

"Just knew," she said.

"Wow, so you know I bought the Jell-O already and was going to make it tonight, but I just couldn't do it, seemed too unfair?"

"No," she said. "But you're telling me now. Remember, there's still one difference between you and your mother in law."

"What?"

"Did you ask them to make your sauerkraut?" Each year, I loved sauerkraut, but this year, I knew that my mother in law was hurting, so I had gone out of my way to tell her not to worry about making it. "No, I sure didn't," I said.

"See? Now you just have to put the Jell-O back in the pantry and set your own boundaries, right?" Stevie's voice was soft but firm.

I nodded.

"What did you say?"

"Oh," I said, "I was thinking you're right, but trying to figure out how to tell her I don't wanna make it."

"Sounds like you already told William and probably her too, so it's up to you whether you're gonna follow through, right?"

I sighed and nodded. Then I said, "I just hate being the oddball here, like the woman who doesn't like to cook casseroles and who can't stand up to her mother in law, or who just likes to write stories and drink coffee at midnight and who talks to angels, it's hard being different sometimes, you know?"

"Sometimes it's easier, less mentally demanding, to accept someone's differentness, uniqueness, plain weirdness, when they're far away rather than in your own community or neighborhood. But that's the proximity to you, where non-judgment and love, the messy, painful unconditional kind, is really most needed. And what's the place or the person closest to you, Sally?"

"Besides you?"

"Yes."

I watched the steam rise on the electric heater, and then I put my wrist just above the steam, and for a moment, the steam obstructed the view of my skin. I was looking at myself, but having a hard time seeing anything. "I guess I'm closest to me, so you're saying I have to accept myself? And once I do that, I can say no more easily?"

"Exactly. Accept that you don't want to make the casserole, no ifs and buts about it. And then don't."

"Just don't," I said.

"Just don't," she said.

Scorecard

100 marbles bought.
100 marbles dropped.
96 marbles found.
One possibly digested.
Three chasing mice.
One soccer game.
One goal allowed; two goals scored. 17 meltdowns.
One mom hiding in closet, crying.
Two fastballs thrown with eyes shut.
One ball lost in woods.
Two pounds salmon.
Two cottontails shredded, in driveway.
One entire box sidewalk chalk beaten, seal pup style, by kids carrying street hockey sticks.
One very angry mom.
One very angry dad.
One toothbrush lost down sink pipe. One disgusting, mucky toothbrush retrieved.
"Don't despair mom. Tomorrow's a new day.
P.S. Mom? I love you."

Chapter 20

Three kids, four soccer games, seventeen library books, six donuts, four Slurpees . . . such is the first equation that best describes the math of our Autumn Saturday.

Between soccer games, we all ended up in the kitchen. With a bottle of water in one hand, I leaned against the countertop, watching as William ate a "Muffuletta" sandwich we'd bought yesterday from The Italian Store in Arlington, Virginia.

Junior sat facing William. "Dad, when I write 'Junior' after my name, it makes me proud to have your name." Junior's voice, still high pitched, echoed against the red walls in our kitchen, and I smiled.

Before I could say anything, my husband set his Muffuletta down and wiped his hands on his paper towel. "Well, son, I'm very proud to share my name with such a great kid. I don't think I've told you today just how awesome you are."

I glanced at William, who was once again grasping his "manwich," and nodded at the clock. He sighed; I sighed; and we started to check shin pads, cleats, water bottles and soccer balls. Fifteen arguments, four missed calls and an entire box of obliterated Munchkin donuts later, I sat in my husband's big, striped fabric chair in the kitchen, typing up some research notes about angels on my silver MacBook Pro. Brett whizzed around me, and we played our "I love you game."

I started. "I love you more than all the leaves in the backyard."

Brett's eyes lit up as I spoke. Before I finished, he danced in front of me. "I love you more than all the trees in America."

"Sun, moon, stars."

He grinned, all dimples showing, and yelled, "Mom I love you more than anything, even God."

I smiled back at him, and put a hand on his shoulder. "Not more than God. You must love Him most." I paused mid-negotiation long enough to mix a smile into my sober response. "How about except God?"

"Oh, okay, except God." He hopped around again. "And I won't let anyone hurt you." Brett grinned at me while he sipped his Slurpee. "And if anyone tries to hurt you, I will protect you. If someone comes at you with a knife, I will hit them, or cut their head off!"

"Um . . ."

Brett jumped up and added, "Look at the picture I drew for you, Mom! It has pink hearts on it, and me, and you."

I glanced over at the drawing of two blue-colored people holding hands and walking through flowers on a scrap of wrinkled white paper. I was sort of expecting to see angels casting fireballs at Lucifer and a host of demons but all he'd drawn were flowers. I leaned over and pointed at the pink hearts and said, "This one's mine, that one's yours, eh?"

"Yeah," he said.

"They're lovely," I said.

"Hey Mom?"

"Yeah?"

"Can we go to the Golden Gate Bridge tomorrow, maybe have a picnic, maybe camp out there too? Please Mom?"

"Wait, you mean the Golden Gate Bridge, as in the one in California?"

Brett gave an almost annoyed nod of his head. "Course I mean that one, silly."

"Um, well, I dunno, I don't think so, it's three thousand miles away from here."

"Three thousand miles? How far is that?"

"Um," I said, "Well, back in Jesus' day—"

"—And Joseph of Arithmea's."

"Right," I said, "And in Joseph's day, we would walk like thirty miles a day whenever we were traveling places."

"Like where would we go?"

"Well, Jesus walked all over Israel and he walked to Egypt and Libya. He also walked up toward Tyre—"

"—That's a big port, right?"

"Yeah, Tyre was a huge port back then. So he'd walk all over, from Bethany to Galilee up to Tyre, probably up to Ephesus in Turkey even, but it was from Tyre where I think they'd usually sail to Cyprus and Crete and Libya and Ethiopia."

"And England too."

"Yeah, I think they might have seen England as well, yeah," I said.

"Are we gonna go to all those places?"

"Yeah, someday soon," I said.

"How soon?"

I pulled Brett into a hug and said, "Well, once my books take off."

"Take off?"

"I mean sell," I laughed.

"And we'll dig for treasure?"

"Maybe, I said. "If you count lost gospels as treasures, yeah."

"Good," he said.

Chapter 21

"Ow!" I howled, waving a newspaper wildly above my head. The fruit fly whizzed past me, and I whacked away at it with the folded up Wall Street Journal, which I hadn't read in weeks. There was never enough time to just sit and read the newspaper, not with all the doctor's visits and the daily word count goals and the marketing phone calls.

"Mom! Watch out for the chandelier," Junior groused, one hand smoothing down his longish, dirty blonde hair. He and Brett had both been growing their hair out for a year, ever since Brett had caught sight of RG3 racing down a sideline, dreadlocks floating behind him as if unable to keep up with the rest of RG3's body.

"I want his hair," Brett had proclaimed with a weird intensity.

William had given me an almost shy glance, and I knew he was remembering back when his hair was long enough for him to catch between his teeth and chew on when he was bored in class. Then we'd giggled at one another. Our white son wanted African-American hair, and there was something cute about the whole idea of it.

"Yeah, sure," I'd shrugged, and William and I had grinned at one another.

I nodded at Junior, who was as sedate as William at all things, so staunchly conservative and cautious that I called him Alex Keaton behind his back, after Michael J. Fox's character in *Family Ties*. And then the fly whipped back in my direction, so fast, and aimed straight for my eyes. I flailed away at him with a massive swing of my right arm, and groaned when I heard my shoulder clicking. "Bastard," I growled under my breath.

"Heard that, Mama."

I glared at Brett, who was sitting at the kitchen table, legs splayed, pressed up against the back of the chair all casual and boyish. A cowlick stood up on the top of his head, and his eyes were lit up. He loved when I cussed, which was awful, because as soon as he learned a bad word, he'd walk around all day repeating it. Lizzie had been working that system all year with hilarious consequences. She kept making up cuss words, like "Zup," and Brett would repeat them at least 50 times in the space of a half-hour, until even Lizzie agreed that teaching Brett how to cuss was a bad idea.

"Yeah, Mom," Lizzie made a snapping gesture with her left hand, thrusting it out like she was a very freckled rap star. "Yo. Heard that."

"Heard what exactly?" I paused and grunted, as I flung the newspaper at the fat insect bearing oh-nine hundred.

"Mom, stop it," Junior's squeaky voice impaled the split-second of silence in our kitchen. "You're going to break the chandelier. Again."

"Nuh-ugh!"

"Is that a cuss word, Lizzie?" Brett leaned forward and barely suppressed a smirk.

"Watch out Mom! Ten o-clock!" The kids had all learned to speak in military terms to me. It was something weird our neighbor Todd had taught them all one afternoon, when he'd showed them how to shoot BB guns at targets on his parents' farm in Warrenton. I'd missed that trip. I was out running one of my marathons.

With one arm behind me for balance, I caught a glimpse of something moving toward me, then it dipped and weaved around me and was heading straight for the curtains over the table. I had a bead on the little beast and I was gonna get him right between the eyes. With a crisp but powerful motion, I brought the newspaper back, and without looking to my left, swung it in a massive arc—

And then all hell broke loose.

I'd swung so hard, I lost my balance, and just as I was teetering on the chair, certain I was going to land upside down and break my temple on the edge piece my mother-in-law had insisted on putting in the middle, actually, of the kitchen, I saw my only chance was to . . .

Grab hold of the chandelier?

In between thinking how bad of an idea this was, and reaching out and grabbing for it, I felt the chair give way underneath me, and then I was flying, not so much horizontally, but diagonally over the kitchen table, and right into the chandelier. I tried not to grab it with all my force, but I saw Lizzie's glass doll lying beside her and I didn't want to break that, so I, well, grabbed the spokes of the chandelier and held on for dear life instead.

Or something like that. It all made sense when it happened. Sort of.

I fell, hard. The chandelier fell on top of me, or half of it did, and the other half sort of dangled from the ceiling, while the kids all screamed, "Mama, are you all right?" in stereo. The chandelier left a few scrapes on the side of my head, and I was a little woozy for a few minutes, so I crawled out from underneath it and gestured toward the freezer.

"Ice?"

Lizzie pushed Junior out of the way so that she could get to the ice pack quicker, and with a tender smile, she held it against my head.

Brett grabbed his fuzzy pillow, and sucking his thumb, sat beside me and patted me on the back.

Junior shook his head, and pointed toward the windowpane overlooking the backyard. "Want me to kill the fly? Or should we just leave him for Dad?"

"For Dad," I giggled weakly. "Sweetie? Can you carry this to the trash please?" I handed him the chandelier remnant, and he hoisted it over his shoulder.

Just then, the garage door mechanism began to whir. Junior met William at the door holding the chandelier remnant, and I tried to overhear what they were saying.

Junior's high-pitched voice carried. "I did NOT do that."

William came around the corner carrying his briefcase. He shook his head at us, and nodded toward the dangling broken half of the chandelier.

I smiled at him, trying to appear wounded and charming at the same time. "How was your day, hon?"

He shook his head again and crossed his hands over his chest. His glance skipped over Lizzie, and rested on Brett.

Brett looked guilty for a moment, and then came to his senses. "I did NOT do that."

William's eyes knifed over to me. I tried another smile, which was fast becoming a whimper-laugh, which was probably the worst response.

"Really? Sally? *Really*? This is the fifth one."

"Hmmm?" I murmured.

Lizzie handed me a bottle of water.

"You can fix it, cantcha?"

William was fighting a smile. And losing.

Chapter 22

Jan. 21, 2014.
Junior's Diary

I am pretty much the best-behaved kid in the family. I have a lot of fun enjoying privileges while the other two don't get screens that much. But, let's tell about more interesting things.

I remember at, ummm... so mom was trying to kill a fly with newspaper and, instead of hitting the fly on one try, she ended up hitting the chandelier and making it fall down and breaking it! I said it was a *glorious* fail. Then, when dad got home, Lizzie, Brett, and I all pointed at the chandelier and, in unison, said, we did NOT do that!!!!!

Chapter 23

I was home with Lizzie one awful cold miserable morning.

Like the start of a horror story cold miserable morning. And like any good horror movie, my troubles were compounded by my tragi-comic internal and external struggles. In other words, I was sick, and though supposed to be hard at work on whatever book I was writing, I was instead stuck at home with an also sick child. And that was before she threw up on the carpet in her youngest brother's room, and before I was like the worst mom ever and actually stormed upstairs and yelled at her for throwing up on the carpet in her brother's room.

On second thought, it was pretty bad that she threw up on his carpet, and not in the bathroom, which was at the heart of my grievance. That, and I am a sympathetic puker. But I had a moment, probably (hopefully) one of my worst moments as a mother, when I reacted most unkindly to my daughter vomiting on the carpet in her brother's room.

"Why did you do this?" I was quivering and shouting.

She groaned and laid down, exhausted, on her bed.

"Why?" My voice was hysterical, dripping in fear of the vomit awaiting me. I probably should not confess that there is yet another permanent stain on the carpet because I did such a terrible *most unthorough* job cleaning it, but really that does not matter because my son's gone and drawn with oil pastels all over the carpet, both surrounding and overtop the vomit, so you can't really tell it's there. Not unless you're me and you know exactly where to look for it.

"Because I couldn't see in the bathroom. I was scared." Ah, she was just as scared of the absence of light as I was of the existence of vomit on carpet.

I paused at the entrance of her doorway. I sighed. She was right. There was no light in her bathroom, nor in my bathroom, nor in any other room in our house. Just as she was loudly vomiting, and I, writing, the electricity flickered once and then ground to a halt. I froze, in fear as usual, and quickly calculated whether I'd ignored the electricity bill—again. No, it was on auto-pay. Then I wondered if God was giving me a sign . . . too much time online. But why were the lights out? He could have just taken out the router.

"You were scared of the dark? So what does that have to do with where you go to vomit?" I heard the sarcasm dripping in each word I spoke, and it sounded just like my mom, which was very bad. So I took a deep breath and tried not to mutter strange expletives under my breath as I was tucking in my Lizzie.

And then I sort of cleaned up the vomit. And called my William to announce my list of complaints. And finally, in sheer boredom, and unable to work, I went outside to rake the last of the late autumn leaves from our front yard. Or most of the last leaves because I can't focus on any task for very long. Especially when power trucks keep circling the house, over and over and over again.

I got annoyed for some reason as I watched the power trucks circling our block. They passed in front of our house five times in an hour, and each time, I ran inside to observe a eureka moment. Power trucks should equal electricity. But they didn't. They equaled a pointless, stupid no that's mean gallant, hard-working search for the broken transformer.

Four houses down, the outside lights blinked at me, a stinking reminder that half our street could see; the other half . . . was blind. I progressed from outrage to whining to despair as the trucks kept circling and as best as I could see, unscrewing green boxes but fixing nothing.

I went inside to check on Lizzie, who had miraculously recovered from her vomiting incident. When I whined about the power, she asked, "you sure the Wi-Fi on my tablet isn't working?"

I giggled. "There's no such thing as a little Wi-Fi. It's like being a little pregnant."

I think that got an eye roll, maybe a snicker.

The rest of the day was moribund. Depressing. Awful. And my dear Lizzie listened to me patiently. After a few hours of this, I saw a neighbor upbraiding a power guy who was messing with our transformer, and I laughed, in relief, because I was not that woman. I was patient and reasonable and full of good cheer. Or at least I wasn't screaming and making a scene like the neighbor lady was.

"Mom?"

"Yeah?" I sighed, and pulled back from the window.

"Let's go to Starbucks. You can work there, right?"

"Yes! Lizzie, how smart you are," I said. And once we got outside, but before I drove off, I greeted the power guy with a brave smile. "So, how's it going?"

"Oh. Not so well. The last crew just left without explaining anything. And now I gotta recheck all the transformers. They thought they'd found the problem, but they forgot to perform a test, so I have to redo everything."

"Oh," I said. "How long do you think . . ."

"No idea, Ma'am," he said.

"Thank you," I said, and tried not to slouch too much.

According to my dear William I kept "bugging" the poor power guys throughout the evening. We walked around the block supposedly to get some fresh air, but it was really so that I could keep asking them when they'd fix the broken part of whatever transformer was causing our neighborhood to not have power.

I grew suspicious by dinnertime because the power guy showed up outside our house for the third time, just when William was saying that inevitably, "Idiots dug around power lines where they weren't supposed to dig."

"Junior," I said, "You been digging for specimens again?"

He fixed his blue eyes on me and shook his head. "I did not do that," he said.

"Lizzie?"

She rolled her eyes at me. "Really, Mom?"

I sighed again. Just then, Brett pelted William with a handful of acorns and raced around the edge of the house and then tripped on something. It was one of our shovels, and it was leaning on the side of the house.

"Brett?"

He looked up and grinned at me.

"Have you been digging?"

"Oh yes," he said.

"Why?" I was still curious more than mad.

"Oh," he shrugged, as he picked up the shovel and looked around. "I was looking for diamonds for my collection. And when I hit something hard, I just kept digging."

William glowered at him. "Wait. Let me get this straight. You were digging next to the green box. The transformer. You hit something hard, so you kept digging?"

Brett pulled an acorn and studied it. "Oh yes," he said. "I got to something really hard and diamonds are a ten in hardness, so I dug harder."

I stifled a giggle. There was something really funny about seeing William angry. "Find any diamonds?"

"No," Brett said.

"Right," William said. "No diamonds. Just power lines." William squared his shoulders and dragged Brett over to talk to the power guys.

We had electricity again a couple of hours later. So did a couple hundred of our neighbors. Naturally, we never told William about Brett's diamonds.

Chapter 24

The good news: the corner kids and I did a chemistry experiment in the kitchen and did not blow anything up. The glass is half-full good news: our granite counter tops have a bluish streak anyway, so I can probably 'splain away the blue aluminum compound spill. Oh! My fingers are blue too . . .

As I just complained online, I can't stop coughing, so my friend JC said to me, "Sally, grab some Vick's Vapo-Rub and rub it on your feet. It will help with your cough." I did that, but then I got overexcited and remembered all those commercials I watched as a kid. So I rubbed it on my throat, under my nose, and yep, on my chest. And now? Now I got burning boobs. No!

So now I got a Vick's problem, a blue granite countertops problem, and I am still coughing.

"So I said to him, 'dang Junior, your cheeks jiggle so much, you need a bra for them.'"

I looked over at my son, who smiled amiably while he crunched on hot Cheetos.

"Man."

"Yep," she nodded. "So he said, 'At least they're not hitting puberty yet, like you are.'"

Junior grinned at us and I shook my head and left the kitchen.

God is in her sleepy gaze.
God is alive in his two dimples,
shimmering like shiny crystals
among his 53 broken crayons.

Chapter 25

We left Brett, who was turning eight soon, with Lizzie and Junior for about a half-hour today, just so we could take a quick walk in our snowshoes. It was the middle of February and we'd just gotten hit with a foot of snow. Brett had not been taking his ADHD meds unless he was at school. I gave him the choice and he said, "Nope, no meds. I like being a wild thing, crazy and fun and all." He'd clapped his hands together and his eyes had gleamed with enthusiasm, and I'd smiled and told him we'd try it. I told him I'd honor his wishes, at least, if I could.

Anyway, Brett wasn't taking his meds. We had a ton of snow. And he'd been driving us nuts all day. We wanted to clear our heads, and we hadn't been snowshoeing in four years, since the Snowmageddon hit in 2010.

It was my idea, leaving him alone. "He'll be fine, come on, let's go. Just for a half-hour. What trouble could he possibly get into?" I'd been standing out in the garage when I asked William this question. We were lacing up our boots and our snowshoes. He'd gotten my boots hooked in my Tubbs snowshoes, so all I had to do was get my boots knotted and tied up. It was cold, and it was sleeting still, and it was glorious. William smiled at me and I thought about how gorgeous he looked in his blue jacket, and I remembered the first time we'd gone snowshoeing out by the lake together, so many years ago, before we had three kids. And now, we were going somewhere alone together.

He smiled back at me, and we stepped toward the snow bank and headed down the hill in our backyard. "You know what?"

"What?"

"This is what it's gonna be like in ten years. When the kids are in college," I said.

We'd smiled at one another again. I was thinking about being alone with William and I was pretty sure he was thinking that too.

Anyway, our walk was glorious. I know I'm repeating that word, but it's all I got, so why not reuse it, kind of like a Kleenex that's stuffed in your pocket from a couple hours ago. Okay, that's a gross comparison. I loved being out with William alone.

And as it turned out, it was fine. At least we thought it was fine. Later, at dinner, I smiled at Brett across the table. He was driving William crazy so I wanted to deflect the heat off Brett. "So," I said, "What did you do while we were out?"

"Threw water balloons. Had a blast," Brett said.

I laughed. I thought he was joking. I mean, it's the middle of winter. We don't even have water balloons.

"Yep," he said. "Got some plastic bags, filled em up with water, and hurled them into the shower. They exploded every time."

Lizzie laughed. Junior laughed. I glanced over at William and he definitely was not laughing.

"Um," I said, "You put them in the bathtub, right?"

Brett smiled. "It was fun, wasn't it?" Brett looked at Junior, who was grinning.

Junior nodded.

"'Specially when they went splat," Brett said. "They broke every single time."

"Wow," I said.

William still wasn't laughing, and I knew I wasn't supposed to be either but Brett looked so happy.

"And did you make a mess?" William said. "Because lemme tell you, if you made a mess, I'm gonna . . ." William looked really mad and I was trying so hard not to laugh. Lizzie and Junior weren't trying so hard.

"I expect more from you, Junior," William said.

Junior quieted down a little.

"Well," Lizzie said, "At least he didn't like flush 'em down the toilet. Like five bags or something like that."

"Oh my God," I gasped. I stared at Brett and made sure I wasn't laughing. Darn it, I was laughing. I tried to look serious. "Please do not ever put anything in the toilet."

"Except poop or pee."

"Thanks Lizzie," I said. "Seriously Brett. We already had to replace one toilet after you . . ." I paused to regain facial control. "After you put Matchbox cars down the toilet."

"Lots of Matchbox cars," Junior said.

"Like how many?" Brett asked.

I shook my head at Brett. "Even one's too many. Really. Please don't break anymore toilets." I could feel William turning red next to me. Almost choking he was so angry. "The last one cost six hundred dollars."

"Wow," Junior said. "That's what an iPad costs."

"Can I have an iPad?" Lizzie said.

"No," I said.

"No," William said. He gripped the sides of the table. "Lemme tell you, all of you, look up at the ceiling!"

Four sets of eyes followed William's finger to the ceiling.

"When you break stuff up in your bathroom . . ."

"Like toilets," I said.

"And bathtubs," Junior said.

"It all leaks through this ceiling. And it ruins more than just the bathroom floor." William was enunciating each word very carefully. "And I do not like it when things in this house are ruined."

"Especially toilets," I said.

"Can I have ice cream?" Junior said.

"Yeah, Mom," Lizzie said. "Can I have ice cream?"

William shook his head. "No more water balloons. Y'all hear me?"

We all grinned at one another. "Yep, you can have ice cream," I said. Then I paused and looked at William. "Um, not Brett?"

"Not Brett," William said.

When William walked out of the room, I whispered, "Hey, Brett, you can have some ice cream tomorrow."

Brett grinned at me and said, "It's a deal."

Scorecard

Two well visits.
Two descended testicles.
Three cards stayed up.
No pinching, vomiting, hitting or other incidents.
One somewhat unmentionable infection.
Many Ritz crackers ingested.
Two lunches eaten en route to doctor's.
One howling collie.
One bra-obsessed fifth grader.
Three Thursday folders.
17 forms to fill out.
"Stop chewing in my ear—it's gross."
One soccer practice.
One Cub Scouts meeting.
One therapist visited.
One impromptu playmate.
and a mission to find Mom's birth gem.
One serious pep talk after I wrote depressing poetry.

Chapter 26

"Mom, where's the . . .[garbled]?"

"The what?"

"The dice."

"Dice?"

"Oh my God, Mom, the DICE."

I was stumped. I just sat there, staring at Lizzie. Then I mumbled, "Um, I dunno."

"Oh my Gawd. Mom. How could you not know where the dice are? Like, oh my Gawwwwd."

"I'm sorry, but—"

"—Mom! Where are the dice? You and Junior used them last. Like, how could you not know where the DICE ARE?"

"Um—"

"—Oh my Gaaawwwwwwd. Mom! You're impossible." Daughter stamps from room. Mom giggles helplessly. Goes back to work.

•••

A little later, it was almost dinnertime, and I wasn't sure where the kids were, but I had a pretty good idea that they were over bugging Todd. When I stepped out the garage door, I spotted Sandy pulling up into her driveway from work. She waved, and I stood beneath the crape myrtle and waited for her to get out of her sedan.

Sandy was in her early sixties, and she was a pediatric nurse. I cannot emphasize how much I loved having a pediatric nurse as my neighbor. Sandy had helped me figure out how to breastfeed Brett. Sandy had looked at many a scraped knee and bashed-in forehead, and probably saved me a half-dozen trips to the ER. She was your salt of the earth Midwesterner, with a deep voice and a girlish, melodic laugh. She was as kind to my children as she was gruff to Todd.

It was probably because of his automobile collection. He had seven to nine cars at any one time, and to evade getting fined by the Homeowner's Association, he would drive the newest of the cars around the block and park them in different places every night. One of his finest jalopies was a broken down, busted up, absolutely dilapidated 1975 El Camino. The soft black top had more holes in it than fabric remaining, and it was, as Brett had proclaimed, the color of boogers and vomit. Unfortunately, this fine jalopy was parked in front of Sandy's house, with its front bumper about three inches from the opening to her driveway.

Sandy slammed her door shut and called out, "Hi there!" She limped over to the edge of her driveway and grabbed her newspaper.

"Hi Sandy, how was work?"

"Not bad, we got a new computer system in, it's driving me a little crazy, but I had a lot of field visits today, so I got to see three new babies." Sandy beamed a little.

"Aww, were they cute?"

"They were tiny! Every one of them was less than a month old." Sandy's brow knotted together and she paused to swat at a gnat. "Bugs are awful tonight."

"Yup," I said. The gnats were swirling around me too.

"Where are the kids? Is that them down there?" Sally pointed a few doors down, to where six more of Todd's vehicles were keeping his home company. Beside the 69' blue Mustang fastback that was up on blocks in his driveway, a gaggle of children was assembled, and if you squinted, you could see Todd's boots sticking out from under the engine.

"Yeah, I reckon they're helping him with his Boss." As Todd had once explained to Junior, the name Boss came about when the designer of the 69' Mustang was asked what project he was working on. All he would say was, "the boss's car" because the project was a secret.

Sandy shook her head and grumbled, "Then we're gonna take a walk over there, hold on, let me put my trash out."

I followed Sandy into her garage and grasped hold of her dark green trashcan before she could get ahold of it, and I dragged it to the curb.

Sandy was right behind me, and she put her hand on her hip and made a clucking sound with her tongue. "I can hear the oil dripping from the oil pan, I know he's trying to avoid getting fined, but this is really too much."

"Well, he knows you'll never report him, right?"

Sandy cinched her pants up and gave the El Camino one last disgruntled stare. "Doesn't mean I can't make him move it, come on Sally, let's go fetch your kids."

I giggled and fell in beside Sandy. She grumbled on and on about oil stains and leaking undercarriages, and I kept laughing because there was a Ford Pinto parked in front of my house, and it had no rear bumper and no passenger side door. It was a shade of green that was somewhere between fir and mint with none of the pleasant attributes of either color. The kids loved to dive in and out of the backseat and climb through the rear lift gate to the roof, from which they had a good leaping-off point to get to the back doors of another one of Todd's projects: a baby blue 1964 Chevy Corvair Greenbrier van. I loved it because it reminded me of the van the kids drove in my favorite cartoon as a kid—Scooby Doo. The kids played house inside it, and even though its entire left side was rusty, the floorboards still held and the van drove pretty well on the few occasions it left its spot in front of our house.

Sandy, meanwhile, was still clucking and shaking her head. "Golly," she snorted, "Never figured out where he stowed them at Christmas."

"Oh," I chuckled as I waved at Junior and his friend Ed. They were climbing through the rear doors into the interior of the Scooby van. "He took 'em down to the Bernstein's. They were out of town and they never put up votives anyway."

"Harrumph. At least they're at the end of a cul-de-sac," Sandy said. The Bernsteins' cul-de-sac was up and around the street from us, maybe a half-mile away, and because the Bernsteins were Jewish, they didn't celebrate Christmas like the rest of us did.

As we reached Todd's property, Todd emerged from beneath the Boss. He wiped his hands on a towel Lizzie handed to him, and I could overhear him telling the neighborhood kids about the history of the Boss.

"It was first built in '69 to compete with the Camaro ponies, they put a 302 into her belly and tuned her up right good. This beauty is worth at least one-fifty once I get her fixed up, she's the belle of these here parts, I'm gonna tune up her eight, the G-Code engine was rated at two hundred ninety horses; however, that's underrated, on the dynos she can pull three eighty, she's gonna be a beast for sure." Todd reached for a plastic cup and spit a string of tobacco into it. Brett was watching all of this with saucer-wide eyes; so was Joey and Alex. Tunie was parading up and down the street waiting for one of the boys to notice her outfit, which was modeled on the ever-popular High School Musical. And Rhodie stood about a half-block away, looking uncomfortable in a tight ensemble, preening for the boy she was seeing.

"Oh hiya Ms. Sandy, hi Sally, how y'all doin'? Todd was tall and gangly, skinny everywhere except his gut, the likes of which was fueled by cans of Budweiser and Coca Cola that were strewn in the general vicinity of his royal blue recycling bin. He had lanky, long blonde hair and I always assumed he was teasing when he said the reason he had dark streaks running through it was because he washed it in motor oil, but Lizzie swore it just meant he was a hard core motor head from West Virginia.

Sandy issued one of her brisk nods. "Hello, now here's the thing," she said. "I know that's yours, Mr. Todd, I know that old brute is yours."

Todd held his hand out and said, "I need the nine wrench, Brett, Alex, Joey, the nine."

All of Todd's tools were numbered with duct tape that had been threaded and then cut out to leave a number. Before Brett could grasp hold of it, Alex had a wrench that was almost as long as his forearm in hand, and he winced and then used his other hand to hand the wrench to Todd.

Todd grunted and said, "Now see here kids, this here Boss is gonna get shined up, we'll get the stripes repainted, and I ordered the original blue—"

"—Mr. Todd," Sandy said, "I know the El Camino is yours, and you can't keep parking your truck in front of our house, there's oil stains—"

"—Lizzie, grab me another beer from the side fridge will ya?" Todd turned his baseball cap around backwards and pulled a rag from the back pocket of his jeans.

At this moment, Tunie sauntered over and typed something with emphasis into her cell phone.

Everyone ignored Tunie, and she stalked away with a flounce and a head flip.

Lizzie mumbled, "Yes Mr. Todd, coming right up," and scampered into the garage.

Sandy cleared her throat and tapped her foot with a commanding air. "Mr. Todd, listen, you better move it from in front of my house down the block walk, you can afford the extra far walk home. You need to put that wrench down and get it out of my way now or I'll take that damned old bumper off." Sandy finished up her speech with her Midwestern drawl pulling the last few words out almost deadpan. She looked serious, and with her arm outstretched, she added, "Lizzie, you don't need to go fetching him beers, he's a grown man, grown enough to move a dust heap from his neighbor's yard."

Lizzie returned from the garage already holding a can of beer. She handed it to Todd and he nodded and popped the can open.

"Um, Miss Sandy, it's not—" Junior started to say.

"—Shhh, Junior," I said. I knew he was going to correct Sandy on the meaning of yard, and somehow so did Sandy. She liked Junior, so her words were fairly tame. "It's parked in front of my yard, that space is mine sure enough, whether it's defined as mine or not mine, Mr. Todd here knows he ain't sposed to park seven cars, or is it eight? Around the neighborhood, you're much too nice

Sally, but Mr. Todd here is gonna move his dust heap, isn't he?" Sandy put a hand on Junior's shoulder and motioned for Lizzie to come closer. Once Lizzie did, Sandy smiled at her, and then added, "Right Mr. Todd?"

"Awww, Sandy, you wouldn't call the Association on me, you don't like em' anymore than I do, ain't that right? Todd took a swallow of beer and gave Sandy a mischievous grin.

"Don't test me, now I better go walk the dog," Sandy said.

"Oh, can I come?" Brett hopped up and stood in front of Sandy.

"Me too," Lizzie said.

"Sure, make sure that thing's moved before Grant gets home." Sandy gave Todd a short, appraising stare and a hint of a smile made her cheeks move a little. "He's liable to call a tow truck."

"Aw shucks, a tow truck? That ain't nice." Todd was smiling now too. "Are you grilling ribs this Saturday?" The neighborhood was holding a pot-luck dinner, and Sandy was hosting it. Sandy's husband Grant grilled the best ribs in Virginia, or so Todd liked to say.

Sandy chuckled and shook her head. "Maybe, maybe not, Mr. Todd."

"Okay Sandy, I'll move it." Todd nodded, and Sandy, the kids and I walked back toward the Scooby van.

"Think he'll move it in front of the Scooby van?" Lizzie asked.

"No telling if it can fit, don't know," I said.

"Crazy ol' coot," Sandy muttered.

"He's younger than you are," I laughed.

"Still is a crazy ol' coot," Sandy said.

Chapter 27

"Hey mom? What's an {word garbled}?"

"What's a what?"

She didn't miss a beat. "An erection."

William walked past me and whispered, "Tag, you're it." I gripped the spatula and stirred the soup, trying to sort through my answer. She was reading a book, so it must have come up . . . oh crap. She was reading the book I wrote. I grimaced. "It's what happens when a guy gets turned on and," I paused and decided to spell it out. So I did.

She laughed. "Oh my gosh. That's hilarious!"

William's eyes twinkled. "In Scotland, they'd say, 'Oh! The little man's gone all angry!'"

"Thanks a lot William." I rolled my eyes.

"Oh my gosh Mom, you two are so funny," Junior said.

Brett walked past me. "Can I go to Target with you?"

"No. You gotta help clean your bathroom. Start with picking up all toys off the floor."

Brett started to cry but it was his fake cry.

I glared at my fake-weeping child. "What? What do you want at Target?"

"Um, a plane?"

"No. Your toys are all over the bathroom."

"A magnet? Please? Promise me."

"I promise I will throw away all the toys that are in the bathroom if you don't pick them up."

Then William took over and it was glorious. It sounded like he was delivering a speech to military troops and he was the general. "You're not showing your mother the respect she's due—I mean, she spent all this time cleaning the bathroom, YOUR bathroom, and you defile her work by spitting toothpaste all over the faucet? It's either clean when she gets back from Target or all three of you lose TV for a week."

•••

Later that night, I was on the phone with Stevie, and I giggled midway through the call. "Uh oh, a black Caprice keeps circling the block. Unmarked."

"You think it's a detective? Something going on?"

I giggled and shook my head. "No, Todd's got himself another vehicle and he's looking for a place to park it."

"And how many's that? Wasn't it eight already?"

"Um, he was up to eight, but he sold his Camaro, oh that was a pretty one, I think Sandy's husband wanted to buy it."

"Shut up! Sandy would have blown a gasket," Stevie said.

"Yeah, but I think he said he sold it for thirty-five grand, he's actually doing pretty good, I just kinda wish he'd get a storefront." I moved away from the window shade and grinned again. "Then again, I like all his cars. And this Caprice . . ." I paused and heard a door slam, and peeked out the window one last time. "Ohh, sure enough, that's Todd, and he parked it in front of Aaron's house, and now Bad Doggy's barking, oh my gosh, that dog . . ."

"You should say something, right?"

I sighed and left the front study. "Nah, I dunno, so hey, did I tell you Jesus was telling me about being kids? He said I was always hanging off the chandelier at the Frat, is that true? And he said I was always in trouble, I was like, 'Who me?' And he was like, 'Oh yes, always eating everything in sight and breaking things and making things.' Is that true? And was he really my dad when I was Mark?"

Stevie was quiet for a moment. As if she were choosing which question to answer. Sure enough, she volunteered in her high northeastern accent, "Yes, you were always hungry as a baby soul, always were eating everything, and bouncing around, and getting into trouble."

"Why did I eat everything? Do souls eat?"

"Course they do, they need energy, and when they're young, they'll eat just about anything," she said.

"Huh," I said. "Like furniture and whatnot?"

"Uh huh," she said.

I thought about it for a moment and tried to picture a soul eating a sofa, and the image that came to mind made me smile. And then I thought of another question. "Um, when our souls are in our bodies, are they a separate consciousness? Like, do our souls think and talk and direct what our bodies are doing?"

"It depends." Stevie paused and answered a question about tacos Desi was asking. Then she said, "Our souls go into our bodies and our souls have a different consciousness. The soul is connected to the human brain by two or three tethers. These are energetic connections that tie the soul's core to the brain stem and to the part of the brain that's responsible for deep thinking, or what we know as intuition. The mind is a separate entity or consciousness altogether, and some people go their whole lives kind of asleep, like their soul never wakes up, so their brain controls everything, all the information they get, all the thoughts and feelings they have, but many other people do wake up, at least some, and they start to be able to connect to their souls. This happens a lot more easily if a person has a near death experience, say, or if the person meditates a lot."

"So is that what all the yogis taught in the Upanishads and the Gita about getting free of your senses, of getting absolutely still, so that your brain is essentially empty of inputs, of questions, of thoughts, of feelings, because all of these act as interference that keeps us from hearing what our souls have to say?"

Stevie was quiet for a moment, and then she said, "In a sense, yes. If your soul is a different consciousness and if it contains all your memories of Home, of past lives, of your early childhood . . . then basically your brain, anytime it's working, is sending energy that blocks the signal from your soul. It's like if you're trying to tune the radio, and there are two radio stations situated in different places, but you're in between both stations, so they're interfering with one another's signals. You have to move closer to one station or the other and pick a signal, otherwise, you hear the strongest signal, and that would be your brain until you get used to silencing it. And doing that requires practice . . . it's not as easy as driving your car closer to one radio station or the other. You have to move your consciousness away from your brain in order to hear what your soul has to say, but you still must be connected to your brain, so it's only something most people can do during meditation, when they're absolutely still and quiet."

"Only then can they hear their soul's transmission?" I was walking around the downstairs, stepping over stuffed animals and Legos. "Thank God I have slippers on," I muttered.

"Why?"

"I dunno, just stepped on a Lego, almost died," I giggled.

"Oh," she said. "They're pretty painful."

"Yeah," I said. "So, wait, I don't mean to ask the same question again, but you're really saying that we have two different, totally separate consciousnesses?"

"Yes. Hey, go into the kitchen and grab two bowls and set them out on the counter."

"Huh? You want me to make some soup or something? I'd rather brownies."

Stevie chuckled and said, "I don't know how you can eat like you do and still be healthy, it just kills me."

"What, I shouldn't eat brownies for dinner? I think it's a great dinner." I was grinning, but I was also pulling bowls down from the cabinet as I talked. "And what's this about you being vegetarian? I don't know if I could do that."

"If you saw how the animals were treated, you might change your mind. But that's not the main reason I don't like to eat meat, it's more of a health thing, and most meat makes me sick. I can eat fish, but everything else is pretty hard on my stomach." Stevie's voice deepened and she said, "Okay, you got the bowls?"

"Yes ma'am, they're white and blue with pretty little swirls and drawings on them." I smiled and touched the inside of one of the bowls. The surface was hard but smooth and it felt good on my fingertips.

"Okay, now take one of the bowls and put it inside the other one," she said.

I lifted the bowl on my right and placed it inside a slightly larger bowl that had the same design pattern etched on it. "Okay, I did it," I said.

"Now look at the bowls. Imagine the inner bowl is your soul. The outer bowl is your mind. To get from the outer bowl to the inner bowl, what do you do?"

"Um, I dunno, you move the inner bowl back out from the outer bowl? Do you mean you have to float your soul out of your body in order to get free of it?"

"Well, that's the easiest way yes, like when you die, when your body dies, the inner bowl does float out, and it goes back Home. It has all of the memories from this life stored in its core, and it also has all your memories from before this life stored in there. But what if you can't get out of the outer bowl? What if your soul is tied in there, which it is, with those tethers—how can you travel from the outer bowl to the inner bowl?"

I stared at the bowls for a moment and felt stumped. Then I said, "Um, you could pour water on them both, so that they're now connected to one another by a substance other than air, and then you could move back and forth between them more easily."

"Good!" She said.

"But how does this translate to our ability to move from the mind, the outer bowl, to the soul, or the inner bowl? What is the water? Is it like spirit, or something energetic?"

"Yes, the spirit is the water living inside all of us. It's through spirit that we can travel from mind to soul."

"That's the Holy Spirit you mean?" I paused and stared at the bowls again. "Is the Spirit what Rumi called the 'living waters?' It's something that may not be visible to the eyes but it does exist, and it is energetic, it's a form of energy, it's real, we all have it, but we simply need to will to use it?"

"Yes, I know you want to over-complicate it Sally, but the spirit is real. We all have it. Spirit is what allows the mind to access the soul, it's what allows us to connect to our soul, to Home, to our past, to our other lifetimes, and to other spirits or souls who may not even be in human shells. Spirit exists in all things and in all bodies, but it also exists outside our physical existence."

"My head hurts, it's a lot to take in," I admitted.

"That's okay, you need to eat, why don't you make yourself something healthy? Like some eggs or something?"

"I was just thinking an omelet would be good, like with some mushrooms, some peppers you think?" I opened the fridge and searched through the veggie rotter. "Oh! I have some scallions, I love them too!"

"I love omelets, alright, go eat, and text me with your questions," she said.

"How do you know I'll have questions?"

Stevie laughed. "Really Sally?"

"Love you," I said.

"Buckets," she said.

Scorecard

1,500 words written.
78 e-mails read.
First game, artificial turf.
Seven goals allowed.
One goal scored.
"2, 4, 6, 8, who do we appreciate?"
One aching heel.
One aching head.
Three dirty yellow t-shirts.
Two hours times two boys, one dad,
Equals six hours total service.
Three pinches, two punches, one tantrum.
Four Slurpees.
Two Gatorades.
One bag green, blue and pink cotton candy, shared.

Chapter 28

I was groaning all morning because my editor was trying to kill me. She's making me not only research Outside Looking In: BD Guide to Making it as an Indie, she's making me outline it. I think she might have even raised her voice, LOL. Or used all-caps. As in, Sally: YOU MUST OUTLINE. Then I was crying. Real tears.

"Oh um yeah, hey, Sally, can you write a TOC?"

"Huh?"

"Table of contents."

Sally sighs dramatically. "Man, that sounds . . . organized." Sighs again and squints at phone. "Yeah. I guess so—wait!"

"What?"

"You're not trying . . . to fool me into writing an outline are you?"

"Oh my God. Sally. Write that ********* outline!"

"Huh? What did you say? Reception is horrible—"

"—You said you would—"

"—Oh, my God! Brett's teacher is on the other line! Gotta get that!"

Editor glares at phone.

•••

I stayed up all night last night, or almost all night. I tried to stop working at 4 a.m., but the document I left on the big iMac followed me around as I tried to nod off. I had taken on this project pro bono, as we used to say in law firms, for a friend of mine who paid all this money to get her book edited, and the editor had left the formatting in complete, total, disarray. So I'd offered to help, knowing it would take at least a few hours. And once I got into it time lost meaning. I couldn't, wouldn't stop working. It's always like that when I take on technical work, or mechanical jobs, like formatting a Word doc.

So I lay there, cuddled up against William, and I tried to absorb myself into his calm, steady heartbeat. I wanted to slow down, and rest, just like he was. But . . .

What if I moved the stuff from the front, like the Acknowledgments, the Dedication, and the infernal Table of Contents, to the back of the book? That would solve my pagination problems. Maybe my editor won't mind. I really should move the TOC. I should get up and move it now. No. No. I shouldn't do that.

I close my eyes, and the words from her book run across my mind's eye, kind of like a newsreel. I can slow it down if I try really hard. But nothing's moving slow right now. I can't slow it down, so I just let the pages race past me. Sometimes I spot a misspelled word, or what would my editor call it? A predicate? A boring predicate? Honestly, predicates are about as interesting as gerunds. I don't like them either. I wonder what page she is on, or was on, when she went to bed. At what? Midnight?

Man, I should just get out of bed and fix it. But what if I have a seizure? My synapses are bugging out right now. Like, zing. Ping. It's like my head is filled with some of Junior's missing electrons. Carbon's missing four electrons. Sodium has one extra. And once you combine that with chlorine, which has one extra electron, they get stable.

"Oh," I'd cracked to Junior, "So that's why they call it table salt. Because the salt is stable."

He'd laughed out loud at my first and only chemistry joke.

• • •

"Hey, guess what Todd just brought home?"

"Hello to you too, Sally."

"Oh," I giggled. "Hi Stevie. Guess what?"

"Um, Todd just brought home two geese? And six ducklings?"

I grinned. "Close. More like the ugliest duckling you've ever seen, he brought home what looks like . . ." I paused and took a glimpse out the dining room window. "It's a . . ." I started to giggle uncontrollably.

Stevie laughed and waited for me to gain my composure.

"Um . . ." My voice dropped to a whisper. "He parked a monster truck out front, and it's almost as tall as my house."

"Why are you whispering? And as tall as your house? Get out."

"Oh, I don't want William to hear, he might get mad."

"I thought you were worried about Sandy finding out about it." Stevie laughed again and said, "And what, like William's not gonna notice in the morning?"

"I dunno, he leaves for work when it's dark out, and maybe he won't notice, I hope he doesn't, because as strange as it sounds, I think it's hot."

"The truck?"

"Um, yeah, what else?"

We both were laughing now, and I sat down in one of the dining room chairs and took a few deep breaths. "Okay, okay, how are you?"

"I'm okay, just tired."

"You feelin' okay?" I was worried. I knew Stevie had just been into the hospital for another round of immunotherapy shots.

"Yeah, I'm fine," she said. Her voice was steady and confident.

"Well," I said, "I'm working on understanding some stuff."

"Like what?"

I twirled a ringlet of hair around my index finger and stared at the lines in the skin and the sheen of my blonde hair. "You said there are twenty eight jumpers and that I also jump. Is this body mine? Did I jump or is this an incarnation?"

"Incarnation."

"So I've been in this body my whole life?"

"Yes, it's your body from the start."

"Okay," I said. "Is yours' an incarnation too?"

"Yes, I was born into this body."

"What about the times you weren't born into a body? You take them over? How do you do that?"

"There's always a dialogue about it. The person in there usually is struggling, doesn't want to continue, or they agreed before the lifetime that they were going to be jumped out for. But we don't hurt the people. The first time I jumped—"

"—Oh yeah, wasn't the woman being tortured? Like by a dragon or something crazy? And you were watching, watching, this was after the Watchers got called off the earth, so you were watching, but the only way you could legally help is if you took the body over, and you couldn't stand the suffering she was being put through, so you took over?"

"Basically, yes."

"What did God say about it?"

Stevie gave a quiet laugh. "He wasn't happy about it. He didn't want me to leave."

"But did you take all of you down? Or did you split your energy?"

"That time, I took all my energy down. We didn't know how to split consciousnesses at that point."

I tried to picture how a soul could split their consciousness, and I saw an ethereal machine of sorts, with souls surrounding the machine, talking quietly, going over the scientific applications involved. It looked like a friendly laboratory of sorts, and I knew that Stevie was inside the machine but also outside it . . . as if she was . . . already split into two. "Whoa," I said, "You were the first one to split into two, weren't you?"

"Yes. It was a decision that came about from my penchant for jumping down from heaven into distressed bodies."

"You weren't getting your duties done at Home then if you were jumping, so this was a way to solve that problem. You could stay Home and also come down, right?"

"Yes," she said.

"And now it's very standard, souls only take part of their energy down when they incarnate or jump, and now a lot of jumpers will split their energy in three, you split even more sometimes don't you?"

"Yes, I will sometimes split into four, but it's rare. It's pretty hard to do much more than a short jump with less than twenty-five percent of my energy on hand."

"Which you can do more than most human souls," I said, "Because you're more powerful, you have more energy. And so do I, but I don't split quite as much."

"That's true, you're never down in more than three bodies," she said.

I paced around the dining room and passed into the kitchen, and tried to imagine being in more than one place at a time. The thought of it felt a little strange.

"It's not that weird really if you think about it," she said.

"Huh," I said.

"There's a lot that needs to get done, and if we can serve, we will."

"Yeah, I understand that," I said. "But there's one other thing. "Am I somewhere else right now? Like in California maybe? Or is it possible to be in a different body in a different time period?"

"Time is different back Home," she said.

"Like there's no clocks or seasons?"

"No, not that. There is time, but it's different back Home."

"So are they in a different time period back Home?" I shook my head and chuckled. "Like things are in the future, and I'm . . . we're . . . back in the past? I guess that would make prophecy more like a magic trick than a gift, I mean, if we're in the future back Home, and we're in the past here on earth, then it's like cheating to tell people here what's about to happen?" I giggled and added, "You didn't tell me if I was in more than one body here on earth."

"You have some of your energy reserved back Home."

"But am I anywhere else on earth right now? Or in some other period?"

"Do you think you are?"

I contemplated it and finally shook my head. "No, it feels like all of Sally is Sally, except the part of my soul that's at Home. Is that right?"

"Yes." Stevie was quiet for a moment, and I heard Desi asking her a question. Stevie said aloud, "I need to run to the hospital to take something there for a friend."

"One of your friends is sick?"

"Yes, and I need to go check on her."

"But I thought you weren't feeling well." I opened the fridge and grabbed a water bottle.

"I'm fine, and it won't take long."

"You always do stuff like this for people?"

"It's nothing." Stevie was smiling as she spoke.

I smiled too. "Okay, I won't keep you. It's nice that you're helping her, that's all."

"All right, I love you."

"Love you too," I said.

Chapter 29

And continuing with the grinding inability to write *Outside Looking In* amid bedlam, the neighbor's bad dog won't stop its incessant yipping. I keep practicing my forgiveness lessons, but every other ten seconds or so, a prayer is interspersed with a cuss word. *Sigh I MUST NOT SCREAM AT MY NEIGHBOR.*

Message from God: you are working too hard and doing too much last minute work to get this book out in the next couple of days, so stop it. Close your eyes and listen and I'll give you things to share. But you can't listen if you're worrying about stuff. You're not hearing Me.

I am not hearing Him. So you know what? It's time to put my work aside and go listen.

Before I heard anything, I started talking. "God? Is that you? Are you there?"

It took a few seconds, and then I sensed an entity standing next to me. I started to smile and then couldn't stop smiling, because the presence felt so warm and comforting. "Is that you, is it God?"

"Hi Sally, it's Jacques."

"Jacques?"

"We could go over this for an hour, and you wouldn't understand what I was telling you, so I'll just say it's God. It's smart to ask who you're talking to, always. And if you don't get a name, then you should go with how the spirit makes you feel. How do I feel?"

I closed my eyes so I could see better. It's hard to describe that, but I feel blind when I talk to spirits unless my eyes are closed. It's almost like the physical world distracts me from seeing and hearing. Once my eyes were closed, I felt almost like my soul was humming. I felt peaceful and comfortable. Safe. "Feels good, like you are protecting me, is that what you mean?"

"Yes, Sally, it's God, and you should feel safe when you're talking to me."

"Which is the opposite of how I'd feel if I were talking to a demon, or to Lucifer, right?"

"I think so. Lucifer and the other fallen angels can feel pretty reassuring, though, remember, they were once angels," He said.

"But they would try to get me to do things that didn't feel right, and they might promise me things that made me feel uneasy . . . um God, what do you want me to tell people?"

"My main message is no more blood."

"Does that have to do with the Crucifixion?"

God laughed softly. "That's way too complex, my message is much simpler. No more blood just means no more fighting, no more hatred, no more killing, no more wars over religion or over land or over petty differences, or even major differences. No more blood, Sally, it's that simple."

"Okay," I said. "So you want me to teach love and tolerance and unity? Acceptance of others? Peace?"

"Yes."

"But is it sometimes okay to fight wars? What about the Civil War? World War Two? The Revolutionary War?"

"Those wars were justified."

"They were fought to preserve human freedom you mean? Or to save the lives of the oppressed?" I tried to think about all the wars that were ever thought in human history, and suddenly I pictured bodies piled on bloody battlefields, and I could hear men crying, and other men crawling over top the slain bodies, whispering sweet words of comforts to the fallen.

"Yes. Some wars had to be fought, you know this, don't make it more complex than it needs to be. You know the difference between fighting to save lives or ensure freedoms and wars fought for greed, for gain, for power. You know this, right?"

I was quiet for a moment, and then I nodded. "Some wars are fought for the craziest of reasons. There's always a justification, but usually it's vengeance or power or greed. Like the Thirty Years War . . . that was fought for the craziest diplomatic gaffe ever. That was one of my favorite lessons in high school history."

"You're talking about the window-throwing incident?" God was reading my mind, because I was picturing one large, bearded European man hurling another man through a third story window. The room was dark, dimly-lit, and full of smoke and the din of loud voices shouting threats back and forth.

"Yes!" I chuckled and said, "They called that the Defenestration of Prague. That's French for 'to throw out the window,' and it caused thirty years of war. Or World War I was started when the Arch Duke Ferdinand was assassinated, I don't even remember what nation he was from."

"Austria-Hungary."

"And the assassination was by a Serbian, so Austria-Hungary declared war on Serbia, and all of Europe jumped in on one side or another, and this led to four years of slaughter."

"Yes."

"Not a great war, huh?"

"None of the wars are great, Sally." God sounded sad, and I felt bad for trying to joke about it.

"It's okay Sally, sometimes we have to laugh about these things because they're painful. But so rarely is war necessary. So rarely is any sort of fighting necessary. Every human comes from Home and returns to it. Every human has something in common. There's no reason to fight over all your differences when you have the same Home. That's the common thread that ties you all to one another."

"The same Spirit?"

"Yes," He said. "Same DNA is in each human, not just in the human body, but in the human soul. Everyone comes from the same source. From All to each."

"Kinda like the motto of the United States, but backwards." I thought about it for a moment to make sure I had it right. "E Pluribus Unum. It means, 'From Many, One.' But what you're saying for the human soul is, 'From One, Many.'"

"I love that!"

"Awww," I said. And I smiled.

"I like it when you smile, I like it when all humans smile," God said.

"Thank you, it's hard not to smile when I'm talking with you," I said.

We talked for a few more minutes, and then I fell into a deep and peaceful sleep. I was still smiling when I woke up in the middle of the night. I stayed awake just long enough to text Stevie and tell her I had figured out a new motto. "What's Latin for, 'From One, Many?" I typed.

In the morning, I read her response:

Ex uno multa.

And all she wrote afterwards was, "Sounds like you had a good conversation with God."

Weekend Scorecard

One soccer game. Four goals allowed.

Four goals scored, one in the last few minutes.

And 26 bagels.

One sick mom. One book close to deadline, time ticking.

"Hey Mom?"

"Yeah?"

"Wanna take a walk with me?"

"Sure. Just gimme a min."

In the mirror, my 8-year old makes a fist and punches the air, creases dividing his broad cheeks with a joy that spreads to me. One walk around the lake. Two long arguments, about reading and video games. Mom won this round.

Two women plus one bad doggy equals new business venture.

A game of catch. Two sore right shoulders.

Some sadness, some joy, some frustration, and little pain.

And that's a wrap.

Chapter 30

I was woken up this morning by a bugle; a squeaking clarinet; and the clarinet player screaming, "Argh! I'm going to break it if it doesn't stop that!!"

I called Stevie and announced, "I need for someone to please invite me to visit them for a few days. I'm quiet. Oh okay, no I'm not. I'm charming."

She laughed and said, "You are that."

"Right? And I don't eat much. I don't do much except write and drink coffee. I am hyper and never shut up. But I'm . . . charming."

"Charming indeed," she said.

"Ugh," I said, "William bought Junior a bugle."

"A bugle?"

"Yeah," I groaned, "He bought our nine-year old son a bugle."

"They are kinda noisy," she said.

"Yes! As in a very noisy brass bugle! Gah!!" I sighed and sipped from my coffee cup.

"Drums?"

"Huh?"

"You were thinking, *what's next? Drums?* So I answered you." Stevie paused and quietly answered a question from Desi.

Then she said, "And you're wondering what you were like as a kid, and you are also wondering if you can talk to Jesus, but you're not sure about what, which is ridiculous because you grew up together, of course you can ask him, and what were you like? Come on, you know exactly what you were like, right?" Stevie's voice rose at the end, and I giggled.

"Um, I was very, very loud, right?"

"Yep."

"And we were always getting into trouble, like what did we do?" I closed my eyes and smiled, because I could picture two souls walking beside me, and they were both male for sure, and they were laughing as they walked beside me.

"Why don't you ask him?"

"Who—Jesus?"

"Who else?"

"Like, just say 'Jesus, I wanna ask you a question,' and he'll come?" I chuckled and then thought of something else. "Is that even his name?"

"Well, he will answer to it."

"To Jesus?"

"Yes," Stevie said.

"But isn't his name . . . don't I call him . . ." I paused and felt the muscles around my eyes tightening in concentration. "Isa?"

"Yes."

"And that's short for something, something fancy, right? Longer, with three syllables."

"Ysgawayn," she said in a gentle voice.

I shut my eyes and sighed. "Means one who's devoted to God if I remember correctly?"

"Yes, you remember correctly, why don't you go talk to him, I gotta drive into town and get some light bulbs."

I giggled. "Light bulbs? Huh, I think I need to get some too, I keep getting the wrong size."

Stevie laughed and after we talked about light bulb sizes and said goodbye, I hung up and wondered down into the backyard, where it was quiet. I headed left on the walking trail and was thinking about Jesus. The wind rustled the trees, and just as I was thinking, I wonder if we got in trouble as young souls like Lizzie and Junior and Brett always are, and that's when I heard a voice whistling through the treetops.

Always getting into scrapes, yes, hi Sally.

I whirled around and searched for the voice, and I got a glimpse of a man, almost like he was translucent, but real . . . he had long, wavy brown hair. He was about five-ten, maybe five-eleven, and of average build. He had a smile on his face, and he was wearing white robes and brown sandals. I couldn't help but grin at him.

"It's you," I murmured.

"It is me, yes, you're not sure are you Sally?"

"That it's you, or what I should call you, the first word that popped to mind was Isa, is that what I should, is that . . . who you are?"

"It is I." He twirled his arm a bit, and I nodded and smiled as the edge of his robe rose and then flopped on his wrist.

I mustered a shy smile and then realized I was close to tears.

"It's good to see you too," he said.

I took a deep breath and swallowed, and he gestured toward the asphalt path that lay between the tall, dark brown pen oaks, and he began to walk, so I followed in step, and we were quiet for a few moments, walking side by side, not talking.

"I have so many things I want to ask you."

"About the Jesus lifetime? Or about Home?"

"Both," I chuckled. A sparrow alit on a post to my left, and I pointed at his tiny feathers and said, "But sometimes it's all I can do to share the sparrows with you, is that how I was when I was your son, I was your son when you were Jesus, right?"

"Yes, and yes, we liked to watch the birds, that's what I have at home actually." Isa paused and nodded toward the sparrow.

"A sparrow? Or something a little different, I'm seeing, like a parakeet? And he talks all the time, he sings . . ." I giggled and glanced at Isa. "He sings naughty limericks, doesn't he? And isn't he called a Laniel?"

"Yes, Mary and I have a talking bird, he's very pretty, and he sings what I'd prefer to call 'Welcome Songs,' but unfortunately Michael and Tiziel taught him fight songs, and then the fight songs led to chants, and the chants led to some limericks, and now Mary is trying to curb him of welcoming visitors in quite so robust a way." Jesus smiled fondly while he talked, and I pictured a very bright and colorful bird flitting around the room, squawking out funny poetry and then I caught a flash of a beautiful woman and I knew it was Mary Magdalene, and before I could ask, Isa said, "Yes, Mary Magdalene, you're remembering."

"So she was my mom, you were married to her?"

"Yes, and don't forget to ask me who Tiziel is," Isa said.

I shook my head and before I could ask, I got a sense of Brett's floppy hair and pictured him hopping in front of me on the pavement, yelling about avenging Bad Doggy. "Oh, wow, Tiziel is Brett?"

"Yes, and do you remember where he lives back Home?"

I waved at the sparrow and avoided stepping on a large tree branch, and then leaned over and pushed it off the trail. Then out of the corner of my eye, I pictured a swirl of colors whizzing around a chandelier. I knew somehow the whiz was me, because I felt a sense of glee—the type you feel when you're being a little naughty but not too naughty. Then I heard a voice, and it was an older brother's voice. Somehow I knew the brother was Tiziel. "Iz," he was saying, "You better get down from there before Mama sees you, you broke it last week and she's gonna be mad if you break it again." I giggled and instead of listening, grasped hold of the chandelier and then was tumbling down the stairs, giggling but a little frightened, and there was Tiziel waiting, and he caught me, and we both fell backwards a few steps, and landed at the bottom of the staircase, and sure enough, Isa was there too, and he gave me a stern look and then smiled at me.

"Wow," I said aloud, "He lived in the Frat, like me, you must have lived there too?"

"Yep, all of us were together, Tiz and I for two thousand years before you came along, that's what I'm telling you. We grew up together, more or less, but you were the very noisy young one."

I grinned and nodded. "Sounds about right. So, are you gonna tell me more about your Jesus lifetime? About what it was like, about how I was as a kid then too?"

Isa swung his head back and forth and then raised an eyebrow. "First you need to study, you need to know all you can know, and then I will tell you more."

"Ha! You sound like Stevie," I said.

"The word is important though, you know that. And you tend to learn best when you read and study first, then ask questions. You were asking for a Prophet Handbook weren't you?"

I gasped in surprise and then spluttered, "You knew about that?"

"Yes. And if you remember, one of the rules is a prophet needs to listen, and another rule is you need to study hard, which is easier for you than listening sometimes, right?"

My cheeks moved up into a one-sided smile. "Yeah," I said.

"So reread everything you can find about that lifetime, and then come and ask questions. Right now, you don't even know what to ask, do you?"

I thought for a moment, and a jumble of mixed-up questions surged into my mind. I waved my hand and shook my head. "Yeah, I could ask fifty questions and I bet thirty-five of them could be answered if I took my time and thought about it, read and studied."

"Thirty seven," he said.

"Thirty-seven huh?"

"Uh huh." Isa put a funny emphasis on the 'huh,' and I chuckled, because the sound of the word felt familiar. But before I could ask him if my soul always said it, Isa said, "I gotta head back Home, I love you."

I stopped and gave him a long, slow smile. "I love you too," I said.

"I know," he said.

•••

The corner kids and I were still up, so I enlisted them in Mission: Clean Brett's Messy Room.

I duct-taped a couple of his bed slats back together (duct tape is the bomb, and it's especially neat when it comes in pink camou color patterns).

Lizzie was on closet detail.

I was on dirty/clean clothing separation detail and scrub the crayons off the furniture and carpet detail and rearrange the seventeen hundred and sixteen rocks detail; and Brett . . . I don't know what Brett did, besides tell us stories and talk up a storm.

At first, he just smiled at us a lot. Funny how far three dimples, a scar, and a cute, rakish smile can take a kid.

But after a few minutes, he began to talk.

"You know, Mom, as a baby soul, you used to drive me crazy. You EXASPERATED me. One time, you took a crayon out of a building and the whole thing crashed down around you. I had to jump into a bunker to avoid the carnage. And another time, you ate Triniel's pet bunny. And another time, make that many times, you ate my furniture. And whenever I'd yell at you, you'd go tell on me, and I'd get in trouble. And you wrecked everything! Everything! And when I'd hit you for it, you'd tell on me or you'd make such a racket, Mama would holler at me to cut it out, and you'd just sit there and giggle." Brett's voice rose, and he pointed at his chest. "I'd get in trouble. Can you believe that? I got in trouble every single time, how is that even possible?" Brett raised both hands above his head and shook his head with an expression of rueful self-pity.

I chuckled and said, "No, that's not how I remember any of it. Specifically, you'd hit me, and THEN I'd go tell Mama, and she'd tell us to cut it out, and then we would, for about five minutes, and then I'd touch one of your models, you always had models of worlds and planets, and you'd hit me, and I'd cry to Mama, and then we'd both get in trouble, uh huh, that's what I'm remembering."

Lizzie put her hand on her hip and tried to flip her hair back, but most of it ended up hanging down between her eyes.

I reached over and wiped a few thick strands out of her eyes, and she continued to stare at Brett with a look of comical disdain. "Really, Brett," she said, "You're saying Mom was loud and you're saying Mom was messy, have you looked at your room recently?" Lizzie opened the drawer that sat at the bottom of Brett's bookcase and with her nose squished up, she dangled a few wrappers of string cheese in his direction. "This is gross, Mom, have you seen what he's got in his room? I bet this has mold, oh yuck, yuck, Mom, Brett's been eating cheese in his room."

I opened the trash bag and held it in front of Lizzie. "Ew, throw it in there, Brett, we're gonna have mice if you keep eating in your room."

"Ew," Lizzie said.

"I love mice," Brett said.

"You're disgusting, really, that's so gross." Lizzie pointed at the drawer and grabbed Brett by the elbow. "You need to clean that out, you're the one who made the mess, you should see how much nicer my room looks."

Brett twisted out of her grip and smirked at her. "So? I'm Mom's crown jewel."

Lizzie flounced and then rolled her eyes. "Mom, you hear him? Tell him to clean his mess up. I am not touching his cheesiness."

I giggled.

Brett smiled winsomely. "No, I don't have to, I'm Mom's crown jewel."

"You're ridiculous, you are not," Lizzie said.

I shook my head and smiled.

Brett hopped over a few of his toys and appeared at my side. "Aren't I, Mom?"

Lizzie reached down and grabbed a pair of scissors. Without looking at Brett, she grabbed his teddy bear and mumbled, "I think Gertie needs a haircut."

Brett got a startled look on his face. And then he said, "Mom, make her stop that, do you see what she's trying to do?"

I smiled and glanced at Lizzie. I knew she wouldn't miss the irony.

She didn't. "Um, Brett," she said, "Who's the one telling now?"

Brett looked mad for a moment. Then he flung his hands up and in a good-natured voice replied, "Well, if you touch Gertie, I'll put a mouse in your bed and when you jump out of bed screaming, I'm certain you'll remember that I'm Mom's crown jewel."

Lizzie opened and shut her mouth. "You wouldn't," she finally said.

"Yes, I would." Brett was grinning now.

I put my hand out and said, "Better give me the scissors."

"Fine, but I'm done helping." Lizzie handed over the scissors and started to leave Brett's room.

"Hey," I said, "Hug him first."

"But Mom . . ."

"I love you both, now hug and then go to bed." I corralled Brett, and gave Lizzie a commanding stare.

She was about to argue, but her left shoulder dropped a little, and then she put her hands out and took Brett in towards her.

He bear-hugged her back, and they almost toppled over.

Lizzie put her head on my shoulder, and I hugged her. Then she said goodnight and shut his door.

"Mom," Brett said, "I know I'm your crown jewel."

I hugged him and laughed. "Night, Love you," I said.
"Love you too," he said.

Scorecard

One Ping Pong ball chewed and flung within millimeters of a mom's head.

Two knees skinned and bleeding; one badass kid shrugging and walking for another hour.

One man wearing a grey suit and red tie picked up at noon from Metro stop.

Three marbles still at large.

Three kids now able to explain a furlough, a budget, and a Do-Nothing Congress.

One new book idea launched: *Shutdown*.

Two hours busted, working on website issues with horrid Hostgator.

One epic search for literary excellence, coming to a close, pending final proofing.

And that's . . . a wrap.

Chapter 31

"Yes."

"No."

"Yes."

William threw up his hands. "I'm done arguing!"

Sally snickered. "We're not arguing."

"Ha! I am not taking that bait!"

•••

That argument arose because of the antique coffee table. It had been months since we had more or less finished the ark, and William had been staring forlornly at it for the better part of three months. Every time we watched TV, he would set his mug of tea down beside one of the glue glops, and he would frown at it, at the glue glop, at the paint stains, at the shreds of paper held to the table surface by the paint and the glue. And I would grin and say, "We'll get her fixed up, I promise."

For his birthday, Brett asked for a model battleship, circa World War Two. And for days, William would come home from work, Brett would greet William and without giving William time to set the mail down, Brett would talk about building the battleship.

William would look at me for help, and I would shrug and say, "Why not?" And William would say, "But you haven't fixed the mess on the table," and Junior would interrupt and say, "We could build it on the deck, on the metal table," and Lizzie would also interrupt and say, "But we would forget it was out there and it would rain and ruin the paint and make the boards rot," and then Brett would hop around and wave his hands and say, "Please Mom, it's all I want."

And I would of course say "Yes" just as William would open his mouth to say, "No," and so it continued for quite some time, until I just ordered the ship, but also made a trip with the kids to the hardware store. I picked out an ample supply of steel wool (which removes glue and paint without destroying the wood surface most effectively), cherry wood stain, paintbrushes, as well as a brand-new throw mat to catch any paint that could leak onto the floors. And I set all of that on the countertop by the laundry room, knowing Will would see it just before he set the mail down.

William was not amused. "So now you have to completely resurface the table?"

"We'll make it look like new," I promised.

"And then you'll build more models on top it, and you'll probably ruin it all over again."

"Don't be such a pessimist," I said.

"Don't be all rainbows and unicorns," William said.

"Oh, I like rainbows and unicorns," Lizzie said.

"But unicorns bite," Brett said.

"Do not," Lizzie said.

William had removed his tie, and was headed upstairs, and he didn't speak about the table anymore that night. So I set all the supplies out on top of that old table of ours and I waited for William to go on a business trip so that we could work Project Restore.

Chapter 32

I couldn't concentrate. It was Bad Doggy's fault. So I was on Facebook complaining about it, which is definitely not getting old for all my fans. William says I am a minor Internet Celebrity and I told him he should make me a t-shirt that says I am, and he told me he would also write on the shirt, "It's all about me," and I said it was.

Anyway, while I was on Facebook complaining about Bad Doggy's forcing me to get on Facebook because he wouldn't stop barking, I liked this friend's or should I say "friend's" status update. I forgot we weren't talking I guess and I know it's naughty to giggle about stuff like this but . . . I guess she's been mad at me for a long time.

So when I liked her status update, and I swear it was about her cat, she unfriended me. I know it's absolutely insulting when someone you dislike LIKES one of your status updates. It's almost as bad as when you . . . steal their last candy bar or slap them silly upside their face. Not that I would EVER do something like that. I mean, like, steal their candy bar.

And I really do like cats. I even liked the woman who unfriended me, but that's only because I forgot how mean she is. Or was, because now I don't see her or her status updates about her cats and I really miss her.

And I know this probably has nothing to do with the woman who unfriended me after I liked her status update about her cat, but I realized something after all this.

I was just thinking that Jesus hung out with people like me, you know, the messed up ones especially, and the thought of it made me grin. And then I realized I was yet again trying to seem extra special, and so I let go of that too. Even though I'm a total mess-up, Jesus loves us all the same—no more, no less. And that's pretty awesome.

Meanwhile, I was cleaning Lizzie's room and I came across her diary. I'm not sure what to say about what I read. I'm hoping it's just a sample of creative writing. Here's what I found.

•••

The TP Disaster

Sally was really annoyed about how the dog was barking its head off.

And Aaron was playing the bagpipes to appease it. Sally kept pacing all over the house saying she had no idea Jingle Bells could sound *so* annoying!

So, she was so annoyed *so* much that she didn't realize that she'd let me have friends sleep over the very same night Petunia was having her friends over for a sleepover!

Anyway, Petunia and her BFF'S looked at Lizzie's snazzily decorated house and Petunia *must have felt* a surge of jealousy.

Then Petunia must have gotten a rare fresh idea. It was also, as is typical of Petunia, a nasty idea. She and her BFFs grabbed dozens of rolls of toilet paper and TPd Lizzie's house.

When Lizzie saw what they did, she walked over to her BFF'S, held up a roll of toilet paper and said, "This is war!"

Sally was *so* annoyed about the dog and Aaron, that she didn't notice that the house was TPd. Anyway, Lizzie raced over to Sally and said: "YO mom, can ya take me to Target?"

Sally nodded, grabbing the car keys. Lizzie jumped in the car and Sally started up the car. When Lizzie got inside Target, she dragged Sally through endless aisles and aisles of merchandise, occasionally grabbing something and when they finally got home, Lizzie raced upstairs and told her BFF'S the plan. When they were done, this what it looked like:

It had a picture of Petunia's crush, Justin Creeper, and underneath this is what it said: Justin Creeper + Petunia Sluggard=true suck. They sneakily got a ladder and set it up against the side of the house. They hung it up with permanent glue and permanently glued super bright Christmas lights on it.

When Petunia saw it she screamed out "I will get you Liz!"

Petunia knew Lizzie hated that name.

Lizzie of course wasn't finished with Petunia.

To be continued . . .

•••

As I set Lizzie's diary down, I started thinking about what sort of things I'd been teaching my children. I needed to think about all this for awhile actually. And I also figured I'd talk some with God about it. After all, a little toilet paper goes a long way so to speak.

And the last thing I wanted them doing was fighting. That was not why we were here.

Chapter 33

But before I went and talked to Lizzie, I searched through the computer and came across Junior's diary. Sure enough, he had something to say about Petunia as well. I wasn't too happy with what I read.

Junior's Diary

Today was one of the weirdest Saturdays ever. Mom destroyed the chandelier when trying to kill a fly with newspaper; Bad Doggy ate Petunia's MP3 player, and SO much more.

Oh. I forgot to tell you that Petunia TPd our house. Lizzie was plotting revenge against Petunia. My friends and I are too. We are going to do graffiti on Petunia's secret meeting place.

And . . . MO-OM! Gotta go, she's calling me.

Thirteen annoying and tiring minutes later . . . Sorry for all that fuss. Mom had asked me to clean up the TP with Brett. I am really pissed off at Petunia for TPing our house. She should've thought twice about TPing our house, because now she has got two people on her case.

Jan. 14, 2014.

I asked mom if we could go to AC Moore, because I needed spray paint to do my revenge on Petunia. I got purple, red, green, yellow, blue, brown, and a lot of other colors.

Mom asked me why I was getting so many colors, and I said, "You'll see soon."

I saw Lizzie making the revenge poster for her revenge against Petunia, oh, and tiny reminder: Lizzie does not include my revenge against Petunia in her document diary. I asked mom if I could play with my friends, and she said yes. I went to Dan's house and told him what had happened, and after getting a big laugh from him, we started calling our other friends, and we all got the plan started. Thankfully, she and her friends were not having a meeting.

We made our painting really creepy, un-girly-girlish. Here is the design: we put Angry Birds, Skylanders, and all the other characters from games girls don't like. We also put 2 angry, and creepy eyes that said: WE ARE WATCHING YOU.

We also painted a lot of Barbies and other stuff girls love, and with the red spray paint, drew a huge X on it. We ran off just in time, because they were about to come in and have a revenge meeting.

•••

With a deep sigh, I flipped through Lizzie's diary and Junior was right: there was nothing about the toilet paper. There was, however, another one of Lizzie's revenge stories. It was more of a sketch than a story—not quite as well-written as the first one she'd penned.

•••

School War Time!

Lizzie got on the Yellow School Bus and sat down on one of the gray seats.

Petunia of course flounced on in last because she was a safety patrol. When Petunia passed everyone, she gave all of the people she hated warnings. She pranced around after that, spun twice, and then with an evil cackle, she gave all of her friends AWOL notices from class.

When Petunia passed Lizzie she whipped out a report slip. She was actually yelling the words as she wrote: "**Lizzie Brookman Under Report Because She Said Several Bad Words And Is Not Respecting The Dress Code.**"

Lizzie did not react. Lizzie silently plotted her revenge. Petunia was not going to get the better of her THIS time.

During class Lizzie quickly grabbed Petunia's **Private** paper and wrote in Petunia's handwriting:

Dear Mary,

Whoa doesn't Timmy look hot today?

Love Love Love,

Petunia

P.S. Doesn't "Ms. Stupid" look so frickin dumb? I can't believe how easy it was to give all you BFF'S of mine AWOL notices and all my *Not Friends* warnings! And it was so fun giving Lizzie a report for no reason, and yelling it *out loud* so she was super duper embarrassed! Muahahahaha.

Carefully Lizzie skidded the note across the worn out tiles so that Mary didn't notice it, and then she screamed, "Mary get the note!"

Ms. Einstein turned around slowly from degrading Brett about bringing his pets to school: a hamster, a chickie, and a Burmese python. "What's going on?"

"Nothin'," Lizzie said.

Ms. Einstein looked on the ground and she noticed the note, and after she read it, she made Petunia read the note to the *whole* class.

Petunia lost her patrol belt. Because of this, there was an opening in the safety patrol squad.

And so Lizzie finally got her safety patrol belt.

The End.

•••

I sighed when I set this story down. It wasn't real. I mean, Brett didn't have a python—right?

Chapter 34

I waited an hour or so before I approached Lizzie's door and knocked gently on the painted white wood. She was reading the Bible, which made me smile.

"Hey, Mom, I'm reading your gospel," she said.

"Ah, Mark. Good." I beamed at her and then said, "You know, those were some good times, but it was hard after Dad died."

"Did you write about that in here?"

"Nah," I said.

"Why not?"

"Well, when we left, it was because the Sanhedrin, which was the Jewish council, had gotten to one of the Apostles and the Romans were coming after us. We busted out of there and told the other Apostles not to tell anyone about Mom and me and Sarah, otherwise we'd have been killed."

"Who told on you? Was it Peter? That would figure, you know," she said.

"Nope, wasn't Peter. It was Andrew, his brother."

"Did you wanna kill him?"

I thought back to that lifetime and kind of shrugged. Then I admitted, "At first I wanted to, yeah. But Mom wouldn't let me. She said it wasn't what Dad would've wanted. And then I could hear God saying or whispering, 'No Mark, you must forgive, you must not fight. No more blood.' And the thing is, Mom forgave him. Anyway, the Sadducees and the Pharisees and the Romans would have come after us at some point. Andrew probably did us a favor in a way. So we left Bethany and that's when our long journey began. And after fifteen years or so, Andrew was dead and we had more to worry about than who was leading and sharing the Word." I wasn't telling Lizzie just how hard it had been for Mark to follow Peter and Paul. I wanted her concentrating on the forgiveness bit.

Lizzie's eyes got wide. Then she said, "Yeah, but you met back up with Peter right? Why didn't you write about the family then? I mean, you were like his assistant or whatever, right?"

I groaned a little. Even now that stung a bit. "Yeah, I was freaking Peter's assistant for awhile and believe you me, it felt like he lorded it over me." I paused and felt a pang in my heart. "Also, he was usually quite fatherly and good to me. So it wasn't like he didn't care about me. As far as who we were, well, I think by then, the story was already kind of set in stone and Peter didn't want us talking about Mom and the family."

"Why not?"

"Well, the way it had gone down led to Peter being the leader of it all so by then he was in charge and he wasn't gonna give that up."

"Ooh, did you wanna punch him?"

I chuckled and thought about it. "Well, it wasn't easy being Mark. I really did wanna kill Andrew when he told the Sanhedrin about the family. And there were times I wanted to punch Peter in the head, yes. Absolutely. But I never did, you know?"

"How did you not punch that fool?"

"Awww Lizzie, he wasn't a fool. He wasn't the brightest of the Apostles but he was a good soul, and he was doing a lot of good sharing the Word. When he got me really mad, I'd try and laugh about him, or I'd try and think about the things I liked about him. Now, sometimes that was a short list," I paused and grinned at Lizzie.

She laughed. "Mom, will you tell me the story of when he tried to walk on water?"

"Oh, maybe. But only if you will promise me one thing."

"What? Pray for Tunie?"

"Well," I said, "How about tell me one thing you like about her?"

"Okay, it's a deal," she said, "You first."

"Well, sure," I said. "So the wind was blowing over the Sea of Galilee and Jesus went off to pray, right? And it was a little chilly with the wind blowing, and it got real dark and really fast and some of the apostles were freaking out. Okay, Mark was freaking out a little too. It was pretty gnarly with the waves beating against the boat. I mean, it was wild, and . . ." I switched over to first person about halfway through the story, right about here. Lizzie was used to this. I was always going back and forth between being Mom and being Mark.

"So we were all so tired. Dad could make bread and feed people all day long; never tired him out, and he pretty much just laughed and got everyone eating and he smiled and taught while everyone was eating. I was following right behind him of course, and it was the best thing, and he kept passing me loaves and people were touching his robe and grown men were on their knees and crying when he stopped and touched their heads. It was amazing and exhausting, you know?"

"So the boat was pitching about and what was Peter saying?"

I chuckled. "He was complaining that Dad was taking too long and the boat was leaking and Andrew had forgotten to patch it up and Philip kept sticking his stinky feet where they didn't belong, and Andrew was saying he did patch it up and Peter should have done it better, and Luke was real quiet and so was John. Honestly, I sorta thought the boat was gonna tip over, it was wild, and I was thinking I should have stayed ashore with Dad, I mean it was wild.

"So anyway, boat's rocking, pitching. Thunder's booming and everyone's scared, either scared silent like me, or scared whining like Peter. This goes on for hours, and it's the fourth watch. We're pulling at the oars; we're all awake, you couldn't sleep through that. And then we see this apparition, ghost really, and it's dad, but no one else gets it. I wasn't even totally sure, you know?"

"You were scared?"

"Oh yeah, big-time. And some of the disciples start screaming, 'It's a ghost.' And they're throwing their hands up in fear and going on, you know, like this." I threw my hands up in the air and screamed like a little kid.

Lizzie grinned at me.

"Peter was one of the screamers." I yelled one more time, and then I was bent over from laughing and Lizzie was laughing too. "Okay, okay," I said, "So then dad yells out, 'Take courage! It is I. Don't be afraid.' And we're quieting down, right? But Peter's gotta prove he's a good disciple, and he clamors over the side of the boat, you know, like he's supposed to walk on water, like he's gotta be like dad. So he takes a couple steps, and then the wind whips up again. I mean, boom, a gust comes through and you could see Peter freeze and look back at the boat, like Oh no, what have I gotten myself into, and in that moment of doubt guess what happens?"

Lizzie was laughing really hard, but she managed to stammer, "He sinks?"

"Yes. He darn well sinks. So dad takes a few more steps, and Peter's screaming, 'Oh Lord, save me.' So dad fishes his butt out of the water and says, 'Oh you, of little faith, why did you doubt? You could have walked if you believed.'" I paused so me and Lizzie could stop laughing.

"So Mom, Jesus saved Peter and then the wind calmed down?"

"Yes, Dad made the wind calm down after they got back in the boat and Dad was pretty mad at us for worrying and all the disciples, well, especially Peter, were saying that for sure Dad was the Son of God. As if they weren't sure after he created thousands of loaves of bread. But he smiled at me, and I was pretty sure we were both thinking of the time Dad asked Peter and Andrew if they wanted to be fishers of men, and I'm thinking if only Dad had known he'd have to fish Peter out of the water." I felt my eyes crinkling up in laughter.

Lizzie looked up at me and said, "That's a funny story too, the fishers of men story."

"Yep. It is. Now you owe me something."

Lizzie groaned. And then she smiled and said, "Shoot. Okay. Tunie is a cute nickname."

"Yeah, I sorta like it too. Anything else?"

"Anything else I like about Petunia?" Lizzie pretended to frown.

"Yeah, come on. Can't be that hard."

"Oh. All right. I like the way she gives out warnings. She actually looks kind of badass about it." Lizzie frowned again and said, "Oh Mom, do you think it was wrong for me to tell on her? She really did look badass as a patrol and now she won't get to report people."

"Well," I said, "I'm thinking that if you're the one who wrote that note and she didn't actually do the things you had her doing in that note, you could fix that, couldn't you?"

"Well, she does do those things," Lizzie said.

"But . . ."

Lizzie looked down at her hands and said, "But she didn't write that note. I mean, Mom, none of that happened, that was just how I wanted things to turn out. But I still sort of wish they had turned out that way."

"You do? Because now you'd be turning yourself in for having done something dishonest and that wouldn't feel so good either, would it?"

"Have you ever done that?"

"Done what? Turned myself in for having done something wrong? Why yes, I have," I said. "One time in 11th grade, one of the guys I was friends with kept asking me and asking me for that day's quiz questions. We had the same AP History teacher, different periods. Anyway, this guy kept asking me and I wanted to be nice to him I guess. I mean, I made a bad decision. I told him the questions. And then I felt terrible and went and told the teacher the whole story. I felt awful and it was hard, telling the teacher I had basically cheated, or helped someone else cheat, but I felt better after I told."

Lizzie was studying me really carefully, as if trying to memorize my facial expressions or something like that.

I held out my arms and said, "Goodnight sweetheart."

She embraced me and cried out, "I love you so much Mom!"

"I love you too," I said.

Chapter 35

Brett grabbed my NIV Bible, which was shoved a bit slipshod into the middle of the loveseat in the family room. I read and study the Bible because I can't stop trying to figure out what parts of it are missing, what parts really reflect the Word of God, and what parts need to be rewritten. God says we're going to update it someday and reissue it under the title, "The Way," but I'm getting ahead of myself again.

"Hey Mom? Which is the one you wrote?" Brett's hair was standing on end and he was perched on one foot, about to swallow the medication that keeps his heart working right. Without it, he wouldn't be here, and at least a few times each day, usually when he's driving me crazy, I remind myself that he died and came back to live with us only after I promised God I'd complete my mission. Because Brett's a jumper, or an angel who incarnates to help humans complete important missions, and Brett's here on earth to help me get my mission accomplished.

I love him thank you God for giving him back to me and oh my God he's really driving me crazy this morning and it's not even eight o'clock yet. I glanced down at my steaming mug of coffee. I was drinking some fancy blend from William's favorite coffee store.

I put my hand out and gestured for Brett to hand me the Bible. It wasn't exactly dog-eared because the pages were gold-embossed, but it was well-loved. I scribble on everything I love a lot and I adore the Word of God. I adore the Bible and I also adore the Hindu Scriptures and I also adore the Quran and I also adore Rumi's Masnavi and I also adore the Gnostic Gospels and I also adore . . . well, I love just about all things written by, for and about God. It's just how I'm wired. Sometimes I think I adore the New Testament the best of all, but that's just because I have spent so much time with it this lifetime. So by the time I'd been through the New Testament several times, there was almost more written by my hand than typeset in the pages.

Brett flew in beside me just after I set my mug down on the coffee table. Brett was always flying everywhere; I mean, he's all over the place. He never sits still. I guess he's like me in that respect, but I swear he's even more hyper than I am. Stevie says it's adorable, or more adorable on him than on me, but I'm thinking Stevie's partial to him because of all his dimples. And because he's made from her wing . . .

"Yeah," I said, Give it here." I flipped toward the back of the Bible. I skipped right over the Old Testament, which is hard to teach to people. I still try and teach it, but now I usually start with Jeremiah 8:8. If you're wondering, it's when the prophet Jeremiah says:

> *"How can you say, 'We are wise,*
> *for we have the law of the Lord,'*
> *when actually the lying pen of the scribes*
> *has handled it falsely?*

In other words, God gave His word to the prophets, beautiful souls like Moses and Abraham and Elijah and Elisha and Daniel. But sometimes what got written down was changed by the people who copied it. Indeed, one thing that most people simply don't understand is how the Old Testament came into being. What we read in the Bible isn't actually what was originally written down. And as far as the New Testament, well, a bunch of what was written by the Apostles didn't make it into the gospels and the Roman Catholic Church eventually declared as heretical whatever gospels the majority came to disagree with, and the church was driven by corrupt politicians, so who's to say the right gospels were excluded?

Besides, we're reading translations of original texts. It's hard to translate things into different languages and even the most well-meaning of souls gets stuff wrong. I know I for one don't always understand what I'm reading or what I'm hearing and that's true for everyone. So the point I'm making is you're not always getting the actual or full or complete or accurate Word of God when you're reading whatever Holy Scriptures you're reading . . .

"Hey Mom," Brett was saying, "Can you tell us what's missing from the Bible?"

I grinned at him. We were always going over some of my favorite missing gospels, like the Books of Enoch, which tell stories about giants and fallen angels. "Well, Enoch for sure," I said.

"Oooh, Enoch was righteous," Lizzie said.

"In general," I said, "The stories from the Old Testament are mostly a history, but only of the Jewish people. It's missing what happened here on earth before and after the Great Flood, as well as the history of the Earth before, during, and right after the Great Fall."

"When Lucifer fought God?"

"Yes, Lizzie." I closed my eyes for a moment and imagined what the Earth must have been like during the Great Wars between the Sons of Beliah (or Sons of Darkness) and the Sons of Light. Then it was as if angels were soaring through the air, great winged-creatures, and their flight was a glorious one. I opened my eyes and said, "The Old Testament's incomplete. It's missing a huge chuck of time, between the first few chapters in Genesis and the Flood. The world wasn't really created a few thousand years ago. God never said it was . . . it's just that the entire story of the world wasn't relevant to the history of the Jews, which is what's really being told in the Old Testament. That make sense, love?"

Lizzie nodded but still looked confused.

"Well, Lizzie, there's just a lot missing, sweetie. But in time, we'll find those lost gospels. We'll find more proof of all those lost civilizations that existed before the Great Flood and before Israel became the Promised Land. Soon. Soon we'll go on wild digs and we'll find all the lost gospels."

I sighed and thought about how much people argue about God and religion and science. I thought about how much easier it was to disagree about everything, to divide into teams and flags and countries and groups than to be peaceful and loving toward those we disagreed with. I thought about how people get mad at me when I speak out in favor of tolerance. I thought of how silly it was to fight over God.

As I was thinking about all this, I was also letting the gold pages slip between my fingertips. About three-fourths of the way through, I paused, flipped past Matthew, and found the intro to the Gospel of Mark. I put my finger on the first page. "Here's the introductory section, which tells you lots of stuff about the time period and about the author."

"You mean John Mark, which is you, right Mom," Lizzie said.

I nodded, and shot a glance in William's direction, but he was ignoring me and Brett and Lizzie. "And then if you flip a couple pages further, you get to the text, which tells Mom and Dad's story."

Brett put his hands on my Bible, and his eyes lit up, as if a beacon were turned on them, or from with inside of him. He turned a few pages and then, as if giving a benediction of sorts, he smiled at her. "You wrote a lot," he said.

"Yeah, I sure did, and this is just a small piece of it," I said.

"Where's the rest of it?"

I smiled over at Lizzie. "We buried it in some cave under the sand, and me and Raz and maybe some other souls are gonna go dig it up in a few years."

"Oooh, can I come?" Brett leaned against me.

"Yeah, me too," Lizzie said.

"Yep," I said. "You both can come."

"Did I bury stuff too?" Brett was slowly remembering bits and pieces of his past lives. His trip to heaven when he was six had refreshed his recollection, so to speak. Brett had been Joseph of Arithmea during that lifetime. He'd run a shipping and mining company.

"Hmm," I said. "I don't know, what do you think?" I tried not to plant ideas in Brett's head. I needed for him to come to the memories in his own way.

Brett was silent for a few moments. Then he said, "Do you have any maps? Maps of that area?"

Of course I had maps. And so began Mark and Joseph's Great Treasure Hunt for Lost Gospels.

Chapter 36

"Mom?"

Lizzie, Brett, and I were walking on the path behind our house, just the three of us, and Brett was jumping around a few feet ahead or behind us depending on the shiny objects he saw.

Lizzie pointed at Petunia's yard and sighed. There was a huge mound of dirt, a lot of stones, and a trampoline. One of those big ones from Costco and as Lizzie explained, "Petunia said it only cost $1,500—"

"—Can we get one Mom, please?"

"Shut up Brett," Lizzie said. "Can we get one Mom?"

I shook my head. "Maybe when I get my next huge book contract we can," and I laughed because at the rate I was going, Petunia would get three more trampolines before I landed even one of those contracts.

Lizzie and Brett didn't get why I was laughing, so it was that much funnier.

"You know, Mom," Lizzie said, "Petunia's gonna have all her friends over and she's not gonna invite me."

"Yep, " I said.

"Petunia's a dumb idiot," Brett said.

"Tru dat," Lizzie said.

"Well, guess you could shoot her with a water gun, I mean accidentally of course," I said.

"That's a great idea!"

"Yeah," Brett agreed.

"Hey Brett," I said. "Do you remember the time you got in trouble for tossing acorns at the HVAC guys?"

Brett grinned at me and shook his head.

"Yeah." I reached over and ruffled his hair. "It was kinda dicey, because I was being really pissy with them cuz our A/C was busted and they kept coming late and not fixing it. So then they were out there, messing with it for the third or fourth day in a row, and I was cranky, you know how I get when it's hot, and then I heard a knock on the deck door.

"'Ma'am?'"

"'Yeah?'"

"'Um, yeah, uh could you tell your son to stop throwing acorns at us while we work?'"

"'Oh my God,' I said, and I knew which boy was doing it of course. So I called, 'Hey Brett, stop pelting the HVAC guys with acorns.'"

"Did he stop?" Lizzie asked.

I grinned at Brett, who was laughing now. "Yeah, but I'm afraid I laughed when he came inside."

Brett took a hop and skip and then pointed at Bad Doggy, who sprinted to the fence and stuck his nose through the slats. "How about if we throw acorns at Petunia? And at Bad Doggy too?"

"Yeah," Lizzie said, and she was shouting really.

I laughed but remonstrated, "Sounds not so good to me."

Brett ignored me. "And in the winter," Brett said, "We can throw snowballs at them."

"Yeah! And ice balls," Lizzie said.

"Um, wait," I said, "No ice balls. That ain't nice."

They were both quiet for a minute. Then Brett wrinkled up his forehead and I could tell he was thinking hard. "Rocks?"

"Oh good God no!"

Lizzie was snickering, and Brett was too.

"Really, you two. No throwing rocks at Bad Doggy, Petunia, or any of the other neighbors or their dogs."

"Why, Mom?" Lizzie said. "Did you get in trouble for that as a kid?"

I groaned a little, thinking about the times my brother and I and his friends would be ducking behind bushes tossing rocks at cars. It was a really bad thing to do and I have no idea why we did it, but we did. Not that I'd ever admit it to my kids.

"Oh no, Lizzie, I never got in trouble for that."

"But did you do it?" She was always persistent like this, just like her father really.

"Hey, Brett," I said.

He looked up at me with one of his lopsided smiled.

"Wanna go get Slurpees?"

Scorecard

Eldest child turns ten. Face contorted, voice rising.
"Today, of all days, I had to step in dog poop? Really?"
Cupcakes for breakfast, snack and dessert.
Three children did not eat their dinners.
Five people. Four upset stomachs. One laughing man.
Culprit? Cupcakes likely.
Blue frosting. Vanilla frosting. Milk. Cake portion thrown into the trash. That means one cupcake's worth icing, zero cake. Times six.
Morale: make more cupcakes next time.
Three bottles of stain remover.
Five pads of steel wool.
Four paintbrushes.
Two hours, fifteen minutes.
One antique coffee table, Project Restore, complete.

Chapter 37

I just got a phone call from some Republican running for political office here in Northern Virginia. They call my husband and me because we vote red most years. Yeah, stupid us, right? Anyway, I almost picked up the phone and started screaming, "I'm mad and I'm not gonna take it . . . ." but I thought better of it.

Upon further reflection, maybe I need to hit the caller ID button and return that phone call. Silly politicians. Dadgummed fools. Really. Forgive my ire. But I'm really angry tonight. I'm a little bit angry at myself, and a lot more angry at the folks we voted for. Sure, I voted some of them into office. But my party has now put my awesome, hardworking, proud to serve and all of that family out of work.

I am so irked I could spit. You know what I wrote?

They really want to say the government is unnecessary? Then shut the whole thing down. Military? Shut it down. FBI? Shut it down. Counter-terrorism unit? Shut it down.

Something explodes somewhere? Oops. No emergency workers. Need to visit someone you love somewhere? Oops, we sent the air traffic controllers home. There are no planes flying the friendly skies tonight.

You need more government handouts? Nope. You're relying on your social security check? Oops. Defunded. Forget about welfare. Too bad you need food stamps. You're injured? Oops. Medicare just went kaput.

You know what? If government doesn't matter, then just shut it all down. You get my point, right? Or if you're a crazy anarchist, you're nodding, and howling, "Right on Sally!!! WAHOO!!"

The government either matters or it doesn't. If you really think it doesn't matter, dear Congress, then shut the whole thing down. Then clean up the mess you've created. Do your own dirty work–even for just a day. Take responsibility for tearing out the walls that bind our collective welfare together.

I've heard some folks argue, "Stop paying Congress. That will solve the problem." You know what? They don't care. Most of them are rich. They won't miss a measly paycheck or two. But you know what? My family will. Oh, we're not going to lose our home. Nor is my friend Joanne. But we're scared. We don't know when we will receive our next paycheck. And it's not like we're raking in money. A federal government salary is solid, but it won't make anyone rich.

I don't work for the government. But my husband does. And he has no opinion on this issue. I do, however, and I speak on behalf of the more than eight hundred thousand men and women who comprise the federal government's work force. I'm too mad to be eloquent, but I need to say my piece tonight.

Dear Republicans in Congress: It's been said that the power to tax is the power to destroy. It's a power you're supposed to use wisely, with great care, respect, and prudence. You're not supposed to use it to further your own ends, or advance your partisan beliefs.

Job One, Republican friends, is to keep the lights on and the electricity running. Now, you refuse to do either.

You're not building. You're destroying. You claim to be protecting the country, but all you're doing is breaking stuff.

You're not keeping the lights on and the electricity running. You won't, unless the Democrats agree to your terms. You know what this amounts to? It's blackmail. You're basically blackmailing the country. And this is a sick misuse of your power over the nation's purse strings. Obama Care may be a piece of controversial legislation, our nation's elected representatives rightfully, duly, voted for it. When challenged judicially, the Highest Court of the Land ruled in favor of its constitutionality.

The Democrats followed all of the procedures, obeyed all of the rules, and now all we're asking is for you to do the same. You lost—we lost—fair and square.

But now, you want to break the rules—the same rules that all of us live by. When we lose, we shake hands and move on. And for more than two hundred years, that's how our country operated: you fight your ass off, lose, shake hands, and get back to work.

The rest of the country has moved on. We might not love the health care bill, but we're making do with it. We're doing the best we can. We're compromising and working the mess out. And all we want is for you to keep the lights on. Please don't make us go home to a much too quiet house on a darkened street.

We the People deserve better.

•••

I was in a much better mood the next day, so I wrote a letter.

Dear Congress:

Re: Please Take My Husband Back

On behalf of all the wives of federal workers, I wanted to thank you for sending my husband home to me. I've loved having him around. Really, it's been great . . . but—would you please TAKE HIM BACK NOW?

Here's why you gotta take him back:

1. His furlough beard is itchy when he kisses me.

2. His quiet creeping around the kitchen is making me nervous. His incessant opening of the fridge is making me nervous. I wish he would go and get groceries. "I can't; the commissary's closed, too." Uh oh.

3. He has reorganized all the CDs and left a stack of at least 100 of them next to my laptop, and won't leave my study until he downloads all of them to the Cloud.

4. He has thrown out at least 500 hangers, which was great, but he also threw out my children's School Picture Forms, and I got a hysterical, slightly accusatory call from our fifth grader this morning. "Mom? Um. Where's my picture order form?"

5. He's making me look really bad in front of the other soccer moms. My kids actually have their hair brushed when they show up at the bus stop in the morning; they're not wearing flip-flops; and no one has worn sweats or frayed t-shirts all week.

6. Is it really necessary to store 50 bottles of water in the basement? Like really necessary? Just checking.

7. C-Span. Nuff said.

8. He keeps walking past the stack of bills on the counter, sighing so heavily, I can picture Al Gore during a presidential debate.

9. He's caught enough fish to feed the family for the rest of the year, and there's no more room in the freezer to store it, so now we're eating it every night for dinner and have I mentioned I hate fish?

10. He's redesigned the family escape plan at least ten times, and now he's making us stop, drop, and roll several times a day.

11. Every time I go to get my nails or my hair done, he gets this look on his face, like, "What the heck do you do with all your free time, anyway?"

12. Fox News. CNN. And more bloody C-Span.

13. No, we don't need to build traps to catch all the squirrels in the back yard, and no, we really shouldn't buy the boys BB Guns for target practice. No. No, no, no!

14. No, I'm not hungry for lunch right now.

15. My daughter can now burp the entire alphabet.

16. My husband has spread enough insecticide to kill entire universes of ant colonies, and now I'm worrying about the neighbor's dog.

17. Speaking of the neighbor's dog, I found three bark arrestor collars on the side counter. We do NOT own a dog.

18. Last night, before I got into bed, my husband was holding his iPad watching baby videos. And when I started to undress, he said something about trying for a fourth. "Trying for a fourth what, exactly," I almost screamed, before I cuddled up against his itchy furlough beard.

19. C-Span. Again.

20. He keeps editing my work. He is editing MY WORK.

Dear Congress, I'm hoping you can understand just how badly you need to take my husband, our husbands, back. Before we deliver them to the hallowed grounds of the nation's . . . oh whatever. Sorry. The phone's ringing again. It's a Republican politician calling for the fifth time this week. I gotta take this call.

Respectfully Yours,

A Soccer Mom in the Suburbs of Northern Virginia

• • •

You know what was really funny about this blog? It went viral and then I got interviewed by the *Washington Post*, which is no doubt one of my shiniest moments. I told the reporter how my husband was alphabetizing all the CDs and arranging all our books according to the Library of Congress something something and had torn the entire garage apart. So I really wanted Congress to take him back.

I had him home for another three weeks. I really am not looking forward to retirement, as in his retirement.

•••

Apparently my nine-year old son got onto my Facebook Page this morning and posted something my husband didn't want him to post, but I think we need to listen to our freaking kids. Congress may be shut down, but the First Amendment is alive and well.

Here's what he wrote:

Hi guys it's me Junior again. We'll get back to weird but true facts later. First I gotta talk about my Dad. About the fiscal year. Fiscal, not physical. It's pretty creepy. They shut my dad's job down. It happened a few nights ago. It makes me angry. And they closed our national parks. I can't believe Congress IS NOT DOING ITS JOB. Dad says we don't have to worry about the mortgage. That's for our house. Dad says we're going to be okay. Mom says we should fire Dad's employers, but we can't, can we? Mom says we can vote their asses out of their jobs.

"Oops. I said a bad word. Is that okay, Mom?"

William found out what Junior had done and made him take it down, but not before the status update got shared like 500 times. So now everyone knows my husband works for the federal government (yeah I know he said he worked for a private law firm in *I Run* but he made me lie) and that we may not be able to pay our mortgage and Mom is mad at the Republicans and the Democrats and pretty much all politicians.

I told Junior he made a bad mistake not writing all this, but telling his dad about it. I told Junior next time, tell me first, not Dad, because, you know, we never tell William much of anything. That is of course how we've managed to stay married for 16 years. Maybe 17. I always get the date and the year wrong. But that's another story.

Anyway . . . my husband is discovering just how annoying-unproductive it can be to work from home this morning. He's the one who's gotta go into school to pick up the picture forms we misplaced, because it's Picture Day. This makes me happy. And did I mention that we have no idea where the forms are?

"Oh, and William," I added, "Don't forget Junior's homework folder."

"Grrrrr."

I kept saying snarky stuff on my Facebook page, like:

> *Back in the 19th Century, there was a party called the Know-Thing Party. I think we should label the current Congress the Do-Nothings. This attitude surely transcends party lines, LOL.*

I didn't tell William what I was saying. Unfortunately he keeps looking up my books on Amazon, and my Twitter feed is linked to my Amazon feed, so he keeps seeing what I'm doing. And I keep saying, "Well, come on William, get out of my business." And he says, "I'd love to, so long as you stop talking about mine."

Chapter 38

We got the battleship built in record time. It was a much easier model than the ark, and we got a little dropper to use on the cement glue that made it much easier to glue the pieces together. We used a gunmetal gray on almost the entire exterior, with a slightly darker shade on the decks, and black paint on the guns and the railings. She was truly, as the kids took to repeating in fake Boston accents (after watching old Katharine Hepburn movies with me), quite "yar."

A few days after she dried up sufficiently to leave her dry dock on the coffee table, Brett took her down to the river in the backyard, and he was gone for several hours except for trips he or Junior and then Lizzie made to the basement to retrieve supplies. I didn't keep an eye on what he was gathering because I was cooking leek stew, but I did notice that he had taken a plastic water pitcher from the cupboards.

At about six, I called the kids in to get washed up for dinner. I called and called, but no one answered me, not even when I opened the deck door and hung over the edge of the railing. Bad Doggy, in fact, was the only one who was answering me. But even she didn't pay much attention to me. She was standing at the far corner of the fence, yipping and wagging her tail periodically in the direction of the bridge, where I imagined the kids were situated.

With a sigh, I switched the stovetop burner onto low, and then exited through the garage and headed down the hill in the back. It hadn't rained much throughout the summer, so dust swirled up as I traversed the steep incline and stepped over ganglion roots from the pen oaks and dodged brambles from sticker bushes. Rows of azaleas threaded the middle of the backyard, and stood sentinel on both sides of a brick walkway that stretched from the back patio to a grassy section that abutted wooden slats that demarcated a small garden area. I cut across the grass, picked up a few tree branches that had fallen on the walkway, and tossed them into the woods that stretched for miles on the other side of the asphalt hiking trail. Then I hooked a left and followed the trail to a desiccated, moss-covered "troll bridge" and peered over the edge.

"Kapow!" Brett screamed. His hands were spread over a sling-shot contraption that he had taped to the deck of the battleship. When he pulled his hand back, a rock launched from the sling-shot and then slammed into the ramparts of the ark—the model ark the kids and I had built some months earlier. The rock slammed into the side of the ark, and then tumbled below, and a wave of brown water rushed over the top portion of the ark. The kids tittered and screeched, and the ark pitched to its side and appeared to almost capsize before it found its center again.

"Hurry, Brett," Lizzie said. "Retaliation is called for!"

"Water aweigh!" Junior said in an quiet but intense tone.

And then Brett leapt to the bank closest to the battleship, grabbed the plastic turquoise pitcher he had taken from the cupboards, and poured a torrent of water onto the battleship. The grey ship flipped first to the right, and then its entire mast ripped off, and it shifted astern and began to sink. Brett filled the pitcher and poured an even more violent waterfall atop the battleship, and it disappeared into the muddy waters and was seen no more.

"Team God is victorious," Lizzie yelled.

"And Team Mean goes down!" Brett screamed.

"Um, hi Mom." Junior had spotted me, and his red cheeks glowed with excitement.

"Hi, dinner's almost ready, um, kids, whatever are you doing to that lovely ship we just built?" I chuckled and shook my head, and what I thought was a plastic grasshopper fell out of my hair and I grabbed it and held it up with an air of disdain. "Don't tell me you're also making grasshopper plagues, ew, no more plastic bugs!"

"Ew, Brett must have put that in your hair when you weren't looking," Lizzie said.

I inspected it more closely and it moved, and I jumped a few inches and let out a surprised squeal.

Brett rushed toward me and climbed the banks of the river in two quick bounds. "Don't worry Mom, I'll get it off you," he said. Brett rubbed my shoulder and said, "You're all clear, no bugs."

I smiled at Lizzie and Junior, who were giggling, and said, "Thank you. So what's this all about? And Junior, please save the battleship, we can salvage most its parts, Lizzie, grab the ark."

"Yes ma'am," the older kids said.

I put my arm around Brett and said, "So what's this all about anyway?"

"Oh," Brett said. "The battleship represents the mean girls at school, like Tunie's gang. And the ark represents our family. The battleship hurls rocks at the ark and almost sinks it, but then God sends aid in the form of His waters, and they obliterate the battleship before it can destroy the ark." Brett hopped back down and cried, "I'll get it Junior, hold on," and he immersed himself waist deep in the water, and came up holding the battleship like it was a freshly-caught tuna.

"Um, wow," I said. But before I could say anymore, Tunie and two of her friends appeared on their back patio wearing bikinis and carrying lawn chairs. Brett emerged beside me again, now dripping water from all orifices of the battleship and from his shorts and sandals. He was smiling a tooth grin, but as soon as he saw Tunie, he stiffened up. I put an arm around his shoulder, and felt all the muscles gripping his shirtsleeves so tight, his shirt appeared even baggier than usual.

Lizzie emerged on the bridge, and Junior was two steps behind her. Lizzie's face did almost the same thing Brett's had done. It went from a big smile to a withdrawn, wan sort of frown. And she stopped mid-sentence; before that, she had been talking at a rapid pace about Noah, but I hadn't caught what she was saying, and now she too was silent. Junior didn't notice anything because he was busily shifting the pitcher to his left hand, while not dropping a spade that was still in his right hand. He didn't notice anything until Lizzie kind of reached back and tapped his torso with her elbow and whispered, "Tunie's out."

He made a face but didn't take his eyes off his hands.

Brett didn't say anything dramatic. He simply walked the long way up the yard, not through the grass, not taking the walkway, but skirting as close to Sandy's yard as he could get. He didn't look back. He just clomped up the hill, and once he got about halfway up it, he took flight, and all I saw was the backs of his shoes.

Lizzie saw all of this too, for she said, "It's not like him to go that way."

"Yeah, I know," I said.

"He's upset with Tunie, Mom," Junior said.

"Why?"

"That other girl, the one with the brighter suit—"

"—You mean skimpier," Lizzie said.

"Um, what's skimpy mean?" Junior got a puzzled look in his eyes.

"Means her suit has less fabric—"

"—And covers her nonexistent breasts less," Lizzie added.

"Shhh, that's not nice," I said.

"Oh," Junior said, "Well, that girl said Brett smelled bad on the last day of school, and I guess Tunie laughed, and then the girl repeated it, said he smelled like cow dung—"

"—She used that word?" I stared at Junior.

Before he could answer, Lizzie said, "No, Mom, he's trying not to cuss, but the girl used the s-word, and then I brought that fact to Tunie's attention, and she shrugged, and then a couple more of her friends started to tease Brett, and he probably woulda punched them if they hadn't gotten off at the next bus stop."

"Yep, that's the size of it," Junior said.

I glanced over at Tunie and she was talking in a loud, condescending tone to Bad Doggy, and her friends were cooing just as noisily. "Come on," I said. "Leek stew is Brett's favorite dinner, I'm sure he'll cheer up."

I headed up to the house. And just like Brett, I took the long way. I didn't feel like waving to Esmeralda, who had emerged onto the patio to talk to the girls. Lizzie and Junior followed close behind me, and only when we got to the edge of the driveway did Lizzie say, "Are you gonna talk to Brett, Mama?"

I tightened my jaw and said, "Don't worry, I'll handle it."

"You're not gonna call Miss Ez, are you?"

"Seriously, Lizzie, I'll handle it," I repeated.

Lizzie blinked her eyes and shrugged her shoulders.

Junior whispered to Lizzie, "I think she's mad, but she's trying not to show it."

"Oh," Lizzie whispered back.

•••

Two hours later, the kids had demolished leek stew and had finished up their showers. Lizzie was lingering around Brett's room, but I knew I needed to talk to him in private, so I said, "Lizzie, I think there's some of your soy ice cream left in the freezer, the mocha fudge." I grinned to myself as Lizzie skedaddled down the stairs. Then I slipped into Brett's room and shut the door behind me.

Brett was building a ship with Legos, and he barely acknowledged me. I didn't want to disturb him, so I sat on the edge of his bed and waited for a moment.

"Oh, hi Mom, I'm building the Titanic, do you like it?" Brett's eyes gleamed as he inspected his ship.

I held out my hand and he thrust his ship into it. The ship was rotund and complicated, with at least five separate layers or decks. "Huh," I said, and pointed to several red rectangles on the top deck. "Are these lifeboats?"

"Yes," he said.

"Very beautiful." I handed his ship back to him and said, "Do you wanna talk about what happened on the bus?"

"You mean on the last day of school?"

It had been at least a week since school ended, and I wondered just then why the children hadn't mentioned anything to me. "Tunie's friend told you that you smelled bad, and Tunie joined in?"

"Yes." An irritated look crossed Brett's face, and suddenly he looked much older.

"How do you feel about it? I mean, do we need to talk about our neighbors, or are you okay?"

"I just think some neighbors aren't very neighborly," Brett said in a matter of fact tone.

"Yeah," I chuckled. "Guess that's the size of it."

Brett grabbed another red brick and affixed it to the top deck. "I know we're sposed to treat our neighbors the way we want them to treat us, but I think that there should be an exception for mean girls who call you names. The worst thing Mom?"

Brett made eye contact with me for a second, and I nodded.

"I liked that other girl, the one who said that, but I'm not gonna talk to her anymore." Brett's brow knit together, and he shrugged. "I don't need her."

"Don't need to be friends with someone who doesn't treat you well?"

"Yes. I know I'm not sposed to hit girls, and I told myself not to hit her, but I don't like the way she talked to me, and she talks mean like that to other people too. So I'm not going to talk to her next year, and I don't want to talk to Tunie either. She's not my friend. She's not any of our friends. So I'm not gonna talk to her."

"That seems fair to me," I said.

Brett set his ship down and then he hopped over to his bed and curled up in it. I kissed his forehead and said, "Ready to go to sleep?"

Brett's eyes shuttered and he smiled at me.

"Night son, I love you," I said. I leaned forward and kissed his cheek.

"Love you too," he said.

Chapter 39

We were all out on a walk and at least for the first mile or so, the only extraordinary thing about it was the copious pocket of vomit lying on the bridge outside our home. It was disgusting and in the morning I'd walked a different route than I usually walked to avoid it—that's how disgusting it was. Naturally the kids wanted to ask who had vomited and what had vomited and what sort of food had the vomiting animal eaten and it was all I could do to forget that we'd just eaten burgers for dinner.

Lizzie was whispering about Petunia as we walked past the bridge and she came within a few millimeters of stepping in the vomit. "Ew, gross," she cried, "Is that even human?"

Brett piled into Lizzie and came within a millimeter or two of landing in it. "Wow," he said. "Is that a dog's?" He bent over and looked at the whitish-brown fluid that looked like it had baked beans mixed into it, and I swallowed and kind of winced because we'd had exactly that as one of our side dishes.

"Bet it was," Lizzie was now stage-whispering and glaring into Petunia's yard, "Tunie, hahaha, or maybe Bad Doggy."

"Yeah, betcha she stole their lunch because Tunie's dieting again," Junior said.

"Oh did you know she's been listening into our conversations again?" Lizzie glanced over her shoulder and kind of shuddered.

Junior, meanwhile, was deep in contemplation and I was sort of picturing him poised over a microscope in a laboratory inspecting samples as a grown man. Lizzie and I were thinking the same thought, which was, *Oh my God, what if the vomit traveled by air and reached out from where it was lying and touched us?*

To get my mind off this I asked Lizzie what she meant about Petunia, and I would regret asking after listening to Lizzie tell her latest tale of Pentunia-woe.

"Well, there's only one reason for her to be out on that trampoline like 24-7," Lizzie said.

"Really?"

"Yes," Lizzie said, nodding and wrinkling her forehead. "Because whenever we say something, she stops bouncing. So that means she's listening to us."

"Oh listening to you eh?" I grinned. Petunia was way too self-absorbed to be that interested in whatever my children were talking about unless of course the subject was Petunia.

"Yes, and so tomorrow we're gonna talk about vomit." Lizzie gestured toward Junior and then grabbed hold of Brett's arm. "Guys, come on, we've gotta talk all about vomit tomorrow. So I want you to give me all your books about body fluids and how things work and all that gross biology stuff y'all are always reading."

"Oooh," Brett said, "I got great stuff on bile. The liver, the kidneys, puke, pee, and other fluids. And vomit, what does it come from? What foods make the most vomit?" Brett was concentrating so hard he almost ran into a jogger and I had a fleeting thought about warning the jogger about the pile of vomit but I just couldn't wrap my mind around what to say. Meanwhile, Brett and Junior were intensely wrapped up in how to torture Petunia, who I sincerely doubt was ever eavesdropping, but if she ever did, she'd know more about vomit than most ten-year old girls would ever want to know.

A little while later, William and I were walking along and I was annoying him, talking about the Chain of Command in heaven. "Seriously, William, it's kind of complicated. I mean, here I come along and I am talking to so and so, and I am being respectful and all that sort of thing, and then he asks me what I think the Chain of Command is. And God is talking to me in the background, telling me 'God gives the orders, then Jesus, then me.' But I know I'm not ready to give orders yet, right William?"

William didn't say anything. In fact, he was sort of tuning me out, but for a few moments I pretended he was rapt and wanting to hear the whole story. I just spoke faster.

"Okay, so then the angel I'm talking to, he keeps asking me what would happen if there was an emergency, and I'm like, 'Well, I'm not ready to give orders yet. I'm not ready for command. So if there was like an emergency, then I'd advise, I'd ask for advice. I'd consult with him and then we'd try to come to a joint decision that was for the best of the kingdom. I also told him I would be ready to give commands the next time I'm here. Like when Jesus and I come back in one hundred and fifty years, maybe one hundred and twenty five." I was picturing the number 2136 in my head but decided not to tell William. There's a lot I decide not to tell William. That's what I'm thinking this whole monologue, because I can sense his discomfort with all I'm telling him.

William looked over at me and said, "Well, yes, leadership can be hard. You have to earn their trust situationally and it doesn't appear that you can do that."

"Situationally—what do you mean? As in wars with the Enemy?"

William kind of shrugged. "Um, situations where you might be interacting with . . . other . . . others."

I realized Brett was bouncing beside me, now sort of listening. He had a way of tuning in whenever the conversation shifted to things heaven-related. "Oh, you mean like smiting Lucifer? I love to kick his butt," Brett said.

I looked over at William to see if he was gonna respond but he didn't say a word. He just put his hands behind his back and kept walking. So then I said to Brett, "Yeah? You're pretty good at that aren't you?"

Brett raised both his hands and said, "Yeah, I like to hurl fireballs at him."

"Fireballs eh?"

"Yes. Especially purple ones." Brett looked over at me, his face lit somewhat by the setting sun. "Purple fireballs are hotter than regular ones."

"And you throw the fireballs at them?"

Meanwhile, I was trying to talk to William, saying things like, "William, how come you never say anything when I talk about this stuff? Who else can I talk to about this stuff?"

William's jaw flexed and shifted and he glanced over at the railroad tracks and the thick reed marshes adjoining the tracks. The sun was following the tracks behind us, laying shade as it slid down to the horizon. "Beautiful night, isn't it?"

It was beautiful, and it's never impolite to talk about the weather but sometimes it doesn't match everyone else's conversational bent and this was one of those times.

Brett gave an annoyed wave at the electrical lines above us. "Everything's beautiful but these are horrible. They don't need those to transmit energy. It can move through the air just like this." Brett took his hand and used a cutting motion as if drawing a wave.

"Yes," William said, "Too bad they didn't listen to Tesla."

"On Israel," Brett said, "We won't have these ugly lines for electricity."

"Oh, how will they transmit it? Will it be like the pyramids, using crystals to create some sort of radio waves?"

"Yes, do you understand how harmonic resonance works, Brett?" William launched into an explanation of how the ear takes in sound waves that vibrate against its membranes and Brett gave a bored shrug. I felt bad and kept trying to get Brett and William to communicate about energy transmission.

Meanwhile, Junior came up behind Brett and said, "How many fireballs can you throw in a minute?"

"Oh not as many as Raz," Lizzie said. She put an arm on Brett's shoulder and patted it. "He's not as powerful as Raz. She can take out entire rows of demons, can't she Mom?"

It was getting darker now. The last trace of the sun had disappeared. The fireflies were out and we were still about twenty minutes from home.

"Yep, she sure can, that's right," I said. I was picturing Raz laying down a field of fire about a mile wide. "She can scorch entire city blocks when she's in battle."

"And destroy all her fingernails in the process, right?" Lizzie was obsessed with the parts of the stories I told that involved Raziel using wrath. I don't know, maybe it was because Raz usually destroyed her nails whenever she used wrath. I guess the burnt nails were illustrative or whatever for my ten-year old. She couldn't quite picture the burning demon bodies but she could imagine what burnt fingernails would look like.

"Yep," I said.

"Hey Mom," Brett said, "Can you try to read my mind?"

I groaned to myself but smiled for his benefit. I was training him on telepathy and we weren't doing so well together. "Yeah, go ahead, gimme a number."

Brett focused his face up and shouted something internally at me.

"73?"

He shook his head and groaned and said, "No, 85."

"Okay, try again," I said. I sighed. William was now walking in front of us. Truth is, it's incredibly hard to guess numbers. I think that's because there's rarely a need to transmit a number so in most cases, the only reason someone would be transmitting a number would be as a game or as proof that one has certain powers. And this really isn't a proper use of psychic powers. You should never use them for things like gambling or to show off to your friends.

Teaching telepathic communication is hard. It's much harder when you're around someone who loudly disapproves of all psychic and what he would call supernatural endeavors. But the thing is there's nothing really supernatural about telepathy. We can all do it. But we gotta have total faith in it and some of us are better at it than others. I was thinking all of this, but I was also trying to listen to Brett.

"Um, 71," I said.

"No! Come on Mom!" Brett threw his hands up in the air and got all loud in his gestures. He does this beautifully whenever he's disappointed with me and it's about the cutest thing, him looking like a seventy-year old man in a child's body. "It was 95. Sheesh, come on, try again."

This time, Brett was positively screaming something at me and for the life of me, I had no idea what he was transmitting. I was also aware of William. I could hear his thoughts or more, his feelings, and what he was feeling was of course hurting my feelings.

I shrugged. "73."

"Oh come on, you guessed that last time," Brett said.

"Seriously, Brett, it's almost impossible to guess numbers, especially when you're so loud. I have trouble separating your voice out from all your internal noise."

Lizzie was beside me and she was nodding. "Yeah, he really is loud."

I gave Lizzie a thoughtful look. She was always talking to God, giving me messages from him. And I could usually find her signature even when it was really loud all around me.

We crossed a street and were about to hit a really loud intersection and Lizzie was saying, "Yeah you should put your hands on your ears to block out the interference, specially when you're talking to Brett."

Brett was saying, "Well, lemme try to send you something, Lizzie."

Lizzie listened for a moment and then she shook her head. "Ouch, it sounds like a pulsing sound and it hurts my head," she said.

I nodded. Then I said, "Lizzie, try and send me something."

"Okay," she agreed. And right away, a gentle tone came through. *Mom, you're the best, I love you.*

"Mom, you're the best, I love you."

"Wow, that was almost it," she said.

I nodded again. She really has a steady gentle voice when she transmits telepathically.

"Actually, what I said was, 'Iz, you're the best, I love you,' so you got it, Mom!"

"Doesn't surprise me sweetie. You're always talking to God and He's always saying how cute you are. It's just hard for you to hear Brett."

"That's right," Lizzie said, "That's because he's transmitting on angel frequencies and I'm on a human frequency and you can communicate on the human frequency and the angel frequency but he hasn't learned to do that yet." Lizzie paused and a gratified and surprised look crossed her face. "Wow, I think God just gave me that."

I grinned. Often when Lizzie said something that was particularly wise or grown up sounding, it would have come from God. What was neat was that she was realizing it and at such a young age. "That's great, Lizzie. I would prefer you didn't try to communicate with Brett just yet. I'd rather you keep practicing by listening to and talking to God. He's the best at this—He can tune His frequency to yours and He can read your mind and hear you really well. I want you to never try this on your friends. You must never use this as a game or if people find out you have these psychic powers, you must never let them test you or play games with it, do you understand me?"

"Of course I wouldn't do that," she said with a sweet smile.

"And you must never use this for your own benefit, but only to serve the kingdom. It's a responsibility, okay? You're like me of course, I mean, you're from the Frat too. We all have skills and abilities—"

"—And we must use them to help others get Home and for no other reason," Lizzie said, as if repeating a solemn oath. Then she got a look of total delight on her face and exclaimed, "Wait, I'm from the Frat too? Does that mean—"

"—Yep," I said. "You're different, like me."

"Wow, am I an angel?" Lizzie looked down at her nails and I knew she was imagining what her nails would look like if she used wrath on a demon. Then she looked up at me with an expression of unadulterated joy and said, "I am, aren't I?"

"Well, my girl, you're actually a hybrid, just like me," I said. Then I put my arm around her and added, "You're made from my wing, actually, mine and Gabriel's and maybe some of Mary's too."

Lizzie gave me a solemn nod, and then she said, "Right, okay, God's telling me I need to repeat the thing about not using these abilities for any reason other than to serve the kingdom and only when obeying Him, is that right?"

"Yes, very good," I said. And then Brett was jumping up in the air and waving his hands. "Look," he said, "I'm gonna make some fireballs explode!"

William was once again a few feet away from us. He'd sort of walked ahead but we'd caught up to him at a stoplight. I wanted to make sure he felt comfortable so I said aloud, "Now, your father is incredible at science and at understanding how things work. So he might not be able to hear telepathically but he sure can grasp how thoughts, for example, might be a form of energy and thus be transmitted from one mind to another."

Behind me, Junior was making explosion noises to go along with the fireballs Brett was trying to make. "Just tiny ones, Junior, little ones that won't light up the entire street or anything like that."

"Oh no, Brett, don't go blowing anything up right now, we're too close to other houses."

William held up a hand and smiled. "Okay, Brett, if you can unload one between here and that corner." William pointed about twenty yards away, "Then you can go ahead and do it."

Brett concentrated as hard as he could. He threw his arms up violently and both eyes were burning and his temple was throbbing. Then he sighed and shook his head. "Nope, cars are too loud, maybe I'll try tonight in my room."

"No, not in your room," I said.

"Just a tiny one."

"Nope, no fireballs while inside," I said, and I smiled at William.

"Okay, fine," Brett said.

"Fine," he said. "I'll try and pick stuff up instead."

"Just don't break anything big," William said.

"Or anything of mine," Lizzie said.

Chapter 40

Brett and I were sitting at the kitchen table. He was staring intently at a piece of paper and every once in awhile, like every two or three minutes or so, he'd whisper, "Mom, Mom, check it out, I made it move, come on Mom watch this."

I was studying the Bible, which is sort of what I do every morning. I think I was on Jeremiah, trying to find a passage that said that some of the scribes who wrote the Bible were liars. Yeah, I know that sounds like an extraordinary passage but if you wanna read it for yourself, go check out Jeremiah 8:8. It's what I always use now when I'm pretending to have an argument with someone who thinks I'm a Salad Bar Christian. I don't really have arguments anymore because I realized God didn't want us fighting over him anymore. But every once in awhile I forget I'm not still a lawyer . . . or someone writes me a mad letter and I think about how to respond to it.

So anyway, Brett keeps trying to get a paper to lift up off the table and fly my way without actually touching it. This is called telekinesis in case you're curious. I'm completely certain that in heaven Brett can do this and his siblings keep saying they've seen him send toys flying off the shelves in his room. While I think they're a little gullible, I also believe that when he gets older, Brett probably will be able to make objects go where he wishes them to go. So I listen and look up from Jeremiah and try to read a few passages in between sips of my coffee.

And that's when William comes into the kitchen and he's got that look on his face . . . the look he has when someone's gone and gotten a note sent home. I'm serious. William has a look for this. It's like a tiny frown . . . I've seen his dad make the same look when his sister burped at the table the first time William had me over for a family dinner. It's that look of parental disapproval is the best I can describe it. And this time he's completely ignoring Brett so at least I don't have to explain the roundabout process for training an angel. In case you're wondering, it's a lot like raising a Jedi warrior, with a bit of Bible-reading thrown in of course.

"What's wrong? Someone get a note sent home?"

William shook his head and handed me his iPad. Sure enough, it was open to an email from Lizzie's teacher, Ms. Funzip.

Hi there,

I just graded a paper Lizzie wrote for a class project and I wanted to touch base about a couple issues. Please ask Lizzie to give you the assignment labeled, "Lesson Learned" and then perhaps it would be best if we spoke over the telephone. I am concerned as well about a situation involving one of Lizzie's classmates, particularly since Lizzie writes about this child in the assignment. Petunia is doing well in English and as I am sure you've heard she has been elected sixth grade class President for the upcoming school year.

Thanks,

Ms. Funzip.

I sort of shrugged when I read this because I could tell from the tone of it that Lizzie had written something awful about Petunia. I was also getting that sinking feeling in my stomach, kind of the one you get when you know your kid's gonna get screwed over and probably deserves some form of punishment but doesn't deserve the exact form she's gonna receive. And then there was the issue of the incoming sixth grade class presidency. This alone was going to ruin my daughter's summer and in truth, probably mine too. "Oh no," I whispered, "Petunia's gonna be prancing all over the neighborhood, you realize that, right?"

William, meanwhile, was flipping through Lizzie's blue binder and then, lips still pursed, was reading over her assignment. After a minute or so, he shook his head and placed the stapled loose-leaf in my hands. "Lizzie! Get down here," he called.

Meanwhile, I read what she wrote.

•••

Lizzie Teaches Sally

Lizzie was mad at Sally. Sally had grounded her for riding Junior's skateboard off the roof and wrecking it. So anyway, Lizzie was sitting in her room, bored, alone, and mad. Suddenly, she came up with the perfect idea for revenge while Sally was screaming cuss words at Bad Doggy. She grabbed a sheet of notebook paper and wrote in Sally's hand writing:

> Will you idiots make that frickin bastard dog stop barking? Did ya know I led the skunk? If you don't make it stop barking, I will kill it!
>
> Your nemesis,
>
> Sally.
>
> P.S. thanks for your consideration☹

Then Lizzie snuck downstairs and grabbed 29 delicious chocolate chip cookies, put them in a box, along with the letter, and put it at Petunia's doorstep, then she rang the doorbell and ran away. When Aaron and Esmeralda found it, well let's just say Sally got a lot of angry phone calls from every single neighbor who owned a dog . . . and was so tired from all the angry phone calls, visits, and letters that it took her 24 hours to discover who did it.

Epilogue: Well, actually Sally thought Brett wrote the note and wrapped up the burned cookies, so Lizzie got off scot-free and Brett got grounded.

Moral: Borrow Brett's skateboard not Junior's.

•••

Lizzie was sitting down at the table looking at least a little chastened. William had been talking to her in a quiet voice for a couple of minutes. At first, Lizzie had been asking me if the essay was at least well-written and I'd given her a stone-faced stare in response. I specialize in those stony stares. Usually my face is almost hyper-expressive, so the stoniness creates a dramatic effect . . . or so I am always hoping when I get like that. I'm usually trying to buy time to figure out how to react but in this case, I was lost in thought, thinking about the Middle East.

I know. Sounds like a stretch. But I'd just seen a movie called Argo, and it was about how the CIA and the Canadian Embassy worked together to get six Americans out of Iran when scores of Americans were taken hostage by revolutionary crowds who stormed our embassy. Note how I used the pronoun "our". That's sort of what I was thinking, or along those lines, as I listened to William talk to Lizzie about the real and not-so-real war she and her brothers were raging against Tunie and her gang.

Gangs. Wars. The Middle East.

"You know what this reminds me of, this whole battle you're fighting against Tunie and her friends?" I looked over at William. "You know what it's like, Will?"

"Carringtons and Ewings mixed into one show as a lark?" William leaned back against the counter and closed one eye, as if picturing an unwritten TV episode from the '80s. He was referring to two separate shows that were popular and involved incessant family feuding. The first was Dynasty and it involved the Carringtons; the second was Dallas, and it centered on the Ewings. "Yeah, imagine if those two shows, those two families got together, imagine the mud that would fly."

William and I chuckled at one another. It was silly, for I had never watched Dallas and he had never watched Dynasty but the shows had been wildly popular and had formed our cultural shorthand in a sense. But something else had also helped form that shorthand. Iran.

"Good one," I said. "But no, I was thinking about Iran. Remember that song we were singing that summer?"

"Yep," he said.

"Bababa-bababa-bomb Iran," I sang as off-tune as ever. Then I looked over at Lizzie, who was looking inquisitive and alert. She was also surprised, I'm thinking, because I almost never talked about my childhood. The kids had long ago stopped asking me to tell stories about how it was growing up, and of course I knew this.

"Oh yeah," William groaned. "We were so young, so foolish about all that."

"What's it all about, anyway?"

Ha, I had her, I smiled to myself. "Ah," I said. "In 1979 your father and I were, what—nine?"

William nodded.

"And in a small country in the Middle East, called Iran, our embassy got itself seized by some angry revolutionaries and they took a bunch of American citizens hostage. They held onto them for 444 days, right Will?"

"Yes," he said, "Sounds right."

"But why?" Lizzie had that look you get on your face when a bug keeps landing on your nose.

"Well, I'll get to that. But anyway, me and Will were kids. We heard everyday about the bad Iranians. And lots of Americans were pretty angry about all this. They didn't understand why our President didn't go and bomb the heck out of the Iranians."

"Yeah, but why did the Iranians take over the embassy?"

"Well, here's the sticky part, the ugly part of the story. Back in the 1950s, the US and England held oil interests in Iran. Meanwhile, a democratically elected leader wanted to nationalize the oil industries. We didn't think that was such a great idea, so we knocked him out of power and helped put someone else in his place. This guy turned out to be an awful leader. For one thing, he modernized the country in ways that upset the mainstream people, who were devout Sunnis."

"What's a Sunni?"

"It's a branch of the Muslim religion, like the main one, and it's pretty traditional."

"Like do they make women wear head coverings and that sort of thing?"

I sighed. Lizzie was making a face and I remembered my promise to God not to go fomenting discord, and I was gonna keep to that. And yet here was an opportunity to teach. I sighed again and said, "Actually, the Sunnis are a lot like some of the Southern Baptists or maybe like some Catholics as far as wanting folks to follow certain rules and yeah, sometimes those rules result in women being treated unfairly."

"Like how, mom?"

"Well, Catholics say women can't be priests and shouldn't teach religion, and a lot of Baptist churches say that being gay is an abomination, and I could go on here." I paused, took another deep breath, and thought about how she was giving me an opportunity to criticize anything that denigrated women, but how I needed to make use of an even more important opportunity to teach tolerance. So I said, "But the thing is, the Sunnis are almost entirely peaceful, and so are Catholics and Baptists. There are only a tiny proportion of Muslims who are violent, they're called the Wahhabis, and they're extremists, they're the ones who go killing folks for no good reason, you hear me? Most Muslims are just like most Christians, they have families, they try to live good lives, and they're just doing their best to get back Home."

Lizzie's forehead was wrapped around itself and she was trying to figure out what question to ask me next. About four different ones were pulling at her, from the looks of the intersecting lines above her brow line. I smiled and realized I was getting off-topic, so I said, "Okay, so you following me about the history of Iran? About how most of the population is Sunni, or fairly traditional, and how the ruler was changing things up and that upset folks?"

Lizzie was quiet for a moment. She was picturing head-dresses and veils, or so I imagined. Then she said, "Yeah, but so what if they didn't like it, I mean, modern is better isn't it?"

"Well, I don't know if modern is better, no, not always sweetie. But that wasn't all he was doing, because this leader that we supported was totally corrupt. He'd fly meals in from Paris and he was supposedly massacring members of the opposition and he was incredibly unpopular and cruel and what do you say William, wasn't he an awful leader?"

I glanced over at William and waited. He was always honest and his family had been (still was) both devoutly Republican and well-informed on all things governmental; after all, his father had worked for the State Department. "Yes, we made a terrible decision, no doubt about it," William agreed.

"So anyway, the Iranians overthrew that leader and they wanted to try him for war crimes. Meanwhile, he got cancer and we brought him here so that he could receive treatment."

"Yeah, they said his 747 could barely take off, it was laden with so many bars of gold," William said.

"That's just awful," I chuckled. "Anyway, Lizzie, we're not trying to teach you about the evils of colonization or give you a dissertation on American foreign policy. It's just, you see, that situation was a terrible one. Mistakes were made on all sides. We shouldn't have put the corrupt leader in office. He was bad. But the Iranians shouldn't have held our guys hostage."

"And Carter should have been firmer with them, should have showed them we were serious. I mean, look what happened once Reagan got elected?"

I glared at William and said, "Yes, but what really could Carter have done? If we'd gone in there with guns blazing—"

"—Yeah, that Marine Captain who said that if even one shot was fired, that everyone would have died, he saved lots of lives," William said. He was talking about a scene from Argo during which a US Marine ordered his men to only fire tear gas at the crowd. For sure he had saved many lives by exercising restraint.

"Yes. And what Carter could and couldn't have done or should have done differently doesn't really matter. It was a difficult situation." I paused and could see Carter speaking on TV, saying that the U.S. wouldn't tolerate terrorism. Everyone agrees with this . . . and yet we've been the target of terrorists many times since the hostage situation and no doubt we will be again in the coming years. I shook my head and continued, "But I do know one thing. There's almost nothing we can do right in the Middle East. The only thing that would work is if every single country agreed to disarm and somehow each citizen who has a weapon or a bomb stashed away somewhere gave up their weapons . . . and if everyone agreed to respect existing territorial lines . . . and if . . ." I threw up my hands and gave a rueful laugh.

"Impossible of course, will never happen," William said.

"Exactly the point I'm trying to make," I said.

"Mom, you're losing me," Lizzie said.

"Well, y'all are fighting a war with Tunie and maybe you have some things you've got a right to be mad about or maybe you once did, right?"

Lizzie was nodding emphatically and was about to lambast Tunie.

I held up a hand and said, "But you and the boys have done some wrong things to her, said some hurtful stuff, yes?"

"Yeah, but—"

"—But what? She's had it coming to her? So what? What does that prove, huh Lizzie?"

"Someone needs to teach her . . ."

"What," William said, "Like someone had to teach the Iranians how to run their own country?" William made eye contact with me and I nodded. He was taking this in a different direction than I was headed, but this would work as well.

"Like y'all know better, like y'all know everything," I said. "Like y'all are perfect in every way and should impose your system on Tunie?" It was the anti-colonial argument after all, I thought to myself.

"Okay, so you're saying I should leave her to her own devices," Lizzie said.

"We're saying that's part of it. I was also saying," I added, "That this war you're fighting over this or that is unwinnable. It's just gonna go on and on and it's gonna get worse not better."

"So what's Iran like now?"

"Good question, Lizzie. They still hate us. A lot of Americans still hate them. We're scared of them; they're scared of us. And the people are still poor and at war with most of their neighbors. It's a mess, Lizzie. I don't even know who's fault it is, you know? I just know the fighting and the hatred hasn't stopped and I know war's just like that."

Lizzie was quiet for a bit. She was taking it all in, probably wondering if she was in a lot of trouble. After she was still for a minute or so she said, "So did the hostages, were they okay?"

"Yeah," I said. "They were all safe. Still seems like a bit of a miracle that they made it home without getting shot."

"Okay," she said.

"Okay, what?" William asked.

"Okay, I'll try not to enslave, fight or otherwise torment Tunie," Lizzie said.

"Or write stories about all of the above," I said.

"Aw come on, Mom," Lizzie said. "I need to retain creative control."

We smiled at one another. She'd been listening to me argue things over with my manager and was picking up some of my writer lingo.

"Creative control, eh?"

"Yes," she said.

"Lizzie," William said, "In all seriousness, and that goes for you too Sally—"

"—Who me?" I grinned.

"Yes," he paused and gave me one of his steely looks. Then he said, "Lizzie, please be respectful to your teacher and try not to write stories about people in your classes while you're in school."

"Yeah," I said, and tried not to giggle.

"Sally, really," William said.

"Okay, okay. Lizzie, you can write anything you want in your journal, okay?"

"Will you read it Mom?"

"You want me to read your journal?"

"And critique it please Mom? I wanna be a writer like you," Lizzie said, and she was absolutely sincere about it.

"You're already way, way ahead of where I was at your age, you know that?"

Lizzie beamed at me. "Really?"

"Yeah, I swear," I said. "Now, did you hear your father?"

"Yeah," she said, and her eyes had a little bit of a dreamy quality about them.

"Good, and your Mom knows talent, Lizzie," William said. "So if she says you got it, you got it."

"Wow, thanks Mom, thanks Dad," Lizzie said.

"Right," William said. "Now get on to bed. We love you."

Chapter 41

I woke up bored. And maybe that's a good thing, because when bored, I often lose my filter. And as William always says, "Sally without her filter is just a few steps short of Roseanne Barr." Except of course I'm a lot funnier. William also says I'm "too sensitive," am "not being logical," and am "acting with my emotions." Of course only a man could have said this—a man who isn't attending to his own karma. The way I see karma working is you don't tell a woman she's being too sensitive or else she will bring the woman's ire to the karma, as the saying sort of goes.

I'm trying so hard to avoid cussing, because whenever I do, Brett copies me. And that's no good. But the saying just needs to be stated. I was riffing off the expression, "karma's a bitch," which is a ridiculous expression really, unless you want to say that karma is an angry female.

Wait—that actually makes sense. Karma is like that, as I like tell my kids: if you behave well now, things will work out for you later. But if you behave awfully, well, you are gonna have to face the consequences. In other words, karma's like when you misbehave and your mom tries to tell you to cut it out but you don't listen, and she finally cuffs you. She doesn't just tell you to wait till your father gets home, no way. Mom handles it. After all, karma, like Mother Nature, is female.

Anyway, I woke up bored, and then I got to designing or redesigning my website. Soon enough, I got lost in what I was doing. I know just enough about website design to be extremely dangerous to myself. By the time the kids got home from school, I'd destroyed my existing website and was contemplating reading the instructional manuals I'd refused to read before I started the redesigning, and I was almost wishing I wasn't allergic to instructional manuals.

That's when Lizzie and Junior and Brett piled into the laundry room. Lizzie was yelling at Brett and Junior was telling me about his spelling test and Brett was asking if he could have some whipped cream. I gave my website one last woeful glance and shut the computer off, and for a half-hour, Brett and I struggled through his homework while Lizzie and Junior sat in their assigned chairs, getting their work done and trying to help Brett get his done too.

Homework's not the quietest time of our day. In fact, there's no quiet time during our day, not really, especially not when Lizzie's wanting to talk about what's bugging her at school. I waited for Lizzie to go on about Petunia's latest perfect writing score, which really bugged Lizzie. It was so unfair Petunia got a better grade than Lizzie and it was unfair that Isabel was also getting lots more attention with her writing and it was pretty pathetic that Matthew couldn't string together two sentences without using an explosion sound and why wasn't Lydia paying better attention during the assembly, and why couldn't the bullying assembly had addressed the actual bullies in her class rather than having goofy play-acting?

It was going on and on like this and I was trying not to get an ice cream headache from it. "Lizzie," I said, "How about if you stop worrying about what everyone else is doing and concentrate on your own stuff?"

"What do you mean Mom?"

I stopped and looked at Lizzie. I didn't want to tell her to stop talking, not exactly, not in so many words. So it was going to have to be one of my indirect stories. One that would make her pause for a moment, at least, and think.

"Do you think that this is the best thing for you to be doing with yourself? Is this the best thing to talk about?"

"Well," she said, "I don't know, I'm just talking about my day, you know?"

I said, "Once upon a time, back in the days of Muhammad, maybe a little later—"

"—Is this one of your Rumi stories?"

I nodded at Lizzie and continued, "So anyway, there was a rich old man and he knew he was about to die. He had three sons and he wanted to leave his fortune to the correct one. So he called his lawyer to him and said, 'Ali, I need you to arrange my affairs so that all my money goes to my laziest son.'

'Laziest son?' Ali said, frowning.

'Yes, the one who's most fit to be a Sufi mystic. The best of the best, the laziest. That's my final wish,' the father said."

"Wait, the father leaves his money to his laziest son?" Junior pinched his nose together and frowned.

Brett leaned forward and grinned and I grinned back at him, and then took Junior in as well with my eyes.

"Yep, that's right. So the father dies, and then Ali calls the sons to him and he's gonna test them, see who's the laziest. So he says to the eldest son, 'Tell me how you're the laziest,' and the son says, 'Okay, well, when I meet someone, I will let them talk for a few days, just talk and talk, and then I'll figure out what they're thinking from what they're saying, like I'll be a great listener, and only after three days of just listening will I say anything.' So Ali turns to the next son and says, 'Okay, how about you?' And this son says, 'I will read their facial expressions and will know what the other person is gonna say before they even talk, and then I'll kind of nod at them or shake my head to show them what I'm thinking, oh, and I will let my wife do all the work, yeah, and I definitely won't water the camels or feed the pigs or anything like that.' So the second son was pretty satisfied with himself, right?"

I turned and made sure Lizzie was following me, and she was kind of nodding, and Brett was still grinning. Then I said, "So Ali turns to the third son and he says, 'Okay, your turn, what would you do?' And it was the most annoying thing, because the third son just sat there, completely still, and wouldn't answer or didn't answer. He was like mute, dumb, not speaking, saying nothing. Ali thought maybe the son was deaf so he kept asking, and of course the first brother kept trying to answer for him and the second brother had this look of intense concentration like he was trying to read the third brother's mind—but nothing. No answer."

"Oh my God, Mom, so what's the point?" Lizzie folded her hands together and gave me one of her disgusted stares, and I was quiet for a moment. I was thinking about it, hoping she would answer her own question.

And sure enough, she said, "Wait, Mom, did the third son get the money?"

"Yep," I said.

"Because he was the laziest?"

"Yes, Lizzie, he was the best mystic, the best Sufi so to speak, do you get what I'm saying?"

Lizzie shook her head and then she grimaced a little and in a meek voice, she said, "Are you telling me to be quiet?"

"Well, sweetie, not exactly, but sort of. What the Sufi mystics teach is that you gotta get silent in order to learn, and you gotta empty yourself of all your carnal soul issues if you're going to be able to hear and get closer to God."

"Hey Mom," Junior said, "What's carnal mean?"

"It's greed and selfishness and lust and wanting stuff from this world; it's also caring about what other people think of you, or vanity so to speak, and that's what I am trying to tell Lizzie to stop doing, if that makes sense, Junior."

"Oh Mom, is the carnal soul the donkey soul that Rumi always talks about?" Lizzie was now grinning, even as she was getting corrected, because she loved when I talked about our donkey souls. It was one of her favorite expressions from Rumi's sacred scriptures, or the Masnavi he'd composed centuries ago.

"Yep, Lizzie, the carnal soul is like a donkey. It's stubborn and it can carry our bodies, no problem, but it's constantly needing to be fed and caressed and persuaded and congratulated, just like you're wanting your classmates to feed and congratulate you on your writing, yes?" I smiled at Lizzie gently, wanting to lesson the harshness of the lesson I was teaching.

Lizzie smiled back at me and said, "Okay, so stop feeding my inner donkey and get quiet like one of your Sufi mystics, okay,

okay, so will you tell us the story of the mouse and the frog? I love that story."

Junior walked over to the fridge and poured a glass of grape juice. Brett jumped out of his chair and almost collided with Junior.

"Wow, watch out for that inner donkey, Brett," Lizzie said.

Brett made a face at Lizzie, and then she asked him to bring her a glass of grape juice too, and he smiled again. I smiled too, thinking he was a kind soul.

"Okay, there's a frog and a mouse and they meet up with one another every day, just for maybe an hour in the morning and a little bit more in the evenings, like before bedtime, and they're kind of in love, right? So the mouse wants to spend more time with the frog. The mouse keeps saying, 'Frog, I miss you when we're not together, I miss you awfully, I miss you every minute we're apart, it's killing me, we need to be together more, we need to be tied to one another and never apart,' and the frog isn't so sure about this. He's thinking, okay, I love the mouse, but I don't wanna be tied to him, not exactly, I wanna go home to my own frog family at night, but the mouse is very charming and adorable, and the frog's in love too, so he doesn't exactly say no. Anyway, the mouse keeps begging and then the mouse comes up with an idea. He finds a rope when he's scavenging through some garbage and he ties one end of the rope to his foot, and another end of the rope to the frog's foot. He's so excited about this, so excited that the frog sort of forgets his misgivings. The mouse is like, 'Frog, frog darling, whenever one of us wants to talk to the other, we can just tug on the rope, just like this,' and the mouse gives a little tug, and pulls the frog to him, and they kiss, and it's so beautiful."

"Oh Mom, come on," Junior said, "Aren't they both boys?"

"Yep," I said, "They sure are, and their boy-kissing is just as beautiful as a boy and girl kissing is, okay?"

"Yeah," Lizzie said, "Totally right."

Junior gave an affable nod, and then he said, "Okay, so they're both boys. Go on."

"Well, they go on as best friends and soulmates and all, keeping up their endless conversation that never gets old. And then one summer night, a raven swoops down," I moved my hands together to illustrate the night attack, "Grabs the mouse, and flies off with him. And attached to the rope of course is the frog, so he's flailing around, hanging down from the rope, flying along thinking, wow, what did I get myself into, I should have listened to my inner voice and not agreed to this, and then the raven finishes eating the mouse and the last thing the poor frog sees is the raven's beak coming toward him.

"Ew, Mom," Lizzie said.

"Clomp!" Brett slammed his hands together.

Junior made a swallowing sound, and he and Brett giggled at one another.

"And the point of this awful story?" Lizzie was still making a face at me.

"Well, there are a couple of points," I said.

"Like mice and frogs shouldn't be kissing?" Junior was still focusing on the kissing part of the story.

I smiled. "Well, more like frogs belong to water and mice are always scurrying around, getting into other people's business, they're kind of yucky if you think about it. And if you're going to associate with other souls, you maybe wanna pay attention to what they do in their spare time, or how they conduct themselves, before you tie your fortunes to theirs, right?"

"So is that like the saying, 'birds of a feather flock together'?" Lizzie asked.

"Yeah, Lizzie, it is," I said. "We really do benefit from keeping company with other souls who are swimming in the right direction as we are, which is not to say that we shouldn't have friends with diverse interests or that sort of thing. But we truly do tend to act like the people we're with, so when we choose companions, we should choose wisely." I got up and poured myself a glass of grape juice and then I said, "And do you think the frog had an inkling of this before he agreed to the mouse's rope idea?"

"Yes," Lizzie said. Then she held out her glass. "Can I have some more juice?"

"No," I said. "So what did the frog do wrong again? As far as that inkling he had?"

"Um," Junior said, "He didn't listen to it?"

"That's right, Junior," I said, "In other words, he didn't listen to that inner voice of his, what we call intuition, or what do your teachers always tell you as far as writing down your first answer or your first guess on a problem that's hard? Don't they tell you to go with your first guess?"

Junior sort of shrugged and then Lizzie snapped her fingers. "Yes, yes," she said. "For our SOLs," which is what the state of Virginia calls the Standards of Learning Exams elementary school children take. "Yeah," Lizzie said, "We're supposed to go with our first response because that's usually the correct one?"

I nodded. "Listen, kids, what they're referring to there and what the frog was not listening to was his intuition. Your intuition is your sixth sense and it's actually your most powerful sense of all, and you know what else? It's what the Sufi mystics were talking about when they taught that you had to get really quiet in order to learn best. And you know why? Because it's through that sixth sense that you're able to talk to God—so that's the whole point of both stories. Be quiet. Stop talking so much. And listen. Listen to your inner guide, your inner voice, your intuition—"

"—And don't get eaten by the raven," Brett said.

"Yep," I said, "And don't get chewed up by the nasty raven."

Chapter 42

Junior sauntered into the kitchen and spun around as if dancing to a tune. Then he said, "Hmmn, Mom, do you like ABBA?"

I kind of groaned. "I don't know, love, the real question in my book is whether ABBA's way too cheerful for a Monday morning?"

Lizzie stumbled beside me and almost slammed into Junior. She heard the crack about ABBA and that's when Junior started to sing, "Dancing Queen" and it's about when I went searching for the Motrin, all the while humming the chorus. Of course.

The kids got home from school and they were all yelling about Petunia's goings-ons and how unfair it all was. "Oh my god, Mom, she gave Brett a warning for saying 'Chickie Chickie Chickie Hamster Chickie' too many times in a row." Lizzie put a protective arm around Brett and hugged him tight. "Poor kid."

"Well, he did say 'Chickie Chickie Chickie Hamster' a lot of times," Junior said. Junior was pouring a bowl of chips and I shook my head and asked for the bag at about the same moment the chips got out of Junior's control and flooded out of the bag, on the countertop and all over the floor.

As I knelt to pick up the chips, Lizzie helped me. And I said, "Well, about how many times then?"

Brett shrugged and reached down, grabbed a chip and shoved it in his mouth before I could stop him.

"Ew, Brett, that's disgusting, and I guess you best go ahead and tell Mom the rest of the story before she opens her email."

"Shut up Lizzie," Junior said, "Stop tattling."

"No, you shut up, you said it too, and I wasn't tattling on you, least wasn't gonna till you opened your big mouth," Lizzie said. Then she turned and flashed me a loving smile. "Here Mom, let me help you with this, you shouldn't be doing this, not with your bad back and all."

I stood up and sighed. "Okay, boys, what else did you say besides Chickie and Hamster? What's the word du jour?"

Junior folded his hands in front of him and his cheeks looked red and plump, like they always did, just more so when he had done something wrong and wanted to apologize. This was him at his sweetest and he knew I never stayed mad long when he stood before me like this. "Well. Brett may have said the word 'Vag,' and it was an incorrect usage of course, so I whispered to him the correct word and then when he couldn't hear me, I said it again, and then he yelled, 'I can't hear you did you say 'vagina?' and that's when Tunie heard him, and so she gave him a warning and instead of just saying nothing, he repeated it the rest of the ride home and told her she had mustard on her chin."

"Well, did she have mustard on her chin?"

Brett shook his head and snickered.

I tried very hard to keep a straight face. "She didn't?"

"Nope."

"Nope? Is that how you're gonna play this? Nope? Is that respectful?"

"No Ma'am it isn't, ma'am," Brett said, and this time he appeared somewhat chastened.

"Well, Lizzie, go get me my Bible please."

"Yes ma'am," Lizzie said. She was gonna play up this 'yes ma'am' thing for the rest of the day, right up until it was time to brush her teeth and go to bed, I reckoned, and I was fine with that. I was also ready to do some teaching.

Lizzie handed me my marked-up copy of the Bible. I nodded and ordered all three children to grab a chair.

"Okay, how about something from the Sermon on the Mount? That's one of Jesus' best speeches."

"Were you there for that one, Mom?"

I smiled at Lizzie. "Yep, but he used to tell me the same stuff whenever I got in trouble with the other Johns in my class. Before I went by Mark, one of the monks used to call me John and he'd call us Johns over to him and tell us we were needing to act less like sons of darkness and that used to make me mad, so I'd go home and rant and complain about mean old Brother Aaron, and so dad would tell me all the stuff he'd teach to the other disciples. By the time I got to this sermon, I'd heard it dozens of times but you know what? Probably could hear it all again. This stuff never gets old."

The children each nodded at me and then I began reading aloud from the Gospel of Matthew.

> *"You have heard that it was said, 'Eye for eye, and tooth for tooth.' But I tell you, do not resist an evil person. If anyone slaps you on the right cheek, turn to them the other cheek also. And if anyone wants to sue you and take your shirt, hand over your coat as well. If anyone forces you to go one mile, go with them two miles. Give to the one who asks you, and do not turn away from the one who wants to borrow from you.*
>
> *"You have heard that it was said, 'Love your neighbor and hate your enemy.' But I tell you, love your enemies and pray for those who persecute you, that you may be children of your Father in heaven. He causes his sun to rise on the evil and the good, and sends rain on the righteous and the unrighteous. If you love those who love you, what reward will you get? Are not even the tax collectors doing that? And if you greet only your own people, what are you doing more than others? Do not even pagans do that? Be perfect, therefore, as your heavenly Father is perfect.*

I set my leather brown Bible down and said, "Okay, Lizzie, what does this mean to you?"

"Well, it means when Petunia calls me names I shouldn't call her names back?"

"What do you think, Junior?"

Junior gave me a gentle, downright beatific smile. Then he took one of his Matchbox cars and slung it towards Brett.

"Son, get that off the table," I said.

"Yes ma'am," he said.

"And answer the question."

"Um, should not hit her back if she slaps me?"

"How about you, Brett? What if one of the bullies at school keeps slapping or punching your sister? Should you let him do it? Or should you jump on his back and restrain him?"

"If anyone touches you or Lizzie," Brett said, and he was one hundred percent sure of himself, "Then I will beat their heads in."

"Perhaps that is in fact what you should do, my angel," I said with a little smile.

Junior gave me a confused look and then Lizzie said, "But shouldn't you be, what did it say? Kissing or blessing your enemy?"

"Well, it does say that you should love your enemy. And Jesus does teach that, as he would say to me at home, in a perfect world we should practice non-violence. But he also didn't want us laying down for bullies. He stood up to all sorts of injustices. He was always fighting against hypocrites and injustices . . . but in a perfect world, the use of force should be reserved for someone who's not involved in the dispute. Do you know what I mean?"

Lizzie raised her hand as if she were at school and I went ahead and pointed at her. "Go ahead," I said.

"Like when we're bickering and one of us hits the other one and you tell us not to hit back, but preferably to tell you first, and the same thing goes at school?"

"Yes," I said. "In society, neighbors aren't supposed to punch one another, and if they're disagreeing over something, they're supposed to go to the police or to the courts to resolve their differences."

"Oh, so why don't you sue Mr. Aaron and Ms. Esmeralda?" Junior was studying his fingernails as if to discover a missing nub but he'd already chewed all the way down to the final layer of skin.

"Well, I suppose we could," I chuckled, "But that would be kind of silly. It's really up to me to approach them nicely and ask them to get Bad Doggy to stop barking."

"So why don't you?"

I smiled at Lizzie. It was a fair question but a hard one to answer easily. "Well, I have a few lessons to learn this lifetime. One of those is patience. Another is non-resistance. And the third one is tact. So when I figure out how I can talk to Aaron without snapping at him or whining or crying or raising my voice, I'm thinking I will. But that isn't the issue here so much is it?"

"I don't know, Mom," Lizzie said. Her eyes were focused and she was concentrating on something. "I mean, if you can't make Bad Doggy stop barking, shouldn't you do something about it?"

"That's a good question, Lizzie. The answer is yes and no. Yes, I should take measures that are peaceful to seek redress with my neighbors, but yes I should also try to be tolerant of the barking and yes, I should say something if it interrupts my work. But in the case of y'all being mad at Petunia for doing her job on the school bus, and it is her job as patrol to keep order, is it not?"

I paused and waited for the children to nod at me and they did.

Then I continued, "So she was doing her job, correcting you. She was not at least today slapping you on the cheek, not really, was she? She was not mistreating you, she was not giving you any reason to tumble off the bus saying this and that about her was she?"

The boys shook their heads and both looked sheepish. Then Lizzie made a face. "But she's kind of mean almost all the time to us and she deserved to hear she had mustard on her face because a few days ago she told Robert he had dog poop smeared on the bottom of his shoe and he didn't but he swore he was never gonna wear those shoes again not ever, and they were his favorite shoes."

"Okay, so that wasn't nice, now was it?"

Brett shook his head. "She had it coming to her."

I chuckled. "That would be the law of karma in application."

"What's karma?" Junior asked.

"You do something good to someone, something good is done to you, but if you do something bad, something bad is gonna happen to you."

"See?" Brett clapped his hands and looked smug. "She had it coming to her."

"Well, maybe she did, but it's not our job as humans to apply those laws," I said. "It's God's. It's our job to try and keep the good karma coming our way, so to speak. And how do you think you keep good karma coming your way? Hmmn, what do you think, Lizzie?"

"Um, by loving your neighbor?"

"Yes, and who's your neighbor, huh, Brett?"

I looked over at him and he glanced over his shoulder in Bad Doggy's direction.

"Um, Tunie is I guess."

"Right," I said. "So you make your life better or worse today?"

"Better! I got Petunia back! And now Robert can wear his favorite shoes again," Brett said.

"Really?" I shook my head and caressed the cover of the Bible. "Because now don't you think you got some sort of revenge or bad act, some mustard or some dog poop so to speak, coming your way? Don't you see, y'all? You slap someone back, you hurt someone, and they are gonna do what?"

The boys both shrugged and so I repeated my question. "What's coming back to you?"

"Um, a slap, right Mom?" Lizzie said.

"Yes, Lizzie. A slap, some mustard and some dog poop. So do you see why maybe it's best to turn the other cheek when someone slaps you? Do you see how if someone doesn't stop the slapping, stop the violence, it becomes one long cycle that never ends?"

Brett and Junior still looked a little confused. I stood up from the table and said, "Well, I'd like for you to behave on the bus tomorrow, you hear me Brett?"

"Yes ma'am."

"And an apology to Tunie would be good, okay?"

"Yes ma'am," he said again.

"Okay," I said. "I'm gonna go check the email."

"You're not gonna tell Dad are you?"

I shook my head and said, "Nah, I'll let you tell him, maybe over dinner, best to be the one who tells that story don't you think?" Then I tousled his hair and walked out of the room. Thankfully there was only one note waiting for me and it wasn't by any means the worst note home we've ever received. The word "vag" or any variation thereof didn't even appear in it.

Chapter 43

I sat at the kitchen table cowering before the stack of bills. There was the cable and internet bill, which I always ignore until Cox Communications gets medieval on us and I go to check something on Facebook and get this blinking cursor and then read this on the screen:

> *Your service has been disconnected. Please call customer service at whatever number to pay us the stupid amount of money you owe us for TV channels you never use and Internet you use excessive—no, obsessively. Thank you for making us rich at the altar of your poverty.*

Or something like that. I added the misspelling just to be bad.

So I dial the number for customer service and pay the $404.23 and then the computerized voice tells me not to hang up or else the transaction will be canceled please wait for your confirmation number. And inevitably the computerized man hangs up on me before giving me the confirmation number and I hold my breath until I click the browser and then reboot the computer because that never works . . . and finally, after another 15 minutes, log back online and get back to "work."

As part of my "work," I confess my malfeasance to whoever will listen. I write stuff like:

> *Dysfunction is fantastically funny until . . . it's not.*

And:

> *I just wish God could handle the banking account. Pay the bills. Deposit the checks. Reissue the stale checks without bugging anyone.*

And:

> *Reissuing stale checks is a lot like the atonement. Because after all, isn't God's forgiveness like one massive freaking blank check, paid in the currency of eternal love? Sighing. Well, back to my very messed up checkbook. Thank God there's no checking accounts in heaven.*

So after I work for awhile, I look to God and philosophy to explain my fear of bills. And then I write stuff like this:

> *I'm just sitting around waiting for God to tell me what to do. Sounds simple, doesn't it? Sometimes the messages come from unexpected places, so I'm just going to be grateful and figure out what I'm supposed to be doing.*
>
> *It's kind of a relief, not having to be in control all the time. What if I don't have to figure everything out on my own? What if it's completely okay if I get it wrong? Like hey, He still loves me no matter how messed up I am, or how much I mess up.*
>
> *I would like to say I learn from all this. Really, I would. But about a month later, this happens:*
>
> *I paid my water bill on time. Well. By on time I mean only a month or two late . . . but before we received the disconnect notice, and definitely before the water company sent a truck out to disconnect our water. Well, actually they DID send a water truck out; in fact, they sent three of them. I think the guys just got the wrong instructions because they*

turned the water off, and then told me they were just making sure they could turn it off, and they could. Then they turned it back on. And then I ran inside, found the three water bills, and paid the angriest-sounding one over the phone.

So I want a medal. I'm tapping my foot, waiting.

Nah. I was being silly because I don't like worrying about bills. It's a waste of time. That's what I realized later on, once I stopped thinking about bills. I realized worrying doesn't make you a better soul. It might make you seem more responsible to others but it doesn't get you a pass into Heaven. When you go back for your mission debrief, no one claps you on the back and says, "You did a great job, worrying over that job of yours, worrying about how to afford stuff you can't bring here with you." No, nope, you just don't gain anything that lasts or does you any good when you worry about the things of this world.

I was thinking all those things when I was taking a walk tonight. God was sort of gently telling me to give up my worries and for a few moments, I was inclined to argue with Him about it. And that's when my Lizzie reminded me of what I should be spending time thinking about. It's not something she said really, nor was it the least bit dramatic. It was a simple hug actually, and yet it seemed like a lot more.

I don't know what I'm trying to say, or maybe I do. Maybe I feel the best as a soul when I feel the most bewildered, and nothing bewilders me more than motherhood. I don't know what I'm doing is what I'm thinking half the time. I mean, being a mom is the most humbling thing I've ever been. And yet it's the thing I'm most proud of, you know? And motherhood is so often what I'm most fulfilled by . . . like tonight, when Lizzie spotted me walking down the street toward her from the distance, and I screamed, "LIZZIE!!" and she came running toward me and almost knocked me over with one of her massive hugs.

This makes all the frustrations, worries, and even endless conversations, feel more like consecrations.

Which means: these many seemingly tiny moments feel like holy ones, when I'm with my kid.

Almost as holy as the moments I spend talking with God. That's the point of what I was trying to say. Love is all that really matters. God loving us, us loving our sons and daughters, me loving my Lizzie, her loving me, both of us loving God with all the love He gives us—it's all about the love. That's what we take Home with us.

Bills? We leave them back here.

Chapter 44

Okay, okay. I got too many balls up in the air again. This is my management style, or my way of living. Get excited. Grab project—ball 1. Feel sympathetic—take on someone's case—ball 2—to help them. Hear about something fascinating—ball 3— follow it all the way until I hear about something else that's also amazing. Take detour. Keep collecting more balls, until I get to balls 42 through 43.

Forget about the 43rd ball in the air. Pause. Look for it. And then ducked out of the way when the 1st through 42nd balls come flying through the air. Gravity. That's my problem! I'm warring against gravity. And balls.

The 44th ball is usually God-related. Actually, most of the balls are usually God-related. Like one morning I was researching angels in the New Testament for this book I was writing. It's called *Michael's Hand,* and it's about Archangel Michael. I've always had this idea about avenging angels, and I'd pictured Michael doing some serious avenging . . . particularly of people who hurt kids. When I told one of my friends all about my idea, she'd written me back and "cautioned me" to make sure I knew what I was really talking about before I went creating stories about heaven and God and angels. *What do you really know, Sally?*

Well, she didn't say that; I did. But she did tell me that Michael didn't go killing people in the New Testament except for in Revelations and *Sally that sounds a little severe*. That got me all spooked, like maybe angels had given up wrath not so much for Lent or whatever but for all time, so I went searching for an example of Michael getting medieval on someone.

Then I called poor William at work when I found proof that angels still avenged in Acts 12.

"Guess what?"

"Sally, stop screaming."

"Oh, right. I found out that Michael struck Herod down and turned him into worms," I said.

"Oh." I could hear him typing in the background.

"William? Stop typing."

"So the angel kicked Herod's ass," he said.

"Yep. It was wild. And he turned into worms once he died. So now I can go write the story."

"That's great," he said. "Want me to pick up milk at the store?"

"Michael killing Herod and turning him into worms is so much more interesting than your store list."

"Bye. Love you lots," he said.

At about that moment, Lizzie came up behind me. She'd heard the last of the phone call and she wanted to hear more about avenging angels.

"Mom, when else have angels done some avenging?"

"Oh," I said, "There's Sodom and Gomorrah. Angels took out two cities."

"Why?"

"All the people were evil, just pure evil. It was an ongoing problem after the Great Wars. When Lucifer fell and took thirty-eight percent of the angels with him, the fallen angels trained demons and the demons and the dark angels would go and take over human bodies."

"So can one angel destroy an entire city?"

Brett came up behind Lizzie and he nodded solemnly. "An archangel, like Michael, can," he said.

Lizzie's eyes got wide. "Really?"

"Yeah," I said. "Single raising of his arm could take out 70,000 men, maybe more."

"Wow, that's awesome!"

I put a hand on Lizzie's shoulder. "Well, sweetie, it's just something that's gotta get done sometimes. And while it certainly is awe-inspiring, it's probably not the best part of an archangel's job." I fixed my eyes on Brett. "Wrath is only used as an absolute last resort."

Brett took his arm, raised it, and then let it extend outward from his body. "Yeah, you fling fire bolts like this," he said. "Then boom, those demons go crying home to their mamas."

"Ooooh," Lizzie said, "Awesome, I wanna be able to do that."

"Well, here's the thing," I said, "No archangel enjoys flinging fire bolts or using wrath, not when it's for real and not just practice."

Lizzie was still smiling. Now she nodded towards Brett. "He knows how to use it?"

"Well, Brett's practiced it in heaven."

"It's fun, I'm good at it," he said.

"But you're not as powerful as Raziel," Lizzie said.

"You two," I said, now in a sterner voice. "Listen to me. Wrath isn't fun. It's necessary sometimes, but it's not fun and it's not the sort of thing angels ever do for fun. They do it only when they're following orders, carrying out God's will. God hates giving that order—the one to use wrath. He doesn't like using wrath. It hurts him. He loves all his children. He only uses it when there's absolutely no other choice. And keep in mind that the whole reason we're supposed to turn the other cheek is because there's someone who, as a final resort, will stop evil. It's God's job to fight. Not ours. He takes on that burden, that sacrifice, for all of us so that we don't have to and He does it because He loves us that much."

Lizzie got a sober look on her face. "Is that what you're writing about in *Michael's Hand*? Is he coming down to help people who've been raped and murdered? Or is he coming down to save souls? To help and take care of people?"

"A little bit of both, I think. I want to show how God feels about the sex trade. I want to show Michael helping good people stop it, and some of what Michael will be doing will be helping those who've been raped and abused, who've been taken in by the sex trade—"

"—What's the sex trade again?" Lizzie asked.

"It's when bad people take kids your age, maybe a little older, take them away from home, get them addicted to drugs, and sell their bodies for sex."

Lizzie made a horrified face. "But that's awful. That will never happen to me, I never will talk to strangers."

I glanced over at Brett and got the distinct feeling he was practicing flinging fireballs in his head. Then I said, "Well, most kids aren't taken by strangers. Most abuse, and this includes the sex trade, occurs when relatives or close family friends hurt kids."

"Like you were hurt?"

"Yes," I said. "The thing is . . . it's an evil that is just as much a scourge as slavery—it's modern day slavery and it's gotta stop. So if God's gotta send Archangel Michael down here to destroy all the people who are doing this to kids as well as all the places that sell films made by enslaved children, then so be it."

"Is that what's gonna happen in *Michael's Hand*, Mom?"

I sighed and nodded. As usual, talking about the slave trade was hitting a little close to home. Kids who are abused grow into being adults like me and talking about it always hurt a little, just as it hurt knowing that there were millions of children I couldn't help, no matter how much I spoke out or how many books I wrote.

"Is it true that anyone who rapes kids is gonna get soul death?"

"Yeah, Lizzie, it's true. If you think about it, some souls are past saving. There's nothing anyone can do to help those souls. The best thing for them, the best thing for everyone, the most humane thing actually . . . is to put that soul to rest." I motioned toward Lizzie and she leaned into me for a hug. She knew I was done talking about these things, at least for the moment.

Chapter 45

Later that week, it was Friday, and I was annoyed. Bad Doggy would not stop barking. The way my brain is wired, noises get to me, particularly shrill ones over which I have no control. I kept saying I had to do something but I had no idea what to do. I wanted to ring Aaron and Esmerelda's doorbell. I wanted to ask. Ask nicely. But for some reason I just couldn't. As ridiculous as it sounds, I was scared. I was scared of making waves, of making trouble, of bothering them, of giving them some reason to hate me.

I guess I'm like a lot of abused kids in that way. It's not usually in my nature to walk around with my head always bowed, afraid of getting in trouble so to speak. Only in this lifetime have I been this frightened, this afraid of getting in trouble. Granted, this barking had been going on for months and still I hadn't said a word of it to my neighbors. Worse, I was always complaining about it to William. And I was probably taking it out some on the kids.

Like this morning . . . it started out the way my mornings usually did. I got frustrated at breakfast and it was probably because of the barking, but I told all three children they were eating too loudly. And I felt kind of bad as soon as I said it, and when I said it, I didn't say it in the nicest of tones.

Then William came around the corner. Now, I adore my husband. I never get tired of seeing his gorgeous smiling face . . .

except when we're both working from home. William was home sick but he was kind of working and when he works, he paces. And when he paces he violates my air space, or at least that's the crazy thing I was thinking as he circled the downstairs area for the thirty-seventh time in ten minutes.

"Gah!" I growled, "You're in my air space."

"Air space?" William gave me a funny look.

"And the dadgummed dog won't stop barking."

"Does she usually bark like this? I gotta say," William whistled, "The barking's been going on since I got up."

I looked out the window at the back yard and out of the corner of my eye, I could see Bad Doggy standing forlornly at the deck door. I wanted to reach inside myself and find a way to feel love, to send love even . . . Bad Doggy's way, but I was so annoyed and frustrated and it was all I could do not to open the back door and yell at her.

"Are you feeling any better?" I said to William. "How's your fever?" I was trying to show at least some concern for him. I've never been particularly good at nursing William when he's sick. One time he was throwing up in the bathroom. This was just after we'd gotten married. The sound of it was making me feel like I was gonna throw up too and (I know this is awful) but I called into him, "Please shut the door" while he was vomiting. Later, he said my new nickname was gonna be Florence effing Nightingale. I laughed of course because I deserved being teased.

So now I was trying.

"I'm fine," he said.

"You sure?"

"Yeah, why?"

I reached my hand out to the window sill and took hold of a golf ball. "Because I found this in the garbage disposal," I said.

"You found a golf ball in the garbage disposal?" William's eyes were bugging out a little.

"Yeah."

"And you think that has something to do with me being sick?"

"Yeah, of course it does," I said.

William folded his arms across his chest. "Okay," he said. "This is gonna be good. What's your theory?"

"Occam's Razor."

"Oh come on, that says the easiest, simplest explanation is usually the correct one and that doesn't apply in this case."

"Yes it does," I said.

"How?"

"Because if you were not home, lulling me into the mistaken belief that someone's got a handle on things downstairs, I'd have realized Brett was throwing golf balls into the garbage disposal." I realized about halfway through this explanation that it was ridiculous, but I was really mad about something else. This was somehow connected to the tilting tower of laundry William kept stepping over in the laundry room.

"So it's my fault that—Brett? Did you put the golf ball in the sink?"

Brett smiled at William and shrugged.

"Is that a yes?"

"What golf ball?"

William took the golf ball and held it up in the air. It was a red golf ball.

"I've never seen a red golf ball," I murmured.

"Sally, stop, I'm trying to find out who put it in the garbage disposal," William said.

"But what I want to know is why we even have a golf ball in the house," I said. "And I'm thinking that's your doing too."

"Oh? How?"

"Because your dad plays golf. So my theory is he gave it to Brett." I paused. William's dad would never give Brett a golf ball. Every time Brett touched one of Papa Will's golf balls, something in the house got broken. "Okay, wait. Brett took the golf ball while Papa Will was supposed to be watching Brett."

"But we haven't seen my parents in days."

"True. But it's still your fault."

"Oh, it's my fault," William said. "Okay, that's how your playing Occam's Razor eh? All faults lead back to William?"

"Yes," I said.

"Hey Lizzie," William said. "Who brought the golf ball into the house?"

"Well," Lizzie said, "Actually, I saw Aaron playing fetch with Bad Doggy yesterday and they were using red golf balls."

"Oh my God," I said. "Now I know this is a message from God."

"Wow," William said, "Kind of like Moses' Burning Bush."

I smiled at William and held the golf ball up in the air. "Yep. He's telling me how to talk to Aaron and Esmerelda. I can return their golf ball and mention something politely about the barking."

A few minutes later, I was standing outside, beneath the maple in our front lawn. Like most of the stuff we own, the maple tree's been busted up pretty good. One time, lightning struck it and knocked off about half of it—hit one of the main branches a few feet above where it connected to the central part of the tree. When it first happened, it looked like we had half a maple. Since then the maple's grown and it's not quite as misshapen, but it slants a bit toward our home. It's still a great tree. It gives us shade when we play catch in the front yard.

I walked over and knocked on Bad Doggy's front door. No one answered. I realized, after peeking into the garage, that neither their minivan nor their sedan was parked. So they were gone and they'd left Bad Doggy outside, all alone, unattended. I cut through their yard and leaned over the gate. Bad Doggy came running toward me and started to whine a little; then, a lot.

"Hey, wanna play catch?" I held up the golf ball and Bad Doggy wagged her tail.

I tossed the ball over the wooden post and Bad Doggy ran and retrieved it. She brought it back to me, still wagging her tail. I threw it again . . . and again, and many more times. Finally, Bad Doggy seemed to be shaking her head at me. Then she laid down, still wagging her tail, but not as fast. I sighed and went back inside.

"How'd it go?" Lizzie asked me.

"Oh, they weren't home."

"So what were you doing all that time?"

William was pacing again and I almost told him not to touch the computer. It was ridiculous, as if I was feeling possessive about the computer downstairs as well as the main one I use upstairs. I was a mess. No doubt about it.

When I didn't answer Lizzie right away, she repeated, "What were you doing?"

"Oh, nothing," I said.

"Where's the golf ball?"

I shrugged and smiled, kind of like Brett did earlier.

"Mom! You didn't, did you?"

"Didn't what?"

"Give it to Bad Doggy? Were you talking to her?"

I shrugged and smiled again. Then I said, "You'd best be getting your shoes on, get on out the door, okay?"

"Love you Mom," Lizzie said.

"Love you too," I said.

"Even if you're playing with Bad Doggy." Lizzie grinned at me and I didn't say a word in response. Just smiled.

Chapter 46

It was soccer time. As I told a friend later, "William was so kind to me. He brought me soccer in bed. I promptly spilled it on the white sheets. And I ain't telling either, just to see what he'll say later."

My friend wrote back, "You spilled soccer in bed? Come again?"

I giggled and wrote back, "Okay. Correction. My husband brought me coffee, not soccer, in bed. That's not even a funny malapropism. It's just weird. But I'm weird, so this isn't atypical. But I'm still leaving the stain there, just to see what William will say."

My friend wrote back, "LOL, that's twisted, you're leaving the coffee stain in bed? Is it at least on your side?"

"No, his side," I wrote back. "Kinda like how he eats popcorn on my side of the bed."

"Yeah, that's pretty antisocial . . ." she replied. "Have fun at soccer."

But here's the thing about soccer, and this came to me a little while later, as we were standing there watching Lizzie watch the soccer ball. We collectively, as the Brookmans, suck at soccer. It grieves me.

Later, I was standing alone, trying to watch the game and ignore the other moms. It's a bit of an issue, not a huge one, just a little one, because Tunie's on the team and she's best friends with one of the coaches' daughters. And all or at least most of the moms are friends. They train for triathlons together and a few of them sell things at those parties that I'm sure most of you often get invited to but I don't get those invitations anymore.

I ignore the other moms, not in a rude way or anything; we just don't have too much to talk about. It doesn't bother me most of the time except for when I get a little lonely, which is hardly never, because William's always there next to me. He and I both like to watch the game. Not talk. Watch.

So anyway, these two moms were talking about another mom who wasn't there. It's hard to give complete justice to how Shannon's mom was talking. I was only hearing every other word or so but every word I did hear was ugly. You see, Shannon's mom was going off on a mutual friend of theirs, one who had stopped by the field to exchange hugs and promises to call later to set up a coffee date. And as soon as this friend (who I know as Elise's mom) had waved and headed off to her car, then Shannon's mom went on a bit of a monologue about Elise's mom—who, if you remember, she'd just hugged and promised to call for a coffee date.

Shannon was saying that Elise's mom was something something and then I heard a whole paragraph.

"She posts too much on Facebook and runs too slow and doesn't wear the best of the latest season's fashion. She also didn't buy anything at the jewelry party and now she's wanting everyone to buy her Tupperware, can you believe that? And she's even accepting credit cards which is pretty canny, bet her business is gonna go so well she won't even be able to run the half marathon she signed up for, not that she should've been signing up for that, not with her shin splints and bad knees, but not everyone can run eight-minute miles anymore now can they?"

Shannon's mom just kept going and going, and then she got fixated on going through her own personal bests at pretty much any distance you wanna choose, and she also was going over her swimming instructor and how of all the people taking the class, guess who had the most natural of strokes? And there was something else . . . there was this long list of additional wrongs by Elise's mom.

I didn't wanna hear it, so I moved away from Shannon's mom, trying to be unobtrusive about it. And that's when I bumped into one of Esmerelda's friends and she said hi to me, and I said hi, and then she and this other mom started bugging me about Lizzie's hair.

"Doesn't her hair bother her?" Riley's mom squinted at me, her eyes narrow and her mouth sort of disapproving, or so I imagined.

"No."

"Isn't it harder for her to see?" Esmerelda had a hard look about her and I almost felt ridiculous.

"I don't know," I said. William was standing beside me, and he was smiling a little, because he doesn't care about our daughter's hair either. It's just a haircut. We've even let the boys grow long hair.

"And she won't wear it back in a pony tail? Not during games?"

I smirked. I shoved my hands in my grimy jeans. "Well, you know, she's living my dream. I always wanted to run one of my marathons not only balls to the wall, but hair flying, nay billowing—and you know what?" I interrupted myself. "One of my fans says I shouldn't say billowing."

One of the dads, who is not married to one of the moms, and that was an embarrassing conversation, or bit of a conversation, issued a sly smile. "Fan said that?"

I returned his smile and sighed dramatically. "And I 'splained to that fan that it also sort of pillowed, as it billowed, wildly really, quite wildly behind me, when I ran." I stopped, and giggled. I was talking too fast and this bit, this stray conversation every bit as out of control really as my daughter's auburn hair. And how perfect, how ironic . . . "So I wanted to run an entire marathon with my hair just like Lizzie's, free, wild—"

"—Billowing."

I stopped and grinned at the man who was a dad not married to the soccer mom, and nodded. "Yes, billowing behind me." I waved my hand and waited for the mom who was not married to the dad to catch up to where we were in the conversation. "But by the second mile or so, the bit of stray hair—"

"—Billowing."

"Yes, billowing stray hair, well, it wasn't as wild and free and sexy like I was hoping."

I grinned. Esmerelda gave me an appraising stare and then took her friend by the arm and said something about making sure they got their photo albums synced. Then they walked away but it didn't seem mean, not really. I was okay and at peace with Esmerelda. She wasn't trying to make me feel bad. She really just couldn't understand why Lizzie liked to have her hair billow. And I didn't care if she understood. I also didn't feel like telling anymore funny stories.

It was funny, at least for me, but suddenly I didn't feel like sharing my moment of billowing running hair with anyone. Because inside I was smiling too much about all the things we had that mattered and none of those things had to do with me or my hair or how anyone saw me or saw my daughter. And even telling a funny story and having a bunch of people laughing at the stories I had to tell . . . wasn't so important anymore.

Chapter 47

I walked over to the bed and curled up beside William, and reached over to mess with his iPad. Well, to mess with the game he was playing on his iPad, and he told me to cut that out, and I told him he was acting like the eldest child again, and he told me I was acting like the youngest child again . . . so he held the iPad out of my reach and I rolled over on top of him and reached for it.

Lizzie walked into the room wearing pink leopard pajamas. "Oh my God, you guys," Lizzie said. "Are you two enacting some Klingon mating game?"

William whispered in my ear, "We have just witnessed the unholy confluence of family life and too much Star Trek."

I ran my hands under William's shirt and stroked his back. "Yep. How did you know?"

She rolled her eyes at us. "Can I have ice cream?"

"Yes."

"No."

She looked up from her Nexus and put her hand on her hip. "Really? You two can't agree on anything can you?"

"Woo," William said. "Scary words from the girl wearing pink leopard pajamas, which, by the way, give me an ice cream headache."

"But you can't eat ice cream," I said.

"Thanks, Sally, for reminding me." William said.

"Um, Mom, I'm gonna go get that ice cream, K?"

I glared at William and said to Lizzie, "K."

When she left the room, I said, "So you still don't think I'm a prophet, do you?"

William studied his iPad and didn't answer.

"Come on, I know you hear me," I said.

"I don't know."

"What do you mean, 'I don't know?' What does that mean anyway? Do you think I'm crazy? Sheesh, sometimes I think I'm crazy. The stuff I hear is kind of out there, you know?"

"I don't think you're crazy. And the fact you wonder if you are is pretty solid proof you're not crazy."

I nodded. "Yeah, I don't feel crazy. But if I'm not crazy and you're not sure if I'm a prophet, then what do you think I am? Making stuff up? Hearing from Lucifer? What?"

"I think you have a good message. I like how you're spreading God's word." William spoke carefully, picking his words as if ripping rose buds off a thorny bush.

"But how do you know it's God's word? And how do you know I'm listening, I'm hearing Him?"

"I think you're sharing God's message. I think your message is a good message," William said. He looked me in the eye and I contemplated all the things I wanted him to say. But most of all I wanted him to love me . . . and he already did. So what I was really wanting was for him to hug me. So I curled into him and nestled my head on his shoulder and he set his iPad aside and held me close.

•••

After William went to sleep, I took a walk around the block, and after about five minutes, I knew I wasn't alone. I knew it because I was thinking about how William didn't believe me, and then I saw oysters and the image of a sign that said, "Not Oyster Season."

As soon as I visualized this, I chuckled and said, "Is that you God? I haven't thought about oysters in years."

"Yes, it is I," He said.

"You're here next to me?"

"No, I'm talking to you from Home. You were asking how you could persuade William to believe you, and I heard you."

I dodged an acorn that was lodged into one of the sidewalk cracks and glanced up at the night sky. A full moon hung overhead and lit the late night street. "Well, what do you mean about the oysters? They're out of season? I haven't eaten an oyster in years, that's crazy, I really like oysters."

God laughed and said, "I like them too, but we're not talking about what you should eat for dinner. I wanted you to understand that you cannot reach everyone, and that includes William."

A feeling of sadness gripped me, and I nodded with my eyes on the ground. It hurt to think that I couldn't reach William, or that he wouldn't believe me, not ever, no matter what I said.

"Listen, Sally. You can only fish for oysters certain months of the year. You can only harvest them when they're in season. Some oysters will never be in season because they're sick or ill; others are too young to fish or harvest, so don't waste your time fishing for him Sally."

"But he's gonna be around for a lot longer isn't he?" I gulped and thought about Lizzie's dream. And then I was almost in tears.

"Sally, Sally, it's okay, do not be sad. He may be around for a lot longer, but he should really get his heart looked at. Even if he is going to be around, it's about time for you to start your mission, really start it, and you can't really be an effective prophet if you're wasting all your time and energy trying to reach someone like William. He's not open to your teachings, and he's not open to anything I tell him either."

"Wait, you're trying to talk to him?"

"Yes, he doesn't listen." I could visualize God shaking His head and a look of mild annoyance crossed his face. "I've tried, but he doesn't think that I'm speaking to him unless I do something drastic and miraculous, and that's just not the way I usually work. I shouldn't have to do a miracle every time I try to talk to a human, but too many humans, William included, expect it, so they don't listen when I do talk to them."

"Must be frustrating." I paused and carefully stepped over the lid of a driveway. Then I said, "How hard would it be for you to move the moon a little, say, or shine a light on where I'm walking, if I was making you do a miracle to prove you were talking to me?'"

"Are you asking me to move the moon, Sally?" God was laughing.

I smiled too and said, "No, no, I'm just curious. Can you do it easily?"

"Well, no, it's not an easy miracle to move the moon, not at all. It's not like I could snap my fingers and tell the moon to shift backwards. Everything works in symphony, the moon, the earth, the sun, and we control those things at their core, so to shift the moon, I'd have to go to its core or to earth's core, and it could cause damage to disturb the patterns, not to mention unnecessarily scare seven billion people . . ." God slowed down and sent me images of crowds rushing into city squares, and then He sent an image of the moon drifting to and fro across the night's sky, and I giggled, and I could tell He was smiling.

"Well, I like miracles, God," I said.

"So do I," He said.

"Do I have to do miracles for people to believe me?"

"Well, most prophets don't do miracles, Sally. They listen and share the messages I give them, and it's up to each soul to listen or not listen to what the prophet shares."

"So I don't have to do miracles? But what about being part angel or whatever?"

"Or whatever?" God's voice sharpened. "I've told you, so has Stevie, that you're part angel, are you doubting it, Sally?"

I hopped over the driveway and glimpsed the lights overlaying the string of suburbs that stretched from fifteen miles southwest to where I lived and sighed. "Well, I wish I felt more like an angel, I dunno, I thought it would give me special powers or something."

"You're looking at it the wrong way. As if I have to prove something, or you need to prove something to other people to prove that I'm talking to you."

"Ugh," I said, "But it's hard to prove anything if I'm not doing miracles, why can't I?"

"You're living in a shell, that limits what you can do, it's not the same when you're floating around as a soul. That's how we do miracles, as souls outside our bodies. Take the typical story of a guardian angel saving a human being who's crossing a street and about to get run over by a bus—no one sees the angel, but they see the body magically move several feet out of harm's way."

"So the angel is invisible, but he's there, and he's able to move the body or do that miracle, and because we don't see it, we don't want to believe it?" I paused again at the street corner and scuffed some dirt that was on the curb. "But we see the effects of what was done, so we infer the truth, we infer that a force acted on the human body, so that is a real miracle, I bet they happen everyday, right?"

"Right. Think of all the times people die on an operating table. They always give credit to the surgeons or the doctors, but do you really think we're not helping? Do you really think doctors do all the miracles that are done in hospitals?"

I thought about it for a minute and sighed. "It sure would be easier if I could heal people, then people would believe me," I said.

"You need to stop worrying about whether people will believe you. That's not your concern. You don't need to worry about whether the oysters see you fishing. You just need to go out and fish."

"Oh God, you're talking in metaphors again, you're saying I should be a fisher just like Jesus was? But I'm not Jesus! I can't do what he did!" I chuckled and threw my hands up in mock protest. "I got no bread to feed people!"

"There are different types of bread, just like there's different types of fish, right?" God sent me images of at least five different types of bread, and I smiled.

"I like baguettes best," I said.

"Rolls are good too," God said.

I smiled, and He said one more thing. "I love you Sally, just keep fishing."

"I love you too, I'll try to catch some good oysters," I said.

Chapter 48

"Are you finished your showers?" William's voice sailed forth, melodic, pleasant.

"No!" Lizzie was howling, or yowling. "Brett's annoying me and he's in my bedroom in his underwear."

"Brett," William said, "Get out of Lizzie's room! Lizzie, get in the shower."

"I don't need one!" At this point she was yowling and it was as funny as it was maddening.

"Get in the shower. Brett, get out—"

"—He's annoying me!"

I gritted my teeth and tried not to scream from my study. I really wanted to go upstairs and grab my daughter by the hair and put her in the shower myself.

"Get in the shower." William didn't sound as harmonious and sweet. No longer like the honey butter he'd made earlier, for his fresh bread. "Your hair's a mess."

"I don't need a shower!" More cat yowling-screeching fighting noises ensued.

"GET IN THE SHOWER!!!!" screamed everyone else in the house.

As we waited on Lizzie to stop yowling, which is exactly what cats do when they don't wanna shower, William started laughing.

"Oh I forgot to tell you," he said, "I had a moment earlier that encompassed the personality of all three children."

"Yeah?"

"Yes. We were driving out to the store and there was all this gravel where I was taking a left turn. So I launched the truck into a power slide and then we almost flew into the intersection. Lizzie was like, 'Daa—addd.' and I'm pretty sure she rolled her eyes. Junior kind of whimpered. And Brett laughed and went, 'Whew! Drive it like you stole it baby!'" That of course was what William said whenever one of us drove fast and wild.

"He didn't."

"Sure did."

"That really does capture them," I said.

"Yep."

"Earlier today, after identifying several sinking freight ships, Brett cried out, 'look, there's a bird walking on water and it has no head!'"

"Yep, sounds like Brett," William said.

Just then, a ding popped up on my computer. I crossed the room to check on it, and found a note from Mrs. Funzip, and this time, it was good news.

Hi Ms. Brookman,

I just wanted to let you know that Lizzie wrote an essay that I ended up passing along to Mrs. Lawrence, in Gifted & Talented, and she wants to read it to the class. I am enclosing Mrs. Lawrence's comments for you to read. She thinks Lizzie is quite gifted.

Sincerely,

Jan Funzip

I smiled to myself and read the attached file.

Hi Jan:

Thank you so much for sending this lovely essay. It is quite remarkable.

I think we should consider nominating Lizzie Brookman for the advanced academic program. I was quite surprised at how lyrical and beautiful the composition was. I think Lizzie should consider submitting it for a writing contest.

If it's okay with her parents, I would in fact send it along. Would you please cc them on this email?

Yours truly,

Emma Lawrence

•••

Our River

The river has been there for a while now. I don't know how long. What I do know is that all of our memories lie there. It was just a river. A polluted river, really. We discovered the beautiful river in 2007. We argued over names, we threw rocks. It was a hot year, by any standards. My little brother Brett and I were playing Tag one day, and I didn't want to lose.

I ran down the side of our house, avoiding the thorny rosebushes that screamed with their colors of pain and joy, all rolled up into one. Streaked with pink and red, they told a story. They told a story of my mother's hands, spreading the dirt over the plants, giving them life. My hands, bleeding after ripping one out to give to her. The sting of hydrogen peroxide. My brother Junior's hands, pruning and watering. My whole family's hands.

It was a hot and humid summer, the kind you hear about in the fifth Harry Potter book. Well, without the Dursleys. The grass glowed with dew, and the sun pounded out, with its loathsome fists, all rage and hate. I knew that I didn't want to get caught. I wanted to finish my two hours of playing with him and go inside to read. So I went down our hill, through the green ferns, and turned left. Then? Then I saw it. There was an old moldy bridge. The bridge was streaked with green and brown wood. To me, it was an adventure. To some parents, it was a safety concern.

I stomped on the bridge and I heard a creaking sound. I smiled. I HAD to do that again. I checked my curiosity and continued onward. Later, of course. I smiled at the thought of what I was doing, thinking of the knights and fair damsels in *Ivanhoe*. I wanted to be like a knight, I suppose. Nah, a ninja is cooler. I started to think about that, and I started to think about killing people with swords, and I almost walked past the river. I turned back to ask Brett if he wanted to play Ninjas, but as soon as I turned back, Brett, and Junior collided with me.

"Why did you go," Junior panted, "Brett came to my room and told me that you disappeared, so I helped find you!"

" Let's play Ninjas!" I said excitedly, " I call being the Red Ninja!"

"But," said Junior, " Where do we play it?"

Brett pointed. "Down there!"

I smirked and looked at the river. It was PERFECT! I said to Brett and Junior, "Race ya," and pelted down the side. I managed to forget that there was water. The cold water chopped my ankles and absorbed my pink and white sneakers. I wasn't cold, though. I was a bit annoyed, but I forgot about all that in about five seconds. When the boys saw that I wasn't complaining, they followed me.

Wow, I thought. The river had this smell and feeling, a feeling difficult to describe. Here, you forgot about all your troubles. In future years, when we found oil in the river, it was as if losing a baby. We had started something. We just didn't know what.

Brett looked at me with a smirk and waited for me to figure out how to get on a rock and cross the stream. Later, this rock became us. That rock was there for our feet, it seemed. We did other things on it, of course. When we had that heavy snow, that rock was our resting place before we continued to skate and name the "rinks". Now, I had never seen this rock before. It was triangular, a piece of granite. There was dirt imbedded in the rock, as if many weary travelers once stopped there, washing their shoes and faces, and shaking their traveling cloaks out. Then they left, the dust swirling and dropping and weaving. The dust had a story, too. It had swirled from one place to another, seeing the world. Brett thought that some pirates had stopped here and deposited their gold, never again finding it. Junior thought... well, Junior just wanted to get going and see the river so he could finish his science experiments.

We walked through the river, and then stopped. There was a huge pool. We could easily cross it, but, to us, it signified an ending point. Brett raced to a peninsula that bordered off the marshlands. The marshlands were very peculiar. There was a huge tree that had monstrous roots, indeed so monstrous that they formed steps.

Immediately I imagined the river an ocean, and I saw the pirate's ship, and I saw the pirate and his men burying booty in the inlet under the tree under the cover of night, whispering coordinates. I saw him tearing out his beard, yelling in frustration at the sight of the river now narrow, as he came back thirty years later to get his gold. "Lizzie?" Brett tapped my shoulder, " We get this island, and Junior gets that one!"

I glanced at where Junior was standing proudly. There was a fallen log right next to him, our means of getting to the next part of the river. It was a beautiful log, and we used it for about ten more years. Then we had that Frankenstorm, and the log was covered by a hailstorm of sticks and branches. "But what if we need to reach the other side?" I asked Junior with a smirk at how smart I sounded.

"We have to share our territory," Junior said, "But if you want to do something other than cross, you have to get my express permission, or, if I'm not here, you have to keep a record on the sand, where the water won't wash it away."

Brett and I nodded in agreement. This made the most sense. Secretly, I wondered if we should make a blood pact, like I heard about in *Huckleberry Finn*. But no matter. I looked down to hide my sudden urge to giggle. Below me were rocks. Small rocks, white and rose, blue and gold. I picked one up and rolled it between my fingers. It was a smooth, cold rock, white and crystal. My brothers looked on in amazement, and smiled mischievously.

We giggled and shrieked, we threw sand, we threw rocks. Ninjas were forgotten. We felt a new feeling. A feeling of joy. We felt nature. When we got back in the house, we were soaking wet and covered in dark brown mud. We made a promise that day. A promise to always come back there. And that promise? That promise was fulfilled.

We have moved on now. That river stays in Burke, and I sure hope that little kids come there and scream and play. I sure hope that the oil goes away. The river shall always be in my heart, and I know that, all though the oil may destroy it, it will always be there. However polluted, however destroyed, that river is and will always be Our River.

•••

I sniffled and wiped my eyes after reading the story, but I was confused about something. Why did Lizzie think we were gonna move away? I got up, and glanced over at William, but he was asleep, so I went and knocked on Lizzie's door.

"Mom? Is that you?" Lizzie sounded excited, and then her door swung open. "Yay! You're coming in for a late night talk!" Lizzie's eyes sparkled.

I grinned at her and shut the door behind me. "I am, yeah, hey, I just got a note from Ms. Funzip."

Lizzie started to frown, so I held up my hand. "Wait," I said. "It was actually a nice note. She sent me a copy of *The River*—"

"—Oh," she said, "Did you like it?"

"I loved it! And so did Mrs. Lawrence. She thinks you should submit it to some contests."

"Oh, oh." Lizzie was beaming.

I moved over to Lizzie's bed and perched on the back corner. With my knees pulled up to my chest, I leaned against the wall and closed my eyes for a second to enjoy the moment. While my eyes were still shut, I felt the bed jiggle as Lizzie climbed on it, and then she rested her head on my shoulder.

I took one arm and wrapped it around her.

"Mmm, this is nice," she murmured.

"It is." I rubbed her shoulder and felt the soft cotton of her nightgown beneath my fingers. "Hey, I loved that you wrote about the land, about the environment. What made you pick that topic? Was it because you talked about Earth Day at school?"

Lizzie shrugged and then shook her head. "No, it wasn't that."

"What got you thinking about it?"

"Well, in part because of Earth Day actually, because we picked up trash all morning last year." Lizzie reflected for a moment and added, "Well. I wasn't thinking of that time we picked up trash though. I remembered the time in the middle of winter that you took us for a walk and started counting all the McDonalds' wrappers and 7-11 cups that were lodged in the river, and we came back home, grabbed the old stroller, and took some bags, and we filled them with trash, you told us that the river was sad, remember?"

"Oh, gosh, I did tell you that, didn't I?" I chuckled and added, "My hands got sticky and then they froze over, remember?"

"Eww, so did mine."

We were quiet for a moment.

"So that's why you wrote about the river? You said there was a different reason too?"

"Yeah." Lizzie was being unusually circumspect.

"Gonna tell me?"

"Well you told me not to be harsh about Tunie." Lizzie paused and her forehead knit into horizontal lines.

"Yeah, well, just tell me what happened. It's okay, I'm asking."

"I dunno, it sounds stupid now, but for her writing prompt, she wanted to write about getting a brand new car for her sixteenth birthday, a shiny red one, and she went on and on about it, and her friends were talking about all the stuff they wanted, and then they talked about how when they all have cars they can go to 7-11 and get Slurpies whenever they want to, and it hit me. They would probably throw their cups out the window, maybe that's wrong of me to think so, but I've seen Tunie toss gum wrappers on the ground, so why not paper cups?"

"Ew, I'm sorry, that's awful."

"I know, Mom, it's why my river's ruined, because people don't think, and they just want more and more stuff, but they don't want to take care of what we were given, of what we all are supposed to share."

"Wow, Lizzie, that's kinda beautiful, the way you're thinking."

"Really?" Lizzie's eyes got wide, and she giggled.

"Yep." I hugged her one more time, and then moved as if to get up, but then I remembered my other question. "Um, Lizzie, in the story, you said we had moved away from the river. What's that about?"

"I was dreaming the other night, well, not exactly dreaming, it was that moment before you fall asleep, and an angel appeared."

"An angel? What did they look like?"

Her cheeks rose and her eyes glowed with warmth. "He was very pretty! Dark hair. Ringlets. And he had wings, lots of feathers."

"Wow! What color?"

"Pale yellow and blue," she said.

"Sounds like Gabriel!"

"Mmm, I think that's right. He talked to me for a little bit, and then he showed me where we were gonna live, he said we wouldn't live here much longer. Two or three years, then we'd move west. He was very nice, and he told me I should look after you."

"Why is that?"

Lizzie patted my shoulder. "Well, I'm not sure I heard this right, but I think Dad won't be with us?"

"Huh," I said.

"Well, yeah," she said, "But maybe I didn't hear it right." Lizzie waved her hand and watched the shadow it made on the wall. "Do you think you'll remarry if Dad dies?"

"Huh?"

"Well, when Gabriel told me about our new house, I think I saw another man there."

I chuckled and said, "Never thought about it."

"Well," Lizzie said, "The thing is we were happy, that's all I remember, that, and I was writing too, and I saw us working together on a book, it made me happy, I want to be just like you."

"Awww. You keep working, you'll be a wonderful writer."

"You think?" Lizzie wasn't getting tired; if anything, she was revved up and energized from our talk.

I was tired though. With a yawn, I stood up and stretched. "Yeah, you'll be great, it's just work, and it's listening, just like artists draw what they see, writers put down what they hear."

"I can do that," she said. "But are you sure I'll be good?"

"I am," I said. "But you need to keep telling yourself you're going to be a great writer, that's one of the most important things you can do. You can say affirmations, or mantras, like, 'I am going to be a great writer,' or, 'I'm doing God's work, I will do it well.'" I yawned again and gave Lizzie a bleary-eyed stare. "Remind me to teach you about mantras and affirmations tomorrow, I gotta go to bed."

Lizzie nodded and then frowned a little. "Aww, you're going to bed? I love our talks."

"Yeah, I'm sleepy, I love them too my girl."

"Can you take me to the lake tomorrow?"

"Sure, night sweets."

"Night, Mommy."

"Night Lizzie, I love you."

Lizzie clasped me into a big hug and whispered, "I love you Mommy."

Scorecard

Several boundaries drawn,
Several boundaries blown.
One batch brownies baked;
One batch brownies they ate.
Seven showers. One bar soap,
Lost. One deal declined.
One card moved to green.
One letter left unsent.
One man scoring.
One old friendship resumed.
One new friendship made.
"Just say hi, tell her she's pretty.
"It worked for Dad.
"Right, Mom?"

Chapter 49

Lizzie and I were walking around Burke Lake together. William and Junior and Brett were racing Pinewood Derby cars for Cub Scouts. Lizzie and I agreed we weren't going to watch the patriarchy race kid's cars down a track. Lizzie was all over the patriarchy bit and I had too much of a headache to brave the crowd and the noise, especially since William was MC'g the whole thing and William's really loud and when he's loud he makes everyone else loud too.

It was a cold day in February and the trail was muddy. Lizzie and I kept bumping into one another and I grabbed her several times to help her through the muddiest patches. She was annoyed by the mud and that made me just wanna splash in it more, and each time I did that, she wrinkled her nose at me and tried to look all arch and angry, which just made us both laugh.

At the turn point, she said, "I don't see why anyone would run a half. If you're gonna do it, do the whole marathon."

I put my hands behind me to stretch the kink out of my trapezius muscle, and tried not to smile. It wasn't good to encourage this sort of thinking . . . but man, I so agreed with her. *Oh heck with it.* "I gotta agree with you," I laughed. "Halves are boring. If you're gonna do anything let it be a whole marathon. The entire 26.2, baby!"

We both laughed, and I thought about all the times Lizzie had asked me how many times around a track each distance represented. Lizzie in particular never got tired of these calculations, which is a definite sign that she might end up being a marathoner when she gets old. I also thought, and this with a bit of regret, that my marathoner days are mostly likely over, which means I won't be running em with Lizzie . . . unless she asks, and I'm a sucker. *Stop that now*.

"I don't think there's anything wrong with an eight-year old and a twelve-year old running a marathon, you know what I mean mom? But everyone else was saying there is."

"Everyone else where when?"

"It was in this Scholastic News article. Everyone was saying it was bad for the girls and it was gonna hurt them, and people were just going on and on about it, you know?"

I nodded and thought about it some. I wouldn't have minded if my daughter wanted to run a marathon, not if she really wanted to do it . . . it would be pretty near impossible to get a kid to run that far if the kid wasn't really motivated to run was what I was thinking. I thought hard about what to say and while I was doing that, I asked, "Did they interview any doctors and get an actual medical opinion?"

"Well, they got a sentence from one doctor who said there could be long-term damage; well, possibly but he wasn't sure."

"Exactly," I said. "He wasn't sure, nor was there any reason to be sure, and for goodness sakes think of all the worse things kids could be doing with themselves, you know?"

"Yeah, like drinking lots or using drugs . . ."

I smiled at the frozen lake to my left. We were out walking; often, we'd been out running here. And yet on a gorgeous day, albeit cold one, the park was almost deserted.

"Yep," I said. "Or the kids could do nothing and have diabetes, or be really unhealthy in general because they don't exercise. But folks are going to attack kids who are actually accomplishing something, eh? And you know what else? If those kids were just running a less ambitious distance, like a 5k or even a 10K (not that there's anything wrong with that, it's great) no one would blink. They'd think to themselves, 'Oh, okay, I could do that, sure, this is great, it's cute, isn't it lovely my kid is doing something, just not something too unusual' because so many people don't like anything that anyone does that's too unusual or too great or too far outside the average or expected or mean or average, right? And if it's not comfortable, if it's too great, too much, even heroic, and certainly not racing blasted cars down a ramp or not even racing them, watching a leader push a button as two cars barrel down a ramp, and certainly not rec league soccer or any of a number of other things that anyone else does, then everyone goes on judging the person who does more or just does different than everyone else. And what's that?"

"Judging?"

"Yes," I said, waving my hand, "It's judging. It's jealous and it's judging and it's condemning something for being great, and who's to say that running long distances hurts those girls? Who's to say? There isn't any study, any real proof it hurts a kid. So it's different. It's way different. But folks spend all this energy criticizing and what good is that? It's just as bad mind you when I make fun of cars going down a ramp. That's no good, no good at all of me. Like everyone else, I fall into the habit of criticizing, of judging, of condemning what I judge and it's not good. We gotta stop, we humans, we gotta stop thinking like that because it's not good for us and it's not good for the people we're judging. Not good, no, not good at all."

"Is that maybe a mantra, Mom? 'Judging is jealous?' Is that what you meant last night by a mantra?"

I nodded and took a deep breath. The cold air felt refreshing, and so did Lizzie's question. "Yeah, a mantra is a simple, easy to repeat statement of belief that we can repeat many, many times a day. That would maybe be a good mantra, but maybe even a better one would come straight from the scripture, like, 'Judge not, so ye be not judged."

"Oh, I like that! Did Jesus say that?"

"Yep, he sure did," I said.

We were quiet for a moment. The wind blew a little and caught my attention because it was blowing leaves across the icy lake surface. I gestured at the ice. "Oh! And look! It's icier in the middle of the lake, and the water's moving on the edges. I've never seen that before."

Lizzie nodded and looked past me. She was on the outside, where I'd motioned she belonged so that she'd stay drier. "Wonder why?"

"It's science and I don't do science," I said. "We'll have to ask dad."

She stopped and smiled at me. "When you get to talking like that, you're all passionate and fired up and you sound like . . . you sound like a leader of society, like a top thinker."

I dragged my eyes away from the ice and the lake water. "Of course I do. I'm a freaking prophet."

Lizzie laughed really hard, and so did I. "Oh my God, mom, the language."

I grinned. "It's true. I wrote the Gospel of Mark. I'm Jesus's son now daughter. Oh hey, let's go look at the lake."

"Oh no, you'll get hypothermia."

"Will not."

"Besides, you said God told you not to go on the ice."

"That was two days ago. He's not saying anything now."

"No no, you are too crazy."

"It's a good idea. Hey, what would happen if I threw the keys out on the ice. Think they'd sink?"

"You better not do that," she said, and she was gasping and we were both laughing, and we kept laughing as we headed back to the parking lot.

Chapter 50

I picked up the phone and dialed William's work number and then remembered he was on his way home, so I hung up real quick and dialed his cell.

"Hey cutie," he said, really happy sounding.

"I just got done sending Ms. Funzip an email after Lizzie came home crying because she's not listening to her assignments and writing what she's supposed to; and, I got off the phone with Ms. Topolator because Junior got 16 out of 30 on his math test and he only took 15 minutes to complete it when everyone else took an hour and a half and he only showed his work on two of the questions."

"Wait, didn't Ms. Funzip send a nice note a few days ago?"

"Yeah, but this note wasn't playing, and then I got a call from Junior's teacher." I sighed and glared at the back window. Bad Doggy was running circles in the yard, yipping at leaves, and Sandy's collie had joined in, and the whole thing was a symphony of yip yaps that was making it hard for me to hear myself think. "So it's been a day."

"How did that call go? And how was the email?"

"Well, um, I answered the email in my own way."

"Oh no."

"It's great. Lizzie said it was great."

"Great?"

"Well, passionate."

"Oh no," William said. "And how did the call go?"

"With Ms. Topo-whatever? Not so good. I told her Junior was bored and he needed harder work and it wasn't his fault he had a 103 degree fever when he took last year's SOLs and I also told her he's gotta retake the test during recess and show all of this work and she said fine and I said he had better say yes ma'am and that was definitely the only thing we agreed on, but I didn't call her stupid not exactly."

"Oh wow. But guess what?"

William hit the garage door but he didn't stop talking on his cell. I watched his car cruise into the driveway and opened the garage door to stare at him as he walked toward me. I got distracted by our *poor student issues* because William looked nice and he distracts me that way . . .

He nuzzled up against me in the laundry room and he whispered *I missed you* in my ear. Brett zoomed around the corner in a head to toe hamster costume and William put a hand on Brett's head. "What a handsome hamster."

Brett squirmed and then made a hamster face, with both hands up in the air and curved downward, as if he had hamster hands. "I'm a hamster," he said again.

"—And he didn't get a note, an email, or a phone call home today, so I'm thinking he's a happy hamster," I said.

William tucked his suit jacket under his arm and we both smiled at Brett.

"Okay," he said.

"Yep," I said.

"You wanna show me the email you sent?"

"What, don't trust me?"

William nodded. "Exactly right."

"But I was lovely," I said, and then waved my hand and headed upstairs to our room. "Come on. You can read it," I said.

Hi there,

I'm writing to ask for your help! We have been working on preparing for our writing SOL in March. I've noticed w/ Lizzie's writing she has good ideas, but she's not using her plan or considering her audience. Depending on the prompt, she can misinterpret it and become off topic. Her writing is too chatty for these types of prompts. I've tried to explain to her a many times the importance of sticking to the prompt and writing for the audience of a teacher. When we write creatively or in a journal her writing is wonderful. I'm not trying to squash her creativeness, but unfortunately knowing what to write when is an important life skill.

Could you please talk with her for me? I think if she hears it from others it will help her better understand. We are providing her w/ some extra teacher support on Thursday's during FOCUS J

If you have any suggestions, please let me know!

Thanks for your help!

Ms. Funzip

•••

Ms. Funzip:

Ugh. Well, she came home crying. I can't remember the last time that happened. I gave her the standard "write to a 5th grade prompt and forget you're a very talented writer while obeying orders" lecture and gave her lots of hugs and told her this didn't mean she wouldn't take after me and be a well-known author, etc. I told her she just needed to get through fifth grade.

Right now, and for awhile now, she's been feeling misunderstood and unvalued and I went through the same thing in 5th grade, and I keep trying to tell her that, but she's not getting it. She needs some love and to be taught more with the recognition that she will be as good as her mom and she is writing at a very high level.

She is not thinking of the x and o's; she truly doesn't care about dotting I's and crossing T's and she really doesn't care what grade she gets. I cared about all those things and I got really good grades, so I can tell you that you won't get through to her via normal channels. But if you can persuade her to write according to 9th grade standards (and still pass the 5th grade SOLs) maybe you'll have a chance. I'm not sure.

But I am thinking we can only reach her by using that zany brilliant creativity of hers, and that's gonna have to start with you believing in her talent (trust me, please, on just this one thing—she is going to be a heckuva of a writer when she grows up) and teaching her up as if she's already on the way to that. I bet if you teach her like that, she will discover the seed of it but if you (if we) don't water that seed, it's gonna shrivel up, not blossom, not bloom, and even worse, she will feel the want of the nourishment.

Feed her. Give her harder books. Give her problems to solve . . . indulge her passion. Let her write about saints and angels and God and Mary Magdalene and Jesus . . . let her fly and maybe if she flies, she can land the plane and get better results on the more earthly pursuits. Meanwhile, she needs strong positive feedback on the stuff she does well, even if it's not what the question asked for or within the lines. As in, "You took a creative approach to this question. It wasn't the question I asked. But let's look at what you could have improved on given the answer to the question you decided to answer . . ."

Gah. And good luck. She needs you to believe in her. That's step one, and even if you don't, pretend you do. For her sake ;)

Sally Brookman

William looked up at me. He didn't look mad, so I smiled tentatively. It was not a guilty oh no am I in trouble smile like the one Lizzie had given me when William walked through the laundry room and past the happy hamster. It was just a little bit . . . well, tentative. "What did you think? Was it nice?"

"Yes, it was nice." He pulled off his tie and walked into the changing room that also has a sink in it.

"It wasn't mean," I said.

"No, not mean."

"And . . ."

"Um, it was very . . . passionate," he said.

"And well written."

William pulled his shoes off and kissed me on the cheek. "Oh yes, phenomenal. Yes."

"Good," I said.

William sat on the edge of the bed and paid careful attention to removing his black work socks. With his eyes on his feet, he said, "Mind if I also send her an email? I gotta see her husband tonight at the leaders meeting."

"Oh my God, for the Cub Scouts? Again? I swear, you're not getting laid tonight. I hate those stupid meetings."

"Not getting laid, huh?" William came up to me and grabbed my hand.

I sighed and then tried to remember how much I hated Cub Scouts. So I glared at him, "What do you all need to meet so much for? All sitting around holding your balls and talking about stupid cars."

"Oh I can tell you, I sit right next to Joe and there's not a lot of ball holding going on," William said.

"Eww," I said.

William called Junior into our bedroom and tried to give him the Cub Scout lecture, or something like that, but we got stuck on him demanding to ask Junior "just one question," and that made Junior's lip quiver, so I tried to make it better, but before I did, William asked the question super-intensely did you do your best, and that made Junior cry. So I tried to make Junior feel better by saying, "Well, it's actually better that you didn't do your best because if 16 out of 30 was your best then you'd be kinda stupid right?" and that made Junior both cry and yell at me. So then William told Junior not to be disrespectful . . . and when all the crying and yelling was over, we tried to talk with Lizzie and that didn't go so well either.

While William was supposed to be writing his email to Ms. not-so-Funzip, I decided to try a more creative writing prompt with Lizzie. I grabbed a video from Godtube or something like that of two babies being born underwater. It's a poignant, life-affirming, adorable video. It's the kind of video that makes women and girls go "Oooooo" and "Cute" and "Awwwww."

Unfortunately, William saw the video. "Oh, wow, how weird," he said. "What are they doing? Trying to drown those poor kids?"

Lizzie laughed.

"Stop it," I said. "It's cute. Life is beautiful."

"See," William said, "That one's shoving his hand in the other's mouth. And the other baby's like, 'Get your hand out of my mouth, man."

Lizzie laughed, which was kind of killing my whole idea of getting her to write about what she saw on the video. "William! Get out of here. You're such a jerk, I mean, really?"

"Oh, okay," he said, and held his hands up. "Make sure you don't write, 'Oh man, I've been with that stinky guy for nine months and now I gotta be with him in this water? And it's cold! And I wanna stretch out; I've been stuck all smashed up next to this goofball and now we're all scrunched together again? And it's cold. And I want my mommy. And oh man buster, if you poop in that water one more time, I'm gonna slap you in the head again, yeah, just like this . . .'"

I was laughing by this point, and I shook my head and went outside to take a walk. I didn't even let Lizzie come with me. I made her do the writing prompt. And she, at least, did not write about pooping in the water.

Chapter 51

Junior had been quiet most of the week and I was a little worried about him. He's not the most rambunctious of children or anything like that, but he talks often and he's usually got a sunny disposition. Well, except for when Brett's bugging him . . . Junior will take a quite a lot (much more than most kids will take truth be told) but there's always a point when Brett knocks over one too many toys and Junior goes off and screams. At least, this is usually the case with Junior. But he'd not been saying much at all and I knew something was wrong.

I also knew better than to ask Junior why he'd been quiet. No, I went to Lizzie with it. She was painting her dolls' nails with actual paint when I tapped on her door, and she gave me a grin of sorts when I opened it.

"Oh, Mom," she gushed, "Thank God it's you not Dad. I'm not supposed to paint in my room, that's what he said the last time I did this."

"Probably didn't help that Brett painted his carpets with crayons," I said.

"Kind of turned out pretty though, didn't it?" Lizzie set one of her dolls down on top of a paper towel.

I crossed the room and kneeled in front of her makeshift salon. "You mean the rainbow look?" Brett's entire carpet was now a different color than the original beige—or perhaps I should say different colors, for pretty much each color in the Crayola 64-Pack Box had been used for decorative purposes.

Lizzie giggled. "Man, he got in trouble for that, didn't he?"

I inspected the nail polish on one of the dolls and chuckled. "Nah, not really."

"Cuz you sorta liked the rainbow look, didn't you Mom?"

"Yeah," I said, "I did. In fact, I told William we should paint our carpet, or draw all over it too."

"No, Mom, really?"

"Really."

"Mom, that's crazy." Lizzie grasped the torso of another one of her dolls and reached out for a jar of paint by my hand.

I handed her the white paint and said, "Good choice."

"Yes, your favorite color. So you don't mind the painting and all?"

"Nah," I said. "Truth be told, if I knew it wouldn't annoy your father so much, I'd tell you to draw on your walls."

Lizzie smiled and began painting the doll's fingertips. "Come on, really?"

"Well, I read this really neat article about a father, I think he taught quantum physics, and he told his son he could paint whatever he wanted on his walls, so the son painted all over and the son turned out to be this great visionary of sorts. So I always thought that when I grew up and had kids, I'd be like that. Just let the kids paint their rooms however they wanted."

"I mean, as you always say, we can't take these rooms with us when we go Home, right?"

"Exactly Lizzie. What matters is—"

"—Our souls, not our shells, and not what our shells live in, right Mom?" Lizzie gave me a self-satisfied little smile.

I smiled right back at her. "Yes. Good. You're listening."

"Course."

"Good. So Lizzie, speaking of listening, is something wrong with Junior? He's been—"

"—I know, awful quiet." Lizzie's forehead wrinkled a bit and I imagined how these temporary wrinkles would become permanent markers of her character as she aged. It was a thought that pleased me. For in some ways our shells, our exterior casing, do reflect the light and the love, the travails and what we learn from these experiences, on the walls that house our souls.

"Is something going on at school, love?"

"Well, I think he's trying very hard to turn the other cheek like you've been teaching us," she said. Her voice was gentle and careful, as if she were picking her way along a cliff's edge.

"Oh, no, is someone giving him a bit of trouble?"

"Yeah, you could say that," Lizzie said.

I was silent for a few moments. I was contemplating some of the lessons I've learned over this lifetime, over past lifetimes. I was also thinking of the time Junior, then a knight during medieval times, killed a court jester. Apparently the jester just wouldn't stop needling the shell Junior was living in. The jester just kept bothering, bugging, and even torturing Junior so eventually Junior put a sword through him.

I knew this story very well. I knew it was important that Junior learn to master his anger . . . I also knew that turning the other cheek sometimes had its limits.

"Thanks Lizzie, when I read to you later, it's mostly going to be for his benefit, okay? So please let him answer some of the questions, kay, love?"

"Ooooh, you're gonna read to us? What from?"

"Ahhh, I got the best story. It's from the Hindu Scriptures . . . but I think I will tell the story rather than read, actually. That way he's more likely to concentrate, don't you think?"

"Sure. Hey you wanna paint some?" Lizzie held up one of her dolls.

"Thanks for asking sweetie, but I gotta get some reading done," I said.

"For the book you're writing?"

"Yes."

"Is this one of the books God's giving you?"

"Mmm," I said. "Reckon he gives me all my best stuff. Okay, sweetie, thank you."

•••

The next morning, I was just about finished my morning coffee and I called the kids over. "Okay, come on y'all, let's talk some about turning the other cheek and how complicated that can be, all right?"

Junior sat down first. His soul was weary today. I could just tell. Brett was grasping hold of his newest favorite toy, which was a car carrier that got carried around most the day. "Brett," I said with a shake of my head, "No messing with toys when we talk about the Lord."

"Yes ma'am," he said. But he was still holding onto the car carrier.

"Brett." Lizzie gave her version of one of my head shakes and hers' was much sterner. "Put the toy away."

Brett put the car carrier on the crowded shelf behind the kitchen table, grabbed his fuzzy pillow, and curled into his chair. He sat closest to the edge of the table and I was at the head, in William's seat, because he's got the most comfortable chair. It's the only one in the kitchen that's made out of fabric and it's bigger than the regular wooden chairs.

"Thanks, love. Okay, so I wanted to start by talking about karma a little bit, and about how we are all different, and how that affects this whole turning the other cheek bit. You see, some of us still have some lessons to learn about standing up for ourselves. Some of us are maybe too meek, too mild, and maybe in past lives we didn't stand up for ourselves too much, maybe not enough. So take Lizzie, gentle soul that she is, eh?"

Junior made a face at Lizzie and mumbled, "Baby soul, still has lots to learn." Junior was the oldest soul in the family and he liked to remind Lizzie of this from time to time.

Lizzie sort of shrugged him off, so I made my rebuke gentle. "Her age is irrelevant. We were all young once." I paused and thought of Mark, which was one of my first lives, or pretty early for me at least. I did so much good and plenty of things bad that lifetime and it's okay.

"Lizzie," I said, "Remember my lifetime as Mark?"

"Yes."

"I did my best as we all do each lifetime," I said. "And I'm fond of that lifetime; I'm fond of the cocky, bratty, game for everything kid that Mark was, as well as the proud, hardworking, way too aggressive and occasionally impatient saint that grew into a man. I love Mark. I love what he was but can see all that he still had to become."

"Yeah," Lizzie said.

"Anyway, me and Iz were cute baby souls together," Brett offered. He was grinning at me, and I knew he was about to talk about fireballs.

"We sure were. And hey, Brett, you've got a mission that requires you to protect and defend . . . so there are times you simply cannot turn the other cheek. Like if someone touches your brother or sister, you're gonna jump on them, aren't you?"

"Yeah, I'm an angel, I'm here to protect and defend and kick demon ass," Brett said. He used a completely flat inflection and I didn't correct his language. Brett got a lot of latitude sometimes, especially when he was talking about the demons he and I could always see. It wasn't easy, seeing their burnt out carcasses, and we both tended to joke around about it, talk tough when we were scared, because that's just the way he could handle it.

"But take another soul, like old Junior here, maybe he's learned to stand up for himself. Maybe he's not afraid to speak out. Maybe his soul has learned some pretty hard lessons already. So maybe, when kids are giving him nonsense, maybe his soul needs a different way. Maybe it's best for him to say nothing. You guys with me so far? About how some of the values Jesus taught have to be applied differently depending on who you are and what lessons your soul's supposed to be learning?"

Brett cuddled with his pillow and sort of nodded. He knew the story wasn't for him. Lizzie gave an encouraging smile and I could tell she was thinking about some hurts from her last lifetime, when her beloved husband kept cheating on her and she didn't or couldn't do much about it. Then my eyes collided with Junior's and I thought about the court jester and it was all I could do not to ask him who was hurting him at school. But I didn't want to make him uncomfortable in front of the other kids.

So I continued, "It reminds me of this story I read in the Hindu Scriptures. There was this young monk studying with this great teacher named Ramakrishna. One day, the young monk was on a ferry and a bunch of the passengers were talking trash about Ramakrishna. They were saying some truly foul things. So the young monk jumped up, and he was a big guy. Just by moving his body this way and that, he was making the ferry start to tip over. So the passengers, they got scared and shut their mouths. But when the young monk got home and told Ramakrishna about it, Ramakrishna was very disappointed with him. He was like, 'My son, you must never use your power to attack others or to convince them of your goodness or your teacher's goodness.'

"So a few years later, another monk, a quiet, gentle, meek monk was on the same ferry and man, I don't know what's up with Ramakrishna. He must have been pretty popular, pretty interesting and controversial, because a bunch of the passengers were talking about him. They were saying he was too this, too that, you know? So the young monk saw all that, and you know what he did?"

I glanced around at the kids and Junior said, "Did he do nothing?"

"That's right," I said. "He did nothing. So he goes back home and tells Ramakrishna about it and he's expecting a 'good on you son' but no, he doesn't get that. Instead, Ramakrishna upbraids him. That means to yell. He's like, 'Son, you can't let folks go running all over the people you love. You must stand up for the honor of your teacher; you must not be weak and lazy in your faith.'"

"But that's not consistent," Lizzie said.

"Nope, sure isn't," Brett said.

"What do you think, Junior?"

Junior looked out the window and followed the light beam down to the end of the deck. "Maybe he could have said something, I dunno."

"Well, let me tell you one more story, okay? Maybe this will help you understand. Just remember, y'all, that each of our souls has different lessons to learn from all these lessons you're being taught. My soul, for example, is learning about nonresistance, about peace, about unity and helping all souls get Home. It's just where I'm at now." I paused. It wasn't where I was at when I walked and talked with Jesus. I didn't understand, not when I was a kid of sixteen, why my dad had to go away. All I really knew is I didn't want him to go so soon. I shook my head and let that thought go because it always made me sad, thinking of the last time Mark talked to his dad before the Crucifixion.

"Okay, there once was a snake. A great, great mean biting viper of a serpent, right? And one day a great teacher, kind of like Ramakrishna, who was sort of a Holy Man in India met this brooding beast of a snake. And lo! The teacher taught the snake all the great mysteries of the ancient faith and the greatest teaching of all, sure enough, was the same exact one that Jesus taught: turn the other cheek. Love your enemy. And the snake bowed before the great teacher and promised to reform his ways and stop biting.

"And he did! The snake became the kindest, gentlest creature in the village. He wouldn't harm any of the other creatures . . . and eventually, some of the bad boys of the village decided to torment the snake. They beat him with sticks and tormented him and he would just pray and ask God to forgive the little boys. He would love them and bless them . . . and after some time passed, this great serpent was dying from all the wounds the bad boys had inflicted upon him.

"That's when the great teacher returned to the village and sought out his old friend. When he found the snake he said, 'Good grief, what happened to you?' And the snake just sighed and said, 'Ah well, I get tired, I pray, I guess I forget to eat.' The great teacher was having none of this. He said, 'No no, that's impossible, think, think my friend, something else must have happened to make you like this.' And then the snake was like, 'Oh yes. Well, a few boys beat me up but,' and the snake stood up a little straighter for he was proud and was sure the great teacher would approve, so he said, 'And I of course did not bite them. I loved them and forgave them for they knew not what they were doing.'

"But the great teacher did not congratulate the snake. Instead, he said, 'How foolish you've been, old friend! I told you not to bite. I never told you not to hiss!'"

Junior clapped his hands and laughed. He laughed for quite a few moments. Lizzie and Brett were amused too, but no one laughed as hard as Junior.

When he was done laughing, I said, "Right, so the morale of the story here is twofold. One conclusion is that sometimes it's right to fight back, and we must live in the real world. We also are, all of us, somewhat differently situated, each of us with different lessons we need to learn in order to grow. But the biggest takeaway here is that if you must fight back, always start with the least force possible, remember to hiss first before you strike, never insert venom, or never be cruel even if you must attack. Does this make sense?"

"Yes," Junior said.

"All except for the venom bit," Lizzie said.

"Well. If you must, I don't know, defend yourself, do it without being cruel, do it with love in your heart, do it out of necessity but never ever be nasty in how you do it. Does that make sense, Lizzie?"

"Yes ma'am."

"Junior?"

"Yes ma'am. Can we go outside now?"

I smiled in his direction and nodded.

Chapter 52

There always comes a time when summer's been going on too long. This year it was August twelfth. We'd gotten record-breaking rainfall and I'd been working and running the kids back and forth to summer camps and that sort of thing. Sometimes I had a great attitude about it and God helped a lot with that. One time, when I was figuring out whether or not I was gonna sign Lizzie up for band camp, I asked God about it. As usual, He listened before He gave advice.

He said to me, "Well, you think you can do it without resenting it?"

I was driving when I was talking to Him. I got to a stoplight and watched the lights play off the streets and the windshield. It must have been raining that day too because I remember the glow and the colors all smearing together. I also remember my truthful response was, "I don't know. I don't wanna be driving her first thing in the morning, when we're both at our worst, and yelling at her because I'm feeling impatient." When I talk to God, I don't waste time trying to seem better than I am. I just tell it like it is, knowing I can't keep anything secret from Him anyway. It's easier this way . . . and He can help me more when I tell it straight.

He was quiet for a bit, and I was seeing images of me and Lizzie joking around and sort of talking in a . . . pleasant way in the morning. I chuckled. He was sending me those images. "Okay, yes, sometimes we get along just fine in the mornings, especially when I try harder to be kind."

"When she tries harder too, right?"

"Yeah," I said.

"But if you can't do it without resenting it you shouldn't and if you can't, you can't."

I turned left on the main road near our house and thought about it some more. Earlier, Lizzie had been chirping in the background, talking about her band teacher and how excited she was about going to band camp . . . "Please Mom can I go?"

"We'll see," I had said.

And now God was talking to me again. He was saying, "Don't say yes because you feel guilty about being a bad mom. That's not the way you wanna be making decisions."

I sighed. He was right about that too. I thought about how I always felt this pressure to be as good of a mom as the other soccer moms, but this wasn't fair. I wasn't a soccer mom, not really. I worked. But I wasn't a working mom. I mean, I'm none of that first. I don't belong to any label. I belong to God.

Yes, you sure do, love.

"Mmm, that's it, love. If I do it, it's gotta be out of love, and if I do it out of love, if I keep dipping into love when I'm frustrated, when I'm tired, when we're both crabby, so long as I keep reaching for you, for your love, for love . . . then I can drive her and not resent it . . ."

"Yes."

"So you're saying . . ."

"No, Sally. I'm not saying what you should do. Just if you do it know how to."

"With love."

"Yes."

So I had. I'd agreed to drive her to band camp and actually it had been wonderful. She'd been cheerful every single morning. So had I. And I'd taken the boys to the Scout Camp. And we'd all managed to pretty much get along throughout the summer. I worked every day from home, just like I did while they were at school. I took breaks of course. We went to places. Pool. Beach. Store. That sort of thing.

And I didn't spend too much time worrying about what the other moms were doing . . . or how much of it. Sure, I couldn't afford to send my kids to all the best camps. And sure, I couldn't spend all my time trucking the kids to as many activities as stay-at-home moms could. But just as I couldn't go judging those moms for what they did or didn't do, I couldn't go judging myself either. I was my kids' mom and I was doing the best I could . . . but I also was more than their mom. I was me. And I belonged to no one. No one but God.

All the same, the Twelfth was the nadir of our summer until we saw the rainbow, but I'm getting ahead of myself again.

First, there was the marble incident, the non-cleaning of rooms debacle, the seizing of the car carrier, the counter-seizure of the Barbies (after which I refuse to type Trademarked just, I don't know, on principle). Then there was the throwing of the deck flowers (think marriage ceremony with petals falling as said Barbie and Ken walk out of the "chapel" in the patio), the hacking into the Ethernet, the subsequent signal failure, the chemistry experiment gone awry in the kitchen. Well, that's a shortened list.

But by the time William's car pulled into the driveway, we were all mad at one another. Junior was screaming about a marble grazing his temple; in fact, Junior was shrieking in the middle of the yard at Brett, who'd hightailed it out of the house. His feet were tapping his butt he was running so fast to get out of Junior's reach. I was trying to keep my own voice down as I stood on the doorstep and summoned Junior back in the house.

Lizzie was standing right at my shoulder, bitterly explaining that Brett had taken a pocketknife (her pocketknife—no one would trust Brett with one of his own) to every single bar of soap in the bathroom. And then he'd gone onto Barbie's hair . . . lots of Barbies' heads of lustrous, ridiculous hair. And then he'd used duct tape and taped them all to the wall. That actually got a rise out of me.

"He did what?"

"Said it was a sculpture. Ode to Barbie. No, Ode to Barbies. And he said modern sculpture, so it's interpretative."

"Oh god, that's . . ." I tried not to giggle. I should have been suspicious when he asked me to buy a Barbie doll for him. A Barbie doll and duct tape had been his precise request. Because he was "tired of war."

"It's not funny, blast it."

"Lizzie—"

"—What? You're gonna punish me? Send me to my room, shut the door, lock it?" She rolled her eyes and crossed her arms over her body, and just then William ordered Junior to "Stop that ridiculous caterwauling and bring in the trash."

I lost my chance to say anything to Lizzie because Junior was still screeching.

"Trash? Trash? Argh, trash?" Junior sounded a lot like the infamous basketball star Allen Iverson when asked about "practice".

"Yes, it's your job, make it happen."

"Trash? Trash?" Junior was out of his mind with the concept.

"He's lost it today," I explained to William.

"Obviously. And Lizzie, did I hear you cussing at your Mom?"

"Yes you heard me cussing," she said. The tone she was using was not aggressive. It was one that was okay with me because it always preceded a very funny diatribe followed by a hug or an I love you. But William wasn't taking it the same way. He was about to tell her a few things.

"Lizzie, you had better not ever—"

"—She's been the only sane one here today, William. The one who's needing a serious talking to is actually Junior."

"Brett too," Lizzie said.

"Well, Brett's not been easy today either, but William," I said, "Junior either needs a spanking and I am not big enough to give him one or he needs some sort of one on one with you." I was getting angrier as I talked because Junior was still yelling outside. I nodded at Lizzie and she understood I wanted her to walk away. Then I continued telling William how upset I was and I was praying about a sentence into what I was saying because I was feeling so much anger.

"He's too big for me to physically restrain him William." Junior weighed almost a hundred pounds and I'm not much taller than five-two. I'm not nearly as strong as I used to be either.

Haven't lifted weights since the accident a few years back, so handling my eldest son was getting a bit more demanding. And in fact we hadn't spanked Junior or Brett in years. It made William too angry and we just didn't like doing it.

William's jaw was clenched and he nodded. "I'm so sorry they've been difficult, Cutie. He can't be yelling and carrying on like that." William hated when any of us made public scenes and Junior was now throwing the trashcan around and screaming about trash and about marbles and about Brett.

I could feel my temple throbbing. "It's killing me, they're killing me. I get no vacation. I mean, how would you feel if you were working at home all summer and had to put up with this nonsense?"

"It's terrible, I'm sorry Cutie. I'll talk to him. I don't want to spank him." William had a troubled look on his face so I counted to ten and stalked off. Sat in my rocking chair and prayed for peace.

Junior came into my room about a half-hour later and he approached me with a tentative expression. "I'm so sorry Mamma, I don't mean to make it hard for you to work." He kissed my cheek ever so sweetly and added, "I'll be better, I promise. I love you."

"Love you too," I said.

William came up behind Junior and I noted just how similar they were, both in temperament and in the way they looked. If the corner kids looked like they were clones of me, Junior appeared to be a copy of William.

"I explained to Junior how I had the same issues with my own temper, both as a boy and as a man," William said. He put a hand on Junior's shoulder and Junior gave him a look of total dedication and respect. Then William continued, "And I stopped acting like that when I asked myself a simple question. 'Is this how I want the world to see me? Is this the kind of man I want to be seen as?'"

"Mmm," I nodded. "I guess I ask a similar question of myself a lot. Like, 'Is this the type of soul I wanna be? Is this how I wanna serve Him?'"

"Yes," Junior said. He was basically agreeing to all he was hearing.

"Okay, I said, how about if we go exploring at Lake Royale?" Lake Royale is about three miles away from us, and the boys, William and I'd been there a few days ago. Lizzie had stayed home and Brett was determined to show her how pretty it was. And to pick flowers to make potions to "heal Mom's migraines."

Junior brightened up. It had finally stopped raining a couple of hours ago and the rain had taken the humidity and the heat away, so it was a perfect night for a hike. "Lake Royale?" He said. "Cool. It's beautiful there."

Brett was excited too. He was also happy that Junior wasn't trying to pummel him. He and Lizzie spent most the drive there concocting recipes for their healing potions. Earlier that morning, I'd helped them with their potions by pouring olive oil into a couple of their potion containers. I wasn't sure this was a good idea. I was envisioning bugs crawling all over Brett's bedroom . . . but I also liked the idea of what they were creating. Not magic potions. Healing potions. Loved it actually.

About fifteen minutes later, we were walking counterclockwise and an injured-looking runner stumbled towards us. Maybe it's because I busted my Achilles and can't run, but most runners had been looking injured to me as of late. "Trail's flooded," she said, and she staggered past us.

Brett grinned at the words, "trail's flooded" and he sprinted on ahead of us. William said, "We should probably turn," but I pretended I couldn't hear him and took after Brett. Sure enough, the trail was completely overtaken by water. In fact, there was no discernible path. And that's when a group of ducks came paddling down what once was the trail. They followed an opening between the trees and cut through the marshes and kept swimming through the reeds until they reached the actual body of lake water.

After I walked for a few minutes in the thigh-deep water, I turned around and waited for William. "Hey, look, look at the ducks near the reeds," I said.

"Reeds?" Junior said. "What's that?"

"It's those tall yellowish plants," William explained. "They used those for writing back in the ancient days."

"Yep," I said, all excited and surging forward against the flow of muddy water. "And they dried up leather and turned it and other things into paper. In fact, we made some of it near the Dead Sea and also in Egypt. Oooh, look Lizzie, look at the ducks."

Lizzie was holding William's hand and she was also sort of leaning on Junior. Meanwhile, Junior was holding his shorts up with both hands. He and Lizzie were grinning, and Brett was bouncing around a few feet ahead of me and he was waving his hands and chattering about how deep the water was. William had removed his socks and shoes and was holding both above his head as he picked his way through the water. I groaned a little when I realized Lizzie was wearing her black combat boots. She'd ruined her last pair in the snow and the outlook for this pair was not good. I was wearing a pair of hiking boots that would never smell good again . . . but we were having a great time, so I didn't mind.

We kept on going through the deep water. The water was cool but not uncomfortable. A refreshing breeze blew in from the trees lining the trail. The sky was that extra clear blue that comes after a storm, with lots of puffy cumulus clouds looming above the treetops.

And then, from across the reeds that reminded me of old Israel came the biggest rainbow I'd ever seen. And it wasn't like most rainbows—it wasn't a mere blur of color, a smidge of green and a little bit of red and orange. This rainbow started out with a thick layer of dark purple on the bottom; in fact, there was a double-layer of purple. Then came a thick half-circle of green . . . and again, it was bright green, almost electric. The same was true for the yellow and the orange and the red . . . all the colors were extraordinarily bright and the lines were pure and thick. It was like the rainbows you draw in school, except it was much more exquisite, more lovely, more vibrant.

I could hear God humming in my ear now. Just a quiet and content hum really.

Thank you God.

You know, it's how I send you all love letters.

I know.

It's my love for you.

I know, I love it. I love you. It's beautiful.

Mmmm, he *transmitted. It is, and I am pleased with it. And you're pleased. I like that.*

You like when I thank you.

Yes.

"William," I called out, "Please take a picture of it. Isn't it grand?"

"What, the rainbow?"

"Yes," I said. "Look at all of that purple."

"It's got a lot of purple," he agreed. He pulled his phone out of his pocket and snapped a few images with one hand.

"I've never seen one like that," I said, and I was smiling.

He smiled back at me. "Never?"

It's a love letter.

"Never, this is the best I've seen."

Yes, a love letter.

Guess this means it's gonna get better.

Doesn't it always?

Chapter 53

Three days passed. Now it was Friday the fifteenth of August and it was perhaps the prettiest day of summer. The high was going to be 79 but in the morning it was almost chilly. The morning is when I take one of my walks and talks with God. Usually I go four or five miles and I walk at either Burke Lake or along the brook that runs behind our home.

Today, I walked the kids to the playground and the whole way, I was waiting for when it would get quiet and I could talk to Him alone. But Lizzie was talking to me the whole way and a few minutes from the playground she wondered, "Maybe I'll just walk with you today so we can talk."

It's funny as a mom. We want the best for our kids. We also want to be the best mom . . . and sometimes we forget to take care of our own needs somewhere in between making sure the ones we love have all they need. Which is to say I kind of wanted to walk alone so that I could be with God, but I also wanted to be with my Lizzie.

The other two kids made the decision for me. As soon as he heard Lizzie was coming with me, Junior announced that he wanted to come too, and as soon as Junior jumped off the swing, a reluctant Brett followed him. Brett's too young to go anywhere alone still and that includes the playground in our safe suburban neighborhood. It often strikes me that someone from our ancient past would find the way we protect our kids from possible kidnappings as downright strange. I think about this sort of thing a lot as I watch my kids play outside and almost every time they're outside, they're the only kids playing. I don't know where the other kids are but I know our neighborhood is full of them.

This morning was no exception. It was a glorious summer day and we had it all to ourselves, or at least we did until we hit the street. We were walking the Unknown Trail backwards, which means that we reached the main road, a four-lane highway, toward the beginning of the walk. As we were trudging uphill, Brett asked if Wyoming would be as crowded as Virginia was.

"Nope," Lizzie said, "Wyoming will be great. It's the least populous of all the states."

Off to our left, a tree with white blossoms stood beside a dogwood.

"Are we gonna have trees like that one?" Brett pointed toward the tree with white blossoms.

"Oooh," Lizzie said, "I want one like that, it's beautiful."

"Yeah, and with birds like that," Junior said.

"That's not Mom's 'Procedure Birds' is it?" Brett's voice was sharper than usual. There was a type of bird in our neighborhood that I'd named "lawbirds" because they screeched, "Procedure, procedure, procedure" all the time. They annoyed me in the spring especially.

"No," Junior said.

"Are they cardinals, the state bird of Virginia?"

"No, Brett," Lizzie said. "And meadow larks are the state bird of Wyoming."

"Ooh, those are lovely birds," I said.

Brett banged into me but not too hard. He was excited about the birds. "What are meadow larks like?"

"They sing," I said.

"Yep, they sing all the time," Lizzie said.

"And they're bright yellow with a 'V' on them, and black," I added.

"God created birds because he wanted something that looked like angels," Brett said. Then he grinned and clapped his hands. "God told me that."

I nodded. I'd heard the same story from God and it was a lovely one. God had been alone on a planet and he missed his angels so to amuse himself, he created birds that sang and soared through the clouds and settled on the treetops above him. It cheered Him up when he was lonely. This was one of my favorite stories that hadn't made it into the Bible. "Yep," I said, "Sounds like him."

"Man," Brett said, "Can't wait to get off this road." Brett put his hands over his ears for a moment and grimaced.

"It's hard to hear God when we're walking near all these cars, isn't it?" I put a hand on Brett's shoulder.

"But it won't be like this in Wyoming, will it?" Lizzie put her hand in the air as a big truck thundered past. "Wow," she said, "it feels like the truck's going to run into your hand until it gets past you."

"I can't wait to be on Israel," Brett said. "Off this planet, this tiny little ol' earth."

"Yeah, me too," I said.

"Wyoming's gonna be amazing, I can't wait to live there," Lizzie said.

"I know, imagine all the flowers we'll be able to collect there to make potions for Mom's store." Brett's voice was rising as the noise from the road rose and drowned out anything uttered in normal conversational tones.

"Yep," Junior said. "Godly Goods."

"There will be potions and Lizzie, you gotta start carving quartz so we can have bottles for the potions," Brett said.

"Can you carve quartz?" Junior was thinking about the shows we'd watched on the building of the pyramids. Again and again it had been demonstrated how the builders must have used diamond drill bits to cut the quartz and granite slabs of massive rocks.

"Great question, Junior," I said. "It's hard to carve quartz, no doubt about it, especially the crystal quartz, or the more precious quartz."

"Yeah," Brett said. "Cuz if you use diamond drill bits and too much energy, the sound resonance will destroy the rock."

"But it's hard to hand carve it isn't it Mom?" Lizzie asked.

"Yes, but it can be done—"

"—Or you can carve it with your mind," Brett said. "After all, your mind is your most precious tool."

We passed by an old farmhouse that was sitting on a hill off to the right. It made me think of one of Stevie's tattoos. She's got a dilapidated church tattoo. It symbolizes the state of religious life here on earth. "After all to be human means to sin," she explained. I thought of how we could rebuild that broken-down structure. The key was fixing each soul, as well as the minds that house those souls. I thought of the Native Americans and how they'd been guarding the skulls . . . and how the crystal in the skulls was said to have the power to heal our very souls.

"Yeah," I said, "Sure is. And did you know that's how the crystal skull said it had been constructed?" I'd been researching crystal skulls for a book I was writing and I'd been thinking about the ancient skulls all week.

"Yep," Brett said. "If I were in heaven, I could make one of those skulls in a day but it would take most humans years and years to carve them."

He was correct. I'd read estimates that the Aztecs had taken hundreds of years to carve one of the skulls. This wasn't right, though; at least not according to the skull itself. When a famous psychic in Canada talked to the skull, she channeled its response to the question of how and when were you made. Basically, the skull said it was 17,000 years old and had been created by thought. Sort of like how God spoke the world into being, advanced ancient souls had thought the skull into existence.

"Hey Mom," Junior said, "Guess what I wanna design?"

I reflected for a moment. Last time I'd checked, Junior had been learning how to code a game he'd titled, "Hamster World," so I figured it was something like a computer game. Before I could say anything, Lizzie piped up, "Yeah, I was thinking also that as much as you don't like videogames Mom, some people, it's the only way we can reach 'em, so what if we created a video game that would have humans learning and going through lifetimes and fighting demons and getting back Home and called it—"

"—Soul Life," Junior said. He glared at Lizzie and said, "Why you gotta be getting in my head and taking my ideas?"

"What?" Lizzie threw her hands up and the sun glinted off her auburn hair. She was wearing a grey t-shirt, camos and combat boots. She managed to carry it off and look feminine in a militaristic, longhaired sort of way. She was kind of like my warrior princess. "I mean, God gave it to me," she added.

"Well," he said, "Okay. So here's what we're gonna do. We'll make it so that there are different types of souls, like human, angel, hybrid, and you can choose what sort of soul you're gonna be."

"Oh hey, Junior," Lizzie said, "How about if the souls start off in heaven, and they get to learn the ropes and get to know their soul family first, then they maybe land in the mother's womb, and we could use that as a teaching opportunity, show how the baby develops in the womb, but not too long because that would be boring. And then we'd show the baby soul born into the light and as soon as they enter the light they forget who and what they are . . . and we could show how rebirth and all that works?"

"Right," Junior said.

I held out my hands and the kids grabbed hold so that we could cross Coffer Woods, which is a two-lane road that intersects Burke Lake Rd. It's one of the main roads that enters our neighborhood here in Northern Virginia. Once we crossed Coffer Woods, we came up to the VRE (Virginia Railway Express) Trail, which we had long ago named The Unknown Trail because we walked on it before the County had gone and paved over top of the dirt. The trail wound alongside a stream and the railroad that headed west, toward Manassas and then much farther out for the freight traffic.

"And each year could last like an hour so that the game's not boring. We can show the soul learning stuff, right?" Junior looked up at the sky and cried, "Wow, look at the moon!"

"Harvest moon," Brett said. "That's why it's so close and so big."

"What kind of learning experiences?" Lizzie was still thinking about Soul Life. "And will you have demons fighting the souls?"

"Yeah," Junior said. "There'll be a flash on the bottom of the screen, and it will say, 'Warning, Demon Alert' or something like that."

"And if they've been possessed, it will say, 'You've been taken' intoned in a deep voice."

"And the sound can't be turned down, so it will be extra scary," Lizzie said.

"No, I don't wanna scare people," Junior said.

"Good, I said. "Do you maybe wanna teach them how to fight back against the demons?"

"Yeah," Lizzie said, "Like give them choices of prayer, light, as in shining it all over, or asking an angel for help."

"Oh I like that Lizzie," I said.

"And maybe they can choose how much demonic interaction they want to have when they're choosing which soul to incarnate as," Junior said.

"Yes," Lizzie said. "So if they're a jumper or a hybrid—"

"—They get tons of demons coming at them," Brett said, and he threw his hands up in the air and pretended he was flinging fireballs at them.

I chuckled at Brett, who had switched subjects and was talking about which flowers would make the best migraine potions, and then I said to Junior, "I love the idea, sweetie. I like that you wanna use your talents to design a game that will teach people about God."

"And make us rich," Brett said.

"Yeah, Mom, you can sell the videogame in our Godly Goods store, and we can even build our own sort of device for the game rather than give the game to Xbox."

"First of all, it's probably best to use the existing devices. It's more economically efficient to use a system that a lot of people already own," I said. "And second, we don't design things so that we can get rich. We should never care about the fruits of our labors."

"I know," Brett and Junior said at the same time.

"I know," Lizzie said. "Use your talents to help others and trust God will provide, right?"

I took a careful look at Lizzie's wild auburn hair, now streaming behind her in the late morning sun, and for a moment it was as if I were beholding her as a grown woman. As I said, "Yes, you got it right," I put my arm on her shoulder and she put her arm around my waist, and we kept walking and talking about Soul Life.

Chapter 54

We were watching a show about the Great Sphinx and I was arguing with the show the whole time. "That archeologist is full of it."

"I agree."

"I mean, how does he know Khafu or whatever built it? And why do they keep playing that stupid music? Khafu is bull."

"I wish they'd stop playing that music and showing the same rock graphic melding out of thin air."

"The what?"

William pointed at the screen. It looked like a checkerboard moving up and down . . . oh never mind. It was actually cool, like taking dominoes out of a box upside down, but the dominoes move up, not down . . . or upward at an angle. Or something like that. I wasn't so good at spatial relations. Just take my word for it.

As I studied the rock graphics and thought *I like Dominoes and I like rocks too*, another scientist appeared on the screen. It was a woman from the USA. I don't wanna say what state she's from because everyone who lives in her state will hate me if I say which state because sometimes we get like that. We identify ourselves based on where we're from and divide ourselves into groups based on wherever or whoever we think we belong with . . . sort of like the way we wave flags and wear scarves at soccer games or expensive jerseys at football games.

"That one is stupid too," I said. "Look, she's not wearing her seatbelt." I tapped William's shoulder. "You awake? Look at that. She's stupid. I am not listening to a scientist who doesn't wear her seatbelt."

"Hmmm. Maybe she's only going ten miles an hour and it's in the desert."

"Doesn't matter. She's still too stupid to wear her seatbelt. Disqualifies her. Oh, and she's from a crappy university and from a crappy state. Well, I assume she's from that crappy state because no one who's from out of state would bother to attend her university because it's crappy."

"Like Radford." William's always had it in for Radford. If you wanna make him really mad, say you think Radford University is really good. I think the first girl he dated went to Radford.

"Two strikes. Crappy university and she drives without her seatbelt. It's irresponsible. There could be kids watching this show."

"Thank God ours aren't," William said.

"Oh," I said, "And her hair pisses me off."

"Come on, she's in the desert."

"Okay. She gets a bad hair pass. But she still pisses me off." The professor with the bad hair drove past us again in her white Range Rover. "Look, William. She's going at least twenty-five miles an hour. Definitely no seatbelt, look."

William grunted.

"William? Wake up. She's not wearing her seatbelt."

"Yeah," he said.

"And I swear if they say one more time that 'this proves this' or 'this proves that' I'm gonna have a fit, I mean, how do they know or not know?" I glared at another scientist who was saying there was no way any of the other theories could be right, *no way, nope*. "Absurd," I said.

"I agree," William said.

"Exactly," I said. "If you're not one hundred percent dead dog sure—"

"—I like that expression."

"You taught it to me." I paused and kissed his hand. "I just don't like when they say they're sure, like they act as if they have the full truth and they're arrogant about it, or when the narrator of this show opines that things must be exactly one way when there's no way he could really be sure he's speaking the truth . . ." I groaned and giggled because I wasn't making sense and I was sounding grouchy, so I tried something else. "But he has nice hair dontcha think?"

We both laughed.

"Or when the narrator says 'this proves' whatever," I continued. "Because until they're sure of something . . . William? You still awake?"

"Mmmm. Sort of. Come here, Cutie," he murmured.

• • •

Sometime after midnight, I tapped on William's shoulder. I wanted to tell William I was sorry for saying mean things about the female archeologist, but by the time William was sleepily mumbling, "Wuzzup," I had already gotten distracted by something else.

"Guess what?"

"Really?" William rubbed his eyes and then frowned at me. "Just tell me." William sighed. "Wake me up from a deep sleep and tell me."

I chuckled. I got excited like this and lo and behold, it was three AM? Then I turned back to William and said, "Okay, I just read that Robert Bauval says that the only hard science about or I mean behind or having to do with the Great Sphinx research is that of the guy who says the water caused erosion that dates it as built in at least 5,000 B.C., if not earlier. And he says the researchers who think Khafu built it 2,500 years later relied on conjecture alone, and as usual the establishment just wanted to reject the possibility that humans could have built stuff earlier than they once thought."

"Isn't Joseph that rogue archeologist?"

I put my head on my elbow. "He's not the rogue. The establishment is rogue. They have decided what they think is right and no matter what evidence is found to the contrary, they are going to reject it. It's like the Bible . . . the version of the Roman Catholic Church is the only accepted version and it's like the scene in Indiana Jones where all those boxes are stacked away and they're hiding all this neat stuff . . ." I leaned over and tapped on William's shoulder again. "You hear me?"

"No," he groaned, "I don't hear you."

Chapter 55

"Mom, why are we driving into DC again? Are we going to see Dad or are we going to a museum, or what exactly?" Lizzie was in the third row, but her voice carried even over the air-conditioning.

"We're going to the Air and Space museum," Brett said.

"No, Natural History, gonna see dinosaurs," Junior said.

"Ugh, we saw dinosaurs this spring, I want to go to the Library of Congress," Lizzie said. "Mom, don't you think the Library of Congress is best?"

"Um—"

"—Wait," Lizzie said, "Or did you say we were going to go to the Supreme Court?"

"Lizzie," Junior said, "She said we *might* go to the Supreme Court, *might* go to the Vietnam Memorial, *might* go to the World War Two Memorial, *might* go to Supreme Court, and each time she said that, you asked for the Library of Congress, Brett asked for the airplanes—"

"—And you asked for dinosaurs or art," Lizzie retorted. "We should go to the Library of Congress. That's the only place to go in DC. All the other places are tourist traps."

I glanced at the signs on I-395. If you went left, you got to the museums quicker; if you kept on I-395 and bore to the right, you got to the U.S. Supreme Court, and it occurred to me that the children couldn't agree on anything, so I would have to decide for us. I glanced over my right shoulder and then swung into the right lane.

"Airplanes?" Brett said in a hopeful tone.

"Books?" Lizzie said.

"Oh Mom, you said the museums were the other way, so have you actually chosen to go where you want to go?" Junior was smiling, almost in triumph, and I thought I understood why. I wasn't favoring any one child, and for once I was making up my mind.

Sure enough, Lizzie fired back, "Mom would never do that."

I laughed, and checked my mirrors. Cars surrounded us on all sides, and I needed to get to the right lane in order to make the exit for D Street. Once I negotiated an opening, I turned on my turn signal and scooted just ahead of a red taxi cab. He laid on the horn, and I held my hand up in protest.

"Mom," Lizzie repeated, "You wouldn't do that, right?"

"Do what? Take you to see something I have wanted to see for twenty years?" We got off the ramp, headed right, and then merged onto C Street. "And we're driving past the U.S. Capitol, look," I said. I pointed to the right, and the great dome appeared.

"Wow," Junior said. "It's taller than anything else down here."

"That's because they passed a law that no other building can be taller than the Capitol," Lizzie said.

"Yeah," I said, "Look, Brett, isn't the architecture beautiful?"

"Uh huh," Brett said. His voice was peppered with excitement.

"Look Mom, there's a sign for the Library of Congress," Lizzie said.

"Huh," I chuckled.

"We're not going to look at books," Brett said.

"Yeah," Junior said.

Lizzie groaned audibly.

We took a right on First Street, trailed around, hooked a left on Constitution, then took a quick left back on First. I scanned for parking, but the entire street was mobbed by people carrying signs. "Uh oh," I mumbled.

"It's a parade!" Brett said.

"Oooh, I like parades," Lizzie said. "Can we join it, Mom?"

I squinted into the sun and tried to find a parking garage, but I got distracted by the signs people were carrying. "Equal representation," read a few signs. "Pray for the Court," said another sign.

"Is it a parade, or a protest?" Junior pressed the button for his window, and Brett and Lizzie did the same.

"Junior, look at my phone, where does it say I can find parking?"

It took Junior a few moments to read what I had pulled up, and meanwhile, I parked in a loading zone and looked around and tried to figure out what was going on. About one hundred blacks had gathered on the sidewalk in front of the Court, and I remembered that protestors weren't allowed on the marble steps that were considered part of the Court's building. Almost all of the protestors wore dark suits, and most of them appeared to be middle-aged men.

"It says the closest parking is at Union Station," Junior said.

"Oh, sugar, that—

"—Look, Mom, they're pulling out," Brett said.

An SUV swung out of a space a few car-lengths from us, and I said, "Wooo! Lucky for us!" And I quickly parallel parked in the vacated space. "Okay, everyone put up your windows, and let's go look around, get out on the side closest to the curb." While the children tumbled out the passenger side door, I looked at the parking meter. "Ooooh, they left two hours on here," I said.

As I took in the scene, Junior read aloud from my phone:

The Supreme Court Building was designed by Cass Gilbert and built from 1931 to 1935. The Court first sat in the building on Monday, October 7, 1935. The building, majestic in size and rich in ornamentation, serves as both home to the Court and the manifest symbol of its importance as a coequal, independent branch of government. Architectural information describing many of the building's sculptural elements may be obtained from the Visitor Desk on the ground floor.

Although the Supreme Court does not offer guided walking tours, visitors are encouraged to tour the building on their own and take advantage of a variety of educational programs including Courtroom Lectures, a visitors' film, and court-related exhibitions.

"Oh, what about the architecture?" Brett craned over Junior's shoulder, and Junior grumbled, "Just a second, let me click on the link."

Brett moved away from Junior and headed toward a stand of trees situated across the street from the Court. I told Junior to give me my phone and shoved it into my pocket. Then I corralled Lizzie and Junior and followed Brett. He paused in front of a short wall and gazed in the opposite direction, toward the crowd of people peacefully arranged in front of the eight marble colonnades, about a hundred feet from the steps that descended from the center of the Court. To each side extended two wings of the court, each rectangular, and these wings were about forty percent the height of the triangular portico that topped the colonnades. Statutes provided ornamental signature at the center, in front of the main hallway.

Once we reached Brett, we stood in the shade of the small trees and listened to a man speaking. From the polished and erudite tone of his voice, I judged that he was a member of the clergy. And after I heard a few sentences, I was sure of it.

And now, my brothers and sisters, we are gathered here to pray, to pray that our leader will be able to appoint an able representative to replace the deceased Justice, praying that at long last we will have more fair representation on this nation's highest court.

I turned and explained to the kids, "One of the nine Supreme Court justices died, and the President has to appoint a new one, and these folks are concerned that the next Justice will not represent their interests."

"Mom, can't the President just appoint whoever he wants?"

"Well, Lizzie, he can, but then the Senate gets to confirm it, so whoever he appoints generally has to appear before the Senate and answer a lot of questions."

"Why are all the protestors black?"

"Well, I think they probably organized it at their church, um—"

"—Yes ma'am, they called it at our church, and we rented a few buses and came down here this morning." A well-dressed black man had appeared at my elbow.

"Oh hello, my name's Sally, these are my kids, they're asking me to explain what's going on, and I'm afraid I'm not completely schooled on the issue," I said.

"My name's Robert," the man said. He blinked behind a pair of wire frame glasses.

I shook his hand, and then he said, "I'm one of the assistants to Pastor Kellings, we're from Baltimore, and we are trying to support the Court by leading prayer today."

"Oh, I'm from Baltimore too, how neat," I said.

"Ah, from the city?"

I shook my head. "Baltimore County, born and raised."

He nodded genially.

"Does this have to do with the death of the Supreme Court justice?"

"Yes ma'am," Robert said. "We want to support the President. He might only have a year left, but he should be able to appoint a justice to fill the vacancy. So we are praying that he can use his constitutional power to nominate a justice that has the professional merit and ideological attitude that represents people of races, gender and faith."

"I've never explained to my kids why this is important, Robert," I said. "We're still learning about the branches of government and . . ."

Before I could finish my sentence, a hubbub ensued about twenty yards away from us. A woman appeared holding a bullhorn, and beside her stood more than fifty people, almost all of whom were holding signs, ranging from, "Black Lives Matter," to, "Stop Killing Blacks," to "No More Dead Children." The woman with the bullhorn wore a black tank top and cargo shorts, and she was waving her arm and chanting, "No More Killing," and a crowd was answering, "Black Lives Matter."

I glanced around and made sure all three of my children were within arm's length, but I didn't see Brett. As I scanned the audience, I thought to look for the statues, and sure enough, Brett was heading towards the steps that led to the colonnades. "'Scuse

me, Robert, Lizzie, Junior, come quick, Brett's heading that way,"
I snapped, and I held out my hands and waited until I felt sweaty
palms in each hand. Then I strode through the crowd of well-
dressed clergy, and I wondered as I walked why the chanting was
getting louder if anything, rather than quieter. After all, I was
moving away from the lady with the bullhorn . . . or so I thought.

And that's when I spotted about ten police officers, each
holding batons, and they were moving toward the same spot I was
moving towards.

"Hurry, Lizzie, Junior," I urged.

And then just behind me I heard the loudest chanting I had
heard as of yet, and with a groan, I realized that the mob was
following me to the stairs. Where I for one knew they weren't
allowed to be. And that's when Robert also appeared at my elbow,
and then a cop was about ten feet away from me, and closing fast.

"Officer, officer, please help me," I gasped.

The officer paused and then pivoted so that he was between me
and the lady with the bullhorn.

"Sir, that's my son, he's about to climb on the statue, his
name's Brett."

Several emotions went through the officer's eyes. He looked at
me, he looked at Robert, he looked at the lady with the bullhorn,
and then he must have seen the sincere panic in my eyes, because
he put his hand on his hip and spoke into his microphone. "The
lady right next to me, says that's her son about to climb on the
statue, name is Brett, I'm going to hold her right here, can you grab
him?"

A voice crackled on his speaker. "Yes, hold her there, I see
him."

I craned but couldn't see over the officer's head. "Don't worry,
Ma'am, just stand here next to me," he said.

I nodded and held back tears.

Then Robert bumped into me, but he had turned to face the
lady with the bullhorn, who was advancing with a crowd that was
swelling by the minute. Several of the crowd members were
shouting, "Burn it," and the lady said into the bullhorn, "We must
be heard, take it to the highest Court, they will hear us."

"Please ma'am," Robert said, "It's the law, you can't go on the
steps."

"That's a false law, we should be heard, we must be heard, they're killing our sons, why are you taking their side?" The lady looked very angry, and I checked on Lizzie and Junior, and their eyes were wide. Lizzie was whispering, "I can see Brett, the cop has him," and Junior was whispering, "Are we gonna get in trouble?"

I brought them both closer in towards me, and then wrapped my arms around each one of their shoulders.

"I understand, I do, listen to me, we're here to protest, but some of you are about to get violent, and you gotta understand, these cops here are just doing their job, look, that cop over there is rescuing this woman's kid—"

"—That white kid? Would they rescue a black kid?" The woman got even more incensed, and she began to yell, "Treat blacks equally, we want access, let's hear it!"

The woman pushed forward, and Robert put out his hands and gently touched her shoulder once, and then let go.

"Please, please don't go on the steps, they will arrest you, and it could get violent, you don't want that."

The woman gave him a withering glare.

And that's about when nine different people walked up at once. The cop—with a hand on Brett. Five more cops, all with their hands on their holsters. And a news reporter accompanied by a videographer, and apparently he had the film rolling, but I didn't realize this at first. The funny thing is, I was so enthusiastic in thanking the cop for returning Brett, and then was trying so hard to explain to the kids what was happening, that I said an entire paragraph on film.

"Thank you so much, officers, thank you, thank you for bringing him back to me."

I clutched Brett close and then Lizzie asked, "Why are they yelling like that? Are they gonna hurt the cops? Is this a mob?"

"I don't know, not exactly, this isn't a mob, this is anger, and it's building up in these mommies, they worry every night about their sons coming home, I know what that feels like, but I don't feel it every day, they're scared, they're angry, but anger can control you if you don't control it, you gotta train your mind kids because if you don't one day those wolves are gonna need to eat."

Then I glanced up and saw one of the moms who had come from Baltimore. She was dressed in her Sunday best, and she was standing a few feet from Robert. She was holding her son to her, and he was exactly Brett's size. I looked at her with gratefulness and sorrow and I said aloud, "See that Mom? The one holding her son? She's holding him so tight, you see that? I bet this is how she feels each day, the way I feel holding Brett." Then I brought Brett even closer and kissed him on the head.

The camera panned away from me then. I never even realized I was being filmed.

Not until later.

Because that clip got played on the nightly news and Will's mother saw it . . . and called Will. So I had a little explaining to do later. But first, we took our time walking the grounds and then took a tour of the Supreme Court. Robert was still talking to the lady with the bullhorn and the police an hour later, and the crowd had swelled to include at least two hundred more people. There was chanting. There was shouting. There were signs. And there were people praying. But no one had advanced past the gauntlet of visor-wearing police officers.

All in all, no one got hurt, and every son went home to his mother that day.

•••

William didn't say much for most of the evening. He attended a Cub Scout leadership meeting, and when he got home, the kids were more or less asleep. I didn't realize he was still upset about his mother's phone call until he said, "You know this minor internet celebrity thing is getting a little out of hand."

I set the copy of Rumi's Masnavi I was studying on the table and glanced up at him, not sure whether I should giggle or not.

"They're saying that you're a peace activist, is that what you told them?"

"Told who?"

"The reporter?"

"Um, she never asked me my name, I didn't even know I was being recorded."

"Don't they need to ask your permission?"

I shrugged, and gave my Rumi book a longing gaze. "It's not like I knew there would be a protest when I took the kids to the Supreme Court. I just wanted to show it to them, wanted to see it too. It's funny, they never took us on field trips in law school."

"Didn't you tour the local prison? We did that my year."

"Yeah, but that's just next door to the law school, I mean, they could've rented buses and taken us to DC. Would've been fun, don't you think?"

William shook his head. "You're changing the subject, you know, you and the kids could've gotten hurt?"

"By who?"

"Protestors, cops, vagrants, any of a number of people?"

"Um, I guess you don't want us volunteering at the food kitchen on Thanksgiving?" I snickered and grabbed my book.

"That's not funny."

"What?"

"I thought we were going to my parents' house for Thanksgiving." William's mouth moved downward.

I flipped a page in my book and said, "We could do it in the morning."

"I thought you were kidding, are you serious?"

"I was kind of serious, but joking too, is that wrong?"

"You shouldn't joke about everything, it's maddening, Sally. And Brett could've gotten hurt today."

"Nah, angels watch over him," I said.

Chapter 56

Summer was on its way being ushered out by fall. This takes more than six weeks in Virginia, and we were about halfway through the ordeal of a scorching September. But it had been a good day. For the first time since May, the thermometer hadn't touched the eighty-degree mark. It was around six p.m., and the sun had toppled towards the tree lines, but was still about an hour from settings, maybe an hour and a half. I was over Sandy's chatting while we waited for our husbands to come home from work. Sandy was weeding her bed of liriope, which is a fancy word for monkey grass.

Sandy had some of the prettiest liriope I've ever seen. It has long, dark green, triangular leaves that loop from the ground, up and then they turn outward and their tips wave at you. And sprinkled throughout the dark green thin stalks are purple flowers that glisten and twirl like violet honeycombs. As Sandy pulled out pockets of dandelions, she said, "I don't know how your liriope grow back so nice in the springtime, mine always seem to grow shaggy."

"I love yours," I said.

"Yeah, but why do yours look more uniform?" Sandy grabbed a hand trimmer and started to snip the tips of the stalks that were closest to her. She paused for a moment and shook her hand, and I noticed that her knuckles appeared red and swollen. Her arthritis acted up when she worked too hard in the garden. Then Sandy attacked another group of toppling liriope.

"Oh," I chuckled. "That's the culprit. You're cutting yours with scissors. Not only is that incredibly time-consuming, and arduous, but it's almost impossible to cut everything evenly. What I do with mine is run over them with the lawn mower."

Sandy gave me a skeptical look. Then her collie started to bark, and she said in a kind voice, "Shhh, Betsy, that's just the kids coming up from the fort."

Betsy raced around to the side yard, which abutted a trail that led behind our houses. If you headed left, you came to my house and then the river; if you turned right and walked for a bout a half-mile, you came to basketball courts and a pond. Right around there was situated a gigantic fort that the kids and I had nicknamed Alamo. It consisted of three separate structures, each one representing a more advanced phase in the neighborhood kids' production and building capabilities. As of late, Joey's dad had been carrying supplies down to the fort in a wheelbarrow, and then Alex's dad had one-upped Joey's dad by borrowing a strange contraption he had found on eBay: it was a scooter with a flatbed attached to the back of it.

As Betsy raced up and down the backyard yipping at what Sandy assumed was the kids walking up from the fort, I kept explaining about my system for managing liriope.

"Yeah, the lawn mower works great. That gets 'em nice and even, and they do better in the winter time if the stalks are cut back really far. Otherwise, they get all damaged by the ice and the snow and the cold."

"You really use a lawn mower to cut 'em." Sandy shook her head and then pulled herself to her feet. Her white pants were showing grass stains on the knees, and Sandy had wiped dirt across her cheek.

I was about to lean over and wipe the dirt off her cheek when I the sound of an engine misfiring made us both jump a few inches backwards. "Oh, good grief, that scared me, it must be one of Todd's latest monsters," Sandy said with a guffaw.

"Yeah, but it's coming from behind the house." I stalked off in the direction of the side yard to follow the noise, and what I beheld was total and complete bedlam. The loud bang Sandy and I heard was repeating every few seconds, and it was coming from the bellows of a white and blue Jeep Willys. The Jeep appeared to be World War Two vintage. It was much smaller than any other off-road vehicle I'd seen, a little wider than an ATV, but about half the size of a modern Jeep. Precariously attached to the back of the two-door Willys was a trailer, and it was swinging as wildly behind the Willys as several boys and two girls were swinging from the rear of the trailer.

I shook my head, wiped my eyes and did a double-take. When I looked a second time, I spotted all three of my kids, plus Alex, Joey, and girl named Rachael, and two other boys who were so thoroughly dirt-encrusted, I couldn't tell who they were. In fact, I was only certain that one of the kids was Brett because he was wearing an old Boonie hat we'd found in an army surplus store a few months ago, right before the kids went fishing.

Betsy, meanwhile, was racing in circles around the Jeep, yipping excitedly. Betsy, of course, was a border collie, and she had an entire tribe to herd as well as a noisy machine to corral. She appeared to be trying to nudge the back of the trailer, and once, she even jumped and took a nip at a piece of fabric hanging down from the side passenger door, and in general, she seemed quite busy. The kids were whooping and hollering, their voices a cacophony of joy and wild abandon. The Jeep kept issuing a throaty, "Droom, droom, droom," rolling and rocking up the path.

As the Jeep crawled up the hill beside Sandy's house, the driver's side tires stuck to the asphalt trail, while the passenger side tires carved thick, muddy tracks into the sloped groove between the grass and the asphalt. The trailer clambered and banged into rocks on its journey up what William had always called "Sandy's Pass," and for some reason I thought of this and giggled, because if ever there was a vehicle that could trundle up a mountain pass, Todd's new beast was worthy of it.

With a final round of thunderous clangs from the exhaust, several more "Droom, droom, drooms," and with Todd concentrating hard on both the wheel and the metal ball gearshift, the Jeep zigged and hurtled past us, and kept on going over the curb and onto the street. Sandy was mumbling several things under her breath, but I couldn't catch the words because of how loud Todd and the kids were. Sandy shot me a look of exasperation and shook her head at me when she caught me giggling, and that made me giggle even harder.

"No help," she said, and I read her lips more than I heard her.

I put my hands up and tried to look concerned.

"Droom, droom, droom," screamed the Jeep.

Sally shook her head and tore after Todd and the kids, who now had a house length lead on us. Dare I say I never saw Sandy move quite this fast. By the time Todd had pulled up to his split-level house, Sandy was abreast of him, and I was about three paces behind.

"What is all this racket, now come on Todd, you just cut a six-inch groove in my side yard, and you got too many kids on the trailer." Sandy glowered at Todd, but he was busy cutting a wide circle with his Jeep, so Sandy kept going. "And none of you should be sitting in the front, it's not safe, I bet Alison is gonna give you a piece of her mind when she sees what you done do to Brian, and Joey, you best be sitting down, you're gonna fall if you don't, Todd, this is too much, you can't be driving Jeeps down my side yard, and you can't be hauling seven, or is it eight children in that makeshift rig of yours."

Todd yanked the wheel hard to the left, and the trailer crashed overtop the curb and then settled precariously a few inches away from Todd's daily driver, a 1975 Chevy truck. The Jeep was making "Droom, droom, droom" sounds this entire time, and then it put-putted to a clang-stop. Todd, apparently, was mid-soliloquy.

"Joey, Alex, let me tell you how this here Willys came into being. No, Willys ain't named after the caterpillars, they're named after John Willys, who founded the company, and you pronounce it 'Wilis'. This here is a Flattie. Flatties or Flatfender Jeeps were first engineered as tools of war. Then they got modified for farming. They started as recreational trail machines when GIs came home and started exploring the woods with surplus military MBs, GPWs (made by Ford) and then civilian Willys CJ-2As. The name 'Jeep' comes from people shortening the word that describes how you use one of these flatties—for 'General Purpose,' or GP. Say 'GP' really fast, what do you hear?"

"Jeep!" Shouted several kids.

"Right," Todd agreed. "So anyway, I wanted a flatfender for more than ten years, didn't find one that had the original four, and I wanted that four, but then I came across this junkyard dog, she's got an old Buick six in her, just needed a wee rebuild, I knew as soon as I saw her that she'd become my first real wheeling flattie." Todd paused, and then patted the steering wheel fondly.

Sandy kept trying to interrupt Todd, and a few times, she glared at me and I tried to suppress my smiles. But then Todd cried, "Oh hey Sally, come look at the seats I installed, you wanna come sit in them?"

I glanced at Sandy, who snorted and rolled her eyes at me.

"Get in, Mom, you gotta try it," Lizzie urged.

"Awww, it's very pretty, Todd," I admitted.

"Mom!" Junior exclaimed. "It's great, get in!"

Gingerly, I approached the passenger side door.

"So after I got the engine running and installed a new fuel pan and a fuel tank, I brought ole jeep home, still wanted to fix the seats."

"What was wrong with them?"

Todd wiped his hands on a towel and murmured, "Easy there Alex, you're gonna smack the brake hand lever one too many times."

Alex was hanging on the piece that attached the trailer to the back of the Jeep. There brake hand lever looked like a big metal question mark, and it was just above the rusted metal winch.

Just then, Joey jostled Alex, and they went careening onto the street. They both had a look of shock when they hit the ground, but they both bounced up quickly, each one bleeding from scraped knees.

Sandy stood between the two of them, put her hands on their shoulders and said, "Time to go home, come on you two," and she marched off with them and their siblings down the street toward their homes about a quarter-mile away. Betsy was in attendance, running circles around their knees and barking.

Brett jumped from the trailer into the back of the Jeep and stood spread-eagled, his hands on the backs of the seats, and he grinned at me.

"Okay, show me what you got," I said to Todd. I glanced around as if to grab a door handle, and felt silly because the Jeep had no doors. Todd extended his hand and once I seized it, he pulled me towards him, and I sat into a seat that felt much better cushioned than I had been expecting. "Not bad, Todd," I murmured.

The sun reflected off Todd's aviator sunglasses, and he tapped his hands on the dashboard. It was a very-stripped down affair, with none of the modern conveniences we are so accustomed to: there was no radio, no A/C, no clock, no glove box to speak of, just a huge steering wheel, a speedometer, an odometer and a tachometer. Two long, metal shifters extended from the center area, and I assumed that one was to change gears, and the other operated the four wheel drive. Two more shifters waved out from the floor, reminding me somewhat of alien antennae. The floor itself was stripped down metal, painted white, and by no means pristine, but not too rusted either.

"Okay, you gonna buckle your seatbelt, Sally?"

"Um, are we gonna take a ride?" I fumbled around and then found a lap belt that was made of red fabric.

"Sure, why not?"

"Yeah Mom! It's great! Mr. Todd, take us back to the fort?"

"What do you say, Sally?"

"Um," I stalled, "Tell me more about the seats."

"Oh, well the factory seats had been replaced a long time ago by high-back seats, and these were in terrible shape, all ripped up and not too comfortable, and I wanted new seats but the Jeep seats woulda cost $300 alone for the frames, then a hundred more for each cushion. So I looked around and found a pair of replacement Toyota forklift seats from a friend of mine in Alabama. These were $200 each, and they have built in seatbelts, and," Todd grinned and rubbed the back of his seat, "They also have these side bolsters, but they're only on the back so they don't get in your way when you climb in and out."

I followed Todd's hand and caught a glimpse of Brett. His hair was sticking out from under his Boonie hat and for a second, I could imagine him as a grown man, driving to a military base, and the thought of it filled me with pride.

"Okay, Miss Sally, kids, let's make one more trip down to the fort, Lizzie, thanks for grabbing the pallets."

Lizzie gave a partial salute, and just then I noticed that she had been dragging a pile of wood pallets from the side of Todd's garage to the edge of the trailer, and just then, Junior hopped down and helped her slide the pallet onto the dusty metal floor. As soon as they got the pallet loaded, they jumped into the trailer, and before I could issue another halfhearted protest, Todd turned the ignition and the Jeep clanged to life.

Todd worked all the levers wordlessly and competently, and then the engine issued its "Droom, droom, droom" scream, and we rolled into motion. Todd backed up, and then took off toward my house. The engine roared and crashed, and we bounced over a stick, and then proceeded past my driveway . . . at the exact same moment that William was pulling his sedan in.

William rolled his window down and at first he didn't seem to notice me and the kids, for he gave Todd a genial wave and cracked, "What old metal trash is that?"

Todd shrugged and mumbled, "Oh hi, Will, see you later," and then William fixed his eyes on me and a look of horror came over him.

"Hi Will!" I grinned. And to Todd I muttered, "Gun it!"

•••

Later that night, after I got the kids scrubbed and the grease and grime cleaned off my hands, I came down into the kitchen and found William making a peanut butter and jelly sandwich.

"Oh, I guess we forgot to feed the kids dinner," he said. "But they probably had, what, Slurpies?"

"Um, Slurpies and hotdogs I think, oh, and Lizzie had one of their chicken sandwiches."

"That was dinner," William repeated.

"Uh huh," I said.

"Right," he said.

"Oh, will you make me a sandwich? Please Will?"

William shook his head, and then I added, "I always forget to add the jelly, and then it's not sweet enough." And I started to laugh.

He shook his head. And smiled. I think.

Chapter 57

I just learned the hard way not to ask William a question to which I didn't wanna know the answer. It all started a few days ago, when I asked William what he was looking at. I ask him what he's looking at whenever I want him to tell me I look sexy or whenever I need a laugh, or in his case, usually both. This time, I asked him because I needed a laugh and I was sort of confused by the book I was reading on ancient archeology. It was explaining there was a conspiracy among mainstream archeologists to keep out proof of more advanced ancient civilizations, and I kept getting distracted by how close the word ancient was to alien.

That alone was proof of conspiracy.

"Whatcha reading?"

"Oh," he said. "Check this out." He turned his iPad in my direction and I saw a toilet with a step-stool underneath it. "It's called a Spotty Potty. And the concept is when you put your feet on the potty, it takes care of this blockage thing that we have in our rectums. By changing the angle it allows you to eliminate more completely." I looked over his shoulder and saw he was reading a Men's Health article.

"Oh my God," I said. "And they use a step stool to make for easier stools." I regretted it as soon as I said it. I knew better than to joke about anything bathroom related, but I said it anyway and I would rue it for days afterwards. "That would make a great slogan, step into easier stools with a step stool."

William smiled. His whole face got animated, and the glint in his eye told me just how much I was gonna regret starting him on this topic and even worse, saying something even remotely funny about it. "Ooooh, see? You're interested in it too."

I tried hard not to smile. "Am not."

"Are too." William tapped a few things on his iPad. "Check it out, the reviews are great." Amazon popped up and sure enough, the elimination device had a million reviews and they averaged a higher rating than any of the books I'd written. I tried not to be sore about it. "Five stars, huh?"

"Yep. What's your average rating?"

"Stop it. Seriously."

"What? 4.8? Dontcha wish you had a clean five stars? Clean as a daisy, just like the Spotty Potty?"

"Stop," I said.

"I'm telling you, they say it cleans you right out."

"I really don't wanna hear about it." I pulled the covers over my head.

"Makes it so you don't get hemorrhoids."

"Oh my God William, do you know how to spell hemorrhoids?"

"Without using spell check?"

"Yep," I said. "It only counts if you don't have to use spell check."

"Ahhh," he said, and showed me his screen. "Indeed I do."

"You're such an old man."

"Yeah, but you had them the last time," he said.

"Hemorrhoids?"

He nodded.

"Ugh, just thinking about them makes my butt hurt," I said. "Anyway, I might have had them last but I never had to do a poop test to see if mine were bleeding." I cringed. "So you were the last person to touch poop."

By the end of this salvo, we were both laughing so hard we were bent over in pain. And then of course Junior knocked on the door, and came in before either one of us said he could open the door. For once we were both clothed. "Hey Dad," Junior said. "Have you seen my desk chair?"

"Oh my God, William," I said, "What have you done with Junior's desk chair?"

Lizzie tumbled into the room behind William. She put her hands on her hip. "Like oh my God, Dad, did you take a chair into the bathroom again? Because I almost like broke my toe on it."

"William? Did you . . . use Junior's desk chair as a makeshift Spotty Potty? Please tell me you didn't do that. Please?"

"An Eagle Scout learns to make do with what he's got," William said.

And this is how I learned the hard way not to ask William a question to which I didn't wanna know the answer.

Chapter 58

Six Months Later

Winter came and left without leaving a trace. Spring had launched with its gorgeous parade of cherry blossoms decorating the street. Todd had sold three vehicles, including the cop car and oddly enough the Jeep. "I found a great home for it," Todd had explained. "A friend of mine runs a quarry, and he needed a little runabout for his hundred acre property in New York State." The most entertaining of Todd's acquired vehicles was a '69 Z28 Camaro, silver, with wide black stripes running down the hood. He was rebuilding her and planned to sell her for a pretty penny, as Todd liked to say.

The kids were doing about the same in school, but because Lizzie and Tunie were in different classes, things had quieted down a bit on the Tunie warfront. Tunie and Rhodie wore bright, new wardrobes. A gaggle of friends usually could be spotted traipsing in and out of their house, and Rhodie had been through at least three different boyfriends. But Tunie and my kids had reached a cold détente that seemed to save a lot of hurt feelings.

I had kept talking with God and with Stevie, and occasionally with Jesus and Gabriel, and I was working more and more on building the ministry. We hadn't volunteered at the Soup Kitchen on Thanksgiving, but the kids and I had gone in the day after

Christmas, when Will had to go into work for an emergency. Now, it was April twenty-third, a Saturday.

First thing that Saturday, I called Stevie up and as usual, I barely said hello. "I read this great article, oh my gosh I gotta tell you about it, oh hello to you too, I hope you got some sleep, love!" We'd been up late talking the night before. I was trying to convince her to come and stay with me for awhile, or maybe she was trying to ask and make it seem like my idea, but of course I'd gotten distracted with some of my latest conspiracy theories.

"Good morning," she said. "Yeah, I did. What are you up to?"

I started to laugh really hard. "Well, no walks with God this morning!" That was code for: *no new big ideas*.

Stevie laughed.

"Listen to me," I said, "There has been a VAST conspiracy."

"Yeah?"

I sipped from my coffee and tried to tune out the bedlam from the kitchen, where William was grilling pancakes for the boys. "Yeah, to discredit any scientific theories that oppose Darwin. God's giving this to Fran."

Fran was a mutual friend of ours, one who didn't get along so well with Stevie—not that Stevie got along with too many people. It's not really in the archangel DNA, this whole getting along with folks. Archangels aren't designed with the concept of working and playing with others built into their job description.

"Anyway," I continued, "She keeps babbling about giants and aliens. It's HER fault. And then I found this site that outlines the vast government conspiracy like remember in *Indiana Jones* and he sees all the boxes hidden in the Smithsonian?"

"Uh-huh."

"We're not apes and we had great civilizations very early and there are other species more advanced than we are; humans aren't the be-all and end-all . . ."

"You guys are going all over," Stevie said. She was using her careful or *whoa slow down* voice.

"Yes we are," I said, with a huge smile. "That's why we need Archangel Gabriel to help write it."

"That can be part of the kids' books perhaps, I don't know." Oh. That's one thing I forgot to tell you about Stevie. She's kind of in charge of running certain aspects of my career. So anytime I get a big idea, which since God started talking to me happens almost every day, I have to run it past Stevie. And if anyone wants to talk to me, they gotta go through Stevie. She makes an awe-inspiring gatekeeper.

"We need a man to write some of this. I know I can't. Oh, and I'm gonna mention it in the lost gospels."

"Okay."

"This stuff is fascinating and just because it's true doesn't mean that the history needs to be boring, right?"

"Oh, Sally, none of the history we've been involved in has been boring," she said.

I was cackling madly at this point. "Hahahhaha, I just love this stuff."

Stevie laughed. "Yeah, yeah, I know."

"And now that I can do this telepathic stuff I can really rock it out. And God's making the lost gospels much funnier than I could have and the characters, even mine, are actually charming and funny."

"You all are a little funny," she allowed. "Not a lot."

I started to laugh really hard. "Oh come on, admit we're funny."

"Okay—a lot funny, but you know what's funniest?"

I paused and grinned. "What?"

"What's funny is how hard you laugh at your own stuff. You can't tell a joke without howling at it. Kind of like Robin Williams—"

"—Oh and how he used to give that surprised chuckle at the end of one of his really wild stories? Like even he couldn't believe where he ended up? Like he was just as caught up in the joy and the fun of his story?"

"Yep. Exactly. You're totally full of yourself, you know?"

"I am grinning. Raz has finally admitted I am funny."

"Yes, my girl, Raz deems you funny," Stevie said.

"That I am—I will totally cop to that," I said. "You know, I've written some of the funniest dialogue ever in the last month. My main character is wild. It's her being irrepressible and enthusiastic and like mad-scientist funny. And it's great, William is rolling his eyes about the giants." I paused and laughed again. "I'm like, 'come on it's right there Genesis 6:4.'"

"I thought you said the Old Testament is BS," she said.

"Yes it is except for some parts," I said. I was of course teasing, well, sort of.

"The weird parts, that's what you like."

"They're the best parts."

"I'm rolling my eyes at you," she said. "Are you in the kitchen? Is William having to listen to all this?"

"Nah," I said. "I'm in the study. Guess what? There's all this stuff hidden at the Smithsonian."

Stevie was quiet. I figured she was rolling her eyes.

"Yeah, when I told him about the Smithsonian, he said, 'Right one of your protagonists is a discredited scientists proving all this stuff.'"

"That's perfect!"

"And 'the only people who receive their PhD's are the ones who vow to preserve the conspiracy.' Isn't that swell?"

Stevie was laughing. "Yes! Perfect!"

"And now Lizzie's saying, 'Hey Dad, can you make me a pancake with giants on it?'" I paused, and asked, "Are you sneering at me?"

"Yes," she said, "A very disgusted sneer."

"'Hey Dad,' Brett says, 'can I have a pancake with a bully's butt getting kicked?'"

"'Brett, go to your room.'"

"'But Dad," Lizzie said, 'It was a bully getting his ass kicked!'"

Stevie groaned. "Aww poor Brett, it was a bully."

"Exactly."

"And yay Lizzie."

"Lizzie gets it all. She loves this stuff. Brett just wants to go digging in dirt," I said.

"Brett get to stay out of his room?"

"I bought him books on geology," I said. "Yep, Brett went to his room for thirty seconds."

"Good. Hard core dad, hard core," Stevie said.

"He came back down laughing about a crocodile that fell in ice and died."

Stevie laughed.

"'Brett, don't touch it just sit down,'" William said. Brett said, 'I kissed it on the lips—can I have extra syrup? Is that the maple?' 'Nooooo, it's Mrs. Buttersworth, you asked for it yesterday,'" Will said. "'Yeah Brett,' Junior is saying, 'No last minute changes.'" I paused and waited for Stevie to stop laughing.

Then I went on. "Okay, so when you coming to stay with us again?" We'd been on the phone trying to figure all that out late, late the night before. Stevie and her daughter needed to come to our area for an extended period of time so that Stevie could get the treatment she needed. She had cancer again. The fifth time. And she wasn't willing to go through chemo. So she was going to try this clinical trial and we were near one of the only treatment facilities.

"Oh man, I'm not so sure I wanna come," she said, and we both were laughing.

"I know, it's a zoo here, isn't it?" I said. I sighed now and took the phone outside with me. "I'm serious about you coming, Mama. We got plenty of room. Entire basement's yours."

"And what does William think about all this?"

Stevie and William had never been exactly close. They didn't really argue. They were like a cat and a dog circling one another, never exactly at arms nor completely disarmed. Naturally, I didn't really plan on asking William's permission ahead of time. He'd always told me it was better to ask forgiveness than permission. It was one of his favorite quips actually.

"He's fine," I said.

"Really?"

"Yeah, just wants you to get well," I said. That wasn't a lie. William asked about Stevie's cancer all the time and he always said to send her his prayers.

"Awww, that's kind of him," she said.

Brett burst out through the back door and skidded across the deck until he ended up in my arms. I laughed and said, "And the kids would love to have Desi."

"Oh, well she might be spending the school year with her dad," Stevie said.

"Hey Mom! Are you talking to Stevie?" Brett was standing really close to me but was still shouting.

"Yeah."

"Tell her I am building Israel with God," Brett said.

"You hear that?" I said into the phone.

"Yeah, put him on for a minute," she said.

I stood beside Brett and watched the birds flitting from branch to branch. There was a robin that often made a home on our deck. Each spring it would build a nest on top of our gas grill—which we hadn't used to cook anything in at least five years. Now, the robin had laid an egg and it was the most delicate of blue eggs. The mama Robin was nowhere in sight but I figured the egg was safe.

Meanwhile, Brett was almost shaking with excitement, which was how he always was when he talked with "Raz", which is what he called her when William wasn't around. He was also being exceedingly polite. I heard a string of "Yes ma'am's" and "No ma'am's" and it was making me grin. If—no, when—Raz came, she'd whip everyone into shape. She always did.

After a few minutes, Brett handed me the phone back and I said, "Love you loads," and Stevie said, "Love you buckets," and then I hung up the phone. Then I put an arm around Brett and thought about how I was gonna tell William.

Chapter 59

I was standing by the sink washing out my French Press when Brett ran into the laundry room shouting, "Mom, Mom, I found this huge piece of bromite in the river and it's covered with strips . . ." The rest of his sentence got cut off by the door slamming really hard. Brett came around the corner holding this huge chunk of something reddish-brown.

"Oh come on that's not bromite," William said.

I inspected Brett. His bright blue coat was streaked with new and old dirt, and so was his face, and all of him was soaking wet. "You're not bringing that mess into the house," I said. I did a mental count of all his rocks in his bedroom, the family room, the living room, the kitchen, the laundry room, the basement, and all of our bedrooms. There were at least 1,000 rocks in our home. I groaned a little. Almost as many rocks as books.

William walked past me. "You know, I'm half-expecting that one day he's gonna bring some alien artifact inside the house."

"Wouldn't surprise me," I said. "You know there's at least 70,000 rock statue-artifact thingies all over the world, and not just in Stonehenge. Every single continent. North America, South America, Africa, Europe, and the other ones too."

William rolled his eyes. "You don't remember the other two do you?"

"Do too. Australia is the sixth." I was stalling, trying to figure out if the seventh was Antarctica . . . it wasn't Alaska. That was connected to Canada. I got distracted by this. "Hey do you remember when Sarah Palin said she could see Russia from her back porch or whatever?"

William chuckled. "That was unfortunate, yes."

"Probably tanked her candidacy."

"For Vice President? Oh come on Sally. They vote for President not Vice President. Wait, you think Alaska is the seventh Continent?"

"No! It's connected to Canada. Brett, don't you dare bring that rock in the house," I said. "And don't bring yourself in either. You're muddier than a miner in—"

"—Alaska?" William was snickering. "The seventh continent."

"Cut that out William. Antarctica is the seventh continent."

"You sure? Is that your final answer? And you can't look it up on Google either."

I paused. An entire day of teasing was riding on getting this right. So I feigned confidence and replied, with extra gusto, "Course I'm sure."

"Nice," he murmured.

"Hey Mom," Junior said. "You only listed six."

"Huh?"

"Six continents mom."

I stared out the window. Now which one did I forget?

William had gotten really quiet, like a cat stalking a mouse. I glared at Junior. "You finish your homework yet?"

"What's the sixth continent Sally?"

"I listed seven."

"Did not," William said. "So which one you forget?"

"Um, North America, South America, Europe, Antarctica," I paused and smirked a little at William, "Australia, Africa and . . ." Crap. What was I leaving out?

"Asia, Mom," Junior said.

I groaned.

"As in Canada, Japan, Korea . . ."

"Shut up William. I know what Asia is."

"Hey Mom," Brett said, "Did I die on the Titanic in a past life?

"Oh please," William said. "That's ridiculous. The past lives thing is ridiculous."

We had this fight at least once a week. I was right; he was wrong, but I was on the fringe with this, just like I was with the aliens bit and the Atlantis bit and the prophet bit, and the direct like to God bit . . . and the angels and demons bits too.

"No, not the Titanic," I said.

"What about the Lusitania?" Brett pronounced it wrong and William and I both corrected him.

"Nope, not that either."

"But I was on the battleship."

"Yep."

Brett looked up and his dimples jumped. "Yes! I got to shoot guns. It was so much fun. We would shoot at these tiny ships, almost like model ships but a lot bigger, and when we hit one it would go boom." Brett stood up and gestured wildly. "The most fun was shooting ice. The pieces would race like a meteor . . . no . . . a comet."

"So you were a gunner?"

He grinned even wider and ran to the sink to grab a glass of water. Before he finished swallowing it, he laughed so hard he almost spat his water out. "Oh and the most fun thing was one time I crashed a party at the beach and the bombs set off and all the ladies fainted."

I pictured an older version of Brett in a military uniform chortling happily when one of his bombs went awry and shot sand in all directions. "Wait, you shot a bomb at the beach and when it went off, the ladies fainted?"

Brett clapped his hands and kept laughing. "Yes. It was so funny. I was the only officer, you know, I was a lieutenant, who did crazy stuff like that. I was wild. It was so much fun." Brett smiled, and William snorted in derision. "And you know all this how? Did Stevie the archangel tell you?"

"No, Brett said. She told me I was on a battleship but I remembered the rest of it."

Lizzie came into the kitchen and said sleepily, "Yeah, Brett was there and so was mom, and Stevie too, right?"

"Oh, and you know this how?"

"Mom told me."

"Really, Sally?"

I turned around and met his eyes. "Yes, William, yes."

"And who told you this? Stevie?"

"God."

"Right, and you've got a direct line to Him."

"Yes I do."

"Because you're a prophet," he said.

"You know, you have no faith. Really no faith."

He was about to respond but he frowned instead.

"If an angel came into this room and stood next to you, you'd say, 'Nope, no way. You're not an angel.'"

"Yeah," Brett said. "You don't believe I'm a jumper."

"That's it," William said. "I'm going to Costco. I'll probably see an angel or two there."

"Nope," I said. "More likely to see demons, or Lucifer. He loves Costco."

"Bye Sally."

"Bye William."

"Bye Dad, please get me chocolate," Brett said.

"And angel food cake," Lizzie said.

William rolled his eyes.

Chapter 60

I was sipping my morning French Roast when Brett came falling-sliding around the corner, carrying a spiral notebook full of sketches.

"Mom, check it out," he said, and pointed to a map he was drawing. I glanced at it and was about to say that it looked like a planet.

"Yep," Brett said, and again he was reading my mind without trying. More and more as of late, he was answering my questions before I said them aloud, but I didn't want him to go guessing numbers and crazy stuff like that because it never worked and frustrated us both.

"It looks like earth except South America is joined to the rest of the lands."

"And this up here?" I pointed at another land mass, and it looked sort of like North America.

"Yes, that's North America, and also it's south, in the place where South America is located," Brett said.

I took my hand and put it on Brett's head and sort of tousled what was already pretty wrecked looking, and then bent down and hugged him, and he gave me one of my lopsided grins and smiled at me. "So this is a sort of map, or in fact a part of a bunch of maps we're working on."

"Maps of—"

"—It's what Israel will look like." Israel was the new planet God was making. The word "Israel" means "Wife of God" as well as "the Promised Land." That's what I am of course. His Wife. I'm just serving down here for now. But in the future, He'll be with me. We'll be helping get souls from the earth to the new world. So that's the true meaning of my soul name. In a future lifetime it would be my destiny—our job—to lead humans to the New Promised Land.

Brett smiled again, this time with a matter-of-fact nod. "God took me there to see it last night, we're building it. Are you going on a walk? Can I come? I wanna talk about God."

I smiled. My morning walks with God were sacred but more often, Brett was accompanying me on parts of these walks. He was talking more and more with God but his talks with God usually occurred while he was sleeping . . . and during his talks with God, Brett received a ton of visuals.

I opened the door and paused. William was looking at me. He knew I liked to go off on my own to talk with God. He also knew that I had been including Brett in some of these walks.

"You sure?" William said.

"Come on, can I? I wanna talk about God."

I put an arm around Brett's shoulder. "Yep, come on," I said.

A few minutes later, we were walking along the water's edge at the lake near home. The trail was wide enough for three to four people to walk abreast, so long as there weren't too many bikers and runners out, so I had Brett on the inside of the trail. In my mind I remembered all the times I'd said to him over the years, "Stay on the inside of the trail so that the bikes don't run you down," and it was a fond thought.

"Okay, Brett, so this was a dream?"

Brett bent down and picked up a small piece of quartz and shoved it into the pocket of his raggedy jeans. "Yes," Brett said, "God likes to take me to see Israel a lot and it's why I go to bed early, so I can see how things are coming along."

I nodded. God spoke to Brett more often in dreams because he was young and his mind was electric, or as Raziel often characterized it—loud. God could get through to him when his conscious mind was resting and God had been talking to him for years that way—by reaching out during Brett's dreams.

"Yeah, you have been going to bed kind of early lately, haven't you?" I turned a bemused eye on my son. Sometimes what Brett reported was more fantasy than prophecy, like when he spoke of visits to Hamster World, but often Brett visited places he'd either been or was going to be; in fact, Brett visited places that were coming into being sometime in the future or even in another dimension, as was the case with the planet Israel. I was learning to take all that Brett said in with a smile and to ask God for confirmation later.

"Yes, so anyway, what I got to see was Israel coming into being. It's starting off inside heaven and the place where it's going to go is invisible."

I sent a transmission to God and he sent back: *Yes, we're keeping it inside the heavens until we're ready to reveal it, or until it's safe. For now I'm protecting it from the Enemy. So it might well seem invisible which is to say it's in another dimension, or is manifested only in the heavenly dimension.*

"So you're getting to see the continents formed and you were saying that it looks a lot like earth but it's upside down and there's really only two big continents, one of which is like a combination of all the continents on earth? Sort of like the old Pangaea?" I was picturing an older vision of earth.

"Yeah, old earth, so it's really neat, I took lots of pictures, God is sending a comet to collide with a meteorite, the meteorite had a orange tail and the comet had a white tail and when they formed an X it made a giant core of quartz that was going to be the core of Israel. I was taking pictures, lots of pictures—"

"—With what? What was your camera like?" I smiled at Brett.

"Oh," he shrugged, "With my mind. It's my angel mind, it's how we take pictures. And the country that's going to be combined will look sort of like Pangaea but it will be spelled, like, a combination of Brazil, Europe and Africa, something like Brazurfrica, oh wait, and Asia," Brett said.

"Cool," I said.

"And there will be water that's going to be made from the power of the sapphire in the middle that's on top of the sunstone.

We will all live along the coastlines and the water will be special because it will be good to drink without us having to run it through all these pipes and underground things, the water will be just like it is when it comes out of faucets so when you want to get a drink of water you just go outside with an empty cup and get some water from the ocean and you drink it."

I was thinking, *so the water won't be saltwater? Really?* That was something else I'd ask God about later. Aloud I said, "Wow, so water we can drink and clean energy that's abundant, I like that."

"Yes," he said, "And don't forget the cars and how they work. When you're riding in a car it will be powered by crystal quartz so when you want to turn the heat on or the AC you can change the temperature by thinking it, commanding it, or turning the button on."

I was picturing the vehicles, which were little pods made from completely white material. It was like I'd seen them somewhere. They used water and quartz for power and the engine looked like a serpentine network of crystal tubes with water running through them. I said aloud, "Does that sound right?" Then I remembered that Brett couldn't hear all my thoughts. "Hey Brett, were the cars like little pods?"

"Yes," he said, "Powered by crystals. And there is quartz underneath the ground and it is protected by a special stone called sunstone and this stone is brighter than anything else in this world and a single sunstone can power homes for one hundred miles. That's how bright the stone is, for it's got—" Brett looked up and wrinkled his nose in concentration. "—Nuclear . . . fission?"

"Um, wow," I said aloud," Nuclear fission without any harmful materials causing the reaction?"

"Well, it's generated by using a very powerful ball of light that could black out your eyes even if you're not looking at it, so if anyone tries to use it for a weapon it will cause them to disintegrate."

Hmm, I thought, *is it made from some sort of hydrogen and crystal implosion, like what they created at the Great Pyramid at Giza?* I said aloud, "Is the sunstone a form of crystal?"

"Yeah at first it is a normal sunstone and then I formed a giant ball of light that could block out any form of light and He threw it into the core and it landed into the sunstone and then the sunstone absorbed it and was guarding the quartz and it was a beautiful orange citrine color and was strong enough to power all of Israel."

"But is the sunstone a form of crystal?"

"Yes. It is a beautiful crystal the color of orange citrine but it's not orange citrine because that's below diamond. The sunstone is before the quartz. The quartz forms everything on Israel—it's at the core of the planet."

I was picturing giant crystals and God told me Brett was seeing a glowing stone and I smiled at both of them. To God I sent, *Wow, so what is the crystal interacting with do you think? Water? Sound waves? Is it similar to the Giza pyramids?*

On the right track, God sent.

"Do you remember what the houses look like?" I loved talking about construction with Brett. During our nightly walks, even when he was six or seven, he would frown at modern buildings, with all their messy stylistic embroidery and embellishment and ugliness and he'd say, "Oh, no, that brick won't do, nor will that form of cement. Brick doesn't last and the cement hurts the land. We must only use materials that don't hurt the land." Then Brett would go on a discourse on which materials occurred naturally and which could be worked with by using substances at hand or how we could create structures without "hurting the land," which apparently was one of his main guiding principles.

In this case, Brett was on a quartz kick. "Yes, they will be fashioned from quartz which is really quite plentiful on Israel."

"You sure about quartz not granite? I mean, well, granite is a harder material than quartz so it would be harder to cut. And quartz sure does have a lot of magical or magic-seeming capabilities. "But wait, quartz's hardness level is less than granite's?"

Brett sighed and with great exasperation started waving his hands around.

I grinned.

Then he explained, "No, no, that's just how hard it is to scratch it. Granite has a bunch of different minerals or types of things in it, and once you meld them together, what happens is," and Brett took his fingers and interlaced them together, "You get a snowflake sort of pattern, like this."

I laughed and said, "But snowflakes are soft," and then Brett had almost glared at me, but in a friendly way, and explained, "No, listen Mom. The hardness of granite results from its interlocking mineral structure. This happens when crystals grow out of a molten state. As different minerals reach their point of crystallization, they form in whatever space is available and after they're all done forming, they've tightly interlocked, and that looks like the snowflakes you draw in class, not so much like the ones that fall except for when they get really big, and that's when the arms, the six arms of the snow flake lattice form according to the varying temperatures met by the molecules as the snow crystal tumbles through the air."

Brett had gone on about hexagons and facets and crystalline lattices but I was having a lot of trouble understanding all of what he was trying to teach me.

So I turned and smiled again at him and said, "Okay, tell me more about these quartz homes. They're built into the land, right? I've dreamed them I think, like pods sort of, green metal, and they're built out of or into the ground?"

Brett was walking and stopping every few minutes to sort through the rocks he was seeing. He paused again and kneeled, his angular wrists sticking out of his shirt, now a size too small, just a week ago fitting just right, and held up a rock that didn't appear particularly special. "Ahh, an excellent specimen of rose quartz," he murmured, and he deposited it into the side pocket of his jeans. Then he said, "Nope, not green metal but metal could work, yes, iron-based, not gold, no, too soft of a mineral. Houses are built into the quartz, which is plentiful. And you can get out of the house simply by thinking it and then you teleport out, in fact, on Israel we can often teleport but we can also use the pods or the cars, and of course lots of boats since we will all live on the coast."

"So Brett," I said, "When you gonna take me there and show me what you and God are making?"

"Oh, Mom, you should come fly with me at night, I'll make one of my fireballs like I used to make in First Heaven." Brett got a really intense look and said, "You remember that one right?"

I threw my arm around him for the second time that day and said, "Fireball, eh?"

His eyes narrowed for a moment and he waited to see if I'd remember on my own. Then he said, "Yes, it was one of the times we were messing around when we were kids, kid-souls, I lit one up and rode it and took you with me, it was epic."

"Sounds epic," I said. Then I realized it was almost ten and we were due back for breakfast. I hoped I wasn't missing too much of whatever Lizzie and Junior and William were doing. I hoped I wasn't, and I also wished I could remember riding the fireball.

Chapter 61

Lizzie had taken to reading the newspaper every evening, after William discarded it beside his comfortable chair. And over the past several nights, she'd been asking me questions. It was a Tuesday night, and she was on a kick, and the effect of it was making me almost sick to my stomach. Because I didn't have any good answers, other than, "Well, we could do better," or, "You're right, that doesn't seem to make any sense."

She asked first about vacant houses. "Mom, it says here that in 2013, there were 18,600,000 vacant houses in America, I think that's eighteen million plus, right Mom?"

I looked at the picture on page six of the Front Page Section and read the caption. "Um, yeah, that's right, wow, that's a lot of houses."

"Why can't homeless people live in them?"

"It's a question of getting them there," I said.

Lizzie was quiet for a moment, and then she said, "But we have military troops in eighty countries, that's eight-zero, so why can't we keep some troops here and have them help people find houses?"

"I think it's because they're not supposed to interfere with domestic affairs unless the National Guard is ordered in."

"Yeah, but I'm reading in article that talks about how troops are building houses in Africa, in the Middle East too, so why can't they fix up houses here instead of there?"

"That's not a bad idea."

Lizzie smiled and primped her hair with her left hand. "Oh, thanks. Mom?"

"Yeah?"

"Did you know that the United States has given more than $151 billion to Saudi Arabia over the last eight years? And this is the same country that makes women wear head coverings, there's a lot else, Saudi Arabia is bombing Yemen and three thousand civilians have died, including doctors, children, women . . . and the corporations who are selling the stuff has donated millions to Senators, why are they doing this? Why fund a war on civilians with bribes to Senators?"

"They're not exactly bribes, corporate donations to elected officials is lobbying and it's legal." I shook my head and felt something akin to a haze descending over me. Like my head was tingling.

"It's legal for corporations to give money to Senators, and in turn they get to sell weapons to evil leaders in the Middle East?"

"Yes."

"But Mom, it says here that the corporations didn't pay any taxes or hardly any, so how is that fair? They sell guns, they make money, but they don't have to pay taxes? Is that because they give Senators money?"

I was feeling even sicker, so I stood up and patted Lizzie on the arm. "I need to get some air. Gonna take a walk."

Lizzie set the paper down and shot me a look of concern. "You look pale, are you okay?"

"Just need some fresh air." I closed my eyes for a moment and took a deep breath. Then I took a step toward the front door.

"Can I come on the walk?" Lizzie's eyes were full of compassion.

I tried to smile. "I think I'll go on this one alone, but we can talk later. You should write your questions down and then maybe write an essay about one of them. Maybe you have some better answers than grownups have. I'm so used to things being this way in the world, I don't look at it fresh. But a fresh look might be good."

Lizzie moved her hair out of her eyes and said, "Say hi to God for me, or are you gonna ask Jesus what he thinks?"

I pivoted at the front door and played with the handle. People always like to ask the rhetorical question, *What would Jesus do?* Maybe that wasn't such a bad question to ask. Maybe I could ask Jesus what he thought. "You know, I think I'll see if Jesus is busy," I finally said.

"Say hi to him for me." Lizzie waved her hand and her cheeks rose into the hint of a beatific smile.

"Okay," I said, and shut the door behind me.

I walked a few moments and felt a gentle breeze buffet me as I headed clockwise around the block. Our street formed a circle of almost exactly a half-mile, so it made for a perfect walking course. The very first baby green or light green leaves were appearing on the maples, oaks, and pen-oaks, but the night brought a chill to the air, and also carried the scent of blossoming flowers on its wings. I thought about wings, and ones that could take a human Home, and then I sent a thought wave to Jesus.

"Hi, are you there? It's Sally."

A few moments passed, and another blossom appeared on a flower beside the sidewalk, or so I imagined . . . and then I felt his presence beside me.

"Hi Sally, how are you?"

"It's you?"

"It is I," he said.

"Jesus?"

"Yes." He was smiling, and walking at my side.

"Lizzie was asking me questions about the news. It all seems so much, so much war, so much corruption, did you know we, the U.S. military, is in eighty different countries? And U.S. corporations are funding all these wars, and all these civilians are dying? And there's shootings, blacks are dying, they're being shot by cops, and cops and being attacked by blacks too, it's all a mess, it seems like the world is crying, dying." I waved my hand and sighed. "Oh, and the neighbor's dog keeps barking, some nights, some days, that's the worst of my concerns."

I glanced over at Jesus. His auburn hair cascaded over his white robes, and he stepped over a patch of crabgrass and I watched his sandals scape against the white asphalt, and almost asked about the environment, but he started to talk before I could. "All those things are true, it's normal you would feel upset. The hardest thing about being awake while you're serving down here is not getting lost."

Once he said that, I felt my chest clutch, and then realized a lump was forming in my throat. So I took a deep breath and felt better. Then I said, "So how do I not get lost?"

"If you read follow the world, make a habit of seeing all it has," he said.

"Not just the headlines that make me sad or outraged?" I paused and said, "Hey, did you hear that? I think the frogs are out for the first time, seems early for them." I cinched up the drawstring on my sweatshirt and breathed in another scent wave of flower petals.

"Yes, I heard that." Jesus smiled to himself and waited for me to ask another question.

Which I shortly did. "What else should I see?"

An image flashed into my mind, and after a moment, I realized that Jesus was sending me a video. Two bodies of water met, and on one side, the waters appeared azure blue; on the other side, they shimmered jade green. Before I could exclaim wow, a man sat on the edge of a window ledge high above the streets. His feet dangled below him, and he was crying. Then two police officers entered the picture, and one of them began to talk in a gentle tone. He asked about the man's family, and that just made the man cry harder, and it felt certain he'd jump, but then the police officer said, "Do you like football? Who's your team?" And the man hesitated and said he did like football, and a few minutes later, the man took the police officer's hand and allowed himself to be saved.

"Oh, that's wonderful," I said.

"And there's this," Jesus said. A contraption attached by a harness to a trawling ship opened its mouth, and trash floated into it. "Two surfers in Australia worked for twelve years to create this, it's a floating trash can and it doesn't kill fish," intoned a commentator. The video shifted again. Now a homeless man stood on a street corner, and a conversion van parked next to him. The homeless man climbed in, and a few moments later, stood under a shower head. "This non-profit goes around and offers showers to the homeless," Jesus explained.

"I think I could watch these all day, actually," I said.

"Whenever you feel dizzy or weakened from what you're reading or hearing, go find these stories. You don't need to passively accept the world that's painted and then given to you. Create your own nightly news show, and you will create a different, a better inward reality," Jesus explained.

"Sometimes it feels like I'm just inundated with stories when I go on-line, it's like I can't escape the carnage or the pain of everyone."

"You do have a choice in that regard," he said.

I scuffed my running shoe against the sidewalk to knock out a pebble.

"Do you have to go online so much?"

"There's a pebble stuck in my shoe," I said.

"Because you walked over it, you can always choose a different route, right?"

"When you say it like that, yeah, but—"

"It's still your foot in the shoe, right Sally?"

I glanced at the grooves on the bottom of my shoe and gave a reluctant nod. "I get what you're saying."

"Which is?"

"Only I can change the road I'm on?"

"Yes," he said. "You don't have to be sad, it's not that you shouldn't try to help others, but you aren't necessarily helping anyone when you constantly immerse yourself in others' pain, especially when they're far, far away from the road you're traveling, it's still a choice."

I sighed and finally dislodged the pebble from the groove and said, "I can change my road, change what I see, change my reality?"

"Yes."

We walked in companionable silence around the street, and I said again, "The frogs are out for the first time."

"It's a pretty song they sing, isn't it?"

"Yes," I said.

Chapter 62

William was making bacon for BLTs. I crossed to the fridge to find the lettuce and groaned. There were two green things in the rotter. One, some kind of fancy lettuce, was most certainly unsalvageable. The other . . . I grabbed it and turned it over hopefully.

"That's cabbage, cutie."

"Doggone it," I said. I'd used up way too much lettuce the night before making burgers. I had pretty much wasted half the head in a pointless pursuit of leaf perfection. And tossed the rest. I shot William a mournful look.

"You used it all up last night?"

I nodded and managed a weak half-smile.

"Wow, how did you do that?"

"Um . . . how about if I go out and grab some lettuce," I said.

"Nah, we can skip it," William said. He was trying to be kind to me.

"Don't need it," Brett cried.

"Can't eat bacon without lettuce," Lizzie said.

"It's okay," I said as I grabbed my keys. "I got this."

"See kids?" William was saying as I shut the door. "That's called finding a solution to a problem."

About ten minutes later, I got back home with the lettuce, and I only sort of felt like a conquering hero. It took a minute to peel the leaves apart, and this time, I wasn't gonna get all picky about which ones to use.

I handed Lizzie lettuce and bacon, no bread, no tomatoes.

"Brett?"

"Bacon, no lettuce, no bread, and no tomatoes."

I groaned and handed him his plate. Then I gestured at a plate piled high with bread. "Come on y'all, no bread? These are BLTs."

"Nowhere in BLT does it say bread is required," Lizzie said.

"True," William said.

"Hey, where's Junior?"

"No bacon, no lettuce, no tomato, no bread," Brett cracked.

"He's taking a shower," Lizzie shouted.

I shrugged and spread mayo on my bread.

"So kids," William said, "I am starving. It was a tough day."

"Mine was worse," I said. Then I realized I was being an ass. "Not to be competitive about it."

William laughed. "Okay, I had a bunch of meetings. How was your day bad?"

"Well, I'm a prophet who's wrong at least some of the time. So how can I be a prophet?"

William tried not to snicker. He didn't believe in this whole prophet thing. And sometimes I wasn't so sure either. But that was my own lack of faith, which is a kind of funny thing for a prophet to lack.

"Well, either I'm crazy. Or I am seeing stuff as literal when it's meant as symbolic. Or I am fantasizing about it all. Or I am seeing stuff in the future that will happen, just hasn't happened yet. Or I am seeing five possible outcomes, with the most likely outcome being shown and the other four just being suggested until the event gets closer." I sighed. "And the fact that I understand that all five possibilities are possible means that the first one is not," I sighed dramatically, "true."

William shot me one of his skeptical looks. "Maybe you just tell good stories?"

"Hey Mom," Lizzie said. "Speaking of your stories, did you realize you got the hardness of diamonds wrong? It's a ten, not a nine."

I shrugged. "Yeah. So? It's fiction."

"Yeah, but the hardness of a diamond is a fact," William said.

"It's okay, Mom," Brett said. "I get mixed up between nines and tens too."

"Well which one is it, Brett?" After all, he's the one who gave me all the rock hardness facts. You know, the seven-year old who I trusted so much I never subjected his info to any sort of fact-checking whatsoever.

Brett shrugged. "Ten."

"Yeah, and Mom?" Lizzie said. "Hematite is wrong. It should be Hermadite."

"As in the rock? I thought it was Hematite."

"Well, doesn't that mean girl's body parts?" Lizzie made a face, a funny one actually, somewhere between confused and amused that I'd gotten not one but two facts wrong. Batting oh-hundred as I was so far today.

"Nope," William said. "That would be hermaphrodite."

"What's that mean?"

"It's when a girl also has boy parts, right William?"

"Sounds about right," he said.

Lizzie made a face. "That's not possible."

"Yes it is," I said. "Remember, the body's just a physical shell and if it's messed up or different, doesn't matter. God still loves us just the same."

"Yeah," Lizzie said. "Anyway, being a hermaphrodite might be better. Means you're more muscular."

I smiled.

"Hey Dad?"

William looked over at Junior.

"Can I use your Spotty Potty?"

"Sure! It's great isn't it?"

"Ugh, William, stop, can y'all please not talk about bathroom stuff at the dinner table?"

"Sure, Sally. But you started it."

"No, I was talking about parts that can potentially be used in the bathroom. You're talking about using those parts in the bathroom."

"Hey Mom," Brett said. "I am sure I died on the Lusitania."

William rolled his eyes.

"I don't think it was the Lusitania," I said.

"I'm sure it was," Brett said. Then he moved his hands around wildly. "The bomb went boom! And then some coal fell and hit me on the head. No, it hit Joey. He was there too."

"Who's Joey?"

"He's in my class," Brett said. "And then it hit him again. And then I tried to get on the lifeboat." Brett grinned at me. "But it was too heavy. Then I gave up in despair."

"Oh," I said, and thought about how much it hurt me when William didn't believe my past lives. I wasn't gonna do that to Brett, especially when I didn't know for sure he hadn't been on the Lusitania. I knew for sure he'd been on a Russian battleship in the 19th Century. He'd been a gunner. "Well, good. I mean, not good that you gave up in despair."

"It's okay," Brett said. "Then I got back to heaven and hung out with Stevie in the frat and we got ready for our next mission."

Chapter 63

I used an indirect way of letting William know Stevie was coming to stay with us. I had heard of this documentary called Burzynski. It told the story of a Polish-American scientist who developed a safe and effective treatment for cancer called antineoplaston therapy. For decades, Burzynski fought against efforts led by the FDA and the Texas State Board of Medicine, as well as from rival pharmaceutical companies and the leading cancer research institutes to shut his operations down. Nonetheless, his therapy appeared to work.

The documentary was pretty compelling—much more so than the Wikipedia article I'd read about Burzynski. According to Wikipedia, Burzynski was pretty much a fraud . . . but William is a big believer in small government, as am I. In fact, we both loved this Jefferson quotation:

> *The error seems not sufficiently eradicated, that the operations of the mind, as well as the acts of the body, are subject to the coercion of the laws. But our rulers can have authority over such natural rights only as we have submitted to them. The rights of conscience we never submitted, we could not submit. We are answerable for*

them to our God. The legitimate powers of government extend to such acts only as are injurious to others . . . . Was the government to prescribe to us our medicine and diet, our bodies would be in such keeping as our souls are now. Thus in France the emetic was once forbidden as a medicine, and the potato as an article of food.

This quotation comes from Jefferson's *Notes on Virginia*, and it's an issue William and I debated often, especially since he was an investigative attorney for the government. And no, I'm not allowed to say even which agency he works for . . . he gets really mad when I talk about his job. He would say I need to stay out of his business . . . and in fact he has said that.

I always reply, "Exactly! Just like the government needs to stay out of our business, right?"

William usually agrees with me on this, but he always reminds me of the good things the government does, like prevent fraud, build roads, provide protection against foreign enemies . . . sometimes I use that opportunity to start an argument about the Middle East or about modern colonization actives. Oh, that's another thing I forgot to mention: William and I often vote opposite parties. As of yet, we've not placed conflicting party placards in our front yard, but I've always teased him that I'm planning on doing that when a woman runs for President. Then I laugh and say, "And what would happen if I were that woman?"

William and I always laugh really hard at that point. He says, "Well, you'd certainly be amusing to the media, Cutie."

At which point I usually grin and say, "Kind of like a female version of Charles Barkley, eh?"

And we end up laughing really hard, because everyone knows I am unable to shy away from speaking the truth, whatever the consequences.

Anyway, after we watched the documentary on Burzynski, William asked, "So, how's Stevie doing, anyway? Didn't you say her cancer was back?"

"Well, I said God told me her cancer was back but I didn't have confirmation from Stevie yet about it. But now I do, yeah. She's got it in some of her main organs, like stomach, lungs, that sorta thing."

William made a sympathetic noise. "What kind of treatment is she getting?"

"Well," I said, "You know how cruddy the military is." Stevie had served several years in the Navy and still had military insurance of some sort.

"That's a crime," William said.

"I know, isn't it?" I got a little choked up and looked away as I gathered my thoughts. It killed me how badly we treated the men and women of our armed forces. I didn't always agree with the wars we were fighting but the people who fought? I sure did appreciate each and every one of them.

"Yes," William said.

"So, she's not wanting to go through more chemo, said it destroys her immune system, which is already really weak, and she's not sure she would survive it again," I waved my hand and waited for my emotions to stop surging through me. I'd lost Stevie many lifetimes, grieved her, missed her, and knowing I'd see her again soon helped of course, but losing someone you loved as much as I loved Stevie still hurt.

"I'm sorry, Cutie." William put a hand on my forearm and I looked into his eyes and thought about how gentle he looked, how solid, how kind.

"Thanks, Will," I said.

"So what's she gonna do? If she's not gonna take chemo . . . is she getting into any of these trials?"

I placed my fingers on his hand and entwined mine in his. "Yeah, they're actually offering trials here, somewhere near INOVA."

"Oh wow," William's eyes lit up. "That's great news. You know, if she needs a place to stay when she gets into the trials—"

"—If she gets into the trials," I said.

"Oh, aren't you the one that's always telling me to have faith?" William's eyes twinkled and I smiled at him. In fact, the smile was already turning into a smirk.

"Whoa," he said, "I recognize that smirk. She's already gotten accepted into the trial and you've already told her she can stay with us, haven't you Sally?"

I was grinning now. "How in the world . . ."

"Come on, Sally. How long we been married? You don't exactly have a poker face."

My grin got wider. "So it's okay, she can stay with us?"

William started kissing my neck. I took that as a 'yes' and stopped asking questions.

•••

I had told William many times that if an archangel was sitting in front of him, he wouldn't believe it and sure enough, it was time to test out that proposition. Stevie was due in a couple of days and we had a lot of things to do to get the house ready. I was remembering one of my conversations with Stevie as William and I cleaned the basement up, tried to make it reasonably nice for my angel-mom.

I'd been bugging her, trying to get her to tell me what the plan was as far as where God wanted me to live. See, that's part of Stevie's job. She's supposed to kind of make sure I get where I'm supposed to be, whether it's meeting with reporters or helping take out some demons, Stevie's usually in charge of where I go and when.

So I'd said, "So when you gonna tell me where I gotta live? Can you tell me yet? Can you?"

"Why do you wanna move so badly? And uproot William? You know he doesn't wanna be uprooted," she said.

DC was burning. I'd seen it many times already. I shook my head and shivered. Then I looked around at the red room, which was littered with toys and papers and notebooks and newspapers and maps and books, not to mention bookshelves all categorized according to the Library of Congress. That was of course William's doing. "Because, because I don't wanna have to clean this dumb house. It's a mess."

"Oh my God. Just clean it. That's ridiculous."

"It would be easier to move than to clean it. Anyway, you know I'm a mess."

"Yeah," she said. "Every single time you are."

We both laughed. We laughed a lot about how much of a mess I was, how messy God was too, how messy I kept my room in the frat, how many papers and books and research projects scattered all over the place. And now I was thinking about that as I actually cleaned the house for my Stevie. That made me laugh, and it's while I was laughing that Lizzie came up to me and said, "Gosh, Mom, you know your eyes are absolutely lit up, like glowing white, and you're smiling. You talking to God right now? That's how you look, you know, when you're talking to God."

"Awww," I'd blushed a little. "Sort of. I'm also thinking about how Stevie says I'm always a total mess in all my lifetimes, and now here I am, getting the house cleaned for her."

Lizzie shot William a look of mild concern. He still didn't believe all this stuff about past lives and he didn't believe I was a hybrid or a prophet for that matter, and the kids all knew it. Sometimes we argued about this stuff in front of the kids. We weren't perfect. We'd always try to hug and make up when we argued, but the kids knew we didn't agree about God, not completely. Then Lizzie whispered, "Does Dad think Stevie's an archangel?"

I gave her a sardonic smile. A tired one. "I don't know, love, why don't you ask him?"

Lizzie picked up a paper towel and grabbed the Windex bottle and started to spray one of the windows. She was always helpful like that. "Okay, Dad?"

William was quiet for a few moments. He seemed intent on what he was doing. Then he said, "Like I told your Mom, I don't know."

"So you don't believe?" Lizzie was also seeming intent on what she was doing. I was thinking she was trying not to seem too aggressive in how she was asking William questions. I'd told her many times that we needed to respect everyone else's opinions, and that included her Dad's. Honestly, I told her this so that I'd hear it too because sometimes I also got frustrated with William. But whenever I did, whenever I went to God and asked him what to do, He would tell me to give love, unconditional pure love, and be patient. And when I asked Stevie, she always said to me, "The two of you are on the same side, okay? You're doing good, so is he. So it doesn't matter if you agree on all things, so long as there's love, right?"

"Actually, Lizzie, that's not what he's been saying," I said.

"But he says he doesn't know," Lizzie said.

"Yes, Lizzie. I don't know. But I believe in what your Mom's doing. I believe in her message. I love her message," William said.

I smiled and then very quietly I said, "God's message, Will. I'm just the messenger." Then I walked over to Lizzie and kissed her cheek. "It's good of you to help. Now can you run upstairs and check on your brothers?"

I waited for Lizzie to pound her feet on the stairs and then slam the basement door. She was loud in all she did so the wait was not an uncertain one. Once the door slam stopped reverberating, I tried to smile at William. I was frustrated again, and part of me wanted to argue. But I could hear God whispering, *you want him to hold you Sally, so just ask for what you want and don't go picking a fight.*

William came toward me. Made it easy for me, not even having to move from where I was standing. I held my arms out and curled into him and we didn't say much. Just hugged.

"Looks pretty good for Stevie down here, doesn't it?" William said once we disentangled.

"Yeah," I said. "It's nice of you, helping like this."

"Well," he said, "I guess she's like family to you, right?"

I nodded. Once again my eyes were welling up with tears. She was really all the true family I had—Stevie, Will, and the kids. I was thinking it didn't matter what we were, or what we all thought the other person was or was not. What mattered was that we all had love. And of that I had little doubt.

Chapter 64

Stevie arrived on a Tuesday. She showed up late morning, during one of my walks and talks with God. In fact, God told me to turn around and head back to the house before I got to the train station, which is my standard turning point. *Stevie's at your door*, he explained. *Yeah, I know, she texted you in the middle of the night but your phone's never charged is it*? It was one of the last days of summer, one week before school started.

When I got to the house and climbed up the hill, I saw Stevie's white sedan parked in front of the house. She wasn't outside, so I went in through the garage, traipsed past the laundry room, and there she was, sitting in the middle of the kitchen at the table. She was surrounded by Lizzie, Junior and Brett and they were all talking to her at once. She seemed completely at home. Nonplussed. Relaxed. And beaming.

The first thing you notice about Stevie when you see her is how her eyes glow. All angels glow like that, but archangels have incredible eyes. In fact, mine have changed since God activated me. But Stevie's? They're a shade of green but there's light surrounding her irises and there's these lines across her pupils, or maybe wings. If I were a man, I'd probably get lost in Stevie's eyes . . . but as her child, which is what I am in heaven, I get lost in them too. And as a writer, I try to think of ways to describe them, make their beauty real, but it's almost impossible to capture the light and the love that reflects back to you from the eyes of an archangel.

But I wasn't lost in my soul-mom's eyes this morning. I fell into her arms and I was crying. It sounds intense but that's how I am around the people I love.

Stevie held me close. She knew just what to do. She didn't try and make me laugh or anything. She just held me and patted me on the back and sure enough, the kids were hugging me too.

"Aww, Mama," I said after a few minutes, "How I've missed you."

Stevie pulled away from me and that's when the light shone from her eyes. "I've missed you too, love."

It was simple, really, but there was so much emotion in her words and in her eyes. There was pride and acceptance, the sort you get from the soul that always is with you, lifetime after lifetime, teaching you how to be a better soul, holding you when you're hurt, leading you when you're stuck. There was joy. There was tenderness. There was a strictness and a seriousness, a sobriety, all in keeping with who she was.

Then I switched channels and sent her this telepathically. *It's been too long, Mama. Can't believe this is the first time I'm seeing you this lifetime. God, I've missed you so much, I love you Mama.*

You look beautiful, my girl, she sent back. *And yeah, it's been way too long, but I'm here now.*

And it's my time to take care of you, I sent back.

Care of me? Nah, I'm fine. Stevie smiled at me but it was a tired smile.

Aloud, I said, "How about if I make you some coffee, love?"

Stevie folded her hands and nodded.

I kind of chuckled to myself. Wondered how many times I'd fixed coffee for Stevie during our lifetimes.

476.

476?

Yeah, 476 times, she sent. *Give or take a few.*

I ground up the coffee and bustled about the kitchen and enjoyed the hum of conversation. Everyone was talking at once and yet there was a peaceful feeling, a happy hue about everything.

I had this sense of wanting to capture the moment, hold it, make it last forever. It was too precious to film or take a picture of or do anything other than inhabit. I kept smelling the coffee beans as I waited for the water to boil and I was sort of listening to the kids pelt Stevie with questions as well.

"So how was Iz as a baby?" Lizzie asked.

"And did I really tell an archangel to wait while I was getting my shoes on before my last mission?" Junior asked.

"Oh man," Brett groaned, "Iz was agonizing as a baby soul."

"Yeah, what about the time she switched the electricity on while the pump was going in the pool you were building and it knocked out an entire grid?" Lizzie loved to hear stories about my childhood in First Heaven. She usually got the story messed up when she told it, and sure enough Brett corrected her.

"It was a jackhammer she got ahold of," Brett said.

"Come on, a jackhammer?" I scoffed from where I was standing. "And whose fault was it I got ahold of a jackhammer?"

Stevie put her head on her hand and languidly rolled her eyes. "Sounds like your Mom's got a point, Brett."

"Yeah, well you would drop her off at my lab and say, 'Tiz, can you watch Iz for a few minutes?' I'd be like, 'Yeah, sure.'"

"She'd leave me for hours, wouldn't she?"

"Yes!" Brett cried. "Hours!"

"And would have the audacity to tell you not to torture me, right?" I looked over at Stevie and said, "What was it you always told them?"

"I told them not to torture Iz, just keep an eye on you for a minute."

"A minute that became an afternoon," Brett said.

I poured a mug full of coffee and placed it in front of Stevie. I also passed her the Splenda and the Creamer.

"Can I have some too, Mom?"

"Yeah, sure Lizzie," I said. I poured her a half a cup and passed her the sugar.

"Mom?" Brett said, "Can I have some hot cocoa?"

"Me too, please, Mom," Junior said. He beamed and his cheeks were all rosy. He even tried to wink at me, which was a habit he'd picked up from me.

"Yeah, yeah, all right, all right," I murmured.

"So what all did I do when you looked after me anyway?" I poured creamer and then coffee into a mug and watched as the black and the white swirled into brown liquid.

"You were agonizing," Brett said.

I set Brett's hot cocoa down on top of a place mat with the spoon beside the mug. He didn't like when I left the spoon inside the liquid because the metal conducted the heat too efficiently and he didn't like drinking from a burning spoon. Then I set Junior's mug in front of him on a place mat, spoon inside the mug.

"Like when she shoved a crayon inside a skyscraper joint and brought the whole thing down?" Lizzie had heard all these stories of course.

"Yes!" Brett was stirring his cocoa and now blowing on it and I pictured him blowing ashes at a campfire for some reason. "To this day I have no idea why she did that with the crayon, it was awful. The entire building, and it was like ten stories, came crashing down, but as usual, Iz managed to hide and not get hurt."

"Don't forget the time she destroyed a giant soul university we had all built and ready to open," Stevie said.

"How did I do that?"

"You just collapsed all the columns," Stevie said with a shrug.

"Who was harder to raise," Lizzie asked. "Iz or Tiz?"

Stevie took a sip of coffee and half-closed her eyes. "Oh, Iz, no doubt about it, she was always a handful."

"She was just agonizing," Brett repeated. He flung his hands up in mock disgust and grinned at me. "See? That's why I'm getting her back now, as her kid." Brett smiled from across the table. "Mmm, thanks for the cocoa, Mom, this is yummy."

"Yeah, thanks Mom," Lizzie and Junior said in tandem.

Stevie gave me a quiet nod and murmured, "Good manners, y'all, that's beautiful. Doing a good job with 'em, love."

Chapter 65

The next morning, I came downstairs and Stevie had already made coffee. I didn't try to say 'good morning' before I poured my first cup of Costa Rican Habiernos. Stevie and I have grumbled through enough early mornings together and neither one of us feels much like talking until we've seen the bottom of that first cup. I did summon one of my half-smiles and I hugged Junior when he crashed into me. Brett too.

"Hey, go getcher pajamas off, okay?"

Junior gave a rosy smile and headed upstairs.

Brett grabbed his fuzzy pillow and bounced after Junior.

"Don't forget to brush your teeth and make your bed, Brett, you hear me about brushing your teeth?"

Brett didn't answer. I sighed and crossed the kitchen. Wanted to ask Stevie how she was feeling, how much she was hurting; wanted to make everything that was broken right.

"I'm fine, love," she said.

My shoulders flipped out a little when she said that. And then I watched the cream swirl and then turn brown, which was one of neatest things I got to see every day, at least twice, because I always made two pots of coffee. "Crap. You heard my thoughts," I said.

"You're kinda loud, you know?"

"No one's louder than Brett. He gives Lizzie a headache whenever he tries to send her a thought. It's like his come screaming in, magnified, at level eleven on a zero to ten scale." I smirked at my joke, which wasn't even a little original, but it was pretty good for early morning.

"Oh come on, it's eighty-thirty," she said.

I grinned and sat beside her. "Whatcha doin? Kids being okay?"

Stevie had a stack of bills and papers spread out like a fan atop the table. There were sticky notes and multiple colored tabs and notes penned all over the documents and I felt that sense of dread that attaches to all things official or medical-related. It doesn't have to be this way but in 21st Century America it is.

"Yeah, they're fine."

"The boys weren't torturing you and all?"

"Nah," she said. She squinted at a document and then wrote something down on a yellow notepad.

"Whatcha doin?"

"Ahhh, I gotta try and get the military to pay for these treatments, course they wanna go and say it's experimental, course they'd prefer I take the chemo that never works on this kinda cancer anyway, but it's what the oncologist is recommending, and what's he gotta lose anyway?"

"Knowing the way it works," I said, "He probably is paid by the company that makes the drug he's prescribing."

"Actually," Stevie said, "I checked on that."

"Is he? And why did you check?"

"Yeah, he gets a yearly stipend for his lab from them. Took me some digging but I found it."

"Why'd you check?" I rubbed my cheek, which had some anointing oil on it that hadn't been mixed in well enough.

"Mmm, you smell good," Stevie murmured.

"Thanks, so why'd you check?"

"Ohhh," she said, "I gotta write this letter or these letters and I was trying to think of ways to go about doing it and I contemplated exposing the hypocrisy of the entire governmental-medical-insurance-pharmaceutical industry."

"Yeah, it's a mess, ain't it?"

Stevie sighed. She was in the middle of a sentence, I could tell, and I was interrupting her, wanting to talk about the philosophy of the whole system, and all she wanted to do was to get a letter written. In some respects, that was the story of our lifetimes together. "Yes, it's a mess."

"And too vast a mess to go challenging, trying to fix, trying to fight, 'oh my God Sally, please stop talking at me so I can get this letter written,' eh?"

Stevie laughed.

"Well, you want me to help get that letter written? You know I used to write those sorts of letters for a living," I said.

Yeah and you hated it.

I grinned at her. Communicating telepathically could sure save a lot of time.

"True, but I'm happy to help, just ask, and now I'm gonna go walk and talk with God, tell the boys not to bug you if they keep talking at you like I always do," I said. I slurped down the rest of my coffee and headed out the back door.

God and I had been talking about the Holy Spirit Matrix for days, and I led with a few questions about it. I'd been reading about Jesus and how he told his disciples that he was leaving them with something. He would speak of it in other speeches; indeed, in the Gospel of John, Jesus explained that he was sending them a gift, one even more important than his sacrifice on the cross. He was sending them the Holy Spirit:

> *Unless I go away, the Advocate will not come to you; but if I go, I will send him to you.*

"So in effect, God sent a piece of himself down to all of us, right? That's the 'Advocate' you're talking about? And isn't it funny I'm a lawyer this lifetime?"

God was shaking His head. "Is this still not clear? Come on, Sally, go back in the house and ask Stevie to teach it to you if you're still confused."

"Nah, then she'll get mad at me cuz she's writing an appeal letter or something for her treatment."

"You will write that letter for her of course, but only after you annoy her all morning," God said.

We both laughed. "Okay, at the end of this walk, I'll go ask her and maybe we can teach the kids about it."

"Don't worry Sally, we're going to go over it all week until you get it. Basically, it comes down to the key lying within all humans in the form of the holy spirit."

"Yes, yes," I said, "I know the key lies within us, and the key is the Holy Spirit, and hey, is that what Jesus was going looking for when he went to Egypt? And is it true Mark was born in Libya? I just read that this morning and it comes from the Coptic traditions, but—"

"—Yes, Mark was born in Libya."

I groaned. I'd written one book on Mark and was only just learning this now? How did I not know that yet? And was it true that Jesus hung out with John the Baptist as monks near the Dead Sea? Was it true that Mark went to England? And did he go to America too? Was it true some of the lost tribes went to America? Did Mark really get stuck in a stargate? "

"—Sally! Shut up now!"

I hadn't realized I was saying all of this aloud, but telepathically I guess I was, and God had let me go on one of my long askologues for a long time but He really just wanted to answer the first question I asked, which was, "How does God live within us and how do we live within God?"

"Okay, seriously, you just need to shut up, be still, and listen, okay dearest Sally? You need to learn this. You, all humans, are all able to communicate telepathically with the part of your soul that lives in heaven while you're living in this shell."

"Oh, so is this the great mystery that all the early religions all over were teaching? And what Jesus was looking for?"

"No! Oh Sally, please, just stop. Stop trying to find the answer in books and in the ancient past or in hidden teachings, for this is a new teaching. The Holy Spirit was a new innovation, brought to earth with Jesus. We'd been experimenting with it in heaven, but it was new. Jesus gave it to his disciples before he left."

"Oh, so that's what Jesus gave his Apostles before he left? He gave them light? He gave them a piece of you? That's what the Holy Spirit means? As in you created it, you willed the Holy Spirit into existence, and he gave it to his followers . . . "

"I spoke it into being before Jesus died, yes. It was made to help humans communicate better with God, and to make it easier or more efficient for God to reach humans."

"Because you, as in your soul, you can't . . .well, wouldn't want to, I mean, there's nothing you can't do, but it wouldn't make sense for your soul to speak with seven billion souls all at once, and even if it would be possible, it wouldn't be a sensible sort of solution, so rather than try and talk to everyone, you put a piece of yourself in all of us."

"Yes. My light is now in all souls, a piece of me, but each soul must choose to turn on the switch, to accept the Holy Spirit. You see, Sally, it's like a matrix, and it surrounds everyone."

"Oh my God, of course, a matrix. Oh my God, so that's like the ley lines and the grids that some mystics can see in holy places, when a lot of souls are meditating or praying or connected to you?"

God groaned. "You know I'm not a big fan of people worshiping reaching of a state of higher consciousness as an end in itself." Which is what happened ever since the Beatles made transcendental meditations the coolest thing in the world. As the Beatles and others learned, you could use drugs, meditate, and tap into the Matrix . . . which was great, but lots of people did that and then they sorta checked out of their missions here on earth. Our missions always involve using our special skills and abilities to make the world better, to serve others by doing what we love most, and if you are always in a state of higher consciousness and thus are checked out of this world, well, you're only really serving yourself.

"Right, that's the problem with it, yes Sally. It's great to reach that Holy Spirit, it's great to check into me so to speak, not so great to just check out."

After he finished reminding me of all that, He said, "Yes, it's a matrix, Sally yes. The Holy Spirit is like a matrix surrounding us, and there's also a piece of God within each one of us. We are always able to communicate with the Holy Spirit that lives in us, but we must choose the light, we must choose, all souls must choose to turn on the light."

"Oh gosh wow," I said, and looked through the hazy late summer light at the little league ball fields on my left. I imagined there was a light grey matrix of Holy Spirit connections, sort of like a grid, with each soul plugged in or out of the grid according to the will of the soul. It was wild. I kept imagining this grid encircling the heavens and the earth and all the other worlds God has made, and I laughed aloud because it was so incredibly cool.

"Hmm, but it's real? We're real?" I shivered a little, because in the movie *The Matrix*, minds are just plugged into this matrix and the people are all dreaming, not really living, and the enemy lives off the electrical power generated by all the dreams created in the minds of enslaved souls.

"Yep, it's real, you're real. The world is real, this life is real, earth is real, it's not just a dream, humans are not mere playthings, no, that's not how it works. In fact, although we do have a plan, the fact that humans have free will, well, that is always changing the plan, just as you and I are changing the plan for all seven billion human souls as a result of what we're going to be doing during your next lifetime."

We'd been going over the revised plan again and again every day just about, and it changes almost every day. It might sound scary, I guess, the concept that the plan for our existence is changing, but that's a whole lot less scary than the concept of us all being a slave to some soul's crazy dream, isn't it?

"Okay, right. The matrix is real . . . and so God, as in the Holy Spirit that you created, that now surrounds us, and also exists inside of us. The Holy Spirit is in us."

"Yes."

"And we are all in God, as in our souls are within the Holy Spirit Matrix that you created, that exists outside your soul, the one I am talking to."

"Yes. Not everyone talks to me, it wouldn't be possible, not really, nor would it be reasonable." God ran an example transmission of what even 700 souls all talking at once to Him would sound like, and it was disorderly, to say the least. "You see, I have always chosen to speak through a few messengers to the people. I mostly speak through angels, and I also speak through prophets."

"Basically, you talk through those souls who live in the First Heavens with you." Within the First Heavens lives God, Jesus, Mary, the 20-something Jumpers (or the "Frat" as Stevie calls it), the Master Archangels, and several of the human prophets? Or do the prophets live somewhere else?"

"Ah, don't worry about all the prophets. A few spend a lot of time in the First Heavens . . . basically, the connection between each human soul and the Holy Spirit is not as strong as the connection between, say, Jesus, the angels, the jumpers, and the prophets . . . to Me, but it's nonetheless a priceless tool for all souls."

"And this is why you want me to stop focusing on interpreting all the gospels, all the stuff that's been written? I've been getting obsessed, yet again, with finding and interpreting all the words spoken by Jesus. But the way I understood it was that it wasn't fatal to reject Jesus, not really. In other words, people really should accept Jesus; they really should accept messengers and prophets sent from God to call them Home, but it wasn't fatal to their soul to reject these prophets or the Messiah. It was fatal though, fatal in a way, to turn off the Holy Spirit, or to disconnect from the grid.

Or as God put it to me a bit more gently this morning, "Once we turn off the light that leads us Home, once we choose darkness over light, or reject what I've given each one of you, you've opened the door to the Enemy. Effectively, you're handing over the key to any demon, or to any powers of imaginations or darkness which wishes to take its place within you. So long as you leave the light on, so long as you accept that God is in you, your soul will be safe and headed Home."

As soon as I got home, I grabbed a sheet of paper and started taking notes and drawing what I thought the Holy Spirit Matrix would look like. The kids have grown accustomed to seeing some of my mad writing efforts. These writing jags often come after one of my walks and talks with God. Jeremiah described the feeling of what it's like to receive the word of God. He said it was like a fire was burning inside of you, burning until you stopped everything you were doing and wrote it down or shared it with the people near him.

God's word has always felt a lot like that to me. Like it's just gotta get written down before I forget exactly what he's told me and how he's phrased it. Especially when he talks poetically, which   is   much   of   the   time.

Chapter 66

After I scribbled about a page of notes, I looked up and took a deep breath. Lizzie was grinning at me. She must have woken up and gotten Stevie to pour her some coffee, because she was staring at me from over top one of our blue seashore and seagull coffee mugs. "Oh my gosh, Mom," she said, "God's given you something important, hasn't He?"

I smiled and finished my sentence before I replied, "Yeah, man, this is cool, it's called the Holy Spirit Matrix. Oh, where's Stevie? You thanked her and all, right?"

"Yes, she thanked me." Stevie came around the corner from the direction of the study and nodded toward what I was drawing. "Looks kinda familiar, whatcha drawing?"

"Holy Spirit Matrix," I said.

Junior popped his head in from the other room, where he must have been working on the computer. "Is that real? Like a computer matrix?"

I smiled. "Do you realize how strange it is for you to think a computer program or software is real but not think the Holy Spirit Matrix is a real thing?"

Junior gave me an appraising look. He was, like William, of a scientific bent, and this wasn't something I wanted to discourage by any means. But I knew I had to explain things to him in a sort of different way; after all, if he couldn't see it, examine it, then it was going to be hard for him to understand it.

"You're asking me how do we know it's real if we can't see it, right?"

Junior kind of nodded.

Lizzie was starting to lecture Junior but I held my hand up and said, "Well, how do we know a computer virus is real? We surely can't see that either, can we?"

"Oh gosh, wow, Mom, that's brilliant," Lizzie said. "Yeah, Junior—"

"—Hey, Lizzie," I said, "No piling on, remember?"

Lizzie frowned and then I motioned for Junior to come sit with us. Stevie was washing her mug out at the sink and Brett had flown around the main hallway and was a few steps from banging into the piece of furniture we called the Lifestyle Piece, but he managed to avoid banging his toe into it at the last minute. Then he was hopping around and being loud, so I shushed him and continued talking.

"See what I mean about the virus Junior? It can't be seen by the eye, right? But it exists within the software and it can cause all sorts of trouble can't it? It can affect millions of computer users all around the world; in fact, it can take out mainframes and even destroy routers—and we're talking about something that's just computer code and has no actual physical form, aren't we?"

The look on Junior's face was one of respect. Stevie walked past me and gave me a quick kiss on the cheek. She whispered, "Go ahead, tell them how easy it is to dial Home, tell them the key, it's good for them to hear all this," and after she patted me on the back, she said aloud, "Y'all listen to your Mama. She's preaching the Word."

"Okay," I said, "So the Holy Spirit is like a matrix surrounding us. Imagine if you can these light grey lines and they run from our souls all the way back up to heaven, okay? Each one of our souls is connected to the Matrix; it's like this Matrix is here and there are lines crisscrossing, running in all directions. In some places, holy places, like where people are praying or where there's someone really holy praying even, the Matrix is brighter and stronger. Like a cathedral or where monks or holy men live, the Matrix gets really strong and bright."

"Can anyone see the Matrix?" Lizzie asked.

"Yes, Lizzie, some people have the gift of being able to see ley lines, which are invisible geomagnetic lines that run along certain places on the earth. These are places where there is increased electromagnetic flow and where humans are better able to talk to God, and ever since prehistory there have been people within each culture who could see where these lines ran."

"Wow, is that anything like reading auras?"

"Yeah, Lizzie, that's another gift some people have, yes, how did you know about that?"

"Oh, I've been reading the Edgar Cayce books," she said.

"Excellent," I said. "Cayce taught that the most important thing any of us can do is to look within ourselves for the answer. Do you know why he said that?"

"Yeah," Brett said. "God's in us."

"Good," I said.

"Wow," Lizzie said. "Brett seems to understand all of this."

"Well, you understand it pretty well too," I said. "And Junior, I think you're understanding it too aren't you?"

Junior smiled at me.

"All I want you to remember is to look within for the answers because within us is the key to figuring out all your problems. You got me? Whether you're a scientist or an author—"

"—Or a builder," Brett said.

"Yes, or a builder," I said, "Just phone home. Dial God. Look inside you for Him. That's where the Holy Spirit lives. There's a piece of God within each one of us. We are always able to talk with the Holy Spirit that lives in us, but we must choose the light, we must choose to talk and to listen, we must choose to turn on that switch, the one that dials God. God's always waiting. But only we can choose to turn on the switch, to accept the Holy Spirit."

"What happens if we don't turn on that switch?" Junior looked a little worried. I decided not to sugarcoat it too much.

"Not turning on the switch is pretty bad. Or rejecting its existence altogether, well, it's worse than rejecting Jesus."

"How is that worse, Mom? I thought Jesus was the answer—doesn't it say that in the Bible?"

"Well," I said, "I think Jesus said something like that, yeah, but you gotta understand the context. Here he was, an actual god standing before his people, and he was conducting miracles left and right, just as a Messiah is supposed to, and yet many of his people rejected him. Certainly those people who rejected Jesus, the ones who saw him in person, really messed up big-time, okay? But as far as people like you, two thousand years later, who maybe don't understand exactly what Jesus was, maybe that's not as bad as rejecting the Holy Spirit."

I paused and made sure the kids were listening and they were. So I explained, "The Holy Spirit is the key, and connecting to the Holy Spirit is the single easiest way Home. It is actually more important to accept the Holy Spirit than to accept Jesus and *all* of his teachings. Why? Because the Holy Spirit is an actual piece of God *and* it's inside of us, inside our souls, so as soon as we make the incredibly simple step—easy enough for a mere babe to understand, hence simple, but not always easy, at least for our skeptical modern cold hearted selves—of accepting its existence, we've grasped hold of the immediate key to our salvation. Once we accept that the Holy Spirit is within us, we've unlocked the way Home.

"You know what, go get me the Bible, I got the perfect verse from Mark that explains why it's so bad to reject the Holy Spirit."

Lizzie grabbed the Bible and handed it to me. Then I turned to Mark 3:28-29:

> *"Truly I tell you, people can be forgiven all their sins and every slander they utter, but whoever blasphemes against the Holy Spirit will never be forgiven; they are guilty of an eternal sin."*

After I read this, I held the Bible and thought about how to make this clear enough for the kids to understand it.

Then I said, "In other words, if you reject the purity of what is from God that is within you, you have effectively rejected God. God is in you; He's in your soul, so if you reject your soul, you're rejecting God."

Junior got up from the table and brought my laptop back to the kitchen. Then he opened up a page that had pictures of the power grid.

I smiled and said, "Awesome, yes. In the physical world, there are matrixes for the energy grid, for example, and that's a lot what the Holy Spirit Matrix appears like. It's like a power grid, or an energy matrix, with lines running not only into and out of each soul, but running all around us, from one side of the earth, of all the worlds souls live in, and connected all the way up to the heavens.

"God, as in the soul I talk to every day on my walks and talks, is both outside and inside the matrix . . . as in He created it, and He's connected to it as well, but it's a grid, a thing that has consciousness and a thing that exists outside of Him. God is a soul just like we are, but the Holy Spirit is a bit different. It's a connection, a living, pulsing piece of God, and we're all capable of communicating with it, with the Holy Spirit, because a receiver of sorts exists within our souls."

"You know, Mom, this is all incredible," Lizzie said. "It's so confusing, and it's almost like, I dunno, too good to be true?"

"Yeah, I hear you sweetie. But I'm thinking most new things are confusing. Don't be afraid of what it is, for it is what it is. Fear gets you nothing; it only takes you back into the darkness. God lives in the light, and so when you're not sure where to look or where to go, look for the light both within you and outside of you."

"God is in the light," she said, softly.

"Yes," I said. "And that's where your home is too. The truth is the light, and the answers to all your questions are stored within that light, within the Holy Spirit, the piece of God that's within you."

Chapter 67

It was Thursday afternoon and I was sitting at the kitchen table reading aloud from the kids' supply lists. Stevie was also at the table. She was still glaring at medical reports; in fact, she had two massive collapsible binders that were labeled as "Medical History," with her full name printed on the sides of the file folders. The file folders were overflowing with papers, some of which had come loose from their moorings.

I read Lizzie's list first.

6th Grade Supply List
- 1 pair small headphones
- 1 pack of pencils sharpened
- 1 small personal pencil sharpener
- 4 large glue sticks
- 1 pair of scissors
- 24 count crayons
- 3 single subject-wide ruled spiral notebooks
- 2 packets of wide ruled loose leaf paper
- 1-7 pocket expandable file

*Please label all school supplies with your child's name. As supplies run low, they will need to be replenished.

Lizzie was leaning over my shoulder as I sorted through the supply lists. We had ones for 4th grade and for 3rd grade as well. "I'm so glad I'm starting Sixth Grade. Then I can leave Tray Dale and go on to Middle School and it won't be as stupid, as much a waste of time," she announced.

"In a hurry to learn harder stuff, are you?" Stevie mumbled.

"But why do we all need headphones? I mean, is it gonna be like last year, watching silly movies all the time when our teacher decides that since she doesn't really like to read, we shouldn't have to waste all our time on old methods of inculcation?"

Lizzie mispronounced inculcation, so I quietly corrected her. Then I said, "Is it true Mrs. Funzip doesn't like to read? That's crazy."

"Yep," Lizzie said. "She only read stuff like the Genius Files because at least when she read that, she could talk to her students. What I don't get is why not read the classics, like Hamlet, and then she could teach us the really important lessons."

"Hamlet's great," Stevie said.

I nodded. I loved the way Stevie didn't talk down to the kids or make a big deal out of Lizzie's reading interests. Lizzie was reading Shakespeare and Tolstoy when she was nine. Needless to say, she was bored in fifth grade. And even worse, her teachers just assumed she wasn't interested in learning. The reality couldn't have been much farther from the truth.

"Well, you know what your Dad always tells you about elementary school, right?

"Yes," Lizzie said. "'Don't worry, you'll like high school and you'll love college, when they start teaching the interesting material. Just get through fifth grade, and now sixth grade,' right, Mom?"

"Yeah, Lizzie. And don't let them ruin your love of learning. Maybe that's one good thing about the headphones, eh?"

Lizzie made a face. "You mean I won't have to get other people's ear wax touching my ears?"

"Oh, yuck, that's pretty disgusting," Stevie said.

"Well, yeah, it is," I said. "But no I mean if you've got the headphones on, no one can bother you, right?"

Just then Brett came skidding around the corner. "I was just working with God on Kronosh. We've scheduled it to explode at 1 p.m. tomorrow." Kronosh is the planet where the evil gray aliens live. We just call them the grays around here, and I've warned the kids not to talk to any little gray aliens if they show up, because the gray ones are controlled by the Enemy.

"You're blowing up Kronosh?" Stevie gave him an amused eye roll. "How exactly?"

"Ohh," Brett waved his arms, "We're taking a big meteor to it and BOOM! Meteor, meet Kronosh!" Brett laughed wildly and Stevie and I shook our heads at one another.

"Hey Mom, I've decided I'm gonna drop out of school for now. They mess up everything, and I saw that they've got American History on the syllabus for third grade." Brett shook his head and waved his hands again, now as if he were swatting away an annoying fly. "You know they get it all wrong. Total waste of time."

"Huh," Stevie said. "So what is it they get wrong, Brett?"

"Well, for one thing, they say Columbus discovered America, I mean, how screwed up is that? We were here centuries and centuries before Columbus. We were down in Yucatan too, and South America and don't forget Bimimimi—"

"Bimini," I corrected.

"Right, right," Brett said. "And then the stupid Spanish came and they were so greedy, you know Mom?"

I nodded. I'd heard this particular argument a few times before and rather enjoyed it. "Yeah, they sure loved their gold, didn't they?"

"Tru dat," Stevie mumbled. She licked her fingers and flipped through another set of documents.

"Gold? They love gold and they're so stupid about it," Brett said. "They used it to make little baubles and silly stuff, ignoring how great of a conductor it makes, never corrodes, is also incredible in all sorts of electronics, and is great in vehicles, can work with all sorts of other solids; they ignored how well it lasts, never tarnishes, is great for space travel, great for lubrication of joints in spacecraft, may even be useful for protecting against the sun's rays . . . and yet the Spanish wanted to collect it, wear it, turn it into useless decorations?" Brett gave one of his dimple-intensive shrugs and then concluded, "But we don't learn about all that. We don't learn about the maps the Spanish stole from ancient cultures—"

"—Don't think they stole the maps, Brett," Stevie said.

"How did they get them, Stevie? Did they come from the Islamic World, who got it from the Gnostics in Alexandria, who saved it from the Priests in Egypt, who in turn got them from the Atlanteans . . ."

"Something like that."

"Oh come on, don't get like this!" I threw my hands up in the air and said, "Come on, I know we were there, preserving all the ancient knowledge. We helped the Cathars get it from King Arthur and all those guys, and we helped the Knights Templar hold onto it after the Holy Wars, and then we got it up through the Renaissance, come on Mama, I know we were in the middle of all that, and so was Prince Henry the Navigator right here." I grinned at Brett, who grinned back at me.

"Something like that," Stevie repeated.

"Gah," I said, disgusted. Then I put a hand on Brett's head and tousled his hair. "Now, my little angel, you're still too young to be dropping out of school. So just try and hang in there, learn as much as you can—"

"—And you'll be free of Tray Dale in no time," Lizzie said, with an attempt at a comforting smile, for she was, typical of Lizzie, very concerned for Brett's peace of mind.

"Well, if they try and teach me 'bout Columbus, I'll set em' straight."

"Maybe claim you're part Native American," I said.

"Are we?" Lizzie's eyes lit up with excitement.

"More like part-alien," I said.

"Part-alien? Come on Mom," Junior said. He had come around the hallway that connected to the laundry room and then to the dining room, which my kids treat more as their *toss all their bags into* room.

"Well, our souls all start in heaven, you know? So none of us just starts here. Our only true Home is heaven, right? So in a sense we're all aliens on earth."

"Yeah, but what about us, are we part-Indian?" Lizzie wasn't going to let this go.

"Well, I dunno," I said. "Wanna hear what the Indians say about where we came from? It's about the coolest story ever."

"But is it true?" Junior said.

"Parts of it are true I think," I replied, "Right Stevie?"

"Something like that," she said.

"Okay," I said. "So according to Native American tradition, in the beginning there was peace. This blue earth, this beautiful blue earth, enjoyed a Golden Age. And on the earth lived a different type of human. We know them as the Neanderthals. During the Golden Age, the Earth People, as the Neanderthals were called, could talk to animals and they lived in harmony with the animals."

"So they didn't eat animals?" Brett was looking at me, probably thinking about his beef jerky habit.

"Well, I think they might have eaten fish, but scientists have found when they studied Neanderthal skulls that they were pretty much vegetarians."

"How can they tell?" Junior asked.

"Their teeth," I said. "So anyway, the Earth People, their brains were getting bigger and bigger and so were their heads because their brains stored all their people's memories."

"Wow," Lizzie said, "Like a One-Mind? How cool is that?"

"It's not too far off what our minds really are, at least from what I've been reading Lizzie," I said. "But let's stay focused here." I chuckled a little and so did Lizzie.

"So heads got bigger, more moms died in childbirth, and it got to the point that the whole species was threatened from so many moms dying. And you know what? Childbirth was incredibly dangerous even fifty, maybe a hundred years ago, one in four women died from it, so this isn't too far out, okay?"

Lizzie got a really sad look on her face. "You almost died when you had me, right Mom?"

I put a hand on her elbow and stroked it. "Well, I was fine because I was in a great hospital, had great doctors and nurses, but yes, my love, had I been giving birth back in the day, I'd have died. We're very fortunate, at least in some respects, to be living when we are. Technology can be a blessing. Anyway, y'all have heard of the missing link, right?"

"Yeah, from where apes became humans, right?" Junior was paying rapt attention and he read science textbooks for fun, so I wasn't surprised he was answering.

"Yes, son."

"Course we don't really come from apes," Stevie said, her eyes still on her papers.

"No, that's the thing y'all. We don't."

"Wait, Mom, so Darwin's wrong? As in all the science we're learning—"

"Junior, here's the thing." I paused and gave him my kindest eye crinkle. "Scientists do the same thing I do for a living. They look at the world and when they think they've got it figured out, they tell stories, or come up with theories to explain what they see. But really, their theories are stories . . . or constructs to explain things so we can understand them. Some of what Darwin taught was correct, absolutely. As in we do evolve slowly over time. But what Darwin wasn't able to explain was how we took gigantic leaps forward. In other words, there is literally a missing link, or a step between apes and humans; there was also a huge leap between homo sapiens and the thing that we are, homo sapiens sapiens . . . as well as a huge leap between homo erectus and what followed them. I don't want to bore Lizzie, so what I do want you to do is to remember you want to study this and go look it up later, okay?"

"Yes ma'am," Junior said.

"Okay, so anyway, scientists couldn't explain how we humans took this huge leap forward. They don't know how it happened or why humans advanced so quickly. What the Indians believe, and what their crystal skulls teach is that at about the time Earth People were facing a population crisis, these sky gods, or aliens I guess, came from the Pleiades, from Orion, from Sirius. Indeed, it's what we see on all the great architectural monuments left from the days of prehistory."

"Like your pyramids, Mom?" Lizzie flashed a conspiratorial smile at me and I couldn't help but laugh.

"Well, I wouldn't call 'em mine Lizzie, but maybe you can ask Stevie to tell you about them, I'm pretty sure she was there for all that," I said.

Stevie shook her head.

I laughed and kept talking, "So these lovely beautiful people come from planets that are located near the Pleiades, near Sirius, near Orion's Belt, and they're also looking for a new home because something bad's happened to their world. And when they come, they bring incredible gifts for us of course. They bring these crystal skulls that contain all the knowledge of their people as well as the knowledge of the original twelve planets, combined. The skulls have everything: science, math, astronomy, philosophy, spirituality, archeology . . . just a massive outpouring of knowledge. These skulls were also," my voice dropped to a whisper and all three kids leaned forward, "A template for a brand-new species. You see, the genetic memories we had been storing in our brains now got transferred into our DNA."

"Wait," Junior said, "The skulls allowed them to change our DNA? And store all our . . . total knowledge, like as a people, within the DNA?" Junior was caught between scoffing and gasping in astonishment, so he was sort of doing both in the way he asked the question.

"Yeah, the crystal skulls contained the blueprint for humanity. The thing is this: the people from these other worlds weren't going to be able to survive on earth for long, not unless they mixed part of their DNA with ours. You see, they were silicon-based and we're carbon-based. They needed us; we needed them. So we made a deal. We would mix our carbon with their silicone—"

"—Sounds like a Reese's Cup commercial," Stevie said.

"Oh my gosh, your chocolate, my peanut butter, yeah, I remember those commercials," I said. I paused because I was picturing pieces from my childhood. Of sitting in front of the TV on the shaggy orange carpet and wishing the screaming and fighting would stop. I traded a tender smile with Stevie, who sent to me, *I know, we had it rough then didn't we*? Like me, Stevie hadn't had an easy time of it as a kid, and yet we both found the memory of the commercial comforting.

"Mom . . ." Lizzie tapped on my arm.

"Oh right, so the sky people or the aliens knew how to splice DNA. They took their silicone strand and mixed it with our carbon strand and that's how it came about that we had two strands of DNA. They saved their species and it lives on in us humans, and we were able to make our brains stop growing to store all this cultural memory; now it's stored in our DNA."

"So which Indians believe this story anyway?" Junior asked.

"Well, all over the world, actually. Like the Sioux, the Mayans, the Cherokee, tribes in Africa . . . they all say that their ancestors come from the sky, from Sirius, from the Pleiades, which has a double star system by the way. In fact, they told us that but we didn't believe them, didn't believe that Sirius had two stars . . . not up until we developed telescopes powerful enough to detect that there were actually two stars up there. Now, remember, the Bible says we come from earth . . . and that's also correct. There's two strands of DNA, there's also a long history of humanity and some of that history, in fact, lots of it's missing from the Bible. Because of course the Bible never tries to tell the entire history of the earth. It's really only telling the history of a single people, the Jews. And that history ends two thousand years ago. So as far as details, there's really only about 2,000 years of history in the Bible. But humans have been on earth for hundreds of thousands of years."

"See? Mom? This is history," Brett declared. "You should write the history books we use at school, you know?"

I laughed and said, "Well, that would be fun, wouldn't it be?"

"Yeah, Mom, really, it's fascinating, all of this stuff is amazing," Junior said. "I mean, if this is true, then wow, so what about the crystal skulls?"

"Well, that's a long, long story itself, the one about the skulls. All I can say for sure is the skulls contain the history of the earth and of all the planets and the technology the skulls use is very similar but much more advanced than what we use in electronics and modern computers. Tell you what," I said. "Ask me about crystal skulls tomorrow. I, for one, am tired and I have been meaning to ask Stevie if she needs help with this letter she's trying to draft."

Stevie held up her hand and groaned. "I'm stuck, just need to go out for a drive and think. Maybe tomorrow you can help me."

"Oh, Stevie," Brett nearly shouted, "Can I come on a drive with you, please?"

"Wait," I started to say, "Brett—"

"—Yeah, sure, you can come," Stevie said.

"You sure you don't need peace and quiet?"

"Ah, well, Brett and I haven't gotten a chance to talk much yet, it's fine," Stevie said. And with a motion of her hands she said, "Washing my hands of this mess, for now, at least. Ready, Brett?"

"Ready," he said.

And with a winsome smile, he said, "I'll grab your keys," and then he tore off and headed down the basement steps. A minute later, he was back, holding her purse, her keys, and her shoes, and she was smiling and not looking too tired.

"See you, love," she said, and Brett followed her out the front door.

Chapter 68

The next day, Stevie was sitting at the kitchen table when I left for my walk. She was still there a couple of hours later, after I showered and was reading the *Bhagavad Gita*. Or to put it more accurately, I was sort of reading the *Bhagavad Gita*, or Gita as it's usually called, sort of commenting on what I was reading, and sort of asking her questions about both the text I was reading and the documents she was perusing. Because of course Stevie knew the substance of the *Bhagavad Gita* as well as she knew the Bible, which was pretty much as well as anyone I'd ever met. Well, except God. He knew the material really well too.

But Stevie? She was every bit as good a teacher as Jesus. And Jesus was the best teacher I'd been with, here on earth or in heaven. So naturally, as I was going through Krishna's responses to his pupil and prince Arjuna, I was asking Stevie for her thoughts on it. Brett was also sitting at the table. He was drawing all over one of our historical atlases, recording the shipping routes he'd used during one of his past lives.

"Hey Stevie, did you know Gandhi called the Gita his spiritual dictionary?"

"Yep," Stevie said.

"Hey Mom," Lizzie walked into the kitchen and was brushing her thick hair. It was after eleven and she was just getting up, kind of on the early side for her. "Were you Gandhi?"

I laughed. "Oh God no, no, haven't been in India for many lifetimes. But Gandhi was a great, great soul."

"A lot of what you teach sounds like what he taught." Lizzie paused and then grimaced a little as she fought through a tangle in her hair.

"Well, I agree with a great deal of what he taught, that's for sure," I said. "You know, it's kind of interesting to me that Gandhi cites the Gita as his spiritual dictionary because in fact Krishna does tell Arjuna that Arjuna should go and fight his battles. There's this great scene, actually, when Krishna tells him that all the people who fight in the battle, they're pretty much already dead, and Arjuna's merely the instrument of Krishna's will. Basically, he was telling Arjuna that Arjuna was doing the will of God and was fighting a righteous battle and because of that, it was right for him to go ahead and take the sword to his now ex-friends and family."

"So Gandhi, who represented the nonresistance movement, said that in some circumstances it was okay to fight, Mom?"

I glanced over at Stevie, who kind of grunted at me. I hid a smirk and said, "You should ask Stevie. She fought in Iraq, right Stevie?"

"Yes, I fought, and yes sometimes you need to fight for what's right," Stevie said.

"Like Abraham Lincoln, Lizzie, right?" I said. "He led our country into the bloodiest of our wars and as much as he didn't want to be having brothers fight against brothers, he had to do what he did. Souls needed to be free." I could hear the words of the *Gettysburg Address* jumping about inside my head. It was hard to hear anything else, the words were so loud.

"Were you Abraham Lincoln, Mom?" Lizzie asked.

I laughed and said, "Go get changed, okay?"

"But Mom—"

"—Go. I am busy, I gotta bug Stevie some more."

"Still writing that letter, are you?" Lizzie had her inquisitive, grown beyond her years look on her face.

I held my arm up and pointed toward the stairs.

"Fine!" Lizzie flounced off dramatically.

Brett, meanwhile, was drawing lines all over the Mediterranean Ocean. Whenever I made eye contact with him, he would point to one of the islands and start talking about where he'd buried gospels. "Hey Mom," he said, his pen circling the tip of Cyprus. "Here's where I buried most of the gospels, on Cyprus, right at the top, at Andreas. I buried it in caves and it's dark there and not many people have explored them because they're scared of the dark."

"Should never be scared of the dark in caves," Stevie said. "Just keep walking and you'll find light."

"Exactly," Brett said. Then he jumped up and threw his chair back. "I gotta go harvest some quartz, be back soon." He ran outside, slamming the door at least twice after he forgot to bring one of his digging tools.

Then it was just me and Stevie and I was scribbling stuff down in the margins of the Gita and I kept sneaking peaks over in Stevie's direction.

"Hope I'm not disturbing you," I said.

"Disturbing me?"

"Yeah, like scribbling too loud and whatnot."

"It would be great if you were only scribbling but you're saying, 'Oh wow, isn't this passage amazing,' and 'wow, Stevie, did you write this passage" and 'oh gosh, this is so beautiful' and 'is the Self the same thing as the Holy Spirit' and on and on," she said.

"I am?"

"Yes," she said. "And that's the funniest thing, you don't even realize how loud you're being when you're trying to be quiet."

"Am I always loudly quiet?"

"Yes. When you were a baby soul, I'd bring you with me on these meetings with God and—"

"—I'd sit in the corner reading and I'd only be content if you kept sending me everyone's Akashic Records and other secret writings, and even then, I'd be making sounds the whole time, but happy ooooooh and ahhhhhh sounds, so you wouldn't really be able to tell me to cut it out, right?"

"Well, I'd start to tell you to hush and then God would be like, 'Iz is fine, leave her alone, she's just a happy learner,' and you know how He is with happy learners."

"Yep. That's about the highest compliment He gives, isn't it?"

Stevie grunted, which I took as her sign the conversation was ended.

I was quiet for at least two minutes. I know because I timed it. "And now Stevie's like, 'Stop breathing so loudly oh my God,' and then Stevie's like, 'Stop watching me so loudly oh my God,' and then Stevie's like, 'You're about to ask me another question I just know you are so I am waiting for it, I know it's coming . . .'"

Stevie was laughing and shaking her head. "Yep, pretty much." Then she ran her hands through her crazy-colored hair and sighed. "I'm just stuck on this letter, that's all."

"And I'm just loudly waiting for you to ask me for some of my genius assistance, you know I'm waiting, dontcha?"

"I'm stuck," she groaned.

"And I'm waiting for you to ask me to write it. You know you want me to, and you know this is how it always is, right? It's inevitable that you're gonna ask me to write it for you. And knowing it's inevitable, I'm gonna keep bugging you until you finally say, 'Please write the letter for me?' But until then, you're gonna groan and complain and say I'm bugging you, making it so you can't write the letter . . . but the question I have for you is how long you been not writing this letter anyway? Days? Weeks?"

"I don't know why it's so hard to write. It's just impossible and it's gotta get written."

"Weeks?"

Stevie gave a sort of helpless wave of her hand. "Yep."

"Ready to ask me?"

"Fine."

"So you want me to write it?"

"Fine," she said again.

I started to laugh. So did she. And then I put my hand out and motioned for her to pass me the medical records.

"Come on," I said. "I'll have it written by five. Can you believe I used to do this for a living? How many lifetimes have I been a lawyer anyway? Was never much good at practicing law, but man, I can write a really good letter can't I?"

"Oh Sally," she laughed. "Yes, yes you can."

Stevie stood up and moved toward the fridge to grab her water bottle and she grimaced a little. I didn't want to notice it but I did.

And she heard what I was thinking because she turned and said, "I love you too, and I'm fine. I'll be fine, I promise."

"I know," I said. "Just don't like seeing you in pain."

"It's nothing, I'm fine," she said. And she smiled at me and it didn't look too forced.

I knew she was going to be okay. It wasn't her time to go yet. We still had souls to help.

Chapter 69

On Friday, I was trying to get a little bit of writing done and I was also waiting for Stevie to head out for her first session at the doctor's. She had already told me several times she wanted to go alone, no, she was fine, really she was, it was better if she went alone, really, it was, and yet I was hoping she'd let me take her. Meanwhile, Bad Doggy had been on a barking jag all morning. She'd been yelping and yapping and howling and woofing since I woke up and I was distracted and frustrated, so much so that I didn't realize Stevie was standing behind me with her arms crossed.

"You gonna say something to them or do I have to get medieval on them?"

"Oh man, it's bothering you too?"

"Come on, Sally, this is ridiculous. The dog's not happy, you ever stop to think of that? Or are you too busy worrying about what the poor dog's owners will say when you have the compassion and responsibility to bring the situation to their attention?"

"Um," I was frozen. "I guess . . . I don't know . . . ." Stevie was never gentle with me, hardly ever at least. She always got right to the point of whatever she was trying to teach me and she didn't wait to see if my feelings could take her correction. That's just how she was. I realized my eyes were filling with tears so I shrugged and looked down.

"Uh-uh," she said. "Look at me. Cut that out. You're fine. You're fine, Sally. What I'm saying is you're trying to work aren't you? Do you think your neighbor is constantly being interrupted while he's working? Do you think he would stand for it? Do you really think he'd think his work wasn't important enough to deserve his full attention, which he wouldn't be able to give it if a dog was barking all day at him?"

"I didn't, I don't . . ."

"Shhh. Sally, don't go feeling bad about it. Just be honest with yourself and take your work as seriously as you should. Take yourself seriously and be an adult. You're not a kid anymore. Do what you need to do, do the right thing and don't worry about your neighbor getting mad. A decent neighbor wouldn't get mad, they would want to know if their dog was creating a disturbance, so just assume they're going to be decent, and even if they're not, you can't control their response but you can control the way you respond, okay?"

"So I don't wanna be mean about it, you know?"

"How is it mean to tell your neighbors you're trying to work and you can't because their dog barks for hours on end at a time? And let me tell you something," Stevie added.

"Uh oh," I said.

"Yeah," she said. "If you don't talk to them, I'm liable to and we both know you're gonna be nicer about it."

We grinned at one another. Then I said, "Please let me drive you, please Stevie?"

She shook her head and then tossed some papers on the counter. "But would you maybe mind mailing these off for me? Please, love?"

"Yeah, sure, I'll even print out the mailing addresses," I said.

"Oh and make sure you keep that separate from your business expenses," she murmured.

I started to roll my eyes and then I said, "Well, wish me luck, I'm gonna go call Aaron."

"Don't be silly, you're fine," Stevie said.

And I was fine. I was better than fine. I dug up Aaron's work number and got his answering machine. Even though I was shaking, and I'm not exaggerating, I really was, I called. He didn't pick up, said he was in a meeting, please leave a message. So I left a really polite message. "Hey Aaron, it's Sally, hope you're doing well and are having a good day at work. Speaking of work, that's actually why I'm calling. I don't know if you know that I work at home and you see the thing is, your dog has been barking for a few hours and it's making it hard for me to concentrate on my work. Well, I hope you have a good day, bye." I felt okay after I left the message but I was still scared I was going to get in trouble or create a problem or something like that.

But I wasn't in trouble and I hadn't created a mess, not at all. In fact, Aaron called me back a little while later.

I played the voicemail he left. "Hey, Sally, It's Aaron. I just want to thank you for calling and letting me know that Cally is barking. I am so sorry for the disturbance. We know she can be a pain but we had no idea she was being this difficult so we're really grateful to know about it. And we'll figure something out, I promise. Sorry about all this, and thanks again for calling."

Later that night, after Stevie had gotten back from her appointment and didn't look any worse for the wear, I was getting back from a walk and I ran into Aaron and Bad Doggy right by our mailbox.

He hailed me down with a kindly smile. "Hey Sally, how are you?"

I smiled, feeling a little shy, a little scared I was going to be in trouble.

But Aaron was still smiling and he said, "I just wanna thank you again, Sally, for calling and letting us know about Cally. I know she can be hard to live next door to, I know she barks too much, but we didn't realize the full extent of it, we just had no idea, in fact, that's what I was researching tonight, seeing if we can get a bark collar or some other sort of system that will keep her barking down. So I wanted to say we're sorry and we promise we'll get the problem fixed."

I smiled and thanked Aaron. And then I went inside and told the kids about it. Lizzie was the one who patted me on the shoulder and said, "Good job, Mom, it was about time, I'm proud of you."

I giggled and shrugged. "Proud of me? Why?"

"Well," Junior said, "You turned the other cheek as much as you could, and then I guess you sort of hissed, right?"

I laughed and hugged him. "Well, actually, I don't think I had to hiss. We're lucky, I can't believe I'm saying this, but it's true. We're lucky to have such good neighbors."

"Good neighbors?" Brett gave me a scoffing roll of his eyes and Lizzie and Junior said in tandem, "Come on, really?"

"Okay," I said. "Good people who live as our neighbors. I mean, listen to me, it took true goodness for Aaron to handle my phone call as he did. He acted with humility, with decency, and with a sense of responsibility."

"Okay, Mom," Lizzie said, "But what about Tunie and Rhodie? You think they're good too?"

"Well," I said, "Remember what Jesus said about throwing stones right?"

"Don't throw a stone at someone else if you live in a glass house, or something like that, right?" Junior said.

"Something like that, yeah," I said. "So what does that mean?"

"Um," Brett said, "Throw mud balls instead?"

"Yeah," Lizzie giggled, "Throw cow poop."

"Oh come on, you two, stop it," I chuckled. "What does it mean, huh? Another formulation of that saying is from the Gospel of Matthew. It goes:

> *Why do you look at the speck of sawdust in your brother's eye and pay no attention to the plank in your own eye? How can you say to your brother, 'Let me take the speck out of your eye,' when all the time there is a plank in your own eye? You hypocrite, first take the plank out of your own eye, and then you will see clearly to remove the speck from your brother's eye.*

"Do you guys understand that?"

The kids nodded, so I continued, Or the gospel of Luke says:

> *Why do you see the speck in your neighbor's eye, but do not notice the log in your own eye?*

"See how in that formulation, the person who didn't commit the bad deed actually has worse deeds of his own, as in his neighbor has just a speck in his eye, but the main person has a huge log of his own? Do you see how when you're focusing on what Tunie and Rhodie are doing wrong, maybe you're not catching the mistakes you're making? First concentrate on taking care of your own soul, right? Or as Jesus says in the Gospel of Thomas, 'You see the speck that is in your sibling's eye, but you do not see the beam that is in your own eye. When you take the beam out of your own eye, then you will see clearly to take the speck out of your sibling's eye.'"

"Does this mean that once we're perfect, or once we fix our own soul, we can help Tunie fix hers?" Lizzie was concentrating and thinking.

I put an arm around her and said, "Well, as a kid, I would focus right now on getting your own house in order so to speak. It takes awhile to learn all these lessons and yeah, someday, when you're older, you can help her but remember the golden rule, the most important rule of all is to treat your friends the way you want them to treat you. And do you, Lizzie, really want your friends telling you how to live? Or would it be better if your friends just hung out with you and were there to help you after you made your own mistakes?"

"Oh Mom," Lizzie sighed, "There's so much to learn. Will I ever be as wise as you? I feel like I'm forever gonna be in your shadow."

I rubbed Lizzie's back and said goodnight to Junior and Brett. When they both lingered, I said, "Gimme a few minutes alone with Lizzie, okay you two?" Then I hugged them both and waited for them to go upstairs.

"Lizzie, I felt the same way when I was with Jesus. It was one of my first lives, or at least pretty early on for me as a prophet, and you know, and I was with one of the wisest soul that's ever lived. I wanted to be just like him, you know? But it seemed like I'd never be able to make as long as a shadow as he made."

"He must have been an amazing father," Lizzie said.

"Yeah, the best," I agreed. "The thing is, you're young."

"I know, it's just my fourth life."

"And you're doing great, sweetie. But also remember, you're young in this lifetime. You're the same age I was when Dad found his ministry and started to teach. I was so much like you then. I was wise for my age, and really only wanted to hang out with adults, and I was smart among the adults too, but man, I had so much to learn and sometimes I was totally confused and sometimes I even missed just being a kid. What I'm saying Lizzie is you're doing great and in no time, you'll be just like me."

"And now you're just like Jesus," she said.

"No, no, I'm really not. I still can't tie the thongs on his sandals, but I'm becoming the best me I can be. And as far as shadows, well, I'm pretty comfortable with the one I'm now casting, eh?"

"Mom?"

"Yeah?"

"Is it true I'm destined to be a great writer?"

"Well," I said, "I don't know about who will define whether you're great. If you mean will you follow in my footsteps and continue writing books that helps souls get Home, yeah, I think so. It's what your mission is, it's why you were given to me, it's why you were put in this family, to continue on with my work, yeah."

"But will I be famous?"

"Well, what do I always say about the point of my writing?"

"Renounce the fruits of your labor. I still am not sure what that means," Lizzie said.

"It means I am serving my brothers and sisters by doing what God wants me to do and I'm not worrying about how much money I earn or how many books I sell."

"Or about what your reviews say, or what people write or say about you, just like Jackie didn't worry about what the tabloids said about her and Robert, her and Jack, all that gossip." Lizzie was obsessed with Jacqueline Kennedy. She identified with her a great deal and sort of looked up to her.

"Yes, good, Lizzie. Your mission will be to use your talents as a writer and to write stories that help souls get Home and you're not to worry about the results of all your efforts. Nothing but God's opinion matters, right?"

"Do you really believe that Mom? You really don't care what the world thinks of your work?"

"Yes. I really don't care. I used to, though, Lizzie. Used to drive me crazy."

"I still care," she said.

"Give it time, Lizzie. Someday you'll react exactly the same way when you get an A as when you get a D. And that's when you will know you've understand the secret to your own happiness."

"The secret's not caring what others think of you?"

"The secret is using your talents, the ones God gave you, to do your work in the service of others and not to care about the results of what you do. So yeah, do your best to serve God, to help others, and worry about no one's opinion except for God's."

"Not even your opinion?"

"Well," I said, hugging her, "I'll always be proud of you no matter what, so you don't need to worry about my opinion, now do you?"

Lizzie laughed. It was a laugh full of joy and happiness and wonderment. Then she said, "Thanks Mom. I love you."

"Love you too. Now go to bed, okay?"

"Yes ma'am."

Scorecard

18.3 gallons of gasoline
    7-8 beach towels
    2 Fuzzy pillows
    3 duffels bags, 2 small suitcases
    5 bottles of sunscreen
    1 laptop
    4 reading tablets
    10 books
    A zillion disorganized extension cords
    One SUV packed and ready for a late August trip to the beach.
    One archangel already there, waiting for family.

Epilogue

It hasn't gotten totally and completely one hundred percent resolved but things next door sure are a lot quieter. I guess for the sake of wrapping up this story I should tell you I've stopped getting annoyed by Bad Doggy, but that would be a lie and I'm too old to tell many of those. More importantly, it would belie the lessons I'm trying to share with you. For we've learned a few. We've learned about turning the other cheek. We've learned about reaping what you sow even if you have to wait for the fruits of it all. We've learned about tolerance. We've even learned about when a snake's gotta hiss a little bit (but never, ever strike with venom).

I'd like to tell a tall tale or two more about Tunie and Bad Doggy. Like how, for the sake of my own sanity, maybe Bad Doggy and Rhodie and Aaron and Tunie could have moved to Siberia. I'm sincerely (stop kicking me William! None of the neighbors ever read the stories I write) praying, okay not praying because that's an inappropriate use of my special connection to Him . . . that they move to Siberia.

I'm still waiting for that. And I've tried earplugs and sometimes I open the deck door and get all flustered and I howl, "STOP BARKING" at the dog. I do. I know it's ridiculous but I do it. I have not, however, thrown rocks, balls, acorns, or anything at the dog. And if nothing else guarantees me automatic admittance to eternal glory, this will.

I joke of course. We all find eternal life; well, pretty much, and this is not the place to talk about what happens to corrupted, sick, demon-ridden souls. Let's just say it's worse than getting coal in your stocking.

But Siberia seemed . . . justified. And they wouldn't have to live there for eternity. Just until they got good and cold and realized that the dog didn't deserve to be good and cold all the time. Oh and it would be great for them to live in the country because their dog won't annoy a poor sensitive soul like me because they won't have any neighbors. And that way Tunie and Rhodie, sometimes difficult kids that they are, won't torture sensitive goofy wonderful kids like Lizzie, Junior, and Brett.

Hey. A woman can wish. The odd thing as of late is I've been having visions of snow-covered mountains. They look strange but familiar, as if I see them more every day because I'm supposed to see them. I love these visions. Sometimes I even dream that I'm in an SUV and I'm driving to a mountain top, and while we pass over the landscape, I'm talking and teaching; the kids are asking questions; and we're all happy.

Meanwhile, the kids have gone back to the way they were, but older and wiser, before the fighting with Tunie threw our household into almost daily chaos. They don't talk to Tunie much, and that seems to be for the best. Lizzie wrote a story about saving dolphins on the way to the beach. Brett brought the ark to the beach and said he was gonna release it to the oceans. And Junior is collecting fossils from the banks of our river. Says he's searching for the "missing link," and I smile and tell him to keep searching.

Todd has nine vehicles currently. He sold the Mustang but still has the Camaro, the El Camino, the Jeep, and a brand-new project that's driving Sandy a little crazy: a beaten up, tie-dyed VW bus that leaks oil and chokes and barks loudly whenever Todd starts her. Sandy and Grant are about to retire, and Sandy says they're going to sell their house and move to Florida, maybe as soon as next year. The kids don't like this idea, but Lizzie holds out hope that a family with nice girls will move in if Sandy leaves.

I've also had a couple of nightmares. I've dreamed that William was clutching his heart; I've even seen him lying in a coffin. He was lying there, and I was saying goodbye to him. I woke up after that one and tried to talk to him about it, but he patted by arm and told me he had a great internist, board-certified, and he trusted that if there was anything wrong with his heart, his doctor would've said so. Hopefully the messages Lizzie and I have been receiving got jumbled somehow, and there's nothing to it. Still, I worry sometimes.

Anyway, maybe we didn't get our happily ever after ending; no let me correct that: we didn't get the happily ever after ending I anticipated. We got a much better one. We got something we really needed, and it's cute and it's furry. Funny, how life works out sometimes.

•••

It all started with one of our trips down to Virginia Beach. Me and the kids love these trips. William endures them but he hates sand and he has a really bad habit of losing his glasses in the ocean. Lizzie also hates sand and so do I. Yet we all love the idea of it so much that we spend most of the year looking forward to it and we all want to live down there; well, except for William but he goes where I go.

Anyway, I knew ahead of time that Stevie was gonna be there. I guess by now you've figured out Stevie's my best friend and she's also an archangel. I hope you believe me but it's okay if you don't. It's a lot harder for some people to believe than most of the other stuff me and the kids talk about. William said he's suspending disbelief for now but he's always polite to Stevie, which is all I expect. Okay, I want him to believe but it's fine. My kids believe me and that's of course how it works. Before the world destroys your innocence and robs you of your natural wisdom, it's much easier to not only believe in God but to hear Him. The same is true for angels.

I knew, actually (which is one of Lizzie's favorite words, along with 'technically') that Stevie was moving to Virginia Beach permanently, once she finished her treatment. I also knew that I was working behind the scenes to buy a beach house down by the water. I'd just gotten a big advance and investing in land has always been the best thing to do with money because land tends to appreciate. William says it's not good to buy beachfront land on the first row, closest to the ocean. His plan, or so he said, was to buy on the second row. Then, when a hurricane came through, the second row would become the first row, and even more appreciation would ensue.

This is a conversation we had years ago, but I'd remembered it. And that's why I had rented a second row house which I'd known was about to go on the market. "Just give me a week, okay," I said to the realtor. "Just a week to work on my husband."

The realtor knew who I was, minor internet celebrity and servant of God and all that. It didn't hurt that she was a lay minister on the side. "Okay, Sally," she said. "One week."

During the drive down to the beach, I worked on William, which consisted of me grinning and trying to keep my secret while I asked him about his views on property, rentals, and tax write-offs. Between that and mediating scuffles between Lizzie and Brett and sometimes Junior over who got the top bunk and when . . . made the time go by fast.

We got down there at around 4 p.m., which gave me time to herd the kids and put away some of our massive stash of stuff while William gathered groceries. It was almost 7 p.m. by the time we got settled. The kids had been running around the yard, which was a horrifying mix of sand, burrs, and dead grass. Lizzie had boxed her brothers out of the top bunk, and Junior, as usual, had been the only helpful child. Junior's like that: he's a Boy Scout, totally sweet, and really easy to raise.

I'm not saying I like him better than Lizzie and Brett. It just seems like I don't write about him as much as I should, which is ironic but of course true for most middle kids. He's not forgotten; he simply doesn't demand as much attention as the corner kids.

By the time we got to the beach, it was Golden Hour, which looks different by the water than it does in the forest. It's just as beautiful as it is in the forest . . . maybe more so. The seagulls congregate on the sand more and the crowds thin. I like the seagulls and I've never liked crowds, so I was especially happy that night. I also knew we might run into Stevie because she was staying really close to the house we were renting, and she usually walked during Golden Hour with her daughter and her dog.

I love these walks by the water, and they seem the most magical the first night we get to the beach. It's like the kids fall in love with the ocean all over again, and for me, it's like reconnecting with something that is not only full of life, but which makes me feel more alive than I do anywhere else.

We walked for almost an hour and then we turned. Off in the distance I saw two dogs chasing a ball into the water. One dog was kind of a mixed breed. A mutt. And the other dog was a puppy, not a tiny one, maybe six months old. "A chocolate lab," William said, and he was smiling because you can't see a chocolate lab puppy running into water after a ball without smiling.

We watched the dogs race into the waves from a good half-mile off. The mutt usually beat the puppy to the waves, but the puppy never stopped trying to keep up. It was almost high tide, so the water was pretty choppy, but the mutt was splendid. She'd slam into and under the waves, never letting the puppy just win one, but every once in awhile, I'd see her glance over her shoulder, like she was making sure the little one was okay. I don't know how I knew the mutt was female; maybe it was the way she glanced backwards and checked.

William was smiling as we got closer to the dogs. There was a woman throwing the tennis ball, and the setting sun was shining directly on her shoulders. Almost like God was anointing her . . . then I knew it was Stevie. Only an angel could create so much happiness without even trying. It was so funny and beautiful and wonderful, and I held tight to that vision of Stevie throwing a ball to a mutt and a puppy, I held it tight, as we approached, until my heart was bursting with joy.

And then I bent down and whispered in Brett's ear, "That's Stevie up there, and I think that puppy might just be for us." I don't know why I said that. There's no way Stevie would get me a dog. There's no way any friend would get me a dog without asking me ahead of time. But Stevie was no ordinary friend.

Brett didn't wait for me to say anymore. He ran as fast as he could, heels not even touching the sand, longish hair floating behind him, and he skidded to a stop in front of Stevie and almost collided with her and with the dripping, sandy, messy puppy. I saw

Stevie grab the ball from the mutt and then she bent over, tousled Brett's hair, and she handed him the ball.

He looked up at her; and she looked down at him. Their dimples matched, and so did their smiles. The light in his eyes reflected the light in hers, and I wasn't sure if it was from the sun or from within both of them. All I knew was that God was near and in them, in their smile, was His love and the promise of another rising dawn.

I smiled too, and waved to my angels.